FIONA McINTOSH

REVENGE

TRINITY: BOOK TWO

www.orbitbooks.co.uk

ORBIT

First published in Australia in 2002 by Voyager,
HarperCollins*Publishers* Pty Limited
First published in Great Britain in 2006 by Orbit

Copyright © Fiona McIntosh 2002

The moral right of the author has been asserted.

A CIP catalogue record for this book
is available from the British Library.

ISBN-13: 978-1-84149-458-6
ISBN-10: 1-84149-458-5

Typeset in Garamond Three by
Palimpsest Book Production Limited, Polmont, Stirlingshire
Printed and bound in Great Britain by
Mackays of Chatham plc, Chatham, Kent

Orbit
An imprint of
Little, Brown Book Group
Brettenham House
Lancaster Place
London WC2E 7EN

A member of the Hachette Livre Group od Companies

www.orbitbooks.co.uk

For Monnica and Fred Richards,
my parents and close friends

Acknowledgments

Book Two means even more people to thank! Pip Klimentou remains committed to waking the household with her daily call, for which I am indebted to her. Friend Paul Meehan has created a terrific website — please visit soon. Sonya Caddy is warmly welcomed as draft reader, alongside the much appreciated Anne Maddox. Plenty of other people have been fantastically supportive — too many to list here, but I hope they know how much I appreciate their continuing enthusiasm — particularly Graham Richards, my lovely brother; Kim Bleeker, my 'other brother'; and Lynne Schinella, whom I think truly believes in my magic and the importance of fairy dust!

My editor, Nicola O'Shea, is not only a joy to work with but is supremely talented at her craft — I am fortunate indeed. Thank you to all at HarperCollins, especially to Linda Funnell and Stephanie Smith for their support. I'm in some awe of the fact that Robin Hobb and Sara Douglass are associated with this trilogy and I will be forever grateful for their generous comments and encouragement.

Finally, to the wonderful and sometimes eccentric trinity I share my life with. May I voice once again my love and thanks to Will and Jack, who keep pulling me back from Tallinor into the reality of family life, but especially — and always — to Ian. Fx.

PROLOGUE

The tendons on Themesius's neck stood out like stakes as he strained in a silent scream. He was bearing the brunt of the attack. Figgis, so fiercely unyielding all of these long years, had finally weakened. The cracks in his mental armour were widening rapidly.

Pitching their wit and their magics together, the original ten-strong Paladin had held for centuries. Gradually, though, time and their prisoner's inexhaustible power had worn down their unified strength. He worked on them constantly, sometimes as a group, mostly on individuals.

Kyt Cyrus had fallen initially and would for ever be known as the First. The Second was Cloot of Rork'yel and the Third, Solyana, magical beast, succumbed soon after. There was a long wait for the Fourth but fall she did: Juno the Esian. Adongo of the Moruks was Fifth, followed by Saxon the Kloek, Sixth. The minstrel, Sallementro, was Seventh, and later Arabella the Priestess was Eighth of the Paladin to capitulate.

Only Figgis the Rock Dweller and Themesius of the Giants still held, although Figgis knew his time had almost come. Somehow these two pushed back against the god's relentless whisperings, the wave after wave of astounding power which crowded their minds and battered at their resolve.

Themesius roared as he fought the monster.

Orlac laughed. 'Such spirit, Themesius. I must work harder on you.' He turned to Figgis. 'You had better rest now, my short friend, for soon we shall lock our minds again and then, I fear, I may see your end.'

Nanak, Keeper of the Paladin, watched in bitter silence as his brave warriors rested, their tortured expressions slowly relaxing. He could see the toll this ancient battle was taking. It would not be long now: Figgis would fall, but bravely. Nanak's only comfort was an ever-increasing belief in Merkhud's assurance that these courageous friends would re-emerge to fight again. Merhkud had told him that their spirits fled to the Heartwood where they were restored amongst the living to prepare to fight the next battle. Themesius, bedrock of the Paladin, would succumb last and bear the final humiliation of Orlac's victory; of this Nanak was certain. If only the Giant could maintain his strength long enough to give them the time they desperately needed.

Hold, my brave Paladin, he gently passed through their minds. *The Trinity will come. You are its torchbearers. Buy us the time we need.*

But both were too lost in their despair to respond. Nanak understood. He too yearned for the moment of release, when the Custodian would relieve him of this formidable task.

The silence was shattered by Orlac's manic giggle. The god was staring at him now. Those strange, piercing violet eyes penetrated his own ancient and bewitched soul. Nanak shivered and closed his eyes, shutting out the vision of Orlac whilst he awaited the next attack. He must trust Lys. She would guide them through this and bring about Orlac's destruction.

There were brief moments when Nanak felt a flash of sorrow for Orlac. Prince of the gods, revered son of the Host, stolen from his birthright and forced to live a mortal life. A tragic character. Nevertheless, Nanak hated him. He lived for the time when retribution would be visited on Orlac on behalf of the suffering souls of the Paladin.

Lys had promised salvation. She was the Custodian. He would obey her.

He sensed Themesius and Figgis stiffen and the barriers were thrown up in their minds again in a blink. Orlac was on his feet, dancing madly, rejuvenated. The fight to the death had begun again and Orlac was enjoying himself.

He was not alone.

Watching silently was the god Dorgryl. Excommunicated from the Host and thrown into the Bleak to ponder his sin for eternity, he had watched this battle for centuries, invisible to all, and had celebrated every one of Orlac's victories.

If he had arms, he would have hugged himself on this day. He could sense Orlac's coming release. A release which the mighty god Dorgryl would turn into his own personal triumph.

I

A New Beginning

'The anointing syringe!' bellowed the midwife. 'We should save the soul of the stubborn wretch before we leave them both to die.'

Alyssa Qyn stepped back in disbelief as one of the assistants hurried to hand the imperious midwife the strange contraption. She looked towards the grey-faced woman slumped on the birthing stool. Sweat dribbled through her lank hair and her expression was a combination of exhaustion and untold sorrow. She was too spent even to understand the heartless decision being made for her. Midwives only called for the anointing syringe when they believed the child would perish; it was a means of symbolically cleansing the babe prior to its death.

Alyssa felt an old grief grip her; she was still vulnerable to those hurts coming back to haunt her.

Jayn Elkin was a decent woman; wife to one of the courtiers, kind to everyone, gentle of voice and with an equally soft smile for all who passed before her eyes. She did not deserve to die like this, with her child ready to be born and she herself too weak to bear it.

Snatching the contraption, the midwife pushed one end into the now still mother. Depressing the plunger at the other end, she squirted water onto the head of the child.

Except it is not the head, Alyssa wanted to scream. Even her unpractised eye could tell as much. The midwife carelessly offered some rote words of blessing before withdrawing the syringe, throwing Jayn Elkin's skirts down and standing to stretch her own back.

'Clean her up,' she said to Alyssa. 'She's going to her gods now.' Her task apparently complete, the woman swept importantly out of the chamber with her wide-eyed assistant trailing behind.

It was a cruel scene but it was not out of the ordinary. Alyssa recalled her own labour. It was a blurred memory; she had been robbed of the actual birth. Perhaps the pain had bludgeoned her into a stupor? She had never understood how it had happened; how could she have been unconscious and still deliver a child?

And yet during that period of unconsciousness, her son had been delivered by Arabella the priestess and had died in his father's arms in the Heartwood barely moments later. He had cried his first and last breath without a mother to soothe him and been buried in a shallow grave of forest foliage with no ceremony. Cruel, indeed.

Harrowing though that picture was in Alyssa's mind, it was the father's memory she dreaded most whenever the haunting came. Torkyn Gynt's handsome face, smashed and bleeding from the execution stones. His beautiful blue eyes no longer bright, but dull; unseeing. His bloodied corpse hanging limp from the cross. Many had gathered to touch his feet, to pay their final respects to a man whom the city of Tal had loved.

When Alyssa was sure Tor was dead, she had deliberately turned to look upon his murderer: King Lorys. She had sworn then that she would always look upon that sad, haunted face with hate. And that would never change, for as much as she loved his Queen, she despised the sovereign. He could have averted the execution with a simple command. But he had chosen not to and she had never understood why. Tor, after all, had been a cherished friend to the royals as well as being their healer.

That winter, four years ago, had been a traumatic time. Except for Saxon, all those she had known and loved had disappeared, including Cloot, Tor's loyal guardian. Where had the falcon gone after Tor's death? And what had happened to Royal Physic Merkhud? She had seen him momentarily in the stairwell as she was being escorted back to the holding chamber after Tor's execution. The old man had acted so very strangely that even the guards had commented on his behaviour. She knew Merkhud had taken Tor's body to its final resting place but no one had ever told her where that was. She had wished so many times since that she had asked the physic of its location. And now he too was gone. His few awkwardly spoken words had told her to watch out for Sallementro; that he was a friend. How could the old man have known this?

Sallementro *had* come into her life a few weeks later but he claimed never to have known Merkhud. And Merkhud had followed his words by blowing her a kiss. What had it meant? There had never been any love lost between the two of them. She had despised him and he knew it. She had always blamed him for stealing Tor from her in the first place. What could the old man have been thinking of to show such a public act of affection?

Alyssa heard a whimper from behind her. It was only then that she remembered Jayn Elkin's serving girl was trembling in the shadows.

'Elsa?'

'Is she going to die?' The girl's voice sounded shaky.

Alyssa expected no less but she tried to sound confident. 'Not if we can help it. Make her comfortable, then go and fetch Sallementro as fast as you can.'

Whilst Elsa laid moist folded linens on Jayn Elkin's brow, Alyssa scrubbed her own hands clean. It was something she noticed none of the midwives did. She had learned this from Sorrel. 'Clean hands do not carry disease,' she had often told Alyssa.

She pushed thoughts of Sorrel away. She had never heard from the old girl again. They had shared and overcome such harrowing events together and it was just another blade in Alyssa's heart that her great friend had deserted her in the Heartwood after the death of her son. Perhaps she too was dead.

Jayn Elkin's eyes flew open as the pain of a vicious contraction gripped her. She screamed weakly. Alyssa heard the door bang as the girl fled to find Sallementro. She took a deep breath and lifted the woman's skirts once more. What she was about to attempt scared her. She was going to test Sorrel's suggestion that a trapped baby simply needed to be turned gently.

Alyssa was perspiring, nervous at what she was about to try. She whispered comforting words to Jayn, pushed her own sleeves up and, after oiling her hand, began an examination.

Some time later, when Elsa burst through the door

with news of Sallementro's arrival, Alyssa was alarmed the minstrel may follow the girl in.

'Not in here!' she admonished. She walked to the door. 'Sallementro, please play for Lady Elkin outside the window. She loves your music almost as much as I do. It will help her.'

'I shall sing "My Lady, My Love",' he said, 'for both of you.'

Alyssa touched his arm in thanks and closed the door on him swiftly.

'How is she?' Elsa asked, tiptoeing over.

'She is between contractions. They have begun again properly.' Alyssa could not keep the excitement from her own voice.

The baby had been turned almost effortlessly and she was sure now that the child was lying in the birthing position. Perhaps she could allow herself to hope.

Many a babe, she had heard, had been pulled feet first into the world by aggressive midwives. She had seen the evidence of this harsh treatment in the deformed limbs of children around the city. None in the midwives' guild would admit to such a thing, of course, but then being born with contorted limbs was probably preferable to being murdered, she decided. It was whispered that a baby which simply would not come, and threatened the life of someone more important than a mere courtier's wife, would be killed to save the mother. Alyssa had heard terrible tales of midwives attempting surgical procedures to retrieve a dead child or, worse, killing it in the mother's belly and dragging it out, piece by gruesome piece. Luckily Jayn Elkin was not important enough to warrant such trouble.

Sallementro's lovely voice filtered through the open window. He had chosen Alyssa's favourite ballad. It was the song he had written for her when he first laid eyes on her as she stood on that balcony preparing to watch her lover die.

No one present at the execution, save Saxon and Cloot, had known that she and Tor were husband and wife. And Alyssa had never cared to enlighten her captors. What did it matter now anyway? Tor was dead. Her son was dead. There was nothing to do but kill herself or accept this new life amongst the palace servants. The problem was, when she asked herself the hard question of why she forced herself to struggle through each day, she could never come up with an answer.

Saxon and Sallementro insisted they would never give up hope. Alyssa had been surprised to learn that Sallementro was of the Paladin, but the knowledge had been blurred by Tor's death. Without Tor, surely there could be no Trinity? Even though none of them knew what form the elusive Trinity might take, it seemed obvious that Tor was the critical figure.

If only she had kept her books, the Writings of Nanak. Alyssa had never got the chance to read the second book but felt sure it would have provided the most important revelations in the story of Orlac. Lys had told Tor that the vengeful god would return to Tallinor to finish what he had begun.

Sitting here now, listening to Sallementro singing and seeing Jayn Elkin grimace with another contraction, it seemed just that – a story. But when Alyssa had read Nanak's words, they had chilled her and she knew she had been reading the truth. Now those books were as lost to her as Tor, Sorrel and her friends from the Heartwood.

As for Lys, she too had disappeared from their lives. Not that she had ever visited Alyssa. Which was strange, was it not? Lys had appeared to everyone else connected to this strange quest.

She shook her head clear of thoughts which had troubled her for so long. The search for the Trinity was over. Without Tor, what was the point?

Jayn's contractions were becoming harder, faster; the woman had begun to bear down.

'Fetch the midwife, Elsa,' Alyssa commanded. 'She's probably filling her ugly mouth in the kitchens. We don't know what we're doing and your mistress is about to give birth.'

Thankfully it was not long before the midwife blustered back into the room and was pushing Alyssa aside. It was almost as though the woman had to see it for herself to believe it. Alyssa felt sure she was not back in this room out of compassion, merely inquisitiveness – or was it for mercenary reasons?

She cautiously offered what she knew. 'She is ready to push, ma'am, but she is weak.'

The woman's mouth twitched a grim smile. 'I had this one down for cooling already in her chambers. Oh well, the fee for a live birth pays me more handsomely. Let's set to.'

As Jayn Elkin pushed her wailing infant into the world, the sight of a gleeful Chief Inquisitor Goth kicking at the forest debris which covered her own dead son flashed into Alyssa's mind.

She felt Elsa tugging at her shoulder, dragging her back to the present once again, her own tears flowing freely. Alyssa glanced at the tiny bundle being passed to Jayn Elkin.

'A son,' Elsa said. 'My lord must be told. He will be the happiest man in the castle tonight.' She turned so that no one else could hear. 'Because of you.'

'Hurry and do your duty,' Alyssa said. She needed no one to know of her interference.

Whilst Alyssa Qyn was turning a trapped child in its mother's womb, the King and Queen were preparing for their early morning ride.

As her stableman checked her stirrups, Nyria straightened her back and breathed in the crisp autumn morning. Ah, how she loved this season. She imagined galloping across the frosty turf of the open moors behind Tal, calling a challenge to Lorys that he would never catch her on Freycin. He always gave chase, roaring his response to her bait, but then she knew he also always let her win . . . and she loved him for it.

Nyria's thoughts were pierced by a shrill cry. She looked over towards the palace gates and noticed a scrawny child being led by one of the guards. The little boy was struggling as the man pulled him along.

She asked a nearby guard what the commotion was about.

He bowed. 'Your highness, the child was tied to the palace gates during the night. We discovered him only during the change an hour ago.'

'But he must be frozen,' said the Queen, staring back at the child and his large companion.

'We gave him a warm ale and some gruel. Prime Herek has ordered him be returned.'

'To whom?' she demanded.

The man shrugged, then checked himself and quickly turned his gesture into words. 'Prime Herek told Orgo,' he pointed to the retreating guard, 'to take the lad into the city and ask around.'

Nyria pulled her right leg from its stirrup. She had always impressed the King's Guard by how she rode like a man.

'Oh, that's ridiculous. Stop him immediately!' she commanded.

King Lorys, who had been consulting with the two riders accompanying them, looked over, confused to see Nyria dismounting.

'Now what?' he said and guided his horse to where his wife stood, purse-lipped, her riding crop slapping at her thigh.

She shook her head. 'I'm sorry, Lorys. Go on without me.'

'What's happened?'

She explained quickly. The King sighed. 'Why must you take in every waif, Nyria? Every child in Tal is not your responsibility. What will you do with him?'

'I don't know, Lorys, but you can't just hawk a child around the city until you find someone who may know him. It could take days.'

The King stared into her pale eyes. He knew he could not win this one. When it came to children, Nyria was as soft as butter. Not having one of her own meant she lavished her affection on every child she came into contact with. He pulled gently on the reins to head his dark stallion out of the courtyard.

'I might ride out a bit further then.'

'Thank you, Lorys.'

She meant it and showed it by squeezing his gloved hand as they heard Orgo and the child returning. The King departed.

Orgo bowed stiffly. He was not used to such close proximity with the Queen. He cuffed the child on the head to do the same. Nyria kept her polite smile fixed, though she would have liked to tell Orgo what she thought of his gruffness. She was glad to see Prime Herek striding towards them. She liked Herek. He lacked the previous Prime's charm and dash, but then the boots of Kyt Cyrus would be hard for any man to fill. She often wondered about his curious disappearance.

Herek was bowing. 'Queen Nyria, may I help?'

'Yes, thank you, Herek. I'm told this child was tied to the palace gates last night and I wish to know more.'

Before Herek or Orgo could speak, the tall Queen had bent low and was eye-to-eye with the tear-stained face of the boy. 'Don't be afraid,' she said, loosing his elbow from Orgo's grip.

'Thank you, Orgo.' It was a dismissal. Orgo looked uncertainly at the Prime, who nodded for him to leave.

The Queen had not taken her eyes from the boy's face. There was a familiarity about him which she could not place.

'My name is Nyria. What's yours?'

'I'm Gyl. I'm almost twelve,' he said and bowed politely which impressed her. 'Are you really a Queen?'

'I am *the* Queen,' she said, emphasising her importance by arching her eyebrows and making him giggle. 'Am I the first Queen you've ever taken breakfast with?'

'I've had breakfast, your majesty,' he answered.

'Well, I have not. Perhaps you'd care to sit with me?'
Nyria took his hand, stood upright again and said to the
soldier, 'We'll be fine.'

'My lady, perhaps I should—'

Her look stopped him saying any more. 'Thank you,
Herek.' Another dismissal.

'Yes, thank you, Herek,' Gyl offered. His cheeky grin
was not lost on the Prime or the Queen.

Alyssa's emotions were still churned up from the
morning's activity. Jayn Elkin's son, runty though he
looked, was already suckling and that augured well for
mother and child. As she crossed the main courtyard, a
page called to her. She stopped whilst he ran towards her.

'Her majesty wishes to speak with you, Alyssa.'

'Right now?'

He nodded. 'I'm to bring you.'

They made their way to the Queen's chambers on the
northern side of the castle. Alyssa desperately hoped Lorys
was not anywhere close by.

'Is the King present?' she asked casually.

'No,' the page replied. 'He went for his morning ride
but is not returned yet.'

Alyssa was led into an antechamber and asked to wait.
It was not long before a lady-in-waiting asked her to enter,
then left her alone in the Queen's private sitting room.
Nyria stepped in from an adjoining room a moment later.

'Alyssa. Thank you for coming. Here, please sit with
me. I have ordered some lemon tea.'

'Forgive me, your majesty. I have come directly from
Lady Elkin.'

Alyssa felt flustered. The Queen looked elegant as

always. Tall and slim, she sat straight-backed so the fine garments, simple but sophisticated, hung gorgeously from her frame. Alyssa felt dowdy by comparison. She wiped her hands on her skirt, more out of embarrassment than need.

'A fine boy for the Elkins, I'm told.'

Alyssa nodded, glad to see the tea arriving with the same lady-in-waiting. They paused whilst the tray was set down. She hoped it would distract the Queen from talk of the morning's birth.

'Thank you, Aileen,' the Queen said. 'Can I pour you some, Alyssa?'

Alyssa nodded again.

Nyria handed her a beautiful porcelain cup. 'I'm also told,' she said, continuing precisely where she had left off, 'that you did something rather extraordinary today which probably saved both mother and child.'

Damn you, Elsa, Alyssa thought, reddening. 'Oh, I don't think I—'

'No false modesty, please, my child. I've lived too long; seen too much cruelty. All of us are in your debt for saving two lives today. Now!' She clapped her hands as though about to share some great jest. 'I have been following your progress these past years, Alyssa, and I've decided it's high time we made use of your real skills.'

'Oh?' Alyssa really did not know what else to say, so she sipped her tea and waited.

'Indeed. I am in dire need of a new secretary. I would like you to take up that role and work alongside me.'

Alyssa put her cup down. She could not believe what was being offered.

Nyria held up her manicured hand. 'There's more. You

will do this work for half the day. For the rest of the time I wish you to start a small school in the palace. I am determined that all the children who live here learn the rudiments of reading and writing. You are more than capable of running my school, so make no feeble protest.'

Alyssa swallowed. This was more than she had ever dared dream. 'It would be an honour, your majesty.' She was glad her voice remained steady.

Nyria rang a small bell next to the tray. She looked delighted with herself.

'And I have your first student,' she said, standing to greet the child being led into the room. 'I want you to meet Gyl. Gyl, this is the lady we spoke of.'

Alyssa, who was not very tall, found herself looking directly into the lad's greyish eyes. He seemed strangely familiar but she could not put her finger on the resemblance. He held his hand out politely and she took it. She looked at the beaming Queen and back at the child.

'I hear we are starting a school together, Gyl. Will you help me?'

'I would like that,' he replied.

2

A Messenger Hastens

The man was sitting in a straight-backed chair he had made himself. His hand rested loosely around the half-empty mug on the rickety side table, also of his own design.

'I have a secret,' he said quietly, as he regarded the apparition which floated in front of him.

'Tell me,' it whispered, like a sigh on the wind.

'It's a terrible secret, Yargo.' The man paused; his impossibly blue eyes held hers intently. 'But I need to share it with you.'

He dropped his gaze to stare at the earthen floor. The translucent creature, faintly tinged with green, hovered in silence. She knew when to stay quiet with the man and moments passed whilst her robes billowed around her. They were forever moving and it was hard to tell where they began and her long, silky hair ended.

In almost four summers, she had neither discovered the reason for him being here nor found out anything about his past. It was clear he was educated and his manner suggested courtly training, but he was more closed about his early life than any of the dusty books in this cottage.

He had intrigued Yargo from the moment she had been given the task of watching over him and had drifted gently into his life. She had become much more than an observer, however, which was a clear breach of the rules laid down by the Custodian, Lys, who had sent her to stay close to this mysterious fellow. Yargo, a young and popular member of the Host, had beseeched Lys to find a task for her when her disgraced husband, a god, had fallen seriously foul of his King. Yargo was determined to make up for her husband's shame and so Lys had contrived a special role for her in watching over this precious man.

Yargo had fallen in love with him from the second he had turned those clear, sad eyes upon her. It would come to nothing, of course; she was a spiritual creature only in his world, unable to enjoy physical contact. But the fascination she felt for him was as physical as it was mental.

He was strangely tall — too tall, it seemed to Yargo, for most men of this world — and he possessed the broadest of shoulders. His frame had filled out with the manual work he imposed on himself daily. He told her that the physical exertion calmed his mind and prepared it for the equally rigorous study he carried out each day.

Yargo had learned from Lys that the old master sentient, Merkhud, had harnessed this man's massive power to wrench his spirit free from its body and deposit it into his own frail form, at the same moment throwing his own spirit into the younger man's body in order to undergo execution by crucifixion and stoning in his stead. It was Merkhud's choice to take the younger man's punishment; to save him from death.

Yargo had been given scant additional information. She knew that the spirit of the man in front of her had travelled awkwardly in Merkhud's body between Tal and the Heartwood, where Arabella the priestess watched over the joining of his spirit with his own broken shell of a body. When spirit and flesh were reunited, Darmud Coril, god of the forest, called down the powers of the Host and together they channelled life back into this man. It was a mighty healing and he was made whole.

It had taken two summers just to get him to talk again. During that time Yargo had watched his damaged emotions mend more slowly than his body. She knew nothing of why his suffering had occurred but instinctively understood that here was a man who had lost everything. He had no reason to live but live he did within a cocoon of silence. It was how he wanted it.

She travelled with him on his long walks, floating swiftly and mostly invisibly alongside while his glorious falcon flew high above. The day he first spoke to her was the happiest she could recall. His voice, scratchy from lack of use, was nonetheless of a gentle pitch and she easily became absorbed in listening to his quiet conversation.

Yargo loved to provoke his smile and thrilled herself if she could cause him to tilt back his head with an infectious and all too rare laugh. He was, quite simply, the most beautiful man she had ever known and she longed with every inch of her insubstantial body to touch him.

She knew she would give her soul to smooth that straight long hair he usually kept neatly tied, or to feel the roughness of the dark beard he trimmed so closely. Beyond this, and far more powerful, was the intense curiosity he stirred in her about the dark past he kept so deeply buried. That intoxicating mysteriousness, combined with a long-held notion that his life may have taken this course because of a woman, constantly fired Yargo's imagination.

As she mused on this, he spoke in his soft manner again. 'I need you to be a messenger, dear Yargo.'

He swallowed another mouthful of the sweet berry wine which he kept chilled in the nearby stream.

'I am listening, Tor.'

Her dreamy tone was soothing and did not betray her anticipation of the secret she had chased all these summers.

'You must hear my story and then you must go and find some people for me. It may take you a long time. I need you to watch over them and when you sense the sign, as you will, bring them back to Tallinor. You must warn them.'

She drifted across the room. 'And what must I warn them about?'

'I'll come to that,' he said, running his fingers through his hair.

She noticed he looked tired; too much study perhaps. Or did he look nervous? She could not tell. She floated after him as he moved with his unique economy of motion to the window. His lean frame was silhouetted against the lowering sun and in the silence whilst he gathered his thoughts, she wondered at the beauty of that body which had been delivered to the Heartwood dead and broken.

Yargo had been summoned by Lys when Torkyn Gynt's life was restored. She recalled exactly what Lys had said to her when she was chosen as his Companion.

'It will take a long time for his body to recover. It will take even longer for his emotional state to heal. He will demand to be alone but I want you to become his friend. This man is the most precious thing we have

in our care. He alone will deliver Orlac. Take it slowly.
Between you and the falcon, encourage his conversation,
laughter, memories. Together you will heal his mind.'

And it had taken four years.

Tor had ignored her at first. Yargo knew he spoke across
a link with the falcon, Cloot. He needed no other company,
yet she had persevered. Darmud Coril and the Heartwood
had mended the broken body beautifully. Arabella the
priestess, Tor's second-bonded Paladin, had watched over
him for many weeks whilst the powerful magics of the
Heartwood restored his health.

And when he had finally awoken, the Heartwood and
its creatures had rejoiced. As soon as he was strong enough
to walk, he had left its sanctuary with no direction in
mind. Yargo, following, knew the forest guided him; but
Tor seemed not to care. He simply walked, with Cloot
ever nearby. Then one day, at the edge of a small copse
where a tiny stream ran by, he chose his spot and painstak-
ingly built this humble dwelling. He hunted and foraged
for his own food and even made his own wine. They had
not seen another person these past four summers, save
visits from Arabella.

Yargo could tell that Tor carried great grief within his
heart. She had wished so many times that she could unlock
it and somehow help him. Perhaps now was that time.
Staring out of the window as the sun began to sink behind
the trees, he began to talk. His normally soft, smooth
voice sounded brittle.

'It is painful for me to remember what has gone before.'

She said nothing.

Shaking his head, he rallied himself. He returned to
his chair and settled back with long legs stretched out

and crossed at the ankles. Refilling his cup, Tor began the story. It was the first time he had allowed himself to recall the chain of events leading up to his death, and the only reason he would permit himself to speak of the past now was because of the powerful shift he felt from the Heartwood.

Another Paladin had succumbed.

Recalling his earlier years would be painful; he knew this and it helped immeasurably that he was, for the second time in his life, getting resoundingly drunk as he began his tale. He spoke for hours; sometimes haltingly, at other moments with words spilling over one another. Yargo kept her peace, incredulous at his story.

His quietly spoken words rang in her ears and the scene of his execution played in her mind. Tor told her that at the end he had felt nothing. From behind the eyes of Merkhud, he had been forced to watch his own body spill its lifeblood, knowing that the spirit of Merkhud had died within it.

'After all his deceits and manipulations, he gave his life for me,' he said sadly.

She wanted to weep when he admitted it was also his final betrayal of his beloved Alyssa. He had betrayed her the first time by agreeing to leave for Tal as the Royal Physic's apprentice. The second time he had betrayed her loyalty by leaving her in the forest, and her love and trust by telling her that the son she had birthed had died. He had not said a word to her about the second child.

'But this was the worst betrayal of all, Yargo. She watched me die. She watched my head split like ripe fruit from the stone of the executioner whilst I hung from the cross. She poured her love towards me and wept tears of despair. And later, stumbling around in Merkhud's body, I stood close to her and had my chance to give her a sign . . . anything . . . but I didn't. I just allowed myself to betray her once again.'

'You must not blame yourself.' The words rang hollow as she spoke them but Yargo was fearful that all the years of effort to get him well again might be wasted if he allowed this maudlin mood to overwhelm him. She switched tack. 'Perhaps you should tell me what you wish of me?'

He did not hesitate. 'You must find them. Find Sorrel and with her my son and daughter. Bring them back to me, Yargo.'

'How do you know it is time?' she asked.

'There was a shift in the Land's force this morning. Did you not feel it?'

'I heard the Heartwood creaking,' she replied.

'Well, I felt the Heartwood groan with despair. It means another of the Paladin has died. I felt Orlac's glee. I wonder whether my children felt it too. We are all connected to the Heartwood — perhaps, wherever they are, they also reacted.'

Yargo did not understand his words, but she knew what he asked of her. She floated until she hovered next to him. 'And so I must go?'

'Yes. Track them down. Lys can travel the portals, she will give you passage. Search. Find my children. Look for the Stones of Ordolt: they will call to you. I gave Sorrel these three orbs before she fled with the children.' He shrugged. 'I still don't know what their significance is, but my father gave them to me, told me they were important.'

'And what do I tell these people should I find them?'

'*When* you find them,' he would allow her no room for failure, 'tell Sorrel that I require her and my children to return to Tallinor. You must go now.'

'Perhaps I should consult Lys first.'

'I already have. She has given her permission for you to do this for me.'

Yargo floated silently in shimmering fluorescence. She was upset and Tor knew it, but he needed her help now. Time worked against them.

Her voice was sad when she finally spoke. 'I shall leave you then.'

'I am indebted to you, Yargo,' he said and watched his Companion's brightness dull until she was no longer with him.

Tor absentmindedly drummed his fingers on the books as he thought about their contents. When he was packing the cart which carried Tor's corpse to the Heartwood, Merkhud had taken great care to include his own most precious books. Since his return to life and settling into his hermit's existence, Tor had devoured their contents.

All except these two.

Merkhud had not known about these books. Alyssa had discovered them beneath the old catacombs of Caremboche and carried them with her to the Heartwood when she escaped the clutches of Chief Inquisitor Goth.

When Tor and Alyssa were captured by the King's Guard and a triumphant Goth, it was Kythay the donkey who had rescued Alyssa's precious books, casually strolling away from the scene with them strapped into the basket on his back.

Tor had no idea how the books had come into his possession but he had found them by his side when he awoke from the ministrations of the Heartwood which returned him to health. Whilst Merkhud's tomes were devoted to the wielding of strange magics, which certainly fascinated and occasionally inspired him, Alyssa's books – the Writings of Nanak – were infinitely more disturbing. He had not opened them since his awakening from death. They reminded him too powerfully of Alyssa and it was hard living with the guilt of being alive when she thought him dead. Tor wanted to put the Trinity out of his mind for ever. His old disquiet over Lys had returned. He knew she was leading them all somewhere and even though he relied on her help and guidance, he hated the manipulation. The books were part of the complex plot, he was sure of it.

Read the wretched books, Cloot said from his nearby perch. He had been hunting again and was cleaning his fierce beak of some poor animal's entrails, an occupation that never failed to make his friend wince.

Tor touched the pale thin scar which streaked across his own forehead, a legacy of the stones and a constant reminder of his grief. It reinforced all that they had come through to get this far. He had nowhere else to go but forward. As he opened the first book, a faint scent of lavender and violets wafted briefly into his senses, lingering just long enough for him to smell Alyssa. She was the last person to have fingered these pages. He tried desperately to catch the fragrance again but it was lost for ever.

He stared at the first page for an hour or more, seeing nothing but her face. Finally, he began to read.

3

Forgiveness

Alyssa was the happiest she could remember since those early days in the Heartwood after her marriage to Tor. At last she felt as though her life had a purpose again. Working directly with Queen Nyria was challenging and always busy but she thrived in the political environment and she loved the Queen. Despite the difference in their ages, they shared a similar sense of humour and an irreverence for protocol, though Nyria was always careful never to abuse her royal status. She knew how to have fun and the pair would share great private jokes and, more often than not, if the Queen was not dining with the King, she enjoyed taking a late supper with Alyssa.

Nyria found her new assistant to be hardworking, intelligent and perceptive, as well as a wonderful mimic of the obsequious courtiers around them. She learned a great deal about the girl during their evening meals. There were only two subjects they never discussed: Torkyn Gynt and King Lorys, though the Queen intended to address the latter.

Alyssa was closed on the topic of her lover and would

not be drawn, but Nyria noticed that the girl listened with shining eyes and a fascination reserved just for these moments when she told her stories of Tor during his apprenticeship. It was sad to think that this lovely woman had missed out on so much of her love's life and was forced to learn of his past from others.

Alyssa's hostility towards the King was obvious, even though Nyria could never accuse her of any direct criticism. No, it was more the cool contempt she displayed which troubled Nyria. In truth, the Queen was tired of the tension that arose whenever her two favourite people were in the same hall, let alone a smaller chamber. Lorys pretended he did not notice but she knew he found it difficult too.

Alyssa's work in her small school was testimony to the Queen's faith in the young woman. The palace children adored her and clamoured to attend her afternoon lessons, keen to please their teacher. It was a joy for Nyria to hear the children singing or reading aloud and she had even been invited to view some of their drawings and writings. Primitive though much of their work was, it thrilled Nyria nonetheless.

Alyssa's greatest success, though, was with the boy, Gyl. The child now displayed the full breadth of his bright personality and wit, which had been dulled by the shock of losing his mother at such a young age. There was no question in Nyria's mind: the boy was a born leader. He already knew how to read and write and so Alyssa's work with him was one of enrichment. They would spend long evenings together reading poetry or creating their own stories.

Gyl flourished in his new life and his growing relationship with Alyssa. Nyria realised that Alyssa's dashed hopes of motherhood had been rekindled. She had slipped immediately and with ease into the role of big sister to Gyl, but recently the Queen had noticed a more maternal attitude from Alyssa towards the lad, who was now fourteen summers.

They had certainly been two lost and damaged souls who had healed each other. Yes, the Queen was pleased with her achievements and if she could just sort out this business between Alyssa and Lorys she would be very happy indeed. Secretly she wondered if Lorys admired Alyssa for more than her able skills as a secretary. The young woman was in the prime of her life. At twenty-four summers, she was by far the most gorgeous creature who roamed the palace corridors; she turned heads wherever she went and was able to twist the pages and young squires around her finger for any little jobs she needed done. The lovely part was that she was not a vain woman. If she knew she was delicious to the eyes, then she hid the knowledge well. Petite and slim with honey-coloured hair and pale green eyes, Alyssa was surely irresistible to any red-blooded man . . . including her husband?

Nyria pushed the notion away. Lorys had never given her cause to doubt his fidelity and after so many years of marriage they still enjoyed their lovemaking. No, she must not doubt him, particularly now, as her plan was to encourage Lorys to take on Alyssa as his own private assistant. Nyria did not really want to relinquish Alyssa's companionship or her unrivalled clerical skills, but the King's faithful old secretary had died suddenly and it seemed there was no one else in Tal capable of stepping into the man's shoes with speed or competence.

*   *   *

Alyssa did not hide her shock well enough. 'Work as the King's private secretary?'

Nyria took a steadying breath. 'Yes.'

'Am I not pleasing you, your majesty?'

'Alyssa, don't. You know how highly I consider your help . . . but the King needs you more.' Nyria touched Alyssa's hand across the table. 'In helping him, you help me far more than you can imagine.'

Now Nyria could see the initial alarm snapping into petulance – or was it defiance – as Alyssa's full lips thinned slightly. She rushed on. 'And my plan is that you will continue with the school, perhaps look at taking on and training an assistant teacher.'

'To take my place?'

Nyria spoke calmly. 'No. To help.'

There was an uncomfortable silence, which Alyssa filled by nibbling nervously on her bread.

'And you've discussed this with his majesty?' she asked finally.

'I have and he admits he would be fortunate to have your service. It will throw you into all sorts of situations, Alyssa, that you will thrive in. I know how you enjoy even the small amount of political intrigue which knocks at my door. At his side you will be amongst it all. And you would have the King's ear; Lorys would be turning to you constantly for support.'

Alyssa knew the Queen was genuine. She felt torn. She would be lying if she did not admit that being privy to such elevated matters as the running of the Kingdom excited her. However, the idea of working alongside a man she despised second only to the former Chief Inquisitor, Goth, made her stomach turn.

At least Goth was dead now. How many times had she thought about killing the King in those early days? Too many. Saxon had sensed her rage and cautioned her. There was nothing to be gained by it, he had said. Why become like him, a murderer? It would not bring Tor back. And there was an even worse end than crucifixion and stoning for those who would commit such treachery.

Alyssa imagined herself being hung upside down, her belly split open and her entrails pulled out to lie steaming on the dusty earth whilst the scavenger dogs and crows feasted on them. She shivered.

'Take this chance, my dear, with both hands and clasp it tight. You will soon become a force in the Kingdom.'

The Queen held her breath. She had played her trump card.

'Nyria . . .' Alyssa had never addressed the Queen so intimately before, 'if someone killed your husband—'

'But he was not your husband, child,' the Queen interjected.

Alyssa bit back the obvious retort. She would keep that secret. 'Nevertheless . . . what would you want to do if someone killed Lorys?'

'I should immediately wish the person killed in return,' the Queen replied flatly. 'But then I might think about it. I would measure the situation. If it was an eye for an eye, that would be retribution. But in Tor's case it was not so. He was convicted of a very serious crime against the Kingdom. He knew what he was doing; I gather he was well counselled prior to his departure. And Tor was ever the one for the ladies, Alyssa – I'm sure you already know this. He left a scattered trail of broken hearts across the capital, which made it all the more important for him to understand and abide by the ancient laws of Caremboche. Precautions were taken.'

Alyssa nodded sadly. 'Your majesty . . . he saved my life.'

'He saved my life too and I will admit it has never sat comfortably with me that we took his life from him.'

Alyssa was shocked to hear this. 'Why didn't you stop him, your majesty? A word from you would—'

'I did try, my child. I begged him. It was to no avail. Lorys has faithfully followed in the footsteps of his fore-bears. He is a good King, and a good man. I believe he thought it was the right thing to do, even though I imagine he has not slept comfortably since he executed a person he admired very much. He lost his best friend through it, too. Merkhud left Tal moments after Tor's death and there has been a mighty hole in Lory's life since then. I'll say this only for your ears, child. I believe that if Lorys could have that moment again, he might choose differently.'

Nyria looked at Alyssa hard. She took her hand and squeezed it for emphasis. 'I want you to forgive him . . . as Tor forgave his King before he died.'

It all came back to Alyssa in a rush: that terrible moment when she heard Tor's lovely voice offer his forgive-ness. She began to cry. 'I don't know how to forgive him,' she whispered.

The Queen took Alyssa into her arms and soothed her. 'You will learn how when you start to give him a chance. See him for the good man he is, and for the excellent King he is to his people. He has compassion, Alyssa. Trust me, just give him a chance. This is all I ask of you. Nay, child, I beg it of you. He needs you and I need you to find the strength to try.'

Alyssa sniffed. 'I'm frightened by my feelings towards him, your majesty.'

Nyria snorted. 'Don't be. Use that emotion. Lorys will benefit from having a female perspective in the throne hall. I'm not suggesting that you will be able to behave differently immediately. I'm just asking you to try. Take on this position. Embrace the opportunity, use it wisely and perhaps somewhere along the way, you might start to allow that old wound to heal.'

She watched Alyssa struggle with the decision and decided to press her point one last time. 'Tor broke our most sacred rule and was punished to the full letter of our law. He's dead, Alyssa, and you continuing to hate the King will not bring him back. So turn it around. Make something of yourself that would make Tor proud. Become someone the sovereign can lean on. You will have everything you've ever wanted for yourself and for Gyl.'

They both smiled at the mention of Gyl.

'He's wonderful, isn't he?' Alyssa said shyly.

'He's magnificent. I've seen him sparring with the guards and I'll be damned if I didn't see him learning how to balance on Saxon's shoulders and walk blindfolded along a rope stretched above the ground.'

Alyssa laughed. 'Saxon says it will make him the most balanced swordsman in the land.'

Nyria shared the moment of mirth. 'You should have plans for Gyl. He is Prime material if ever I've seen it.'

'Do you think so?'

'The Light strike you, girl! Don't you?'

'I dare not wish too much for him. We are both so indebted to your majesty for her generosity.'

'Oh, really? Then repay it!'

Alyssa looked sharply at the Queen and then relaxed; she knew exactly what the other woman meant.

'*Will* you repay me?' Nyria asked, softly this time.

The Queen's heart leapt at the single word she heard in response. It was everything she had hoped Alyssa would say.

Tor had spent the past several moons stewing over the contents of Nanak's books. Everything had been quiet in the Great Forest. No further disruptions to the life force of the Land. The Heartwood was in harmony once again. But Tor's emotions were not.

It had been a chilling reminder to read the story of Orlac. Cloot recognised this and, finally, had begun encouraging Tor to talk about all that he knew of the tale from Lys. They had never discussed it during their reclusive years since the execution, for Cloot had devoted himself to helping his companion remain optimistic and had deliberately avoided talk of Orlac and the Trinity or the hard times which may lie ahead. For himself, Tor had focused on the peace and solitude of the Heartwood and was glad to avoid all discussion of the Trinity. And Cloot was patient; he was of the Rork'yel, after all, and that heritage ran strongly through his blood, despite his transformation from man to falcon. But now the time to talk was upon them.

So the Paladin were selected by the Custodian of the portals, he prompted.

Yes. Lys is the only member of the Host who can safely roam between worlds.

Go on, Cloot urged.

On rare occasion worlds can touch, and at such times passage

*between them is possible via a phenomenon known as The Glade.
That's how Orlac was stolen from the Host.*

Tor put the books carefully back into the sack.

Tell me what you're thinking, said the falcon, swooping
down to the forest floor to glare with one beady yellow
eye at his friend, who was sitting leaning against a tree.

*All right. What we suspected about Merkhud and Sorrel
being Orlac's mortal parents is confirmed in Nanak's writings.
After Orlac wreaked havoc at Goldstone, now known as
Caremboche, he was Quelled by the mighty power of the Host,
wielded through Merkhud. Nanak, one of the Masters still alive,
was nominated as Keeper of the Paladin, who were chosen from
the ten major races alive in the Five Kingdoms at the time. They
were empowered by the gods with magical talents which might
stand them in good stead for their undertaking.*

Cloot clicked his approval in bird-speak.

Tor continued. *We know the Host transported Orlac to a
secret place, which is not named and, I presume, not of this Land.
He has remained there ever since, guarded by the complex and
combined magical strength of the ten Paladin, whom he has
gradually overwhelmed one by one over the centuries.*

How do you imagine the books came back into Tallinor?
Cloot asked, switching thoughts as his mind raced.

Tor was used to this habit. *Yes, that's a mystery. Perhaps
via Lys, though I have no idea whether she can physically enter
into Tallinor. Companions, like Yargo, are not of the flesh so
they could not carry objects between worlds. I don't know.* He
shrugged.

*So that's all the ancient history. Right now, we know the
Paladin are re-emerging.*

Yes, Tor replied. *So far we have yourself, Solyana, Arabella,
Saxon, Cyrus and Sallementro accounted for. Nanak names the*

other four . . . people . . . creatures — I'm not sure — Juno,
Themesius, Figgis, Adongo.

Cloot hopped closer. Tor could almost hear him
thinking across the link. *I see that Arabella and myself belong*
to you, whilst Saxon and, I imagine, this songster Sallementro
stay close to Alyssa. What of Solyana and Cyrus — the ones we
know of? And these others yet to reveal themselves?

I don't know. Lys did say that Cyrus is Paladin and has
his own important role to play, but whatever she knows, she is
not telling me yet.

Why does Arabella not travel with us if she is bonded to
you?

Yes, I puzzled over that too. Lys told me that each of the
Paladin have their own special magic and role to play and when
I spoke to Arabella about this it did not surprise her. She believes
her major role had been fulfilled.

And that is?

Marrying Alyssa and myself . . . watching over me as my
spirit crossed back into my body after the execution and then
helping to restore my health as well as she did. There may be
more though, I'm not sure. If she knows, she is not saying.

Cloot voiced what Tor had often suspected. *I sense that*
Arabella is strongly attached to the Heartwood. I'm not sure she
would be comfortable to leave it . . . perhaps she can't? The
falcon noted Tor's nod of agreement and moved on to his
next thought. *You know, I've never understood why, if we are*
all so strongly linked, we don't feel one another or recognise one
another? he puzzled.

I think you will in time. There must be a connection . . .
maybe a place or an event . . . something which will realign
you all, Tor said. *When I swapped bodies with Merkhud, we*
exchanged minds and experiences briefly. Just for a moment, I

glimpsed his thoughts and possibly he did the same with mine.

You're never mentioned this before, Cloot said, sounding indignant. *What did you perceive?*

It was fleeting. I sensed he knew that only Figgis and Themesius remained to fall. The way the Heartwood groaned recently though, I fear there is now only one left.

And after the last Paladin falls?

Orlac will be free. Lys told me that he will destroy Tallinor and all surrounding Kingdoms in his fury. He will raze the Heartwood, Cloot. He will sense its magic; that it is a special place of the gods. It will be his revenge against the Land which claimed his life; his vengeance against the man who bought him as a child and made him live as a mortal. Perhaps it is also his chance to point a finger at the Host, to show the gods his strength and make clear that the havoc he wreaks on them is in revenge for their failure to protect their prince.

Cloot hopped onto Tor's shoulder. *But Merkhud is gone, Tor. Who will Orlac hunt down to vent his anger?*

Silence hung heavy between them momentarily. Across the link Tor's voice sounded small. *Me.*

You? But why?

Because I am linked to Merkhud. Lys has warned that Orlac will not be satisfied to learn of Merkhud's death. He will fasten onto those whom Merkhud loved.

Can we hide you? Or can you not become the hunter instead?

To what end, my friend? No. Orlac will come. Of this we are sure. All we can do is prepare for that time. I am the prey and we must use the quarry to trap the hunter. Lys has brought us all together for a reason and we must try to work out what she wants us to do with our combined powers and knowledge.

Has it ever occurred to anyone just to ask her? Cloot said, unable to hide his sarcasm.

That is not her way. She wants us to figure this out. If we ask the right questions, we will get the right answers.

All right, the falcon said, stretching his wings and swooping into the centre of the clearing to face his friend. *I gather you are well enough now, and in sending Yargo to find Sorrel and the children, you have obviously made a decision that it is time to move on. So what do we do first?*

Well, Lys once said something cryptic to me, which has only recently surfaced again in my mind. She told me to look to those who would be easily corrupted by power and promises of revenge. She impressed upon me, in her strange, vague way, to think on those who would most enjoy seeing me and those I care for hurt.

Tor, you would make a superb tooth doctor with your fine ability to extract maximum agony. And so?

It's so obvious, you mad bird. Goth! Xantia! That charming couple with nothing to lose any more and everything to gain.

You're right. Goth is evil and Xantia is his pawn.

Oh no, Cloot, she's more than that. Xantia is a master of the Dark Arts. If Orlac reaches them and releases her from the archalyt barrier on her forehead, we might as well burn down Tal ourselves and save them the trouble.

So your plan is . . . ? Cloot prompted, hoping there was one.

We go after Goth. Better we stay close to our enemies.

How?

I'm thinking on it, Tor said quietly.

No, I'm not sure I caught that, Tor. I thought you said we were going to fly.

Tor knew very well that Cloot's hearing was almost as acute as his own.

I did say that.

Ah, said the falcon from the overhanging branch. He began to sharpen his beak, as was his habit whenever he felt uncomfortable or needed time to think. *And how will we accomplish such a feat?* he said carefully, emphasising the 'we'.

Well, I have no magic that will sprout me wings, old friend. So I presume I shall be doing the flying?

Correct. And I shall be doing the accompanying.

I see. So you plan to ride me like a horse then?

Tor did not respond to the sarcasm. *From within my body.* It was not a question this time.

Cloot was incredulous. *You will use the Spiriting magic again?*

It will be no different to when I inhabited Merkhud's body, Tor replied, his voice very quiet.

Cloot stopped his cleaning. Nothing had prepared him for this.

Tor, when you walked in Merkhud's boots, you knew his spirit had already died within your body which was hanging off that cross.

Tor pushed away from the tree he had been leaning against and stood.

Cloot, come to me.

The falcon landed on his outstretched arm. Tor stroked the majestic bird and poured his complete loyalty and love for his strange friend across the link. He waited until he felt Cloot relax, mind and body, before he spoke again.

But you will not be dying. I have given this much thought and in Nanak's books I read of a notion held centuries ago that two could share one host for a short time. I accept it may only have been a notion and never attempted, but I believe it will work.

Tor, my beloved friend, it is not my life I fear for. I am Paladin. I have already died once for you and I will surely face death again to save you. You are everything we have strived for. All of this — this strange life, these terrible ordeals — have been to preserve your life and ensure you meet your destiny. No, Tor. Never think that I care a whit about my life compared with yours. It is you I fear for. I am shocked that you would risk your life with such a dangerous idea.

Tor lifted Cloot close to his face so he could look at him directly. The bird cocked his head to one side and eyed him back.

Don't do this, Tor.

Trust me.

Let's wait for Lys, at least. She set you on this course of thinking; she may have some suggestions, Cloot offered hopefully.

No. Alyssa's life may be in danger from Goth. Lys has conveyed as much to me. I must know Goth's whereabouts. I will feel safer knowing where the enemy is.

Cloot hopped back onto his friend's shoulder. *Goth is not the enemy. You must not lose sight of who your real foe is and where the real danger lies. Orlac!*

Tor sighed. *Well, until that particular enemy shows himself, I must content myself with the one I do know about. Cloot, I'm not saying I'm going to do anything. I just want to know where he is.*

All right. Let's pretend I agree to this folly — no, this lunacy. What do we do with your body . . . your cooling, dying body?

This was a great step forward. Tor wasted no time.

The Heartwood will keep my body safe for a time.

He moved on quickly to outline his thoughts. He did not want Cloot dwelling on possible death; he had already spooked himself enough over the frightening thought of leaving his body once again.

The way I see it, when Goth escaped from the palace prison, he would probably have been ghoulish enough to hang around amongst the mob for my execution. Then he would have used the cover of the crowds to get himself as far away from the capital as possible.

Agreed, Cloot said.

The King's wrath aside, he would have grasped that Herek's pride alone would demand that the Shield track him down, whatever it took, however long it required.

Go on.

Well, I've been thinking on where I would go if I wanted to get as far away from the reach of the palace as possible.

North, of course, Cloot said.

Yes, north. But more than that. It would have to be a quiet backwater, somewhere the threat of the Inquisitors was unlikely to have reached. Goth is too readily recognisable to risk a city or town.

Cloot picked up this thread. *Or a place where criminals can move freely . . . somewhere with an underworld where secrets are kept and officialdom is unwelcome.*

Tor felt the idea slide into place. *You're right! Goth could not survive in a village. His appetites are too large.*

Cloot was silent. He was thinking. Tor knew this because the falcon had a tendency to stand on one leg when deep in thought. It amused him and he smiled warmly for the first time in many weeks.

Well, my friend, he said finally, *the north is your country. Where do you think he hides — Rork'yel?*

Cloot returned to stand on both legs. *Rork'yel is closed to all but my own people. Without a guide who is of the Rork'yel,*

Goth would get lost amongst the rocks. But I agree with you. His appetites are such that he would need the trappings of a town. However, he could not risk going back to Ildagarth or anywhere nearby.

How long do we have to search? he suddenly asked Tor.

You mean before my physical body dies? I would say two days, possibly less. Darmud Coril might tell us. We should summon Solyana and beg an audience.

Cloot swooped up to one of his favourite branches. *He will not like it.*

He wants the Heartwood to survive, Cloot. He will help us.

Then, if you are set on this course, my best guess would be Caradoon.

I've never heard of it. Tor was intrigued.

And that's how its inhabitants prefer it. It is a trading post. You've heard of Kyrakavia, of course? He saw Tor nod. *Well, that's the shipping hub for all regular trade from the northern Kingdoms into Tallinor. Caradoon is a thriving town on the very outreaches of the city of Kyrakavia where all the . . . shall we say . . . irregular trade is done.*

Like what?

Spices, herbs, gold . . . even wine.

That sounds fairly regular.

Cloot continued as though Tor had not spoken. *Children, slaves, the forbidden stracca.*

Tor had never seen stracca but had heard of the secret dens where the leaf was smoked or the sap swallowed. He stood. His jaw was set in a fashion that told Cloot his mind was also set.

Let's find Solyana and you can tell me more about this Caradoon on the way.

4

Flight

Saxon gave a shrill war cry and tossed the orange. Gyl
spun. The kerchief blocked his vision but over these past
few months he had been learning to rely on his other
senses. He judged, struck with the sword and heard a
satisfying squelch as his blade sliced through the fruit.

'Bravo!' Saxon called. 'Another!' He moved hard to his
right, giving the lad no time, yelled again and threw a lemon.

Gyl was not fast enough. The lemon hit him on the
chest.

'Woeful!'

Gyl pulled off the blindfold, laughing. 'I won't be
blindfolded in battle, Sax.'

'Let's hope you never have to face battle, boy. But should
you, I want you to be able to cut a man down when you
have time only to hear the whoosh of his sword coming
towards your head.'

'I know. I almost had it though,' Gyl said, picking up
the lemon and tossing it back.

Saxon spat. It was a curious Kloekish habit. 'Almost
is not good enough.'

'Oh, Saxon, I remember you punishing me like this,' admonished Alyssa, who had arrived quietly.

The older man grunted. Alyssa smiled at Gyl. He had grown tall and his boyish features were hardening into the handsome man he would become. She wondered at how any mother could have abandoned this beautiful child. He reminded her so strongly of someone, but that person had always eluded her. Perhaps it was the distinctive walk. Gyl walked with purpose, with a jaunty, almost arrogant swagger. It was as though he knew he was a fine specimen of manhood – or even born to greatness.

She shook her head at such fanciful thoughts. Saxon shouted at him again.

'Saxon, enough!'

'Don't namby-pamby the boy, Alyssa. He's learning sword skills.'

'And what makes you think he's ever going to square up against someone on a battlefield who just happens to be blindfolded or balancing on a tightrope?' Her hands had settled on her hips; a dangerous sign.

Gyl laughed. 'Touché, Lyssa!'

Saxon scowled. 'Oh, go on with you both then. We'll leave you knitting for the children, Gyl, whilst the rest of us worry about the security of the Kingdom.'

Gyl rarely took offence. He worshipped Saxon. Instead he clapped the older man on the back good-naturedly. At fourteen summers he was almost as tall as the Kloek. 'I already know how to knit, Sax! I'll be back for more this evening with the company, if that's all right with you?'

'It's all right with me if your mother there hasn't got plans to plait your hair.'

Alyssa did not give Saxon the courtesy of a response. Her dark look was sufficient, though she could not help but feel a quiet thrill at the word 'mother'. It was the first time anyone had recognised her as Gyl's mother, including herself.

Saxon raised a hand in the air, feigning defeat. 'I'm going, I'm going,' he said. 'Alyssa, my love,' more sweetly this time. It was the voice she adored. 'A quiet word tonight. Meet me later?'

She nodded, wondering what the secrecy was about. Saxon was recently back from a scouting mission with Herek and company. Although he was not a fully fledged soldier of the Shield, he lived on its fringe and was arguably its most popular member. Perhaps he had some juicy gossip for her, she decided.

'Supper?'

Saxon nodded. 'I'll be late though.' He headed out of the courtyard.

Gyl dragged her attention back. 'Did you want me?'

'Yes, Gyl. There are some books in our rooms which I've been working on. I hoped you might carry them up to the King's private chambers for me?'

'Of course. Now?'

'Please.' He was already taller than her and she had to look up at him when he stood this close. 'You know, Saxon really did curse and yell at me like that when I was young.'

Gyl linked her arm with his. 'Surely he wasn't teaching you swordplay?'

'No. He taught me how to fly.' She enjoyed watching his puzzled expression.

'I've never really told you about Saxon and myself in the early days, have I?'

He shook his head. 'I've never dared to ask. It always seemed to be some great secret between the two of you.'

She was amused by his caution. 'Well, remind me to reveal that great secret to you. But come now, the King awaits.'

It was a balmy night and the scent of early summer flowers hung sweetly in the air around them. Alyssa inhaled it and sighed. She felt intensely happy and peaceful. Life had taken an unexpected and lovely turn. Her work with the children enriched her life, whilst nurturing Gyl fulfilled it. She realised she had not thought of Tor in many months, where before she had counted such times in minutes. She felt safe with Sallementro and Saxon close by, her loyal companions. But the sweetest surprise of all, one she barely allowed herself to admit, was daily life alongside Lorys. It was already early summer and she had joined him at the beginning of spring. Three moons ago.

The King had welcomed her warmly to his staff. Although Alyssa had tried hard to maintain her cool approach, the man possessed the most infectious good humour. Try though she might to avoid it, she found herself falling into his smile. Against her consent, it dragged her in and made her smile back . . . shyly. She had always considered Lorys to be dull and arrogant; however, he was anything but.

The King's humility towards his own people was astonishing. That he adored his subjects and his Kingdom was obvious to his new secretary and she felt moments of great shame about her attitude towards him in years gone. He was a man of peace, clearly, though she sensed enormous strength in him and felt he would not shirk battle if it was the only solution.

Lorys treated her with utmost respect and often took her breath away during meetings with his advisers – all men – when he would turn to where she sat quietly in the shadows recording the details and ask her opinion. This obviously made the group of nobles most uncomfortable and initially Alyssa had shied away from such attention. Now, however, she offered her views when asked.

Nyria had begged her to put Tor's death behind her and give Lorys a chance. It had seemed a far simpler thing to suggest than to do and yet, somehow, the man she had once vowed to stab in the heart should she ever get the chance had plunged a blade into hers . . . except his was one infinitely more subtle.

The first realisation came when she felt gooseflesh as Lorys accidentally brushed against her arm.

She had only felt such a sensation with Tor.

Lorys had reached across to take some papers and their arms had touched. His tanned skin was warm and the soft black hairs tickled for that instant. Alyssa did not think she could have reacted more loudly inside if she had been struck by lightning. Outwardly, she blushed, apologised and pulled her arm back. He hardly noticed her discomfort yet her heart had begun to hammer in her chest, like it was hammering now recalling the incident.

It was as if Saxon read her thoughts. They were sitting back to back against each other on a small hillock behind the palace.

'How goes it with Lorys, Alyssa?'

She gulped her wine, trying to mask her embarrassment. Surely it did not show? It *must* not show. Lorys already had a Queen; one she loved dearly.

Saxon did not sense her anxiety. Good job he had his back to her, she thought. He continued speaking. 'I mean, I know how you've felt about him all these years so I'm very proud of you for working alongside him so harmoniously. I'm sure it takes great courage. But how do you truly feel about this relationship?'

'Saxon, I have changed a lot over these years, you know. Since Gyl. The school. Working with their majesties. It's been a time of growing up for me. I have new responsibilities, ones I care passionately about. There is a reason to live again.' She hugged her arms about her before adding, 'There is so much to look forward to and I want to put the past behind me.'

Saxon turned to face her and pulled her against his chest. He hesitated momentarily before speaking. 'Well said, brave Alyssa.'

She leaned back comfortably against the broad chest of this man she loved enormously; he was like a father to her . . . more so than her own father had been.

'I am happy, Saxon. Truly. Torkyn Gynt is behind me. I am definitely looking forward.'

She felt him tense slightly.

'That's good, my girl. I need you to feel secure because I have to go away briefly. And I have some news which I will not keep from you a moment longer.'

His voice sounded strange all of a sudden. She swung around. He was looking at the grass.

'Look at me, Saxon!'

He did so and she saw pain in his eyes.

'Tell me. Nothing you say could be worse than what I've already faced in years gone.'

Saxon could not think of an easy way to say it so he chose the one word which he knew would sum it all up. 'Goth,' he whispered.

'What?' Alyssa grabbed his face so she could stare into his eyes and search for the truth. He felt hairs rip from his beard with the force of her grip but he did not flinch. Instead he sighed.

'Goth is dead,' she said flatly, already disbelieving her own words because of what she could see in his troubled gaze.

'Maybe not,' Saxon replied carefully, taking her hands from his face and wrapping them in his own. He pulled her close again. Alyssa began to tremble. The joy of moments earlier had fled, to be replaced with horror.

Saxon spoke softly, close to her ear. 'I have just learned that Goth escaped the night before Tor's death, but it was hushed up. The Shield was confident of tracking him down within hours.' He sensed a torrent of questions and squeezed her to prevent them pouring out. 'He escaped with the help of an accomplice. Xantia.'

This time a shriek escaped her but he continued. 'The Shield has not relented in its efforts to find him and has kept a constant vigil in all parts of the Kingdom for years now, but with no success. I want to help them search, which is why I leave tonight.'

Her eyes widened. 'You're going to hunt him down?'

'Now that I know he lives, I must.'

'Where are you going? Why must you leave now?'

'No time to waste, Alyssa. I'm heading north, to Caradoon.'

'Alone?' She looked disturbed.

'Only initially. Herek is headed north as well; the Shield is at Kyrakavia.'

Alyssa shook her head. 'Why Caradoon? Actually, I don't think I've even heard of it,' she added.

'Good thing, too. It's inhabited by the dregs of Tallinese society, those who don't necessarily stick to the laws of the Land. It's just a feeling I have, Alyssa. I tried to work out where I might head if I was a notorious outlaw like Goth and it occurred to me that Caradoon is just the sort of place where someone on the run, who also has such a distinctive face to hide, might go. People keep themselves to themselves up there – everyone's secrets are safe.'

He had more to say but was annoyed to be disturbed by a page running towards them, calling breathlessly for Alyssa to present herself in the royal chambers. Saxon let his irritation show. 'At this hour?'

'Hush,' Alyssa said quietly, 'it is the King's summons.'

The page said nothing further; his large eyes darted between them. He had his orders and did not know how to respond when questioned about them. He was just a lad.

Alyssa stood and pushed her hair back from her solemn face. 'I'm coming, Edwyd. You go ahead.'

The page ran off and she turned back to Saxon, who was on his feet now and clearing the remnants of their supper into Alyssa's basket.

He kissed her quickly. 'I'll be back soon. You are safe – don't worry.'

He left her inside the palace gates, calling back to her, 'Tell Gyl to practise his sword skills. The Swan, in partic- ular – he's hopeless at it.'

*   *   *

Tor and Cloot were deep in the Heartwood, surrounded by the Flames of the Firmament. Solyana and Arabella were there too, silent in the shadows. They had been summoned to keep vigil over Tor's body. For now, however, all were listening to Darmud Coril.

'I will keep your body alive, Torkyn Gynt, but mark my words: you have two sunsets to complete your task. Once the sun sinks on the second evening, so will your spirit . . . beyond my reach. You must return to your body by that time or you will be lost.'

Tor never failed to be fascinated by the hypnotic chiming of the Flames and their dazzling colours but this night he gave his full attention to the god of the forest. There was no mistaking the grave warning which had just been delivered.

'I hear you, Darmud Coril. I will heed you.'

'Cloot,' the god addressed the bird, 'is this your wish too?'

Cloot leapt to Tor's shoulder. Tor instinctively touched him.

The god spoke before the falcon could. He needed no answer. That brief gesture between the two had said enough. The barest of smiles creased his face and flickered in his soft, gentle eyes.

'Brave Cloot of the Paladin, our strength will travel with you. You will need it. The Heartwood will speed you on your journey. Let it guide you.'

There was nothing else to say. Tor linked with the Flames, having memorised their special trace.

Keep me safe, beloved Flames, he whispered to them.

He was rewarded by their chiming in unison, a note long and loud.

Solyana spoke for the first time. *Listen for our call, Tor. Please return to us.*

Arabella added a final warning. 'Don't be reckless, Tor.'

He nodded solemnly and then lay down on the spongy forest floor. The Flames followed, dancing around him. Cloot flew to a branch hanging overhead. The cluster of Flames split into two, one group remaining with Tor, the other sweeping to encircle the falcon in a similar blaze of fiery tongues.

Tor closed his eyes and spoke gently to his friend. *Ready?*

As I ever will be, the bird replied.

The Flames of the Firmament increased in intensity in both colour and sound, surrounding Tor and Cloot with coloured light so bright that neither Solyana nor Arabella could see their shapes any longer. Tor summoned his own Colours and allowed their purity to roar through him. He let them mingle with those of the Flames and felt such an enormous well of power at his call that he suddenly knew the Spiriting itself would be very simple.

He imagined where Cloot was perched, pulled all that was himself into a tight ball and lifted from inside. It felt effortless. For a moment he floated, but he knew not to linger and within another blink he opened his eyes and saw the black and white of Cloot's world through the bird's vision. It was an odd sensation, yet familiar. He recalled this awkward discomfort from when he had thrown himself into Merkhud's body all those years ago.

Welcome, Tor. Cloot's voice sounded even deeper and smoother from within.

Tor felt Cloot stretch his wings and he stretched with them. It was a marvellous sensation.

I am honoured to be here, Tor replied with genuine humility.

Make yourself at home, Cloot said as they lifted off gracefully into the night.

Tor just had time to look down at his own body. The Flames continued to burn brightly around its form. Solyana and Arabella had taken up their vigil and sat one on either side of his body. There they would remain until he returned.

They flew higher. Tor was amazed to see through Cloot's eyes that the Heartwood seemed to be leading them.

Cloot read his thoughts. *We must follow that finger.*

But what happens when we leave the Heartwood?

The Great Forest will guide us. It will show us the fastest way to Caradoon.

Until there is no more forest, Tor thought. But he refused to entertain any pessimistic thoughts. *Cloot, this is the most exhilarating experience ever.* He whooped loudly into Cloot's mind.

The falcon chuckled with him, enjoying his friend's pleasure at something he now took for granted. His keen eyes picked out the sudden movement below.

Hold on. I see dinner.

Before Tor could protest, Cloot had banked up high, turned almost on himself and swooped into a sharp dive which would have made Tor close his eyes if only they were his. He felt a momentary nausea, which vanished in the fascination and thrill of the hunt. He could see the prey now. A young hare.

It had broken cover of the trees and was nibbling on some juicy grasses which were luring it further and further from the sanctuary of the forest. Tor shared Cloot's knowledge and realised it was the young creature's inexperience showing. No adult hare would be this daring . . . or stupid, he thought sadly.

Once again it was as though Cloot was reading his mind. *We have to eat, Tor. It will be over quickly, I promise.*

Their speed was as fast as Cloot would ever go. Shaped like an arrow, the falcon dropped silently from the sky, judging the quarry perfectly and giving it no chance to flee. When the hare realised its fatal error, it was already too late. It turned and made for the trees but Cloot used his immense speed from the descent to swoop, claws outstretched. Tor could almost smell the young buck's fear as it zigzagged instinctively. They hit the hare with terrible force. The falcon's sharp claws ripped through its fur and sunk in deeply, tearing flesh as the bird continued its momentum. Finally they stopped, just inches from the trees. Tor remembered Solyana's warning: no animal may be killed in the Heartwood. Cloot had been very careful.

The dying hare struggled bravely, yet knowing that death was but a breath away. Cloot kept his word. It was over quickly and once his razor-sharp beak had ripped into the creature's neck, Tor had the sensation of tasting blood. It was warm and rich, pumping still as the heart of the hare – now in its death throes – slowed.

A mixture of fascination and horror claimed Tor's consciousness. There was something primeval about this feast which he did not feel he should share. He was an intruder in Cloot's body. This was not his business. He tried to shield. He could not. They were one right now. And so he did what he could and withdrew, pulling himself as far back into the spirit of Tor as possible. Small and silent he waited whilst Cloot fed for both of them.

Later, Cloot perched on one of the highest branches of the tallest tree and cleaned himself of the hare's entrails.

That was not fun for you, Tor. It was not a question.

Is it for you?

More than I could tell you. I feel invincible, all-powerful, during the chase.

Flying with you is amazing. Feeding with you is not. Thank you for making it quick.

Cloot began sharpening his beak. *We'll be off shortly but I must complete my ablutions.*

Don't hurry for me, old friend. My body's just dying back there.

They shared a laugh together. It felt almost like old times when life had not been quite so complicated.

Do we have a plan, Tor?

Not really. Languishing back in the Heartwood felt wrong. Reading those books seemed to snap me out of a stupor. Goth is dangerous and still at large. Orlac is still coming. Alyssa remains in danger and ever apart from me. Nothing has changed.

And we are still none the wiser about the Trinity.

Well, doing something at least feels as though we're trying.

I agree. So let's get on with it.

Cloot lifted effortlessly from his perch and suddenly his wings were beating smoothly and strongly in glorious flight again. *Relax now,* he said gently. *We shall be flying steadily for a few hours.*

5

Old Friends and Enemies

They arrived mid-afternoon at the busy port of Caradoon, which they had found by following the inlet from the main harbour of Kyrakavia.

This is it, Cloot said, landing in a tree on the fringe of the town.

Are you tired?

The bird answered too fast. *Not overly.* Then, more abruptly. *What do you propose?*

Tor paused. He had been thinking hard during the flight on just this subject: what to do once they reached Caradoon? He still had no definite plan but could sense Cloot's impatience.

What about these stracca houses you mentioned?

There would be several.

How could we find them?

Oh, I could just circle about aimlessly and see if we can spot one. Or we could fly down and ask someone. A magnificent peregrine falcon who also talks should not be a novelty here.

All right, all right. Let me think, Tor said, recognising that Cloot was tired and falling into one of his sarcastic moods. Perhaps he was hungry again, he thought unkindly.

Well, I'll just sit here, Tor, whilst you think. Take your time. It's your dying body.

Tor ignored him and they fell silent. He sensed Cloot's anxiety and knew better than to think the falcon was worried about himself. Cloot had never really liked this idea and now that he realised Tor had no genuine plan in mind he probably liked it even less. Tor suddenly felt stupid for getting them both into this dangerous situation. How foolish to think they could just turn up at a town and find the man they were searching for; aside from the problem that they were both in the form of a bird while Tor's own body lay cooling many leagues south.

Could it have been luck? Or fate? Or was it Lys manipulating events? Tor would never know but he suddenly spotted a familiar figure making its way along the main street of Caradoon. There was no mistaking him. Even from this high up and without seeing his face, Tor had no doubt that it was Saxon the Kloek striding below him.

Well, well, well, muttered Cloot, who had also spotted Saxon.

Why would he be here of all places?

Cloot's interest was piqued; all sarcasm had disappeared. *I saw some of the King's Guard in Kyrakavia. He may well be with them. Saxon would know of this place through his travels with Cirq Zorros.*

Of course. Tor's mind raced. *Let's follow him.*

The falcon sighed. *At least it's a plan,* he said and took off, being careful to keep the trees as cover. He had already decided that this was not a place for a distinctive bird to be seen too readily.

They watched Saxon drift into an inn and back out again not long after. He called into several market stalls and looked to be asking questions.

He looks grim, Tor said.

He is searching.

For the same thing as us?

Possibly. But why? And why now?

Let's just assume he is. How can we help him?

Before Cloot could answer, they saw a man giving the Kloek directions. Saxon nodded and thanked him. He set off and they followed him once more, heartily glad for the trees which encircled the town. They lost him momentarily and then saw him enter into one of the side streets towards the northern end of town.

Over there, Cloot.

I see him. Let's get as close as we can.

As they flew over a very quiet part of the town where few people were walking the streets, a strange smell hit Tor's senses. Before he could ask the obvious, Cloot answered.

It's the stracca. Smells sweet when freshly burned but after a while it gets that sour aroma. It's worse up this high than I remember.

They watched Saxon get new directions from a youth, who pointed to a whitewashed building not far from the tree where they were perched, well hidden. The structure stood alone. The smell seemed to be coming from it.

Looks as though Saxon is on the same trail then, Cloot.

I'm astonished but I think you're right.

From their vantage point, they could see all sides of the building. There were a few people milling around behind it, where a path led down to the water. Serving women were cleaning and washing linen; cooks' helpers were scrubbing vegetables; other youngsters were fetching and carrying. It was a hive of activity. Tor and Cloot watched as a woman appeared at the back door. She called out something to a lad at the water's edge. He turned, looking scared. The woman stepped out into the open. She wore a silk scarf over her head. The boy hurried towards her. When he arrived, she slapped him hard across his ear; they could hear its sound very clearly. As she did so, her scarf slipped and her dark and luxurious hair whipped around in the breeze. Both of them instantly recognised Xantia.

Together they said her name and looked immediately to Saxon, who was now approaching the stracca house.

We have to warn him, Cloot.

I can't open a link.

Take the risk. Fly into the open. We can't let him walk into this place. If Xantia is here, then Goth probably is too.

Cloot did not hesitate further. Saxon was just moments from entering the front door and they could see Xantia, her fury spent, also going back into the building. Cloot leapt off the branch and used the drop to gain some speed, flying straight at Saxon's face. At the last second, he veered off, clawing at the Kloek's hair and screeching.

'What the hell . . . !' Saxon spun around, one hand poised in mid air to bang on the door, the other grabbing at his face.

Cloot shrieked again, this time from cover. Saxon peered into the trees. He could not see anything but they had succeeded in grabbing his attention away from the stracca house.

Hurry, Cloot. She could step out any second.

I don't know what else to do, Cloot replied.

Flap!

He flapped. Saxon approached. He could see the falcon now and shock was written plainly across his face. His ear was bleeding from where Cloot's talons had scratched him. The Kloek did not care about that though.

He shook his head in disbelief. 'Is it you?' he asked softly, almost with reverence.

In answer, Cloot dropped from the branch and landed on Saxon's outstretched arm. Then he jumped off and headed deeper into the cover of the trees. They needed to get Saxon well away from the building. Tor was relieved to see the Kloek follow.

When Cloot landed once again on his arm, they were both choked to see the Kloek begin to weep.

'You're safe,' he said over and again, stroking Cloot's head. 'We miss you, old friend.'

I wish we could speak to him, Tor said.

No link. Cloot felt powerless. He allowed Saxon to stroke him until the Kloek chose to stop and lifted him high so he could stare at him.

'You are magnificent, Cloot.'

Thank you, Cloot replied. He bobbed his head slightly so Saxon knew he could hear him.

It made Saxon grin through his tears. 'And what are you doing here, bird? What is your business at a stracca house in sleazy Caradoon, eh?'

Cloot hopped about on Saxon's arm.

'All right, we can't link, I take it,' Saxon said, 'but you can hear me and you can find a way to respond.' Cloot flapped his wings in answer.

'Why are you here?' Saxon asked.

Oh Light! Cloot said to Tor. *This is going to be painful.*

'Apologies. I must say that a different way,' Saxon corrected. He frowned then said, 'Are you looking for something?'

Cloot flapped.

'For some*one*?'

Cloot flapped again.

'For Goth?'

Cloot could have kissed him. Instead he flapped a third time.

Bravo, Saxon, Tor said.

The Kloek frowned again. 'So you know he lives. Let me tell you what I know, Cloot.' Saxon sat down on the grass beneath the trees and began his story.

Tor felt great guilt, for obviously the Kloek thought he spoke only to Cloot, yet he also felt great joy just to see Saxon again.

Saxon talked intently to the falcon. 'I accompany Herek from time to time on various missions. I get bored of palace life and prefer the open road. We were headed for Kyrakavia, which was not in our plan when we left Tal. I questioned the Prime — oh, Herek is Prime now, by the way — and he admitted something which had been kept a great secret for several years. Goth never did burn. The bitch, Xantia, aided him to escape on the eve before Tor's execution. Herek confessed that he was so shocked to lose a prisoner that he kept the information from the King and Queen until after the stoning.

'And then, I am told, Lorys decided that the news should be kept from the people until Goth had been recaptured. Like Herek, he expected the Shield to swiftly track down the former Chief Inquisitor and bring him to justice.

When that did not happen, word was given out that Goth had died in prison, inexplicably poisoned by his own hand. The plan was to execute him in private once he was captured; to deny him the final recognition of a public execution. The whole of Tal was in such despair after Tor's execution that everyone believed the poisoning story; no one seemed to care what had happened to the man who brought it about . . .'

Saxon blinked and paused, seeming to gather himself. 'Why did he have to die like that, Cloot? Is that why you left us? Alyssa was inconsolable for months after your disappearance at the same time as his body. You were all she had of him.'

It was Tor's turn to feel the tumult of emotions now. Cloot soothed him quietly. *Just listen.*

Saxon continued. 'Anyway, after the shame of losing his prisoner, Herek vowed to do everything he could to find Goth. And he had never given up the search. Even now, he has detoured from a routine mission at Martintown to head north into Kyrakavia to take a brief look around. I left in the early hours of this morning to come further on to Caradoon. It seems a fitting place for the likes of Goth.'

Cloot flapped excitedly. Tor could see Saxon was thinking hard.

'He's here?' he asked.

Cloot flapped joyously then hopped to a higher perch and stared towards the white building. Saxon followed the direction of the bird's gaze and his broad jaw set itself firmly.

'Then we keep a vigil until my eyes confirm it.'

The trio remained in their secret spot and watched carefully.

As night closed in on dusk, Saxon stretched. So did Cloot.

'I have to take a look,' was all Saxon said before moving soundlessly through the trees and emerging to walk stealthily across the street.

What's he going to do?

Tor, time is our enemy. I must get us back to the Heartwood.

Tor ignored the caution, shooshing Cloot so they could watch.

Goth lay back amongst the silk cushions. He was dressed in the voluminous silk robes he now preferred; they hid the gauntness which the stracca had imposed on his once stocky frame. The room had a salubrious air, but closer inspection revealed it to be tired and jaded, like its clients. Once the stracca worked its magic, though, nothing else mattered and Goth could pretend he was Chief Inquisitor once again, living at the palace, powerful, rich, respected and feared. He liked the last most of all.

During the long, painfully bright days spent in recovery from the effects of the previous night's stracca, reality bit like a snake. Fast and unrelenting, the truth of his life always struck as he emerged from the haze of intoxication. Sometimes the pain of it could make him weep. Xantia would come and soothe him.

Why she stayed with him Goth was never quite sure. She told him they were kindred souls; reassured him they shared the same enemies, the same dreams and desires. And yet he saw how her lips pursed each time he drifted into his pleasant oblivion. She did not like her life. He was not altogether sure she liked him. But she had saved him from death, brazenly ordering those cringing guards to allow her into his cell. Her plan had been simple and cruel. The old hag, Heggie, was expendable. Bribed with a purse, she had agreed to accompany Xantia into the jail and remain there in Goth's stead. After all, what could the Guard do to her; and, in truth, neither Goth nor Xantia cared if the old woman was punished for her part in their skullduggery. Yes, Goth loved Xantia for that cruelty; her passion for power and her unquenchable thirst for revenge was almost as addictive as the stracca.

Goth remembered how it had been her idea to remain in Tal to watch Gynt's crucifixion. How they had sniggered together beneath their disguises at all those stupid people keening and weeping in distress. It had been more fun than a bridling.

Seeing Alyssa had made the risk worthwhile. She had looked so regal standing up there, proud and defiant. If he was still a whole man he would have been hard with lust at that moment watching her. Curse the Kloek who had taken his manhood. It did not seem to bother Xantia that he was not whole. In fact, if he really thought about it, Xantia was not at all interested in him as a man. But she admired his cunning mind, enjoyed his games.

Watching Gynt's head split open had been the highlight. He had died bravely, Goth would give his enemy that. His forgiveness of the King had been a master stroke, but oh, the delight of witnessing his death. Goth had been forced to bite his teeth together to keep himself from laughing aloud.

Xantia's eyes had been sparkling at the hour of Gynt's death. Goth remembered the high colour on her cheeks. And whilst the rest of the mob stared in horrified silence at Gynt's limp body and the surprising amount of blood gushing from the huge wound in his head, Xantia had turned to watch Alyssa. She had bitten her lip in pleasure until it bled at the sight of the girl's agony and chuckled quietly to see Alyssa holding out her arms, reaching for Tor, then her face, twisted with hatred, as she turned on the King.

Goth wished they could have stayed to witness more of that fine theatre. He had wanted to see Gynt's corpse cut down from the cross, perhaps even to touch it to be sure Gynt had died. Xantia had laughed at him then and mocked him. 'Who could live after that, you fool?' she had snarled.

Fool. Goth turned the word over now in his numbed brain. He did not like to be laughed at. And no one had ever called him a fool before. But Xantia was not scared of him. He could hate her for that. She saw through him, knew his weaknesses. Once she had even brought him an eleven-summers-old girl for his sport. But the girl had cried too much and, anyway, what was the point in his condition? If only he could be within spitting distance of that golden-haired Kloek once more . . . Even with his own hands tied and his ankles manacled, Goth knew he would find a way to rip the man's throat open with his teeth . . . and he would wallow in the blood.

He was fantasising again, but simultaneously he could feel the welcome numbness of the stracca wearing thin. So thin that his greatest fear was re-emerging: someone was watching him, spying on him. He would run back to the King and ask for a reward for revealing the whereabouts of the fugitive Goth.

Goth inhaled on the long glass tube again and relaxed into the drug's reassuring embrace. Too much use took away the sense of taste; removed all feeling, in fact. It was said a man could drink bubbling hot water straight from the pot and not feel it, such was the numbing ability of the stracca. Goth was not ready to test that theory yet, even though it appeared his life was over.

Xantia did not think so though; kept talking about some mad god, hell bent on revenge. He did not understand any of it but he humoured her. She made sure he got high-quality stracca. He had to stay on the right side of Xantia. Sometimes he thought she was actually running the den. 'Patience, patience,' she would coo in his ear. 'I have the good stuff for you tonight.' And he would do as he was told.

What did she want from him? Why did they remain in this flea-infested pirate town when they could climb aboard the first available ship to the Exotic Isles? He thought harder and through the stracca haze managed to recall that it had been Xantia's idea to use the stracca den as a hideout. 'We can lie low for a full moon or two,' she had persuaded him. But how long had it been now? He could not remember.

Goth knew he was hallucinating now. He had to be, for through the window he could see the hated Kloek staring at him.

He rolled over and closed his eyes tightly. If only it were true. If only Saxon the Kloek were this close. He could take his vengeance. He inhaled once more and passed out.

Saxon wanted to crash through the window and end the miserable sod's life. It was Cloot who prevented him making a rash move. Goth looked as if he was unconscious.

The contraption next to the bed of faded cushions

gurgled away; a thin stream of purple smoke drifted up and clouded at the ceiling. The Chief Inquisitor was a shadow of his former strutting self; his face was so gaunt it was almost unrecognisable. But he could not hide the twisted flesh and the incessant twitch which marked him as the person they sought.

Saxon considered his options. Goth was useless for the time being. Instead of risking an error, he could make his way back to Tal and inform Herek, who by now would already by heading back south to the capital, of his find. At the same time, he could warn Alyssa of this new discovery. She must be told, even though he dreaded confirming for her that Goth lived. Then he could return with a full complement of soldiers, re-capture this lowlife and deal with him once and for all, not to mention his nasty accomplice. Saxon nodded. It was a wise decision.

He heard Cloot's warning shriek but it was already too late. Whatever it was hit him hard and he collapsed outside the window.

Saxon came to, groggy and disoriented. He could hear a familiar voice yelling through the darkness. It was a voice he despised. Xantia.

The man holding him hissed near his ear. 'Stay still, stranger, or I'll slit your throat from arsehole to appetite.'

Saxon had a mad urge to laugh at the nonsensical statement, but he also had the sense to remain silent as commanded. He peered through blurred vision and realised he had been dragged around to the side of the stracca den where it was virtually pitch black. Xantia looked like a demented ghoul, lit up in the open doorway as she shouted in their direction.

He realised they were just silhouettes to her and thanked whichever lucky stars were protecting him. She thought they were drunken revellers. She had her say, issued a nasty threat if they were still there in two minutes, then slammed the door.

'You don't plan on making any trouble for me, do you, tall man?'

Saxon spat. He tasted blood as he shook his head. His attacker struck a flint and held it up between them.

'Now we'll remember each other's faces. It pays to know who might want me dead.'

Saxon took note of the livid scar which crossed the man's face where an eye used to be; now there was only a blackened socket. He shrugged, momentarily thinking about taking on 'One Eye', but remembered the blade poised near his throat and figured this was a fight better lost and fought again on another day.

'Where is my falcon?'

It was the first time One Eye had heard his distinctive voice. 'A Kloek? My, my, you're far from home, Goldie.'

Saxon hated the nickname but he did not bite. 'My falcon?'

'Ours now,' the man said, pointing to the bushes where Saxon could make out another fellow. Cloot was held firmly in his grip.

Saxon swung back to stare at One Eye. 'You can have all my money—'

'Already got it,' One Eye said, shaking a purse and grinning.

The light inside the building went out. All was quiet.

Saxon spoke softly this time. 'You must give me that bird or I will kill you.'

'I hold the knife, and my friend over there will break your bird's neck if you so much as raise an arm against me, Kloek. Now, do as I suggest and leave Caradoon.'

Saxon tried a different approach. 'What would you want with a falcon?'

'Birds of prey are rare where we're headed. This one's a beauty. He'll fetch me gold for sure in the Exotic Isles. Her majesty has a passion for falcons. She loves to watch them kill.'

'I meant what I said, pirate.'

'About killing me, you mean?'

Saxon nodded slowly, watching for the next move. He was surprised to hear the one-eyed man laugh.

'Shaking in my boots, Kloek. Until the next time we meet then.'

He laughed again, pushed Saxon hard in the direction of the town and wagged his finger at him. 'Go now, Goldie. I've spared your life because I can see I have taken something from you which matters to you greatly. But don't push your luck. My name is Janus Quist. Remember it.'

Saxon did not hear it coming but he saw Quist's eyes flick to whatever was behind him. Something hard and unforgiving hit his head and the Kloek dropped to the ground like a stone.

'Get him as far south from here as possible. Dump him as close to the capital as you dare. I don't want him returning,' Quist ordered.

6

Breach of Souls

Cloot had been so intent on getting into a position where he and Tor could see Goth sucking on his stracca pipe that he had not heard the man creeping up on him. Careful fingers extracted him from the net which had been thrown about him whilst other members of the gang dragged Saxon around to the dark side of the building. The man then bound his beak with a fine thread . . . but not before he had gouged the man's flesh, Cloot thought, although it was very cold comfort.

Don't struggle any more, Cloot. It will just weaken you. Let's wait and see what they want, Tor cautioned, sounding braver than he felt at this moment, remembering his body so far away.

They felt their combined hopes sink as they realised what their fate at the hands of Quist and his pirate gang was to be. They shared distress as they heard the pirate give the order to remove Saxon and watched helplessly as the Kloek was dragged off down the street.

Now all Cloot could think of was their own precarious situation and the dire need to ensure Tor's escape.

Forget me, you fool! Cloot spat at him. *We have no time to waste on anything but you . . . getting you away from them.*

I will not – Tor began but was cut off fiercely by his friend. He could feel the anger coursing through Cloot's fragile web of light bones and feathers.

You will not put yourself in any further danger than you already have. Now use that powerful mind of yours and conjure up a solution, Tor. There is no more time. Quist is about to stuff me into a sack; I'll lose all sense of direction and then we'll find ourselves on a boat to somewhere in the Exotic Isles and that will be that. You'll die inside me and I'll die of a broken heart and of my failure to fulfil my task as the Second. You cannot do this to me. You will do as I say . . . NOW!

What do you expect me to do? Tor yelled, feeling the stirring of real fear.

Something that will magic you away, Tor! Now think. Think hard on everything you know. The answer is within you. Lys has always told you that you have the answers. You just have to know how to ask the right questions. Do it now. Save yourself.

Save us, he added softly before falling silent.

For a moment Tor felt lost, helpless. Growing up, it was not just the love and support of his parents which had made him feel safe; it was knowing he possessed a power way beyond anything anyone else understood. There had never been anything he could not do. Even when Merkhud had suggested the Spiriting, Tor had trusted he could achieve it. But now, many years later, he felt doubt creep in. His own life was his to lose . . . if he so chose. But with Cloot it was different. Cloot was his closest, most beloved friend; he knew the falcon would die without a second's hesitation if he thought it might save Tor. He steeled his resolved. He would not lose Cloot. He would not let a drug-intoxicated bully, a scheming woman and a one-eyed pirate beat them. He remembered how, years ago when they were children, Alyssa had taught him to turn shame into strength, misery into determination and fear into anger. Now he would display that same courage.

Tor withdrew and summoned the Colours. Cloot seemed distant now. The Colours roared and instantly he felt connected to where his body lay with Solyana and Arabella keeping vigil over it. He needed no guiding star to find it. He had only hours left before his body would die and then Cloot would surely be lost – and so would the Trinity. His anger swelled and the Colours roared brightly in answer to his call.

Trust yourself. Who had spoken? Tor did not know but he repeated it in his mind. Trust yourself.

He leapt.

Cloot called across the link, brave as always. *Travel safely, child. Don't forget me*.

Cloot, Tor whispered, *I love you*.

I know.

The link snapped shut and he was travelling alone. Speed was all he could grasp. He felt nothing else. Emptiness enveloped him and he hurtled through the blank. Where were his Colours? Did they blaze behind him? Perhaps he had become the Colours. Faster, faster. No sound.

How long had he been travelling before it happened?

Cold hit him like a slap. He slowed. He was confused. What was it? A sense of foreboding permeated his consciousness; at the same time he sensed that whatever was reaching for him must not be allowed to touch him in the depths of his haven.

Travel! called voices. They were urgent.

He thought he recognised them but recognition disappeared, to be replaced by fear.

And then another voice. It was wintry. It was the source of the cold.

Ah . . . so this is Tor, it said icily.

Who are you? Was his voice shaking from fright or cold?

I am he.

Panic gripped Tor. He had stopped moving. He was dying with each second he remained here but he felt impaled. *Orlac?*

The voice laughed. Still no warmth in it, but there was genuine mirth. *I am not Orlac, though I am as interested in him as you are.*

Where is he?

Before it could reply, another voice, frosty with menace, came crashing into Tor's head. *Get away from him!* Lys said.

It laughed again. *He was passing. I am lonely.*

Quickly, travel on, Lys commanded, *Time works against you.*

Tor picked up speed again through the blankness, worrying at the sinister coldness of that voice until he heard the friendly voices again. All of them singing to him.

It was the Flames. They echoed his Colours and rushed towards him, dancing around him, begging him to follow swiftly and he did, racing with them.

Suddenly Tor hit his own body with such speed and force that it convulsed. He heard Arabella scream but he could not open his eyes. He could hardly breathe. Did he still fit his body? It all felt so wrong. Breathe.

Solyana growled into his mind. *You frightened us.*

He tried to sit up. Arabella helped him, cradling him in her arms.

'I told you not to take chances, Tor.' Arabella snatched at tears and moved away from him quickly, disappearing into the blur which was now his vision. He was seeing through his own eyes again.

The Flames had quietened and were glowing softly white once again.

Darmud Coril was present. 'I am glad you are back with us, Torkyn Gynt.'

'Thank you for sending them,' he was able to say, his voice gritty.

'They came of their own accord,' the god replied. They fled to you, my son. They were very frightened for you. They told me they must guide you home.'

Tor stroked one of the Flames and it chimed its pleasure. He reached out silently to them all, using his own Colours, which it seemed only they understood. 'Thank you, my friends.'

Solyana padded away. Her posture told him how relieved she was.

Tor could not move very quickly. He was not wearing his body with ease yet but he caught up with her awkwardly.

I'm sorry.

I know, she said sadly. *We have all come through so much. It is terrifying to think we could lose you before you have achieved what you must.*

He hated it when any of them talked openly about his personal destiny — whatever that was. *I have lost Cloot.*

I gathered.

How?

He is not with you. Cloot is your first-bonded Paladin; he would die before he left your side.

He is not dead.

He may be. But that would be his choice. Her voice was even sadder.

Tor rounded on the silver wolf. *Don't speak so, Solyana!*

Death releases us, Tor. You must understand this.

I don't *understand it. I don't understand any of it,* he said, limping awkwardly.

Move around as much as you can. Feeling will return soon. She was matter of fact again.

I shall be walking a long way, he said.

Do you wish for company?

To Caradoon?

Arabella had returned. She heard his last words.

'You're going back?' She was shocked.

'Yes. I leave immediately.'

'You cannot,' the priestess said.

'I must find Cloot.'

'Stop him, Solyana. Tell him.'

Tor stopped. 'Tell me what?'

Solyana, calm as always, spoke quietly. *We believe the Tenth is failing.*

'How long?' Tor asked flatly.

'We don't know.' Arabella's voice was filled with frustration and fear. 'That is why you cannot leave the safety of the Heartwood.'

Tor sighed. 'Arabella, that is every reason why I must leave the safety of the Heartwood. I do no good here. I am the prey, remember.'

He stepped towards her and she allowed him to give

her a brief, hard hug. He kissed her lips softly. 'I promise you, I will take no more chances but I must find my falcon. He belongs to me – and I to him.'

He looked into her smoky, dark eyes and finally she nodded.

The Heartwood will guide you once again, Tor, the wolf offered.

Tor stroked Solyana's thick, shaggy fur and took a moment to marvel once again at its silvery tips which seemed to shimmer as she moved.

Solyana, can I cast myself to Caradoon as I did when Alyssa and I left Caremboche?

No, Tor. You can only bring yourself back to the Heartwood in such a manner. You will have to journey to Caradoon by more traditional methods, though the trees will make it as fast as they can. If it was possible for a wolf to grin, Solyana did so and it puzzled Tor. *Enjoy your journey,* she said. *Everything you need will be provided at the edge of the Great Forest.*

Tor stood by the stream where he had first made love to Alyssa. He kneeled by its gently passing water and drank from it, trying to conjure up the vision of that moonlit night. As he swallowed, he tasted her once again, briefly, and he thanked the stream for such a gift.

Running through the wolf's instructions once more, he straightened, put his hands by his sides and closed his eyes to wait for the sign.

He had learned to trust the Heartwood implicitly. It would never harm him.

Tor felt the branches around his ankles and heard the rustle of their leaves. He opened his eyes and felt a surge of excitement. He steadied himself as the foliage entwined, then took a deep breath before the bent trees catapulted him into the air. Travelling again. He felt the exhilaration of flying once more, this time in his own body, and howled with the joy of it.

Another tree caught him deftly and, before he had a second to let out a breath, he was thrown again. This happened repeatedly. Each time the trees cradled his fall and catapulted him on to their companions. Tor began to laugh. He could swear the trees were laughing with him and he realised he was sending out his Colours towards them, thanking them as he tumbled closer and closer towards Caradoon.

He arrived on the Great Forest's outskirts a day later. The trees had been kind, refreshing and encouraging him throughout the journey, finally setting him down just half a day's walk from his destination. Solyana had spoken true. A small pile of items had been left for him on the fringe of the northern finger of the forest. They had been chosen carefully. Fresh clothes, sufficiently unremarkable that he could pass for any transient in the pirate town. A leather satchel, which he slung across his body, contained a few curios which no doubt would explain themselves later.

Tor cast to Cloot but found nothing. So, with no reason to linger, he turned to the Great Forest, bowed reverently to the trees in thanks, heard their gentle whispers and started forth on what he sensed was going to be a long journey.

7

Alyssa's Secret

Alyssa should have been enjoying a leisurely morning: her school classes had been cancelled as several children had succumbed to a mild fever. It was a rare occasion to have these hours free for herself. The King was riding with Nyria on the moors and was not due back for several hours. She told herself to move from his work chambers, go for a walk, perhaps spend some time with Gyl. But no, instead she found herself touching Lorys's desk, even his chair, tidying and re-tidying documents which no longer required her attention. She just could not bring herself to leave his rooms and inwardly chastised herself for it.

Alyssa walked to the tall windows overlooking the main courtyard and stared out, recalling the last time she had been alone in the King's quarters. It was when he and Nyria were away on their royal tour of the realm. Nyria had had to argue her case with Lorys before he would consider such an undertaking, but finally the King had recognised the value of such an exercise.

When Alyssa first suspected that the King was paying

her undue attention, she had enjoyed the feelings it provoked in her. Eventually, she had come to accept how deeply smitten she herself was with the King. For all her efforts to see him as a darkness in her life, she had to admit that she had come to appreciate him as the sparkling light which illuminated her days. She had missed him terribly while he was away on the royal tour, but had schooled herself never to show her heart openly. Alyssa kept her yearnings to herself, convinced that it was her burden alone. However, now that she was sure of the King's ardour, she felt frightened.

He was definitely speaking to her silently, through stolen glances and smiles. She could feel his attention like a cord, reaching out to attach itself to her. His eyes flirted, yet he had not touched her. Nor would he, she was sure, for he loved his Queen.

Alyssa wondered if she should leave the palace. This was dangerous. She would not be involved in such a scandal and if her presence was tempting the King into something he might regret, then she must remove that temptation.

But it wasn't just Lorys's feelings towards her she was afraid of; it was also her own feelings towards Lorys. How she yearned for his touch, even if it came only by brushing past him; how she craved his presence and contrived to lengthen their working hours together or to meet with him on some petty matter at night. How she revelled in those rare occasions when he might ask her to share a glass of wine with him and she was able to look him directly in the eye and feel as though they were just two friends conversing.

But after such precious times with him, she hated

herself for the feeling that she was somehow betraying her beloved Queen. Did Nyria know of her growing feelings for Lorys? A woman's intuition was powerful indeed and yet the Queen never referred to these occasional meetings or let slip any suggestion that she might resent her two favourites being so close. In fact, Alyssa reassured herself, Nyria openly encouraged their companionship, seemed to want them to form an emotional link with one another.

Alyssa laid her face against the cool of the glass. It would do her no good to leave the palace; neither would it serve the royals or Gyl for her to run from what were probably empty fears. No, she would remain there and continue to work hard for Tallinor. And she promised herself that she would do absolutely nothing to encourage any advances or intimacy with the King, imagined or otherwise.

While Alyssa was making her silent promise, Queen Nyria was out on the moors with the King, riding her beloved Freycin. Neither Lorys nor Herek had minded when she decided to join them for their morning ride, even though she knew it was the time when they discussed the business of the day. Gyl often accompanied them too and Nyria knew that the King genuinely enjoyed the time spent with the young man.

The Queen had awoken early after a strange and vivid dream. A woman had appeared to her and told her she must be with Lorys this morning. The dream, along with her own desire to remain close to the King at this time, had prompted Nyria to instruct her staff to prepare her to ride out with her husband and the Prime. Now that she was out on the moors, she felt glad for the decision.

She found her mind turning to the relationship between Lorys and his young secretary. In the past, she had found herself grateful for the girl's calming influence on him. 'You have a way with the King, Alyssa,' she often told her. None of Alyssa's beauty or charms were lost on the older woman and recently she had sensed that the special look in the King's eye, previously reserved for her, was being turned upon Alyssa.

Nyria felt no animosity towards the girl. If anything, she knew Alyssa was unaware of the effect she had on the men of the palace. Nyria, however, could see that not a male soul on the staff could resist this young woman's charms. She was sure even old Koryn experienced a blood rush when Alyssa was around!

Alyssa spoke kindly to everyone and was generous of spirit. Only the shallowest of women could dislike her, despite the fact that she was easily the most beautiful woman in Tal.

Nyria had noted that the King always requested Alyssa's presence at formal occasions these days. Of course, she shone everywhere she went. Nyria believed Alyssa could wear sackcloth and still look like an angel. Her petite build and radiance set her well and truly above the heavily rouged and pouting female courtiers. If this was not enough, Nyria had known since she first began to work with Alyssa that the girl possessed an extraordinary intelligence and inherent strength. She sensed that Alyssa, if pushed, would be a fearful opponent. Yes, Nyria firmly believed she had done the King a great service by insisting he take Alyssa on as his secretary, even though she knew instinctively that Lorys was falling in love with his beautiful aide.

It hurt of course. She and Lorys had been childhood sweethearts. Nyria, the daughter of a loyal wealthy noble who had fought bravely alongside old King Mort, had grown up at the palace and she and Lorys had played together in the palace gardens while their fathers were in the war room, planning battle strategy. She smiled. Thank the Light that Lorys, during his reign, had never had to preside over meetings in that room. Still, she was quietly grateful for that time they had shared as innocents. And it had been no surprise when their two families had betrothed them. She adored Lorys. She had never loved another. To this day she still loved him with the same intensity. It was a fairytale relationship; she conceded this. It was cruel indeed that towards the end of her days another woman should steal his heart.

Even though she had contrived the idea, could they not have waited until she was gone? The Queen breathed in the fresh air which was scented with lavender. She knew her time was short and she accepted it without a fight. That was why the tour around the Kingdom had been so important to her. It was their last chance to ride through the Land as King and Queen, to meet their subjects, talk with them, eat with them and show their love for them.

Nyria was glad that she had achieved this. It was her farewell to Tallinor and its people whom she loved.

Lorys thought they still had a lifetime together. But young Torkyn Gynt had warned her during that terrible meeting just prior to his execution that she must take care. It was a cryptic message but she had understood that he knew her heart was failing. He had looked inside her long ago and seen how sick she was. He had saved her life then, but he could not save her now. He was lying in his own cold grave, wherever that was.

That lovely young man, decaying in the earth. If Nyria had one regret, it was the blot which Tor's execution had left on Lorys's reign. The boy need not have died. Lorys had not thought it through carefully and had refused to be counselled on the matter . . . not even by his wife. Perhaps, the Queen thought, he had already been under Alyssa's spell even then; making rash decisions because he was blinded by desire. The truth of it was, Lorys could have saved Alyssa's lover if he had wanted to.

Oh, her heart hurt in various ways.

The physical pain was becoming more regular, more intense – in fact, she realised, she could feel a spasm coming on right now. She looked over to where her husband was talking intently with his Prime. As she watched, he laughed. She loved him so much and yet she wanted his reign to go on. Their failure to produce an heir was not for lack of trying, yet it seemed it was not to be. It was the only flaw in a successful marriage of almost thirty summers. But perhaps there was still time for Lorys to achieve what she knew was a secretly held dream.

Nyria hoped that Lorys would choose Alyssa as his next Queen. He could do no better. She was perfect: young, beautiful, brilliant, strong and captivated by the King; though it was obvious to Nyria that Alyssa had not yet accepted that notion herself. She could tell this through the girl's body language. She was still awkward around Lorys. But all the signs were there. Unknown to both her husband and Alyssa, Nyria had watched them for a long time now. She had seen how their eyes betrayed them, following one another, hoping the other would not notice. They did not realise that she had noticed; the quiet observer of their growing love. One day, she thought, they might appreciate the irony that it was she who had insisted on them working together; she who had begged Alyssa to give the King a chance and not hate him for ever.

Lorys was still kind, loving and attentive towards her but his desires were for another. Nyria accepted that now. They had enjoyed a strong and healthy sexual relationship in the past, but as Nyria's ailments had become more persistent, their lovemaking had become infrequent to the point where Nyria could not quite remember when they had last shared such intimacy. She considered this. That long ago? That was not right. Lorys had needs.

As Nyria urged Freycin to catch up with the two men, she felt the pain in her chest intensify. She shook her head with regret at how she had failed Lorys and decided on one last gallop across the moors with him.

Saxon regained consciousness with a mighty headache and a tender lump on his head. He sat up in the ditch and looked in confusion at Herek's men, who had found him lying there and roused him from his stupor. Once he realised what had happened, he made ready to return to Caradoon, but the soldiers suggested he should make his way back to Tal instead as it was much closer than Caradoon.

Saxon tentatively touched the sore spot on his head, grimacing as he pieced together events. Quist must have ordered his men to dump Saxon so far south that it would be impossible for him to return quickly to the pirate town. Saxon realised the soldiers were right: his best option would be to return to Tal.

Filled with dread for Cloot, Saxon journeyed with speed back to the palace. He intended to warn Alyssa against Goth and then return to Caradoon. He had a score to settle with the thief, Janus Quist. He also had to find Cloot. The Second of the Paladin must not be left to die in a sack in the bowels of a rat-infested pirate ship. Only Saxon knew of this crime. It was up to him to avenge it.

On arriving in Tal, Saxon reported immediately to the Prime, who had only just returned there himself. Somewhat confused, Herek accepted the Kloek's decision to leave the Shield. Saxon had never been an official member yet all had got used to his jovial, confident presence. Over the last few years, he had trained many of the men with great skill, imparting secrets of balance and how to rely on the senses rather than just eyes and brute strength. Herek genuinely liked the man and would miss his wit and companionship. He could not draw the Kloek on the reason for this sudden departure but he could tell Saxon was in earnest. Herek was not ready, however, for the second piece of news which his friend delivered.

'You saw him?'

Saxon looked grim. 'Almost as closely as we stand now. He was in such a drug-induced stupor I could have grabbed him as one would a child, but I was clubbed senseless by a thief. Perfect timing, eh?' He smiled ruefully. 'The thief got only a little coin from me but I lost my prize.'

'Was that woman with him?'

'Yes.'

Saxon could see Herek wrestling to maintain his self-control.

'I hear our men found you.'

'They did. I was groaning in a heap by the roadside. The pirates drove me south and dumped me there — gave them the time they needed to ready their ship and be off, I suppose.' He rubbed a spot on his head which was still tender from the blow.

The Prime began to pace, all previous concerns forgotten. He would have Goth and the woman Xantia in his dungeons once more and would personally escort the former Chief Inquisitor to the pyre to burn.

'Do you think they will still be in Caradoon?'

Saxon snorted. 'Would you be?'

Herek's expression was thunderous but he remained silent so Saxon continued.

'It's still worth pursuing. You can start at the stracca den. If the scent is still warm, your men can chase it and hound him down until there's nowhere left to run. If you put out word of a rich reward in Caradoon, I'll wager you will receive informants. They're all vermin in that town and a secret is only safe until the price is high enough.'

Herek nodded thoughtfully. 'And you, Saxon, where do you go?'

'I'm off to see a man about a bird,' the Kloek replied cryptically. He gripped Herek's hand in the Tallinese manner. 'I will see you again, Prime.'

Herek returned the grip. 'Make it soon.'

After much searching, Saxon finally tracked Alyssa down to the King's quarters. With the permission of the King's old valet, he waited in the small entrance room to the suite of chambers. Alyssa emerged from the King's study.

'Saxon! You're back.' Not caring for protocol, the King's personal secretary flew to embrace the huge Kloek. The valet arched his eyebrows but, with his usual discretion in all private matters, turned away and went about his business.

'Not for long,' Saxon said, hugging her hard.

She pulled a face as he set her back down on the ground.

'Is there somewhere we can talk?' He cocked his head towards the valet.

'Don't worry about him. Come over here. We can sit at this window seat. Now, tell me everything about that Caradoon place.'

He looked into her wide, concerned eyes and took her hand. 'I saw him.'

Alyssa blinked slowly as she absorbed what he had just said. 'You saw Goth?'

He nodded.

'Could you have been mistaken?' Her voice was small.

'Goth is too distinctive to confuse with anyone else.'

'Can someone corroborate this? Who else saw him?'

'Only I from the Shield, though another did—'

They were disturbed by the valet who was carrying a tray with two drinks on it. 'I thought you may enjoy sharing a cup with your visitor, Miss Alyssa.' He bowed.

Alyssa smiled. 'Koryn, how kind. Thank you, I am thirsty.'

The man bowed slightly again and left them.

Saxon looked into his cup. 'Ale! You drink ale?'

'Only old Koryn knows how much I love the stuff. I have a cup of it around midday when most of the palace is at their noon meal.' She could not help a conspiratorial grin spreading across her face.

Saxon was pleased to see it. 'Good health,' he said.

Alyssa responded in kind and they both took a long draught of the ale.

Her face became serious again. 'You were saying . . . about who else saw Goth . . . ?' she prompted.

'Yes.' He noticed how pale she looked. Could she take this news? But he was too far into this conversation to pull out now. 'I saw Cloot watching him also.'

Although he had readied himself for some sort of reaction, he had not counted on such stillness.

'Cloot?' she whispered, as though hearing the name for the first time.

Saxon remained quiet.

'And did he know you?'

'He flew to me, Alyssa. See this scratch at my ear?' She nodded. 'He did this to warn me. He sat at my shoulder and we watched the stracca den where Goth lay inside losing his senses.'

She looked at him without understanding.

He shrugged in his unique Kloekish way. 'It's a leaf. People smoke it. Very addictive. Dulls the mind like no liquor can.'

Alyssa nodded. 'Tell me about Cloot.'

'I believe he was there to track down Goth. He found him before I did. Perhaps, like me, he had worked out that Caradoon seemed just the sort of place where two lowlifes could hide for a while.'

Alyssa began to weep softly. 'You're sure?'

'That it was Cloot? No other falcon would be so tame. He even managed to flap his wings in response to my questions. It was him all right.'

Alyssa wiped her eyes on her sleeve and composed herself. 'That's happy news then,' she said finally. 'And what of Goth? Is he a threat still?'

He took her in his arms and hugged her hard. He

could see she needed to feel his strength and safety.

'Sallementro and I are here to protect you, not to mention the Shield and the elite warriors of the King's Guard. You have nothing to fear from Goth,' he promised her. He felt like a traitor, for he did not believe a word of it. He cleared his throat. 'I have to go back to Caradoon tomorrow.'

'Again!' She paused and sipped her drink before continuing. 'You're going to finish off Goth once and for all, aren't you?'

'No, sadly. I have to find Cloot. He was captured by traders and I fear he may already be off the mainland and on his way to the Exotic Isles.'

'Why did you come back without killing Goth first?'

Saxon felt the guilt of his decision bite. 'They beat me unconscious and drove me by cart far from Caradoon. When I came to, I realised I was closer to the main Shield group and you than to the pirate town. It made sense to return and give you this news.'

'Goth is no longer your priority, is he?' she asked, already knowing the answer.

He shook his head. 'No, Alyssa. I am leaving Goth to Herek and his men. I must go in search of Cloot of the Paladin.'

They were not together much longer and spent what time there was talking about Gyl. Saxon took his leave soon afterwards, hugging Alyssa fiercely and promising to return with Tor's falcon.

After he had left her, Alyssa returned to the King's study, even more distracted than she had felt before she left it.

* * *

'But I don't know how to fight, Saxon. I am a musician!'

Saxon sighed. 'Sallementro,' he said heavily, 'I am not asking you to fight. I am asking you to protect her. You are her second-bonded Paladin. You were not picked out by the gods for your vocal talent alone, exquisite though it may be.'

They both smiled. This was old ground; a path they had trodden many times before.

The musician spoke softly. 'Yes, it is a notion I repeat to myself time and again. If I am one of the Paladin, then one must presume I have already suffered great pain to be here now.'

Saxon nodded gently. 'You can be sure of it. This is your destiny. You and I are bonded to Alyssa and must give our lives for her. We are all blind in this, Sallementro. None of us knows what will occur. All we know is that we will do whatever we can to keep our charges safe. Now, I must go and find Cloot. He is in serious danger, I fear.'

'I will keep her safe.'

Saxon touched Sallementro on the shoulder. 'I know you will. And the boy — keep Gyl safe too.'

The two men embraced.

'How long will you be gone?'

The Kloek shrugged. 'I'm hoping to return swiftly but Cloot has been stolen from the mainland, which probably means a journey across the seas and who knows what awaits me there. The sun is high already; I must be gone. It will take me many days to get back to the north and there is weather closing in.'

Sallementro was about to say that he too had heard that grim weather was predicted for the coming days when the palace bells began to toll. Neither man had heard that ominous sound since the announcement of Torkyn Gynt's execution. Without another word they began to run, joining the dozens of men, women and children who had emerged from the palace and were rushing as fast as they could towards the main courtyard.

Gyl came careening down a flight of stairs and bundled straight into Saxon, knocking three or four others with him.

'Strike me, lad!' cursed Saxon.

Gyl began apologising to all and helped one of the cooks to her feet. Saxon looked back at the stairs and realised Gyl had jumped the entire flight. All that training was working.

Together the three men pushed through the crowd, Saxon first, strongly shouldering his way through to the front. Despite the numbers of people, a shocked silence hung over the courtyard.

Lying on the flagstones, her head supported by a folded cloak, was Queen Nyria. She was very still. Her skin looked waxen and a trickle of blood ran from behind her ear and soaked into the pale velvet of her cloak. The King was kneeling beside her, his face contorted with grief.

He looked up and stretched out his arms. 'Won't someone help her?' he pleaded.

The King's most loyal servant, Koryn, put his mottled, bony fingers on the King's shoulders and squeezed gently. He whispered directly into the griefstricken man's ear. 'My liege, she has gone to the Light.'

Lorys roared aloud in his agony. He picked up the Queen's limp body and pulled it to his chest. Now all in the yard could see just how drenched with blood her cloak was.

The Queen of Tallinor was surely dead.

No one moved. All were too shocked to speak. Then a lone voice called out and a woman pushed through the crowd. Saxon immediately recognised Alyssa's voice and Gyl moved towards her just as she broke through and froze, taking in the ugly scene.

Weeping, she knelt beside her King and her Queen, close enough to hear what the sovereign was mumbling over and over into Nyria's bloodied ear.

'I am punished for my sins,' he wept.

8

Shrouded in Violet

Tal was in mourning. As they had done for centuries when a royal passed into the Light, the Tallinese shrouded their city in violet; the colour reserved for death. As a sign of respect, shopkeepers draped violet over their doorways, most of the houses had pennants of violet hanging from their windows and people stitched a patch of the colour onto their garments. Little girls even put the fresh flowers in their hair. The city, indeed the Kingdom, would wear the violet for two moon cycles.

The palace itself had descended into a frigid silence. Only essential duties were carried out and the kitchen prepared traditional mourning fare: bland and meagre. The palace occupants would eat this basic diet until the Queen's body was cremated.

For three days and nights she would lie in state, laid out on a cold bed of stone in the chapel where her subjects could bid their final farewells. Word of Nyria's death had spread like fire and people descended in their hundreds on the capital. The King had released money to provide food for the many who had come from so far on so little to see their Queen for the last time.

And this was where Alyssa found herself, praying, watching, weeping with the Tallinese. She had tried to keep up the school hours but none of her pupils could concentrate. By the second morning she had given up, dismissed the two classes and sent the children back to their quarters. With Lorys shut up in his chambers, receiving no visitors, speaking to no one, she had nothing to do.

Gyl escaped the bleak days by volunteering to go into the hills with Herek and some of the King's Guard for drills and training.

Saxon had left the city altogether. He had remained with her longer than he had wanted to and finally Alyssa had told him to be on his way. He could do nothing to help and she knew that the loss of Cloot cut him far deeper than the loss of a Queen. He had left yesterday and she had cried bitterly, wondering whether she would lose him too.

Only Sallementro remained close but he was so involved in preparing the music for her majesty's funeral service that Alyssa could not count on his companionship right now. And so she sat alone in the shadows of the chapel and grieved, wondering what would happen to palace life now that it had lost its jewel.

She watched a young couple grieve at the sight of their dead Queen and she was reminded of the depth of grief she had felt at losing Tor. Alyssa had never thought she would fall in love again or feel the desire to hold her body close against a man and enjoy his touch. But Lorys had reawakened those feelings and she wept as she remembered, just a few moons ago, wishing the Queen did not exist and Lorys was hers.

And now the Queen was dead. That wish had been answered.

Alyssa hated herself.

She watched more and more people filing through the chapel, shocked and distraught. Many of them had seen their Queen in the flesh only a short time previous during the royal tour. Radiant and elegant as always, Nyria had touched their hearts and shown her joy at being amongst them. They had responded with love. And now her body lay cold before them.

It was faithful Herek who told Alyssa what had happened the day of the Queen's death. As usual, he had taken the morning ride with his King and that particular day the Queen had decided to ride with them, as she often did. She had fainted during a gallop across the moors, had fallen from her fleet-footed horse, Freycin, and struck her head on a rock. A similar incident had occurred when Torkyn Gynt was under-physic at the palace, but that time Gynt had revitalised the Queen's heart and saved her life. Whether the Queen's heart had failed again, or whether it was the blow to her head which killed her, no one would ever know, but she was dead before Herek and the King had dismounted and rushed to her side.

Herek confided to Alyssa how the King had screamed Nyria's name for an hour or more. The Prime had not dared to suggest they return to the palace until Lorys had found some level of composure.

'He suddenly stopped,' Herek had said. 'He mounted his stallion, asked for the Queen to be placed in his arms and then allowed the horse to lead them back to the palace at its own pace. Fortunately, I saw a stableboy walking one of the horses. I told him to hurry back to the palace with my order for the bells of alarm to be sounded.'

That was all Alyssa knew. She had yet to speak with the King since that morning when it seemed she was the last at the palace to discover the tragedy. She had busied herself since in making arrangements for the public cremation. Tallinese tradition demanded that the body be cremated within three days of death; beyond the fourth night it was believed that the soul of the dead would be unable to find the Light and would be doomed to forever roam in darkness.

Lorys would never risk this for his Queen. Nyria would be cremated on the third day.

9

A Secret Revealed

Alyssa saw Lorys at the funeral feast although she still did not exchange a word with him. She could see that the King was gritting his teeth throughout the ceremony and he made an early departure.

Later, young Edwyd, the King's page, brought her an unexpected message.

'He has asked for me?' she repeated, knowing it was foolish. That was what the boy had just said.

'He wishes to see you now, Miss Alyssa,' Edwyd repeated.

'I shall tidy myself and come immediately,' she said, standing.

Sallementro, who was singing a tragic love song to the gathering, looked over towards her. She shook her head and blew him a kiss. She would talk to him later.

Alyssa knocked softly at the main door to the sovereign's chambers. She was relieved to see Koryn open it. He was so old, wizened by Gyl's standards, but Alyssa loved the great wisdom in his rheumy eyes. With Merkhud dead, Koryn was the last of the palace staff who had served under old King Mort and who had known Lorys as a child.

He welcomed her kindly and pointed towards the salon. 'I am sure the King thanks you for coming at this late hour, Miss Alyssa,' he said graciously and offered to pour her a glass of wine.

Alyssa did not really want wine. Her stomach was churning at this unexpected invitation.

'Here you are, Miss.' He passed her the goblet anyway.

'Oh, Koryn, I'm just trying to come to terms with today.' She mustered a smile for the gentle man who stood in front of her. 'How is the King?'

He sighed gently. 'It will take time but you know him: his mind never stops and now that the official part is over, he knows he must get on with running his Kingdom. With him being away on the tour and then this . . . well.' He shrugged.

'I understand,' Alyssa said. She sipped her wine politely. 'Are we to work?'

'I don't believe so. I think he might just appreciate some company, Miss Alyssa.' His last few words were whispered for Lorys strode into the room.

Alyssa stood, feeling nervous. Lorys was freshly bathed and droplets of water still clung to his beard and hair. His dark violet shirt was carelessly open and she could see his broad muscled chest beneath. She put down the beautiful glass goblet quickly. It was either that or break it with her grip.

All the feelings she thought she had put aside came flooding back. He was beautiful. So much older than her and yet he was truly irresistible. His grief just made him more vulnerable, more desirable. She wanted to run but found a shaky smile as he looked at her briefly before addressing his valet.

'Thank you, Koryn, for your help today. Please, have an early night. I will not be requiring anything more this evening.'

Koryn bowed to his sovereign and departed. Drake, the King's huge hound, escorted him to the door. The old man was quite used to this ritual and even wished the dog a very good night.

Alyssa's mind was racing. What should she say? How should she act?

'Thank you for coming, Alyssa,' the King said suddenly. She jumped.

'Are you well?' he asked, noticing how startled she seemed.

'I . . . I . . . it's been a very long day, your majesty. My apologies. I imagine you must be feeling it more than any of us.'

She wished she could bite her own tongue out. What a stupid thing to say. He had not seemed to notice, though, and was pouring himself a goblet of wine. He asked her to sit. A small fire had been lit in the room, making it cosy. The nights were certainly cooler now and Alyssa's mind shifted briefly to Saxon, wondering how he might be faring in the north as winter closed in.

Lorys was never one for small talk. 'I wish to discuss Gyl,' he said.

The topic was so unexpected that she swallowed her wine the wrong way in her surprise and began to cough.

'Light, woman, what is wrong with you tonight? You are so jumpy.' He leapt up to help.

'No, sire, I'm fine. Please . . . I'm just not used to the

wine. I got out of the habit whilst you were abroad,' she spluttered.

It was a poor attempt at deflection but it stopped him pounding her on the back or, even more terrifying, sitting next to her.

'Alyssa, this is pure mother's milk. It is called Morache. You should savour its gentle sweetness. Such an elegant wine, the result of a loving first press from that tiny green grape which grows on the hillsides of Arandon. I chose it especially for you.'

She could not help but feel touched, even amused. 'Thank you, sire. I like it very much – or at least I will as soon as I swallow it properly.'

'Call me Lorys, Alyssa. We are not working now.'

Dangerous, she told herself. 'Um . . . you said you wanted to talk to me about Gyl, my lord?'

Lorys sighed at her formality. 'Yes . . . yes, I did. I have decided that the lad is to be elevated to a new position. Under-Prime will put him just one rank below Prime Herek. He is to be groomed for the top job.'

Alyssa stood. 'But, sire, that's ridiculous!'

When the King shot her a tired look over the top of his goblet, she gathered her wits. 'Oh, my apologies to speak so plainly, my lord, but Gyl has just turned fifteen summers. You cannot expect the soldiers to take him seriously?'

Lorys opened his mouth to respond but Alyssa had begun to pace and continued talking.

'They will make a mockery of him. The men of the Shield can be cruel on a lad, sire. They consider it their duty to turn him into a man and I have seen them torture him – all good-naturedly of course – but torture nonetheless. He takes it in the very best of spirits and always returns for more but it troubles me. He is the only boy of that age in the garrison . . . he's just too young.'

She looked at Lorys imploringly.

'He is no longer a boy, Alyssa. He is a man. Young, yes, but a man all the same. I was being groomed to run the Kingdom by the time I was twelve. I was crowned King when I was not yet seventeen.'

'Yes, and no doubt there was a veritable circus of people teaching you how, your majesty. This child was abandoned at twelve. He has learned to fit into this life at the palace but he was not born to it as you were.'

The King sipped his wine and said casually, 'And how would you know what he was born to?'

That confused Alyssa. 'Sire, your own good wife, the Queen, found him chained to the palace gates. He was left there by his mother. Is that the action of a high-born woman?'

'No. But you have no idea of his background.'

'And you do?' Her ire was up now. King or no King, she would not see Gyl harmed in any way.

'As a matter of fact, yes. I've made it my business to find out more. Surely you grasped when you met him that he was an educated child. He could read, write, do sums. He has a ready wit and manners most gentle. This is no child of gypsies. Has that never piqued your curiosity?'

It had raided her thoughts for the first few years they had spent together. These days she forced all thoughts of his early life to the back of her mind and locked them away. She wanted nothing to do with them. Gyl was her son. He was hers.

'I don't dwell on it, your majesty,' she answered tersely.

'Well, let me assure you that Gyl comes from a very good home.' It was clear Alyssa did not want to listen but Lorys pushed on. 'His father was not known to him but his mother – a good woman who, incidentally, brought him to the palace gates because she knew she was soon to die – did her best to give him an excellent education. She worked hard for this because his father, so I am told, was of noble birth.'

Dangerous territory now. He took a big swallow of his wine.

'Who is the father, sire?'

'There are rumours.'

'How can you be sure they are true?'

'Because older members of the palace staff supported them.'

'Such as?'

'Such as Merkhud. Why are you so tiresome?' he said, frustrated by her cross-examination.

Alyssa boiled over. 'Because I'm his mother!'

Now Lorys's temper flashed. He spoke without thinking. 'You are not his mother, Alyssa! You are merely his guardian. But I am his . . .'

He didn't finish.

Alyssa crumpled. The wine had made her emotional and now the dream which she had woven around herself these past few years had been smashed by Lorys's harsh words. Of course Gyl was not her son and she was not his mother. Her son was dead. His body lay decaying on the forest floor.

And so was his father: Torkyn Gynt, the Kingdom's finest physician and its greatest sorcerer. A man who had gone to his death with greater nobility than any of the courtiers who swanned around the palace. He should never have been executed. He would not have been, were it not for this man in front of her. The man who was staring at her with such compassion and regret. The man who had ordered her husband's barbaric execution.

Alyssa screamed aloud. The horror came flooding back. All the old demons raged forth to haunt her once again. She struck out at the man responsible for it all. Punching and slapping, she felt each blow land on his flesh and she hated him for not stopping her. Instead, he stood there sadly and took her punishment.

Finally her rage calmed and she slid to the floor. Her breath came in ragged starts and she could hear that Lorys too was breathing deeply. Had she made a great deal of noise? She could not hear running in the hallways or knocking at the door. Only the dog seemed to have responded; he was taking a greater than usual interest in her, licking at the tears on her face.

'Go on with you, Drake,' she heard the King say.

The hound loped off and she felt the King's strong hands beneath her arms as he lifted her up to face him. His face was bleeding from a scratch on one cheek and the other cheekbone looked puffy. His shirt was ripped, revealing even more of the body she longed to touch. Alyssa felt sick.

'You should box for one of the Shield teams,' Lorys said.

At that she began to cry. What a hopeless, horrible situation.

'Remind me not to try again to make you laugh with my scintillating wit.'

'Sire, you are wounded,' she said, staring through her tears at his face.

'Just a scratch and deserved. I am sorry, Alyssa. Truly, deeply sorry. I had no right to throw that in your face. You are a wonderful mother to Gyl and he is a lucky boy to have you in his life.'

They were standing too close. He took her hand and held it against his bare chest. Alyssa could feel her own heart banging loudly, or was it his heartbeat she could feel against her palm? She did not know but she did not want it to end. She wanted to throw her whole self against his naked chest and cry her tears. Cry for Gyl and for Tor, for Saxon and Cloot, for the tragic loss of Nyria and for her own doomed love for the King.

'Will you forgive me?' he said tenderly.

'Only if you will let me see to that wound.'

He nodded.

Alyssa reluctantly pulled away from his hold and cleaned up her face with her kerchief, which she moistened in some water from the jug. Then she called to the page, who, mercifully, was asleep outside and had missed the noise. Thankfully the King refused to have his chambers guarded or they would have had ten men banging on the doors by now.

'Edwyd, fetch my herbals basket from my chambers. Gyl will show you. Hurry, lad. After you've returned you may leave for your night's rest.'

The page scurried off. Inside once again, she politely asked the King to sit down and poured him another goblet of wine. She could feel his eyes following her every move but she refused to look at him.

Alyssa was grateful that Edwyd returned quickly with her basket. Closing the door on him, she asked Lorys to lean his head back so she could inspect the wound. She had to sit next to him to clean it with a mixture of washes she had made herself only a few days earlier. They were so fresh and stringent that they made him wince but she knew their application would ensure no infection occurred there. Another trick learned from Sorrel: infection kills, so kill it first.

'I'm sorry to hurt you more, sire.'

Lorys sighed. 'Looking at you, having you so close and being unable to tell you how my heart longs for you hurts much, much more.'

Alyssa stopped her ministrations. Their faces were just inches apart.

'My lord, you must not speak so,' she whispered.

The King sat up and took her hands in his. 'But I must, Alyssa. Or I will go mad from the pain. I love you. I have loved you since the day I saw you in the throne room, wan and filled with despair. You were beautiful in your dignity at the execution of Gynt and though I cannot heal that wound for you, I can beg your forgiveness.

'I could have stayed the execution but I was already too enamoured of you. Too jealous of him for having felt your body beneath his. I wanted no man to have you if I could not. I have been demented these years at having you near. It takes all my courage sometimes to stop myself from reaching out and stroking your hair as we work—'

'My lord, please. The Queen's ashes are still warm,' Alyssa cried.

'Hush, Alyssa. The Queen knew.'

From the table next to him, he lifted a piece of parchment. Alyssa could see immediately that it was inscribed with the Queen's hand.

He continued as he unrolled it fully. 'She wrote this

several days before her death; the day we returned from the royal tour. In it she thanks me,' he barked a sad laugh, 'for being so attentive and loving to her during the Kingdom-wide visit.

'I will not read it all to you, but she admits to knowing how unhappy my nights were during that time and further suggests that I was yearning for something. She writes that I was yearning for the company of Alyssandra Qyn. She says that I am not to feel badly because of this. She blesses any relationship that we may have after her death, which she seemed to know was close.'

He paused. It was upsetting for him to read it again, though Alyssa could see the parchment had already been fingered and read many times. She passed him the wine and he drank the rest of his goblet.

'I must finish this. She hopes that I will consider making you my Queen for she believes that you and I will form the perfect union for a Kingdom that is facing trouble. I do not know what she means by that, but on the morning of our ride – the day she died – she told me that she had dreamed of a woman who told her that Tallinor would face much danger in years to come and it would need strength at its helm to navigate those challenging times. According to Nyria, the woman told her that you are critical to the Kingdom and that Gyl must be Prime.'

'Light, Lorys! And you believe all this?' Alyssa exclaimed, feeling her stomach clench as she recognised the intrusion of Lys once more into their lives.

'I believe that you and I are meant to be together. I believe that Nyria continued unto death the fine and noble character she possessed in life; she has blessed our union and I will love her more than ever for that generosity. I believe that Gyl should be groomed for Prime for many reasons and I believe that our army should prepare itself for less peaceful times. Old man Merkhud used to warn me of it but I never really paid enough attention to our defence. We have never been at war during my reign. The modern Tallinese know only peace and prosperity. But Merkhud was a strange, all-knowing old fellow and this dream of Nyria's . . . this warning — well, I have never taken any other of her suggestions lightly so this too will be heeded. Now, tell me you love me too, Alyssa. Tell me I am not imagining it.' His words were tumbling upon each other as he searched her face for his answer.

Alyssa paused, forcing herself to think. But she was too far into her love for him.

'I have tried not to, my lord. All I wanted was to hate you. But I have failed. I adore you, Lorys. I want you with all my heart, although I feel like a traitor to Nyria.'

His eyes looked misty. 'Be my Queen. Stand beside me and rule.'

Alyssa took a deep breath; she saw Tor's face and bade it farewell as she said the words the King ached to hear. 'I shall be your Queen, my lord, and I will love you for ever.'

He reached for her and pulled her close. They kissed, long and sweetly. All sense of time fled; all sense of the palace around them disappeared. They were one. Their love was sealed.

When they parted, she settled her head against his chest. The sensation of his skin against her cheek made her feel like she was floating. She never wanted this euphoria to end. Then she remembered the archalyt. She sat upright, startled.

'What is it?' Lorys asked, stroking the hair he had longed to touch for so many years.

'I am still Untouchable. I am not permitted to have a lover, let alone take a husband, even though he may be King. You have had people murdered for less, my lord.'

'Nyria thought of everything, my love. She has been lobbying me for years about the status of Untouchables. I was forced to admit to her that since we disbanded the Inquisitors, the Tallinese people have been much happier. I realised we have been clinging to an ancient law which, in its time, was set for the good of all, but Goth and his band had turned it into a means of persecuting anyone they saw fit.

'As for the Untouchables, it is much the same thing. We have promoted the fear that every sentient woman will give birth to a demon who will destroy us. It is an archaic belief. Legend has it that centuries ago a madman, a sentient, nearly destroyed the Land. But I think we are all wiser now and we must grow and go forward, not cling to the past and its myths.'

Alyssa welcomed Lorys's words, but nevertheless felt chilled at his reference to Orlac, whom, she knew from Nanak's writings, would return one day. He was no legend. He did intend to destroy Tallinor. But she did not want to think on that now.

'So, what is your plan for the Academie and the Untouchables?'

'Well, the Academie is very important. It must continue its work and will remain as a haven for young women. However, they will not run there because of persecution. They will choose to enrol there because they are gifted and can contribute something special to our Kingdom.'

'And the archalyt?'

'It will no longer be necessary. I realise that those of you who are already marked will never be able to remove it, but no sentient woman will ever be marked in this way again. And those who do carry the mark will be free to live normal lives. We owe you a debt.'

'Oh, Lorys!' Alyssa hugged him. 'This is what your reign will be remembered for. You are releasing those who have been enslaved for too long.'

He was enjoying her praise. 'And as for their status, the Untouchables will be permitted to take husbands, although we will still keep a register of their children. Old habits die hard.'

'I am so proud of you. Breaking down these barriers will make you sovereign of an even stronger Kingdom. Embrace the gifted and encourage their talents and it will repay itself, Lorys, I know it.'

They kissed again, more deeply this time, neither wanting to part from the other's lips.

When they finally did part, Alyssa realised she was exhausted. She yawned. 'I must go.'

'Can't you stay?'

'No,' she said grinning. 'Not until we are married.'

'Meet me for a kiss at breakfast time then.'

'Do you feel guilt over this?' she asked, pulling away from his embrace.

'I have suffered guilt for years over my feelings for you, but I have never stopped loving Nyria even though I love you so much. No, Nyria has blessed us in this letter; she wanted us to be together after her death and so I feel only joy in this, and relief that I knew her and that she was my Queen for as long as she was.'

Alyssa realised he was right, but she made him promise not to make their love public until a suitable mourning period had passed. Lorys agreed.

'That means no holding of hands or looking at me dewy-eyed, Lorys. We still have to work together as King and secretary for a few moons yet.' She wagged her finger at him.

'I promise,' he said, touching his heart. Her spot.

'Before I go, please tell me what you know of Gyl – I beg you.'

Lorys looked deeply into her eyes and felt safe. With Alyssa, soon to be his Queen, no secrets were necessary.

'He is my son. He is the heir to Tallinor.'

10

Reunion in a Brothel

When Tor arrived at Caradoon neither Goth and Xantia nor Janus Quist were still in town. He found lodgings at a run-down inn. His stuffy room was dirty and contained nothing more than a pallet and rough sheets still unchanged from the previous guest. Still, it gave him the anonymity he needed. He had entered town wearing a glamour to avoid being recognised, but having established that Goth had seemingly fled, he was able to rid himself of the disguise. No one knew of Goth's whereabouts; or if they did, they certainly were not telling a stranger.

So be it. Goth was no longer his first priority; that enemy would have to wait. Tor hoped that Saxon had returned immediately to Tal to ensure Alyssa's safety. He could count on Saxon. For now, Cloot had to be found. Tor needed to track down Janus Quist and he knew he would have to be very careful in how he approached his questioning. The Caradoons were suspicious by nature, mistrustful of everyone; they trusted southerners even less, particularly those from the capital.

Tor decided that although the best and perhaps quickest

source of information would be the docks, his chances would probably be better in the local whorehouse. Grease a few palms, ply a few drinks, play up to a woman's charms and who knew what could be learned.

Quist was certainly not a good-looking man but there was a dignity about him. The mere fact that he had showed his face was testimony to a sense of fairness, not to mention sparing Saxon's life. Yes, Quist definitely had a certain charisma, a powerful one. And where there was power, there were women. Tor had no doubt that Quist would avail himself of the ladies of the town each time he returned from a prosperous journey and so he made his way to the brothel.

Falcons could not be Quist's only trade, Tor reasoned, as he sat watching the comings and goings at the brothel. Quist had admitted as much when he had commented how much Cloot alone would fetch. He recalled what Cloot had told him about the trade through Caradoon: he had mentioned slaves. Human treasure must fetch a heady price so perhaps that was Quist's stock in trade. He had all the arrogance of a successful man. Tor knew he would have to tread carefully.

As he strolled towards the brothel entrance, he wondered what sort of a man would be accepted more readily. A confident one for sure. Any sign of weakness would be pounced on. He knew he was imposing enough in stature, with looks to turn heads, but that was not sufficient. A handsome man won initial interest, but he needed more than that. As he considered this, pausing on the porch, he remembered something Yargo had said to him once. 'You are a most mysterious person, Tor.'

That was it: mystery. Nothing piques a woman's

imagination more than a man who is shrouded. Who had told him this? The most mysterious man he had known in his life so far: Prime Cyrus. Now there was a man whom women fawned over yet they knew so little about him.

'Women are the most curious creatures. The more you hide, the more determined they become to know your secrets. Keep your secrets and you keep the woman.'

Tor smiled to himself as he recalled the Prime's words of wisdom. He pushed open the door and stepped into a surprisingly well kept interior. Considering this was reputedly a town of lowlifes, the last bastion of humanity before the Kingdom stretched into a rocky wilderness, their brothel was better cared for than most. A trio of songsters entertained guests with excellent music, men chatted casually to one another at the bar, pretty women plied their trade and there was an air of brisk business being done. It made Tor think of Miss Vylet's, which was the best run brothel he had ever encountered.

His welcome at the bar was a little frosty initially. He ordered a sorvino: a cloudy yellow liquor which was expensive but smooth on the way down and the quickest way to warm the insides on a chilly evening. He was not especially partial to it – since living in Tal he had become something of a wine connoisseur, favouring the finest drops from the south – however, his choice was double edged: sorvino was made in the north and its expense marked him as a man of means.

Only women served, even behind the bar, which was refreshing. After his third nip of the sorvino, he felt the serving woman's attitude towards him thaw. She even winked as she took his coin. 'What's a good-looking stranger like you doing in these parts?'

'Oh, just wandering,' he said.

'Caradoon is not a place to wander,' she warned, still smiling.

'I like it here. It makes me feel,' he looked away as if trying to choose just the right word, 'anonymous.'

'Oh?' She arched her eyebrows with amusement. 'Then you've certainly come to the right place.'

'I think so,' he said, sliding onto a stool with his back to the wall so he could look around.

'And do you have a name? You know we don't like strangers here.'

He said the first name which came to mind, 'Petersyn,' then raised his glass. 'To anonymity,' he said.

She smiled her acknowledgement and moved on to serve another customer.

Tor realised the place was quite crowded now that he had the leisure to observe. He guessed there must be a dress requirement. All the men looked decidedly tidy for pirates, thieves, cut-throats, murderers and slavers. Whoever owned this place must run it with a firm hand, he decided. Certainly all the laides were dressed exceptionally well – just as Miss Vylet's girls had been.

A delectable creature strolled up and leaned over him to put some cups down on the bar. The movement showed off her breasts at their best. He grinned inwardly; an old trick but effective, he had to admit.

'Good evening, sir,' she said politely, 'forgive me for reaching past you.'

'Nothing to forgive. I enjoyed it.'

'Can I do anything for you, sir?'

'You can fetch me a plate of food . . . whatever's going.'

'Everything we cook here is excellent, Mr, er . . . ?'

'Petersyn,' Tor replied.

'Fish, roasted meat, a superb jugged hare?' she enquired.

'The fish would be most enjoyable, er . . . ?'

'Celya is my name. If you fancy anything else, please ask for me. I can assure you, Mr Petersyn, I am far more enjoyable than the fish,' she flirted, before disappearing into the back of the room, where he presumed the kitchens must be.

Tor took a deep breath. She was lovely and quick-witted. The woman behind the bar came back to offer a top up of his sorvino.

'Who is the proprietor here, may I enquire?'

'Madame Eryna, sir,' the girl responded and she cast a glance towards a small flight of stairs that led to a landing overlooking the main room.

Tor followed her gaze and saw a beautiful woman who cut a striking figure in a deep sea-green gown. She stood with poise and surveyed her brothel with a prac-tised eye. Tor marvelled at how like Miss Vylet this woman was; not in looks but certainly in the way she carried herself.

Her red hair was a shock of colour against pale skin and contrasted magnificently with her green satin gown. She was a beauty all right . . . and young. Tor could tell her youth even at this distance; she wore heavy make-up – perhaps to make herself appear older – and yet her own loveliness still shone through.

As if she sensed him watching her, she suddenly turned and fixed a clear gaze on him. She gestured to one of her girls, who made her way up the stairs. They spoke quietly and the girl looked over at Tor and nodded. Madame turned her gaze towards him again and dipped her head in acknowledgement. He raised his glass to her.

This was obviously the woman he needed to speak with, but how?

As his meal arrived, so did the girl from the stairs. 'My apologies to interrupt you, sir,' she said gently, 'but Madame Eryna wishes to meet with you this evening.'

'How lovely. I would be delighted,' Tor said, marvelling at this luck. 'However, I wish to eat first.'

'But, sir, I'm wondering if we could provide you with a fresh plate after your talk with Madame.'

'And you are . . . ?' he said, looking directly into her eyes.

'Aymee, sir, at your service.'

'Well, Aymee, I am hungry for food rather than conversation at this moment. If Madame Eryna wishes to meet with me, it will be my pleasure after I have taken my supper. Now, if you'll excuse me,' he said, beginning to eat. Raising a hope for Cyrus's creed, he counted on his attitude intriguing the madam, even if it also irritated her.

The girl was flummoxed. She stammered another apology and departed. He felt sorry for her and hoped the proprietor would not take her annoyance out on her. If he got the information he needed, then he would buy Aymee for the night. At the very least, it meant she would sleep in a comfortable bed. When he looked back at the landing, the statuesque figure was no longer there. He hoped he had not missed his chance.

Finishing his fish, which was, as Celya had promised, delicious, he settled back with a mug of ale, this time to await Madame Eryna. Several women approached him during the course of the evening which stretched into night. He turned down their advances, always politely, always offering them a drink and always hoping for some titbit of information which might lead him to Janus Quist. He achieved nothing and one girl even became suspicious and left without finishing her drink. Things were not going at all well and just as he began to curse his luck, Aymee reappeared.

'Madame Eryna asks whether you are ready now to share a glass with her, Master Petersyn.'

'I have been ready for hours, Aymee. Thank you. And perhaps later we can share some time?' he offered.

She just smiled and gestured for him to follow. He was taken to a suite where a merry fire burned in the grate and the furniture was expensive, soft and inviting. He marvelled at a pair of superb tapestries which adorned the walls, their richness of colour and quality of work testifying that they had been crafted by the finest Ildagarthian artisans. This was not the chamber of a madam of a backwater brothel; this room belonged to someone with excellent taste and the experience of city life. Tor knew he was going to enjoy learning more about this woman. He made himself comfortable in an armchair and took the liberty of pouring himself a glass of wine from the exquisite carafe which sat on a table next to it.

Madame was not long in arriving, entering through a back door to the chamber. She took him by surprise. 'Torkyn Gynt, how dare you make me wait!'

Tor nearly spilled the wine on his breeches as he jumped to his feet and circled around to clap eyes on a familiar face. Gone was the heavy make-up and crimson lips, the velvet gown had been cast away in favour of a soft and shimmery shift and her hair was no longer red and curly. It hung straight, dark and thick to her shoulders.

'Well, say something,' she said, hugely amused.

'Eryn!'

She clapped her hands. 'One and the same.'

'Your . . . your hair,' he said, feeling quite the fool.

'A wig. I have many of them.' She laughed, full throated, and walked across the room to take his hands. 'No kiss for an old friend?'

Tor could not stop staring. It *was* Eryn. A few years older, yes, but still that sparkling, lovely girl he could have fallen in love with if not for Alyssa.

He laughed out loud with her. 'What in Light's name are you doing in this town?'

'I own this brothel, Tor. You should be proud of me,' she said, sounding a little disappointed, and moved to pour herself a glass of wine.

He snatched her hand back. 'No, wait! You are utterly breathtaking and I am so proud of you I'm almost speechless.'

She beamed then, that familiar giggle surfacing. He bent and kissed her cheek. They looked long at each other and he kissed her again, properly this time.

'I always hoped I'd taste your lips again, Tor.'

He hugged her hard. 'I want to know everything,' he pronounced, pulling her to a sofa. 'Sit here and tell me of your life.'

'Tor, I will tell you but first I have to know something.' She hesitated.

'Ask,' he said, still grinning from the discovery of his old friend.

'Why are you here and asking questions about Janus Quist?'

His grin faded. So word had spread quickly.

'Because I have an interest to meet him.'

'How do you know of him?' she said, sitting down opposite in the armchair.

This was tricky. He could not tell the full truth. Who would believe that the last time he was at Caradoon he had been in the body of a falcon?

'A friend of mine met him once and told me of him.'

'I see. And your friend's name is?'

'Saxon. Saxon Fox.'

'I don't know him, Tor.'

'Nor would you, Eryn. He is a Kloek. What is your interest in Quist?'

'Well, he's a regular. He's also a local.'

'Do you trust him more than me?'

She sipped her wine. 'I did not say that. But I know Janus Quist. He does not like strangers . . . he likes them even less if they nose around in his business.'

Tor looked her directly in the eyes and sensed she was choosing her words with great care. It puzzled him.

'All right, Eryn. Would it make any difference to you if I told you that he has stolen something which belongs to me?'

At this she laughed. 'But, Tor, that's his profession. He is a pirate. He thieves and trades.'

Tor was serious now. 'That may be, but he took something which is exceptionally precious to me, something which I want returned.'

'If you have not met Quist, Tor, how could you know it was he who took this special item of yours?' she said, twirling her glass and not looking at him.

'Saxon was looking after it at the time. The pirate clubbed him over the head and stole what was mine.'

Eryn looked very uncomfortable, he decided; gorgeous but uncomfortable. She pretended to sip again at her wine.

'Could I replace this item for you? Would that help?'

Tor put his glass down and spoke softly. 'It is irreplaceable.'

'But, Tor,' she said, sitting forward so she was almost touching him, 'Janus would have sold whatever it is. He never hangs on to stolen goods for more than a day.'

'Which is why I am in a hurry to see him . . . Eryn, what is your interest in this man? How do you know so much about him?'

There was an awkward silence between them. She met his eyes steadily though. 'He is my husband.'

Tor had not expected this, but before he could say anything, she held up her hand to hush him.

'Let me tell you about my life after you left Hatten, Tor, and you'll understand.'

She poured him a second glass of finest southern wine and encouraged him to sit back and listen. Tor learned how she had felt unsettled after he had left, how she had been angry with him for not saying goodbye or telling her why he was leaving.

'Eryn, you were the one who forbade any love . . . it was just friends, remember?'

'I do,' she replied and he thought he heard wistfulness in her voice. Nevertheless, she had felt empty after his departure. She had continued to work at Miss Vylet's but when the old girl died suddenly, life changed for the worse. A wealthy couple took over the business; he ran the front of house badly and she ran the brothel nastily. The girls hated her and the custom dropped away.

Tor felt saddened to hear of Miss Vylet. She was a good woman and a valuable sentient. 'What of your brothers, Eryn?'

'Ah, here's the meat to my tale. Petyr, as you may have guessed, was an unhappy young man. I was the eldest, so my word counted, but Petyr struggled with this, being a man. He was not much of a man really, though; he was more like a younger sister, I often thought. He knew it and that just made things worse.'

Tor nodded. Eryn told him of the day when Petyr was badly beaten by a sailor. The sailor escaped to his ship but left Petyr with a broken body. 'And a re-arranged face to boot,' she added sadly. 'He took his fun with Petyr, bashed him up and left him bleeding in an alleyway. I'll never forget his name: Nord Jesper. One day I will find him and I will kill him.'

Tor learned that Petyr had not been able to cope with losing his looks and had fled Hatten.

'He was always an unhappy person; sullen and insecure. It was a great shame, for he used to be a sunny child until our mother died.' Eryn shrugged and continued. 'I went in search of him. I hated my life at the brothel but I loved my brothers; they were all I had. So I decided I'd track him down and we would build a life somewhere else. I even thought of trying to find you in Tal. I had heard you were very popular at the royal court.'

At this they both shared a smile of regret.

'It took me three moons but I finally found him in Caradoon. I was just a few hours too late. He was dead.'

Her voice broke and Tor pulled her towards him. She

nestled up against him, wiped her tears and finished her tale.

'He died from the stracca. He was not a strong person and the witch Xantia kept encouraging him to take more.'

'Xantia? Black hair? Beautiful?'

'Well, I wouldn't call her that, Tor. How do you know her?'

'Oh, we met at Ildagarth. We have a score to settle.'

'You and a hundred others.' Eryn sounded bitter.

'Tell me the rest,' he said. He would come back to Xantia.

'There was nothing I could do. His body was already stiff with death. I was distraught. I had no money, a young brother to care for, another to bury and nowhere to live. So I turned back to the only trade I knew. That's how I met Janus. He was my first client. I could hardly bear him to touch me with that one-eyed face. He knew this and, rather than forcing himself, spent his paid hour with me in talking. Other than you, I can't imagine any other man doing such a thing on paid time.' She smiled to herself. 'And then he came back the next night for another hour, to talk again. You know, he did that four nights in a row. I did all the talking though. He just listened. I think at first he took pity on me, but somewhere during that time he fell in love.'

'And you with him?' Tor asked.

'I don't love him as I once loved you, Tor.' She saw his surprise. 'Yes, I broke my own rule. It was never like that with him. But I loved Janus then for his gentleness, and I love him dearly now for his kindness towards me and his goodness. Tor, if you knew him as I do, you would understand what a just man he is. Yes, he thieves, he's very good at it, but do you know he gives away large portions of his money to help people? He cares for a family just west of here, who lost their crops and animals to fire and then the husband died leaving six children. Janus provides for them all. And that's just one example. I could give you a whole list of people who survive because of him, including everyone here.'

Tor stroked her hair. 'Do you mind that he slave trades, Eryn?'

She shot him an angry look. 'Janus Quist is the only one of the mainland pirates who would never succumb to slave trading. The only one with any scruples.'

So he had guessed wrong. 'I'm not sure what to say.'

She waved her hand. 'Oh, you were not to know any of this. He stole something from you and you want it back. I can understand this, but I would not be living such a good life, Tor, if it wasn't for his benevolence.'

'So you own this place?'

'All of it. Janus bought it off the original owner and gave it to me.' She laughed out loud. 'You should have seen the girls' faces when they found out who the new madam was to be. But I learned a lot at Miss Vylet's, especially about how to look after the people who make the business successful. All my girls eat well, dress well, live securely and many have families whom I ensure they spend time with. I pay them well and they make excellent business for me in return. I really love my life here, Tor.'

'And do you still . . . ?'

'What?'

'You know . . . get involved with the day to day business yourself?'

'Do I give sex for money, do you mean?'

Tor blushed and nodded.

'Sometimes, if they're really handsome.' She grinned. 'Rarely,' she added.

He cleared his throat. 'And what of Quist? He does not mind?'

'Mind? No. I told you, Janus is an amazing man. He married me to give me status in this town. His name protects me because people respect and . . . yes, fear him a little. When he is home, which is not all that often, I am his wife and he my husband. But my life is my own; he does not interfere in my business. The money I earn is mine.'

Tor shook his head. 'And what of that rascal, Locky?'

'Oh, he's wonderful, Tor. He's thirteen, almost a man. He lives here; the girls adore him, as you might imagine, and he plays up to them ruthlessly. My income means I can afford to educate him. I hired a tutor to teach all our girls to write and read. I think it's very important; I'll never forget how much it meant when Captain Margolin helped me with this.' She sighed, remembering another life. 'Anyway, Locky is happy, wants to join the Shield when he is of age and is far too clever for his own good sometimes.'

'He was at eight!'

They both laughed.

'So what will you do then, Tor . . . about Janus, I mean?'

It was his turn to shrug. 'I mean to find him. Will you help me?'

'What has he taken from you that is so important?'

'He stole my bird.'

She looked incredulous as he pushed on. 'We have shared much together, that falcon and I. Janus stole him from my friend, Saxon, and said he would sell him in the Exotic Isles for a high price.'

She nodded. 'It's true. Falcons are prized over there. Could you not make a pet of another one if I was able to, shall we say, appropriate one for you?'

'No. It must be Cloot. I'm sorry, Eryn; he's my companion. I promise you this. When I find your husband, I will not hurt him.'

Eryn threw her head back and laughed fiercely. 'Hurt him? Tor, you watch out for yourself. Janus is a fearsome fighter. He is stronger than ten men. I have seen him fight off six on his own, unarmed.'

'There will be no fight,' he said calmly. 'I wish him no harm. I just want back what belongs to me.'

'And should he no longer have it?'

'Then he will help me to find it.'

'Tor, there's something quite arresting about your arrogance. You have changed from the insecure virgin I met.'

Tor grinned. 'I had reason to change. But you have not changed at all, Eryn. You are still most direct and very beautiful.'

He could see she enjoyed the compliment.

'So will you help me?'

She gave him a puzzled look. 'How?'

'Tell me where you think Janus might have sailed to and then help me get aboard the next ship sailing there.'

Eryn took her time. She sipped some wine and stared at the fire. Tor gave her this time. He knew she was weighing up whether such help could be deemed a betrayal of her husband. Finally, she spoke.

'He sailed to Voronin in the Exotic Isles and on to Cipres.'

'How long ago?'

'Three days.'

'And how long will it take me to get there?'

'On a fast ship with kind weather, probably an Eighthday.'

Tor nodded. 'Would you know anyone who has a ship like this – one which is in port now?' he asked hopefully.

'Yes,' she said. 'But The Black Hand, as we call him, is about as nasty a man as you could be unfortunate enough to meet.'

'I'll take my chances, Eryn. How do I get on board?'

'I can get you on board. He owes me money to begin with and . . .'

'He wants to stay on the right side of Janus Quist, right?'

Eryn laughed. 'Something like that. I believe he's sailing tomorrow. I'll see what I can do, Tor, but tonight, what are your plans? Do you have lodgings?'

He noticed she was fighting a yawn. He kissed her hand. 'I'm staying at The Anchor.'

She pulled a face of disgust.

'Yes, a flea-ridden pit, to be sure, but adequate. I can cope.'

'Stay here,' she said. It was not a suggestion.

Tor shook his head and stood. 'No, I won't impose on our old friendship any further. Thank you for what you may be able to do tomorrow.'

'I absolutely insist, Tor. I can't let that old rogue at The Anchor take your money. That place is not fit for a dog. Stay here, really. We have plenty of rooms.'

She knew he was wavering. 'Perhaps one of the girls has taken your fancy? I noticed how your eyes lingered on Aymee. You might as well enjoy your last night on solid ground. I hear you still enjoy the ladies,' she said, innocently avoiding his gaze and standing to poke around in the fire.

'Well now, Eryn, how would you hear something like that, living all the way up here?'

'Oh, I kept in touch with your career. Miss Vylet seemed to know plenty about you and was always happy to tell me. You must have had a mutual friend.'

'We did,' he said, running his hands through his hair.

She chuckled. 'You know, you still betray yourself by fidgeting with your hair like that. You used to do that when you were embarrassed.'

'Eryn, just how much *did* you notice in that short time we spent together?'

'Plenty. What happened, Tor? Before Miss Vylet died, she said you had gone away . . . on some special royal mission to Ildagarth. I didn't even know where that was then.'

'I did go there,' Tor replied, recalling with clarity the moment he had set eyes on his beautiful Alyssa again at Caremboche. 'And I did not return to the palace or to Tal for a long time.'

'And?' she said, intrigued now by his wistful, almost regretful air.

'It's a long story, Eryn,' he said, sadly.

'May I hear it?' Her voice was gentle as she sensed his pain.

'Do you have a long time?'

'We have all night. I'm not doing anything special,

and I have the most comfortable bed in the whole place
. . . I promise you it won't break either.'

Tor did not know whether to laugh at her reference
back to their last night together or to be shocked at what
she was suggesting.

'I'm not sure I carry enough coin to spend a whole
night with the famous Madame Eryna.' He was tempted
to push his hand through his hair but stopped himself
just in time.

She was smiling at him, a wicked glint in her eye. 'Oh,
this one's on the house, Tor . . . for old times' sake.'

Their lovemaking was passionate and hard. They revelled
in rediscovering each other's bodies, kisses and caresses
until Tor fell back onto Eryn's plump goose-feather cushions, exhausted. This time it was he who snuggled up
into her welcoming arms and marvelled at the soft skin
of a woman. It was the first time he had touched anything
so lovely in so many years; he had forgotten how good
for the soul a loving woman could be.

'You are beautiful, Eryn. Thank you,' he whispered.

She had never stopped loving him and had always hoped
that perhaps one day he might walk back into her life
. . . into her arms. And here he was. Far more worldly
now and able to match her in his creative lovemaking,
but still so like the lost boy she had chosen as King of
the Sea all those years ago. What had happened to make
him so sad?

Tor was stroking her breasts and, despite her mood,
she giggled when she realised he was talking to them,
telling them how much he admired them.

'It's lovely to hear you laugh again,' he said, looking up.

'Tor, it's your turn to tell me everything. You have a tale – I sense it and I must know it or I shall go mad.'

She grabbed his thick, dark hair and pulled it hard. Tor smiled ruefully to himself. Old Cyrus was right. He definitely knew women.

'It is not a pretty tale, Eryn; there are not many laughs to share,' he warned.

'All the same, I want to hear your ugly story.'

And so he told her everything. At the end of it, as the first light of sunrise threatened, they hugged each other hard as though they may never let go . . . and this time they cried together.

I I

Aboard *The Wasp*

Eryn had done well. Understandably amazed and disturbed by Tor's story, she had vowed never to share a word of it with anyone. After a slow, final helping of Tor's body, she left to find the captain of *The Wasp*. Tor did not know what passed between Eryn and Blackhand that day but he was at the Caradoon docks by mid-afternoon, hugging her farewell. She had procured for him a tiny but secure cabin on board *The Wasp* which was bound for the Exotic Isles.

'How to thank you, Eryn,' he said, wishing he did not have to say goodbye to this lovely woman again so soon.

'Just keep safe, Tor. Come back and find your Alyssa. You deserve to be together.'

He tried to lighten her sombre mood. 'Ah . . . and I thought you were hoping I'd stay safe so I could come back to you.' He found his very best smile and used it.

'Your heart belonged to her first, and . . .' she added, very sadly now as she looked at her boots, 'I suspect it always will.'

A young lad scampered up to them, a seasoned member

of the crew by the look of his badly wind-burned face. 'Captain Blackhand is anxious to set sail, sir. You will have to come aboard now.' He did not wait for a reply.

'Please, Eryn, cheer up. I can't leave you so maudlin.'

'I'll be fine,' she said, mustering a smile. 'Last night was lovely. I'm glad you stayed.'

'Er . . . you won't be mentioning it to your husband, will you?' he said, feigning anxiety and at this she did manage a genuine grin.

'Just another paying guest, Tor. No one will be any the wiser. By the way, there's a surprise on board from me.'

He looked at her quizzically but there was no more time. Someone whistled loudly from the deck which meant they were serious about departing. Tor could linger no longer so he kissed her lips, squeezed her hand and walked up the gangplank.

The pirate known as The Black Hand had won his curious *nom de guerre* as a result of the forty-three withered hands tied to the main mast of his ship, *The Wasp*. These were his prizes from the men and two women whom he felt had slighted him seriously enough to lose this precious part of their body. He proudly showcased his spoils to Tor, precisely recalling which hand had belonged to whom and why they lost it. Captain Blackhand, as he had come to be known, used this treasure as a ghoulish reminder to all who sailed with him, and especially those who did not, that he was a man to be reckoned with.

Almost as tall as Tor and twice as broad, he was an imposing figure, loud of voice with a mouth filled with yellowed teeth and bleeding gums. His breath stank so his crew gave him a wide berth whenever they could. He knew this and used his ailment to intimidate them further. Tor weaved a silent spell to counter the stench and Captain Blackhand was surprised when his new 'guest', as he called him, did not recoil the moment he stepped within a foot of him.

The same boy sailor who had called Tor for departure came to his cabin with a terse message from Blackhand.

'Captain hopes you'll take supper with him tonight, sir,' was all he said before disappearing hurriedly.

Well, I simply can't wait for that treat, Tor thought, as he imagined the bleeding mouth of the captain leering at him across the table.

He looked around the airless cabin, wondering what the surprise from Eryn could be. She had done more than enough for him already. Her disquiet at his tale had left them both silent towards morning. She had not doubted any of what he had told her, but he had carefully crafted the story. It would do her no good to know of his sentient abilities and so he had been careful to leave out anything which would be inexplicable without the magical component. And she knew nothing of his public execution. Miss Vylet, Eryn's source of information, had died before it occurred and Tor was glad that news of the famous physic's death had not reached as far north as Caradoon.

To Eryn's ears, it was a tragic tale of love lost, found and brutally taken away again. It appealed to her romantic soul and she drank in his words like sweet wine. He did not like hiding the truth from her but knew that it would not help her to know the full extent of his history. It might even harm her.

Eryn, he realised, lived in a cocoon. All trade was carried

out off shore; the pirates never brought home their spoils, only the proceeds of them. The revenue was ploughed straight back into Caradoon's economy and, with good arable soil surrounding most of it, the pirate town was able to function virtually autonomously from the rest of the Kingdom. Tor had wondered how this could occur, but as Eryn had explained, why scratch at what does not itch. It had taken him a moment to work out her odd logic but then he realised that Tal probably found it more convenient to observe from a distance. Caradoon operated as a very tiny separate duchy might, and providing its dubious population and their ways did not seep further south, why try to police this northern state from such a great distance?

'But what of the slaves?' Tor had asked. 'From where are they sourced?'

Eryn had shrugged. 'Well, not from here and hardly from Tallinor. Most come from the fragmented, tiny islands of the south west which are, as I understand it, linked by shallow waterways. Janus says they are nomadic people who live by moving between these islands. They are not aggressive, which makes them easy to capture.'

A knock on the cabin door interrupted Tor's thoughts.

'Come in,' he called, turning.

A rangy lad stepped into the room. He was of middling height, around thirteen summers, with a thatch of unruly dark hair.

He grinned broadly. 'Remember me?'

Tor looked puzzled. 'I can't say I do,' he said, after a pause.

Green eyes regarded him with mirth. 'A ship on fire . . . a brothel . . . three dukes and—'

'Locky!' Tor exclaimed. 'Light, boy, look at you.'

Eryn's cocky brother showed off his best profile. 'Handsome, eh?'

'And modest,' Tor added, before grabbing the boy's hand. 'It's good to see you, Locky. Eryn has told me so much about you.'

The boy smirked. 'I'm surprised she found the time,' he said, eyebrows arching.

Tor had forgotten how direct the small child of eight had been. The boy of thirteen had not lost the smart mouth; he was simply taller. But Tor was taller still and he used this now to good effect.

'Being disrespectful towards your sister is rather ignoble of you, considering that it is her wealth − no matter how she has earned it − which has allowed you to look forward to being an educated man with choices.'

It was a rare occasion when Locky Gylbyt was speechless. But he was now.

Tor had not finished; he surprised himself at how angry he sounded. 'Furthermore, she is an exceptional woman with more sophistication and intelligence than you would find in all the whorehouses of Tallinor put together. Honour her, Locky, for she is worth every ounce of your respect.'

That hurt the boy, Tor could tell. He knew deep down that Locky was simply being witty but he was not in the mood for it. Seeing Eryn again had reminded him of how much pleasure a woman could bring to a man's life. The physical benefit was obvious, but he could not remember a time since those early halcyon days in the Heartwood, newly married and deeply in love with Alyssa, when he had enjoyed such companionship. His friendship with

Cloot was something else – they had shared their bodies more intimately than anyone could imagine possible – but to hold a woman close, to laugh with her, to hear her thoughts and to love her . . . it was as though one had glimpsed the paradise of the gods.

And now, as he accepted the uncomfortable fact of sailing with Blackhand for at least an Eighthday on a long and tedious voyage to who knows what, and suffering the cramped and stifling conditions of this cabin . . . well, Locky just happened to be a convenient target for Tor's bad temper that afternoon.

'Tor, I'm sorry, I . . . I didn't mean to—'

'I know you didn't. It's all right. Don't dwell on it, just try and remember – when you are insulting someone, be sure they really deserve it.'

'I will. Again, my apologies.'

Tor watched him close the door quietly and instantly regretted the incident. He would have to make it up to Locky later. He knew his heavy handling was an over-reaction; he was worried about Cloot and concerned at how Alyssa would react to the news of Goth being alive. He was anxious that in chasing down Janus Quist, he may have let his real enemy slip through his fingers. Where would Goth run to? Tor asked himself over and again. Would he stay with Xantia? The questions tumbled around until he could stand it no longer and decided to head out onto the deck.

There he found Blackhand's second mate speaking to the crew. *The Wasp's* sails were being swelled by a handy late afternoon wind, which ensured that she cut swiftly through the narrow pass and out into the open sea. Tor leaned against the rail and half listened to the mate briefing the men. *The Wasp*'s first stop would be a rendezvous with Blackhand's first mate at one of the uncharted islands of the Trefel archipelago. Here slaves would be boarded before they made for Cipres, the capital of the Exotic Isles.

Tor had vaguely heard of Cipres, an immensely wealthy city ruled by a Queen Sylven. Merkhud had once told him that it was rumoured she kept a harem of men to 'service her needs'. Tor remembered how they had both smirked at the thought of it. Nevertheless, Cipres was a powerful city within a powerful nation run by a powerful woman. It demanded respect, even though it was involved in only minor trade with Tallinor.

'There's talk of storms coming through,' the deputy finished. 'We must be especially alert.'

The ship's boy, Ryk, who had summoned Tor aboard earlier, sidled up to him.

'This is our last sailing for the season, sir,' he offered.

'Is that right?' Tor replied, turning around to look at the lad.

'Captain Blackhand agreed to one more run, even though the weather's contrary, sir, and he doesn't like to argue with it.'

'Are the slaves so important that he would chance an argument with the skies, young Ryk?'

'Oh, it's not the slaves, sir. It's the guests. Madame Eryna paid handsomely for your carriage and we have another special guest on board. I overheard Captain Blackhand saying this man paid enough coin to make anything else we bring on board cold profit, sir.'

Ryk's eyes widened as he realised he may have shared too much and Tor, keen not to frighten the lad, for he could be useful during the voyage, quickly turned his attention away from talk of money.

'And this other guest – will I meet him tonight at dinner?

'Oh no, sir. He is not to be disturbed for the whole voyage.' Ryk swelled up with importance. 'I am personally responsible for his needs, sir,' he added.

'I see. That's an important job you have there, Ryk. And he must be very important to warrant your undivided attention.'

Ryk beamed at the compliment. 'Oh yes, sir, he is. He is a holy man and very wealthy.'

'Well, if your priest gets lonely for conversation, I shall be more than happy to discuss the argumentative weather with him during the voyage.'

Ryk grinned. 'I shall mention it, Physic Petersyn, when I am next in his cabin.'

Tor realised Eryn had kept his true identity a secret and he thanked his stars once more that she was so quick. Not promoting his real name was extremely wise. One never knew who might be eavesdropping on the Link, he reminded himself, recalling Merkhud's regular grave warnings to be cautious in the use of it while teaching Tor how to shield his mind effectively against outside probing.

The first few days of the voyage were uneventful. The wind had calmed to a light breeze so progress was slow; far slower than Blackhand liked and Tor noticed the captain's good humour draining away during their evening meals. These dinners were tedious but the pirate insisted on Tor's presence. Tor had to sit through hours of Blackhand regaling him with tales of his most prosperous voyages, when he had successfully pirated another ship or filled the bowels of *The Wasp* to overflowing with the Moruk slaves.

'Who cares if half of them died?' he would slur between sips of his strong liquor. 'The live ones fetch a high price in Cipres.'

Tor found the conversation boring and the company offensive. He longed for dry land and the opportunity to do something positive towards finding Cloot. The only moments of the voyage he enjoyed were those spent with Ryk or Locky. Between running errands for Captain Blackhand and the mysterious priest, Ryk was kept very busy, though he always managed to find stolen minutes to talk with Tor, who sensed the boy had something of a crush on him. He could see the awe written on the lad's face. Locky, he discovered, was working his passage to the Exotic Isles but was on fairly light duties because of his connection to Quist.

'Blackhand won't risk giving me anything which might cause him trouble with Janus,' Locky explained.

'Is everyone so scared of him?'

'He is the most successful of the Caradoon pirates and that means they respect him. He's also known for playing fair. When he pirates, he takes only half the ship's cargo and no blood is shed, unless the other ship's crew puts up a physical fight. He quite likes it if they run though. Quist loves the chase, you see, but he isn't partial to the kill.'

'And by taking only half, the victims give it willingly?' Tor said.

'Yes. Because they know he won't kill for the sake of it, it's all quite gentlemanly and amicable. That means he loses no men, it all takes a lot less time and he can profiteer from the captured goods more quickly.'

'He's clever,' said Tor, impressed.

'He is indeed. I'm sure Eryn told you about how he does not get involved with the slave trade, but his network of listeners, as he calls them, are so adept that he knows every ship and its goods even before it leaves its port. He never misses; every voyage is profitable. He also pays his crew well and looks after them properly, which makes a huge difference to their performance. None of the other pirates seem to understand this,' Locky continued, a look of distaste on his face. 'Take Blackhand, for example. He rules with fear and if he doesn't like the way someone looks at him, he'll chop off their hand. Light, he's so thick-skulled! One day someone will finish him off. For now, his crew is made up of the scum of Caradoon; they're the only men who will take their chance with him.'

Tor picked up the thread, thinking aloud. 'Yes, this crew is slovenly and ineffective most of the time. The food is woeful and I've noticed that the ship is not in good repair.'

'You're right. Pray we aren't hit by a storm because, in honesty, I'm not sure *The Wasp* is up to it.'

'I heard this was the last sailing this season. I presume Blackhand will spend the winter in port and fix up the ship?'

'Yes, but I've heard from the men that he should be doing it now, except his avarice ensures poor judgement. You know he's risking this one last voyage because of you and that creepy priest on board. Apparently the priest has paid a fortune for passage.'

'Who is he?'

'No idea. I haven't even so much as glimpsed him. It's

all very secretive. Even Ryk, who would normally blab everything, is terrified into silence.'

'Ryk tells me the man has some sort of physical afflic-tion but will not divulge anything further.'

'Well, that's the story but I think that's all it is. Perhaps he's fleeing something and needs to hide his identity.'

'Hmmm, interesting.' Tor determined to find some way of making contact with the elusive stranger. At least conversation with someone new would be a means of passing the time and would take his mind off his inca-pacity for action whilst aboard the ship.

'Tell me,' he said, switching the subject, 'why are you on board anyway?'

'Oh, didn't Eryn tell you?'

Tor shook his head.

'Well, she thought it unlikely that Janus would trust you. He doesn't trust anyone, to be honest, except Eryn. And no matter how much you tried to convince him, he wouldn't have acknowledged you or your story. Eryn figured that if I came along to vouch for you, Janus would pay attention. You could say that I'm your security,' Locky said, falling back on his cocky nature.

Tor was relieved to see it had not deserted him. 'Your clever sister thinks of everything,' he said, impressed once again by the diminutive girl who had picked him for her King of the Sea when life had been more simple and he had had everything to look forward to.

'Look, I really am sorry about what I said the other day. I love Eryn. If it wasn't for her I—'

Tor squeezed Locky's shoulder. The gesture was enough. It told Locky that no more needed to be said on the subject.

Tor had lost all curiosity about the other guest by the fourth day at sea. The rolling of the waves had given him a queasy feeling in the pit of his stomach and he had decided he was no sailor. But when the cry went up from the crow's nest, he forgot all about his churning belly.

'Weather coming in from the west!' the lookout shouted and the crew jumped into action.

Tor looked towards the angry, purple clouds ahead. Heavy rain threatened. It reminded him of the day when Merkhud had arrived at his parents' house in Flat Meadows. The skies had been a similar colour that evening, and what a great storm had hit, lashing the region with heavy rains and winds.

So much had happened since that night when the Royal Physic had asked Tor to become his apprentice at the palace in Tal. That same night he had shared with Merkhud the image of the three magical orbs, their iridescent colours weaving and circling around and between his fingers. Tor had watched the colour drain from the old man's cheeks when he saw the orbs. The Stones of Ordolt, he had called them.

Tor wondered about the orbs now as he stared at the threatening skies. He had given the three Stones to Sorrel in those desperate last seconds in the Heartwood when his beautiful children were taken from him. It had been all he could think of to give them and somehow he had felt that the Stones might keep the three of them, Gidyon, Lauryn and Sorrel, safe as they fled. The orbs were his only link with his secret past and he hoped they would be his children's link to their true parents.

His instincts had been correct. He had learned from the Writings of Nanak that the Stones were deeply enchanted.

They derived from the three flowers which the infant god Orlac had been holding when he was stolen from The Glade. Tor had also learned that the mysterious phenomenon of The Glade was known to the gods by another name: Ordolt. In the passing through the portals, between worlds, the three flowers had shrivelled and dried to hard stones, the Stones of Ordolt. These three magical orbs had found their way to Tor's adopted parents and had been kept safely by them until he was of an age to receive them.

What were they for? Tor asked himself now. What power would they wield in this baffling quest?

A burly sailor interrupted his thoughts. 'Better go below, sir. She's going to burst any moment,' he said, pointing to the bruised-looking clouds which were almost directly above them now.

Tor nodded and headed below, thoughts of the orbs once again put into a safe place in his mind to be pondered on another time.

Tor spent an uncomfortable night in his cabin whilst rolling seas and rain lashed *The Wasp*. The two days following were mild, but Tor was warned not to be fooled by the calmer weather. Blackhand had ordered running repairs on the ship but neither Tor nor Locky believed much would be achieved. In fact, Tor now agreed with Eryn's brother that if a big wave hit or the storm re-presented itself, *The Wasp* would surely founder.

'How many more days until we reach the Trefel archipelago?' he asked Ryk, who was sharing a few minutes on deck.

'Captain says we've lost some time but we should make the rendezvous point in two more nights.'

'That's good, we're not so far behind the original schedule then.'

'No, sir,' Ryk agreed. 'I have enjoyed you being on board, Physic Petersyn, and hope one day to serve you again.'

Tor smiled at the lad, whom he guessed to be around eleven, possibly twelve summers. He was so slight and had a nervous disposition yet when they relaxed and chatted over trivia like this, Ryk became fluent and charming. It must be Blackhand, Tor decided, who made the boy so jittery.

'Do you imagine yourself being a sailor when you're grown up, Ryk?'

'No, sir, I have always dreamed of being a great chef.'

Tor checked the laugh which formed in his throat as he realised that the wistful look on Ryk's face was real.

'But that's wonderful, Ryk. Tell me more.'

'All the men in my family have been chefs, Physic Petersyn. It is rumoured that my great-great-great-grandfather, Orr Savyl, once cooked in the old palace for the King.'

Tor was impressed. 'Indeed? So how is it that his great-great-great-grandchild is now working for a pirate?'

Ryk sighed. 'Our family has fallen on hard times, sir. Two of my eldest brothers died, as did my sister and mother, from the green fever. My father was left with three baby girls – triplets – and myself to run his dining room at Ildagarth.'

'Your family is from Ildagarth? Well, I never – I visited that city once. It is very beautiful, even in its ruin.'

'That it is, sir. My father ran the most famous of dining halls, called The Tapestry, which was his special way of noting the work which came out of Ildagarth's famous looms.'

'So what happened, Ryk?'

'Hard times, as I said, sir. With all the older children dying and my mother gone, my father could no longer work the kitchen. To be honest, sir, I don't think his heart was in it any longer,' the lad said, his eyes a little misty. 'My mother was a fine cook herself and she was a wonderful person too. I think his heart broke and he no longer felt the love for his food.'

Tor put his hand on the boy's shoulder. 'And so you had to find work, is that it?'

'My father turned to the drink, sir, and there were baby sisters to feed. All my earnings go back to them. My mother's sister cares for them as best she can, but it's a poor life for my pretty girls. You know, sir, one day I will be a famous chef like my father, and his father before him. And my sisters will wear beautiful silks and dance with princes.'

Tor could hardly believe this sad little story from the boy squatting next to him.

'And can you cook, Ryk?'

'Of course I can, but no one on board knows,' he answered. 'I was my father's right-hand man in the kitchen. My mother said no child of hers had ever learned the trade as fast. I learned his recipes and, although I am young, sir, I can recall them in their detail. I knew from seven summers how to run a kitchen.'

'And how old are you now, may I ask?'

'I am twelve, sir.'

'Well, Ryk, if I can ever help you make that dream come true, I promise you I will.'

'Thank you,' the boy said, his eyes shining, 'You are very good to me.'

Ryk heard his name being bellowed by the second mate. 'Back to the scullery for me, sir. It's hare tonight and a pea soup to start.'

Tor dreaded the thought of eating hare after his experience with Cloot. 'I wish it was by your hand, Ryk.'

The boy grinned. 'Yes, Therd is too heavy-handed with the seasoning, sir. One day, Physic Petersyn, I shall cook you a grand meal.'

He scampered away, terrified of the captain finding out he was a moment late for his chores.

Tor shook his head. He would have to see if there was anything he could do for Ryk. Perhaps he could talk with Blackhand that evening.

His chance came as they were eating the exceptionally peppery pea soup. Blackhand was in a foul mood and Tor managed to match it; his stomach lurched along with the ship's motion and his mouth burned from Thred's heavy hand.

'Don't be misguided by this calmer weather, Physic. Did you notice how still it became today?'

Tor nodded, hoping if he kept his mouth shut he would not return the spoonful of dreadful soup he had just swallowed. Some of Blackhand's soup had dribbled down his chin and as he licked at it with his tongue, flecks of blood from his diseased gums contrasted horribly with the green liquid.

'That's our warning,' the captain continued.

'You mean the stillness?' Tor spooned another tiny amount into his mouth, refusing to look at the captain.

'I do. It's gathering. I have to tell you, Physic, it makes

me nervous. But we shall try to outrun it. I have hopes we might just sneak around it and reach the safety of the archipelago in time.'

'I hope so too,' Tor said politely.

'Boy!' the captain bellowed.

Ryk arrived at the captain's side. Blackhand belched into the lad's face. 'More soup! And be quick or I'll tan your arse for you.'

This was his chance. 'Did you know, captain,' Tor said, forcing a genial expression to his face, 'that young Ryk, your cabin boy, is the son of a famous chef?'

'What of it?' Blackhand looked at Tor suspiciously.

'Nothing more than the notion that his services might be put to good use in your kitchen. Rumour has it the boy is adept with food.'

'Is he indeed?' the captain said, staring at Ryk over his bulbous nose as the boy approached with the soup tureen. It made Ryk nervous.

'Yes, captain, sir?'

'Are you adept with food, boy?'

Ryk shot a nervous glance at Tor. 'I . . . I can cook. Yes, sir.'

Blackhand sneered. 'A bloody squit like you? Don't try and foist yourself upon my private guests, boy. From now on you are forbidden to leave the scullery unless on my express order. Is that understood?'

'Yes, sir,' the boy answered, his voice wavering.

Tor was mortified. This was not what he had intended. He had thought to do the young lad a good turn but now he had just made his life worse aboard this intolerable ship.

'Now pour me some more soup, you witless brat!'

It was too much for Ryk's nerves. Terror, combined with the sickening lurch of the ship from a rogue wave, saw the entire contents of the soup tureen spill into the captain's lap. The captain screamed so loud that Ryk turned and fled from the room. Clinging to the table in an attempt to remain upright, Tor had no idea how Ryk had stayed on his feet long enough to get out of the cabin. Fortunately the soup had not been piping hot but Tor did not doubt that Blackhand's agony was genuine. If Ryk had not been the cause, he might have enjoyed it. It seemed like divine intervention. But as he staggered over to help the captain back into his chair, his thoughts immediately flew to how he might save the boy's skin from a thrashing.

As it turned out, it was not Ryk's skin he needed to worry over.

Suffering from the return of the stormy weather, Tor remained in his cot the following morning, wishing the voyage was all a bad dream and that he could wake up on firm land. He woke from a disjointed doze to the sound of Locky banging persistently on his door and calling his name. He sounded very anxious. Tor lurched to let him in; it was the one occasion that he was glad for the tiny width of his cabin.

'Come quickly, Tor, it's Ryk.'

'Oh no, don't tell me Blackhand's punishing him. What now? A public flogging, I suppose,' he said wearily, looking for his breeches.

'Much worse. Blackhand's feeling especially nasty. He's ordered that Ryk must lose a hand.'

That got Tor's attention. Suddenly his stomach was

steady and his mind calm. 'That bastard,' was all he said before pushing past Locky. 'Where?'

'On deck.'

They both ran. On the way, Locky added that the second mate appeared to have miscalculated their course. 'I think we might be in the eye of the storm,' he yelled as they burst onto the deck.

It was horribly still outside. The sky was the oddest colour; a dirty yellow. Tor could hardly breathe. It was as though all the air had been sucked out of the area where they floated. All was silent and eerie.

But far worse was the scene on deck.

Little Ryk had been tied to the main mast with one arm pinioned above his head. He was petrified; his eyes were glazed like those of a terrified deer. Tor saw that the small boy had lost his water in his fright. The crew stood around laughing and jeering whilst Blackhand, limping from his scalded groin, bellowed that this was how he treated anyone who mistreated him. It was a ghastly picture.

All Tor could think of was Cloot. He saw him again as he had first seen him, nailed by his ear to a post and surrounded by a jeering crowd howling for the brute Corlin to inflict more pain on the poor mute. Tor felt the same immense anger rising in him again now. He dimly heard Locky speaking as the Colours roared up inside him.

'Tor, there is nothing we can do, or we shall lose our own hands. These men are frightened of the storm; they know their lives might be lost today. They care little for the boy. They just want to see the blood and let someone else suffer.'

Blackhand raged at the boy. 'Are you ready, young Ryk?

A cook, are you, eh? Well, you'll never chop meat again once your hand is nailed to my mast.'

Suddenly the air turned so thick everyone had trouble breathing. Ryk sucked in great gulps; his eyes flicking from sailor to sailor, imploring for their help. They just laughed. They wanted to see his hand fly off, wanted to watch his arm pump its lifeblood and see the tiny trophy nailed to the ship to bring Blackhand's macabre count to forty-four.

Ryk locked onto Tor. 'Physic Petersyn,' he screamed, 'save me, sir!'

Blackhand looked at Tor. 'This is none of your business, Physic. If you interfere, I will chop off both his hands and throw what's left of him into the sea.'

The wind was picking up. It began to swirl madly around them.

'He's just a lad, captain,' Tor yelled back over the howl.

'He offends me, Physic. Stay out of this.'

'I can't.'

Blackhand motioned to his henchmen nearby and rough hands gripped Tor and pinned him back against the ship's rail. Tor let them hold him; he did not need his arms anyway. The Colours were ready. He could call on them at any time.

The captain smiled and turned back to the child, whose body was now shaking so hard that his knees were giving way beneath him. If it was not for the rope holding him in place, he would not be standing. His fingers balled into a fist as he struggled.

'Help me!' he shrieked as Blackhand stepped up to him.

'Off with his hand,' one of the crew yelled. Everyone

but Tor, Locky and the hooded stranger who had suddenly appeared on deck, laughed.

Locky looked sideways at Tor. 'That's the creepy priest.'

Tor nodded and returned his attention to Blackhand. The captain took a short-handled axe from his first mate and showed it to the crew. They cheered.

'Let it fly,' some wit yelled again.

Ryk was sobbing now and staring at Tor.

Stay calm, Ryk, Tor thought, wishing he could communicate it to the boy.

Blackhand took aim at the boy's wrist.

Tor closed his eyes; he weaved the Colours.

With a loud grunt, the captain swung his arm through a mighty arc. Tor heard a bloodcurdling scream, which could only be Ryk, followed by a thud and then a groan. He opened his eyes to see the axe buried in the captain's chest. Blackhand wore a look of such surprise, it was almost comical. Blood was spewing from the fatal wound and, though he tried to utter something, the words died as he did.

His enormous bulk fell to the deck with a crash, splattering blood on everyone nearby. All fell silent, the only sound the howling of the wind which had increased in intensity.

Ryk's eyes were wide with amazement at still being whole. The men holding Tor let go of him and went to their captain, unsure of how such a thing could have happened.

'Cut Ryk free,' Tor said sharply to Locky. 'Now!'

The men milled around their captain's body; some nudged him with their boots. Locky had to carry Ryk over to Tor; the boy was in such shock he could not speak, let alone walk.

All the while, the storm was gathering in ferocity. A crack of lightning erupted above their heads, so powerful it split the main mast in two, just where Ryk had been tied moments earlier. The sparks leapt to Blackhand's body, which began to burn.

'The liquor!' Locky yelled. 'He drank a whole bottle this morning to dull the pain and spilled another half bottle over himself in his efforts. It's ignited.'

Tor nodded. Another lightning strike and then a loud thunderclap directly overhead. He realised that the ship was beginning to spin in a sickening circle as the water started to boil around them.

'Locky, we have to get off the ship.'

Cracks were opening in the timber. He reckoned it would be barely moments before the whole ship broke apart from the pressure. The wind was still raging. Many men would die today. He saw bodies being thrown against the sides of the ship; others leapt into the high waves, only to be knocked back against the ship. The captain's corpse was being flung from side to side and his blood smeared across the flaming deck.

Locky was terrified. He could taste death. Ryk was no longer whimpering; he had become stiff and silent in Locky's arms.

'Give him to me,' Tor yelled, fighting to stay upright.

Another bolt of lightning hit, but the ship was burning heartily now anyway. It would give itself up to its fiery death in moments.

Locky wrapped Ryk's hands around Tor's neck and the boy buried his head into his protector's shoulder. He was feather-light.

'Now hold onto me, Locky,' Tor shouted over the wind

as they clambered onto the side of the railing. 'Whatever happens, don't let go.'

'We'll never survive this,' Locky screamed back, awed by nature's anger around him.

As they jumped, Tor's sharp eyes caught the movement of a black-robed figure also leaping. The priest. His hood had been blown back and Tor could finally see the man's face.

Amidst the clammy warmth of the storm's eye, Tor felt a chill crawl across his skin. The stranger's twisted, scarred flesh was all too familiar; the small, cold eyes regarded him, just for a fleeting second, with menace.

Tor felt as if his own horror was being mirrored in that terrible face.

It was Goth.

12

The Faintings

'But, Father, the Testings of the novices begins in two weeks.'

Gidyon, feeling uncharacteristically sulky, was standing by the window in his master's chambers. Father Piers remained silent and puffed gently on his favourite pipe, whittled by himself many years prior to this moment. He settled into his worn chair, which creaked as he sat down.

Gidyon turned to face him. 'Father, I hardly know her. I've never met her and I rarely reply to her few and far between letters. What is it going to mean to her if I do go all the way north to Petrine? What am I to say to her? For all I know, she might die whilst I am on the road there and then it will all have been for nothing and I will have missed study time I badly need.'

That was a barefaced lie. Gidyon needed no extra study time. He knew he would pass the Testings with ease. To cover his discomfort at the untruth he raked his hands through his dark, straight hair and returned, with exasperation, to the other side of the desk.

Father Piers regarded his charge. A popular boy of the

fifth Stair, almost ready to take full vows. One more cycle of moons through the sixth and final Stair of the Order of Ferenyans was all it would take. He had grown so tall over the years with them and yet he was probably going to be much taller. Piers acknowledged that Gidyon was often wise beyond his years and destined for a senior place in the Order. He was also of a generous disposition and had a sunny nature, which made his stance on this matter odd.

Piers cleared his throat. 'As I understand it, this is all the family you have. I realise you hardly know your grandmother but she has faithfully paid her donations these last eleven years and, although you don't remember your parents, she must . . . and you should respect this.'

He gave a series of short puffs on his pipe before reaching for the clay mug of herbal tea. He took his time stirring in two heaped spoonfuls of honey as he silently sympathised with the youth. This situation with his remote grandmother was very poorly timed indeed, coinciding with critical tests in the boy's march towards his bands and ordination. He was certainly likely to be regarded for the Blues, skipping quickly through the hierarchy of Whites, Yellows and Greens. He might possibly even go straight to Reds – an achievement previously unheard of, but this talented youngster could probably do it.

He chose his words carefully. 'Gidyon, you are not a student who is struggling with his studies. I think we all agree on this, despite your concerns. I know that attaining your Blues means a great deal to you and we are all very proud of your efforts. But the fact is, your grandmother is gravely ill and it is our duty to make sure you fulfil her simple request to see you before she dies. Abbot Muggerydge insists.'

He held up his hand to stop the boy protesting.

'If, in the most unlikely event you should fail to reach the level in your Testings we all know you are capable of, then Abbot Muggerydge has agreed to accompany your papers with a special mention. Now, that's good enough for me – what about you?'

The boy swallowed a gulp of unsweetened tea and fixed his incredibly blue eyes on his superior. He held the gaze defiantly for just a moment, then dropped it with a quiet sigh.

'You're right, of course, Father. I just feel awkward about meeting a grandmother I don't know, other than by name and a few letters. I'm sorry for sounding selfish – it's just these tests are so important.' He bit his lip and struggled with the decision before saying, finally, 'I'll leave this afternoon then?'

'Yes, yes, that's fine,' replied Piers, with relief. He stretched. 'I hope the old girl keeps her strength to see you. You're a good lad and she'll no doubt be very proud to meet you.' He blew out his lips. 'Anyway, Gynt, it will probably do you a world of good to get away from this place for a few days.'

Oh no, here it comes again, Gidyon thought, the fit, or whatever that thing was a few days ago.

'Very strange business,' Piers continued, 'you passing out like that and giving us all a scare. You've probably been burning the midnight oil studying or something, eh?' He looked at Gidyon over his pipe. It was not really a question.

'I'll be off then, Father. Thank you for the tea.'

Gidyon made his way back to the east wing. True, it had been strange, his suddenly passing out like that in the cloisters, not to mention inconvenient as he had happened to be speaking in front of the new novices. They had carried his rigid body to the hospital wing and later the older novices had excitedly described to him how his eyes had rolled back into his head. Some wit had suggested he also began frothing at the mouth and speaking in tongues. This had caused great hilarity in the hospital before they were all shooed out by the monk in charge. Gidyon had no idea what had happened. It had been an isolated event. He ate enough for six and he had not been burning the midnight oil at all. If the truth be known, he did not have to study all that hard anyway. There was no explanation and he just wanted the fuss to stop.

Gidyon let himself into his small but adequate quarters. As head of the fifth Stair he luxuriated in the privilege of his own tiny room whilst his peers quadrupled up and the younger boys shared with eight, sometimes ten others. He enjoyed the solitude after years of putting up with everyone else's mess, noise and problems in the dormitories. Life at the monastery was still structured and full though and he liked it that way. He had known no other way of living since he had come to this place and memories before that were so vague he rarely, if ever, tried to recall them. He dimly recollected the old lady but, as an infant, she had packed him off here. Who could blame him for not being overwhelmed by her invitation to meet her again before she died? It seemed rather ghoulish, as well as pointless.

Gidyon knew he was the Order's brightest, most gifted novice and probably headed for the Reds. And, although no one wanted to say it, all silently acknowledged that he was probably destined to be Abbot one day, when he would have the ear of the King and a role in the politics of the region. Gidyon was outstanding at sports too; there was no physical activity to which he could not bend his body. Fast, agile, skilled, it was magical to watch him perform, be it on a horse or running in a race. Whatever the sport, Gidyon would be at the front and winning. Tall and good-looking to boot, it seemed he had it all.

He did not much care, however, for the whispers of those who made such claims. They thought he could not hear their idle chat, but his hearing was exceptionally acute. His close friends teased him about it; one reckoned he could even hear the birds breathing in the trees. Their comments amused Gidyon, for at times he could believe such folly himself.

Little wonder that his nickname was 'The Wizard'. He hated it but the moment it was coined, it had stuck like glue. He had learned to accept it with a deprecating shrug and plain good grace. No point in fighting it. Gidyon often tried to imagine what his parents had been like. Which particular aspects of them had combined to produce 'The Wizard'? He would never know. He did not know what had happened to his parents. Had they died? Left him at birth with his grandmother? Left each other? He had forced himself to give up asking such questions. But they would come to haunt him sometimes in his dreams . . . who was he?

Sometimes he heard a woman's voice, whispering to him in his dreams. He could never recall what she had said when he woke. He never told anyone about it. Why would he? As far as he could tell, she had never said anything to intimidate him or make him feel anxious. If he was honest, she was almost a comfort to him. He had never known his mother but he liked to believe she had a voice like this dream woman.

Gidyon stopped staring out of the window and dragged himself back to the task of packing. He looked around the room. The walls were covered with diagrams of all things astronomical. His passion for stargazing and worlds beyond his own was evident and he was single-minded in his desire to pursue the science of the stars once he had taken his vows.

'Black devils! I don't need this,' he cursed as he threw his spare cassock into a small bag. It occurred to him for probably the hundredth time since he had heard the news that he had cost his elusive grandmother a pretty pile in donations and going to visit her before she died was the least he could do. He added to the bag a hat and some rough woollen mittens he felt he may need against the chill of Petrine's highlands. In the small glass on the wall, he checked his long hair was still tied back neatly before picking up the bag to leave.

'Stupid . . . what are you going to do for all those lonely hours?' He pulled his new tablet of rag paper from under the wooden pallet where he slept and bumped his head on the frame getting up. Scowling with pain, he noticed his old stone on the window sill. Gidyon had owned the stone for as long as he could remember. He could not recall precisely how he had come by it but it was a special item of childhood that he always took along to his annual Testings. He rolled the perfectly round, heavy sphere in his palm, watching its faint lights of crimson, gold, violet and emerald. It seemed that only he could see the colours. His fellow novices told him he was mad when he asked if they could see them too. So be it. He could see the colours and they never failed to fascinate him. He slipped it absently into the deep pocket of his cassock.

In the cool corridor, Gidyon yelled farewell to some novices before heading for the cloisters. The friendly taunts of the other students followed him.

'You'd do anything to get out of the Testings, Gynt!'

'Give grandma our regards.'

He grinned as he leapt the few stairs to his favourite part of the monastery. The friendly catcalls and guffaws died away as he entered the peace of the cloisters. He loved the vaulted ceilings and pillars and the beautiful gardens which he helped the monks tend. He breathed in the silence and calm one more time, then stepped through the magnificent archway into the front courtyard.

The old stable master was there, holding a fine horse ready for him.

'Good day, Master Gynt.'

'And to you, Horys,' Gidyon replied. He recognised the horse: Empress. He was pleased this mare would be accompanying him. He had ridden her many times and appreciated her gentle nature and big heart.

He held out an apple he had picked from one of the trees in the cloisters. 'Here you go, girl,' he said, stroking her soft muzzle.

'Thank you, she's one of my favourites,' he said to the stableman.

'His Grace insisted you have a reliable horse for the journey. They don't come much better than Empress,' the old man said, handing him her reins. 'She's provisioned for two days. You'll need to replenish stores at Merbury. Oh, and I'm to give you this note. Father Piers just caught me on my way here and asked me to deliver it.' Horys nodded deferentially and handing him a folded paper.

Gidyon read its contents quickly. Piers told him there was a purse of money in one of the bags and that he should try to live frugally on his travels. He also wrote that a man called Galbryth would meet Gidyon in Petrine township and escort him to his grandmother's remote property.

Horys continued. 'I imagine the journey will take you five, possibly six sunrises. Stick to the main towns from Merbury and veer off towards Three Lakes which will take you directly to Petrine.' He nodded to take his leave.

Gidyon thanked the man again and climbed up onto the horse, which patiently waited whilst he settled himself comfortably. He waved before nudging her forwards onto the road which would lead him away from the monastery and all things familiar. Turning his stone in his pocket, Gidyon allowed Empress to walk at her own gentle pace as he drifted off into a daydream in which he imagined himself a hero on a wild adventure, leading an army, fighting off monsters, with women swooning over him.

He had never travelled north of Leedon so in truth he was interested by the prospect of visiting Petrine. And by all accounts, his grandmother lived so remotely that he would have the opportunity for long, rambling walks and quiet time to prepare his mind for the Testings. Maybe it would not be so bad after all . . . well, as long as she doesn't die whilst I'm there, he amended.

They had reached the open road and he kicked Empress

into an easy trot, dreamily letting his eyes move with the countryside which streamed by him. Absently twisting and turning his stone, he gradually sensed an increasing warmth emanating from it. He gripped the stone and experienced a sense of alarm; the vague feeling that this was a trap. However, a moment later the sensation was broken. Immediately he gave Empress the rein and permission to enjoy some freedom at a gallop.

He let go of the stone and the notion of danger.

'Oh, this is unthinkable!' exclaimed the plump girl.

'Come on, Lauryn, it's marvellous . . . I'd give up pudding for a whole moon cycle for someone to take me away from these books,' said Emyly, Lauryn's only real friend.

The girls had struck up a friendship when they were five summers old, each recognising in the other a genuine need. Emyly was plain, buck-toothed and freckled. She was also hilarious and Lauryn loved her.

Lauryn took no pains to enhance her own obvious assets: large, deep green-grey eyes and thick golden hair. She pulled her hair back severely, refusing to display its glossy beauty, did everything she could to get out of any form of exercise and deliberately indulged in her food. She was a hearty lass, as Cook liked to call her; and that was the kindest description of herself Lauryn had heard.

At the moment, however, she was the talk of the convent, although it was nothing to do with her careless ways. Lauryn had fainted a few days ago in the scriptorium, spilling ink – thankfully only a small amount – on the illumination she had just begun working on. Emyly had become near hysterical when Lauryn, for no apparent reason, had suddenly gone rigid in her chair. Her eyes had rolled back and she had struggled for breath before falling in a dead faint against her friend, taking them both heavily to the ground. As a result, Lauryn had spent the next two days under close observation in the hospital. Sister Benyt had been strict about visits, allowing Emyly only a few minutes with her friend each day. Lauryn had appeared fully recovered from whatever had ailed her immediately upon regaining consciousness, but the much revered head of the Gyrton convent had still insisted on contacting Lauryn's grandmother in Petrine.

Lauryn had no parents; her grandmother was her only known family. She had sent word by return with the messenger politely insisting that Lauryn be allowed to travel to Petrine as soon as she was strong enough in order to spend a few days in the clean, fresh air of the highlands. The request was not open to negotiation, as the Prioress later advised the granddaughter when she protested.

'Lauryn, I have no power to argue this for you. Your grandmother has expressed her strong desire to see you and for you to enjoy a short break. She donates enormous sums of money to the convent to help feed and clothe our community and keep this Order in relative prosperity. And I believe I am right in saying you have not seen your grandmother for eleven years or so? It is about time you paid her a visit.'

Before Lauryn knew it, she was packed up and being driven by horse and cart to meet up with the northern-bound coach. She was furious, though in truth she did not know why. Leaving Emyly was the worst part, but escaping the scriptorium was a blessing. She hated the convent, even though she was good at her work and was one of its most talented scribes. Lauryn knew, deep down, that if she cared she could be good at just about anything she chose to do. It was just that she wasn't really interested in the detailed, often mind-numbing work of copying out two hundred pages of script onto parchment.

No, in all truth, what really troubled her was the fact that she was a lonely girl. Lonely for the love of a mother; lonely for a connection to a family. Lauryn was the only member of the convent who did not have brothers or sisters. For her, the rare holidays highlighted her isolation all the more and if it were not for Emyly's firm friendship, she felt she could disappear altogether and never be missed.

She hated the grandmother the Prioress spoke of so respectfully. What kind of a grandmother never visits her granddaughter or makes contact other than by an all too occasional letter? And those letters brought her no consolation; they gave no insight into this mysterious woman. No, she was a total stranger and Lauryn felt nothing but contempt for someone who could masquerade as a caring relative but gave no emotional support whatsoever to a girl racing into womanhood.

But Lauryn would admit to none of this. She went through life as an observer, taking little interest in anything or anyone, save her good friend Emyly. She felt entirely removed from the life she led; she did not belong in the world around her. And now she was being forced to travel into that world to confront the grandmother she despised. She hoped the woman died before she arrived. Perhaps she could escape out onto the moors where this old girl was supposed to live. Lauryn would not mind that so much. The thought of rambling walks alone through the highland countryside almost made the drudgery of getting there worthwhile. Almost. At least that way she could continue to be alone, which was what she did best.

Lauryn smirked as she recalled a regular comment on her school reports: 'Would make a good leader if only she would participate emotionally in convent life.' What a jest. Who would she lead? Who would want to follow fat Lauryn? No one liked her, except Emyly, and she had no relationship with anyone else. She had been wondering about men lately, about life outside the convent. She knew such thoughts were not permitted, but she had no intention of taking full vows. That would be a shock to all. Instead she planned to wander the Kingdom of Shorell . . . as a visiting scribe perhaps. Such a life would suit her. Would any man ever take an interest in her? Did men ever fall in love with the fat girl? Lauryn grimaced. Well, she would catch herself a fine man one day. He would be strong and witty and a leader amongst men. They would fall madly in love and he would never want any other woman but her. And she would not be plump. She would be gorgeous, as her mother had been.

Lauryn's favourite daydream was to conjure a vision of how her mother and father looked. He was dashing and handsome, her mother incredibly beautiful and slender. They too were madly in love but fate had forced them apart and that was why they had to give up their only daughter. Or perhaps they had died tragically, in one another's arms. Her mother's last words to her own mother, this mysterious grandmother, were always the same: look after Lauryn. And that's when the dream invariably turned into the nightmare. Look after Lauryn! Send her as far away as possible to live life alone and unloved amongst a community of stiff-backed, unforgiving women.

As the cart rumbled along, Lauryn took her stone from her top pocket and felt the comfort it always brought her. Strange; it was very warm. She twirled it in her palm and watched its iridescent colours. No one but her had ever seen the colours within it, but that was all right – it was worthless to anyone but Lauryn. It was just a stone, after all. And yet for Lauryn it was her connection to her past. It was all she had carried with her when she arrived at the convent, other than a tiny sack of clothes. The Prioress had told her that the stone had been carefully sewn into one of her mittens when she had arrived at Gyrton on that frozen late winter's afternoon more than a decade ago.

Shivering and confused, the tiny four year old had cried for hours and been inconsolable for weeks. Her only comfort was the stone, which she clutched tight. It had never been far from her in all the years since and Lauryn liked to think that it represented the soul of her mother, wherever she was and whoever she was.

She came out of her dark thoughts into the bleak and misty afternoon of the town and allowed herself to be helped down from the cart and escorted to the waiting coach. There were other people clambering aboard: a chatty mother with two daughters and a single male traveller. He was very old and entirely uninterested in all of them. That was fine with Lauryn; she intended to ignore them all for the three days it would take to reach Petrine.

She pulled a small book of poetry from her gown and hid behind it, pretending to lose herself in the words, only putting it down to share a small polite meal with her companions or to sleep. The girls tried to engage her in conversation but her fearsome comments on the probability of plague sweeping through neighbouring nations, even those divided by sea, put paid to any plans they might have entertained of making a pleasant new friend. Lauryn saw the old man twitch a smile at her tirade; he was obviously an old hand at warding off unwelcome and trivial chatter and perhaps recognised in her the same rude trait developing.

It was three long and tedious days before Lauryn sensed they had arrived on the outskirts of Petrine. No one else was left in the coach now; the ladies had alighted at Verban and the old man even sooner at Divyn. It mattered not to her that she was alone. When finally they reached the centre of Petrine and Lauryn stepped down from the coach, a man hailed her. This must be Master Galbryth whom the Prioress had said would meet her.

'Here we go,' she muttered and grimaced back at him.

13

Yargo's Message

Gidyon stretched in his saddle as Empress entered the town gates of Petrine. He gingerly climbed off the mare, expecting to be sore after riding through the previous night and all of this day. He stared out towards the darkening of early evening over the Petrine moors. Shaking his head distractedly he again asked himself what he was doing here. Empress grunted and shook her head. She was eager for the comforts of a stable.

'Gidyon Gynt?' a man asked, taking off his cloth hat and smiling broadly.

Gidyon returned the smile and answered that he was. He swapped the bag he'd taken off the horse to his other shoulder so he could shake hands.

'I am Iyain Galbryth, a farmer from around these parts. I live near your grandmother and she asked me if I'd pick you both up as I was in town today. Is that your only bag?' He smiled again. 'You should have some coin left to stable the mare – is that right?'

Gidyon was puzzled. 'Yes, Master Galbryth, just this one bag. The saddlebags are empty now. Um . . . there's only me actually. I'm not sure who else you were expect—'

'Is this the horse?' interrupted a stablehand.

'Evening, Angys,' said Galbryth while Gidyon started searching for the coins Father Piers had instructed him to keep available for the care of Empress until he was ready to ride back to the school. As he turned over in his deep pocket everything he had accumulated on the journey, he was startled to feel how warm his stone was.

'C'mon, Gynt, where's your money, boy?' said Galbryth good-naturedly. 'How is your good woman then, Angys?' he added, turning to the man who held the horse's reins.

Gidyon felt his mind blur and the conversation between Galbryth and Angys faded as the heat of the stone increased in his hand. He was caught by the strange conviction that the stone was klaxoning a warning. The words 'To Tallinor' whispered through his mind. Just then his other hand closed around the coins and then the world refocused. He saw both men staring at him.

'You okay, boy?' Galbryth shook him gently.

'Uh . . . oh . . . er, sorry, yes, sorry. I must be tired. It's been a long journey.' Gidyon laughed stiffly as he obliged Angys with the money, then followed behind Galbryth who was waving a farewell.

As he climbed into an old cart attached to two equally old horses, his hand gripped the stone again; the heat had lessened to a mild warmth.

Iyain Galbryth began to chat amiably as drizzle sifted delicately from the blackening sky. 'Can't get rid of this lovely pair . . . they're my first team you see . . .'

Gidyon allowed Galbryth to ramble on about his horses, the words washing over him as ineffectually as the rain, whilst he tried to make some sense of what had happened with the stone. He was not scared, though he thought he should perhaps feel threatened by it. Instead, he had to admit that he felt comforted by its presence . . . and its warmth. Something about it felt safe, felt right. It always had.

What was that name he had heard?

He strained after the memory of it, leaning on his thoughts, probing and grasping at threads, whilst in the background Galbryth droned on about how ploughing with this pair was as easy as a knife cutting through butter. 'Tallinor,' Gidyon whispered into the darkness.

'Mmm . . . what was that?' Galbryth asked, gently flicking the whip over his lead horse.

'Oh, nothing. It's . . . um . . . a word I've been trying to recall for one of the questions in the Testings.'

The man was not listening anyway. They travelled the next mile or so without speaking, although Galbryth sang a hearty ballad into the rain, getting plenty of the words wrong. Gidyon was grateful for the lack of conversation.

The rain had steadied to a light shower by the time they pulled up outside an inn. The Shepherd and Dog was a country tavern built of whitewashed stone with a thatched roof, low ceilings, dark wood surrounds and a pretty woman behind its ale counter. Her lovely Petrine brogue and figure-hugging blouse, which was tied rather loosely at the neckline, made Gidyon instantly forget the incident with his stone and its strange and alarming heat. He grinned and she flashed a radiant smile back.

'This is the gorgeous Glorya,' said Galbryth. 'We won't be stopping, Glor. I'm just going to pick up the missus and the young lassie and we'll be on our way.' Galbryth pushed through the crowded tavern.

'No time for a quick ale, Master Galbryth?' Gidyon offered hopefully.

Glorya noticed his Ferenyan Order cassock and laughed, tipping her head towards him. 'More like a fruit punch for you.'

Some men nearby caught the quip and laughed too, but not unkindly. Gidyon was enjoying the smoky, merry atmosphere and it seemed all too soon when Galbryth shouldered his way through again, this time accompanied by a short, stick-thin woman whose dark hair was pulled into a severe bun, and a plumpish novice wearing a Gyrton convent gown. She did not look at all happy.

'Hello,' Gidyon said.

She growled something unintelligible at him, which happily was drowned out by raucous laughter from a group singing a lewd song.

'Bye, Glorya,' was all Gidyon managed before shuffling out behind the odd troupe he found himself attached to. Glorya did not hear him but she caught his wave and winked back. I bet she wouldn't do that if I was wearing a shirt and breeches, he thought, wondering for perhaps the first time whether life outside the Order and its vows might be fun. The thought of nuzzling close to the likes of Glorya suddenly made him feel weak at the knees.

Outside, the air was chilling rapidly and the early evening sky was inky black; heavy clouds hid the beautiful starscape he knew so well. The shower was just turning into a downpour and there was no time for introductions or conversation.

'Let's run for it!' was Galbryth's battle cry and Gidyon

instinctively took the girl's arm as they scuttled across the yard and piled into the cart. Galbryth pulled a canvas over their heads.

'I'm Gidyon,' he said. 'I'm not too sure what I'm doing here. All I know is I'm off to see a sick grandmother somewhere around these parts.' He wiped the rain away from his face.

'Oh!' was the young woman's surprised reply.

Galbryth noisily called to his horses and then picked up his singing again, drowning out further conversation. 'I'm Lauryn,' was all she managed to squeeze in.

Swiftly they found themselves out in open countryside.

'I gather you two know each other, being cousins and all that, so no need for formal introductions,' Galbryth yelled over the steady rain. 'Gidyon, this is my wife, Jeen. Your grandmother's not far away now but the laneway is tricky to find so I'll concentrate if you don't mind.'

Is he speaking to both of us? Gidyon wondered. He and Lauryn exchanged blank expressions and Gidyon shrugged and surreptitiously made a gesture to suggest that Galbryth was a bit simple. He could just make out that the girl grinned back.

Jeen Galbryth continued her steely silence whilst her husband cursed and muttered to himself. They hit several potholes, one deep enough to make Gidyon's teeth crunch.

Finally Galbryth relaxed. 'Ah, I knew I hadn't missed it,' he pronounced triumphantly as the cart twisted sharply onto a small track. In the distance they could dimly make out the lighted windows of a cottage. The chimney was smoking cheerfully.

They halted on the soggy grass outside the cottage and the horses whinnied, eager to be on their way to a warm, dry stable. Gidyon was surprised to see Galbryth help the girl down from the cart. Why was she coming too? The rain intensified; it was hardly the time for questions and both children stumbled around to grab their belongings and thanked the silent Jeen, who nodded stoically beneath the canvas. They each shook hands with Galbryth, who was, like his prized horses, in a hurry to get going.

'Oh, no trouble. No trouble at all, wee lassie.' He tapped Lauryn on the shoulder. 'Can you manage that now or shall I help you to the door?'

Lauryn was about to say she could manage when the door of the cottage opened. Silhouetted in the entranceway was a small, round woman.

'You'd best get going. My apologies to your grandmother for rushing off. I'll no doubt see her in the next few days so pass on my best in the meantime.' Galbryth climbed back onto the bench seat next to his wife.

Gidyon decided he was the victim of a trick, which everyone else was in on; yet he could not imagine dry old Father Piers going along with it. The rain was really hammering down now and he had no choice but to run towards the gate. By the time he and Lauryn had negotiated their way through it with their bags, the Galbryths had departed.

If Gidyon had put his hand into his pocket he would have been shocked by the sizzling heat pulsing from his stone. But he did not. Instead, his free hand steadied Lauryn on the slippery path as they nervously approached the figure in the doorway. The old girl had her hand to her mouth and was openly weeping at the sight of the two approaching. She opened her arms and clasped them both to her in a fierce hug; they had to bend to reach her, she was so tiny.

Wiping her eyes, she beamed up at the tall pair standing in front of her. 'Welcome home, children.'

Gidyon, now entirely confused, cleared his throat, uncertain of what to say. He looked over at Lauryn, who appeared equally dumbstruck but wore an angry expression, her green eyes glittering and her lips tight.

The old woman shooed them into the kitchen where a fire blazed merrily. A pot simmered on the stove and the enticing aroma of a stew invited a predictable growl of hunger from Gidyon's stomach. She made them sit down, muttering comforting words the whole time, but the happy scene lasted only a few brief moments before Lauryn's short fuse exploded.

She pulled off the hood of her wet cloak, revealing a small square of white Gyrton linen which covered part of her hair. 'Look, what is going on here? I've been dragged all the way up here to see a grandmother I barely know. A chatty stranger picks me up at the coach point, leaves me in a smoky tavern with his wife who doesn't talk at all, and then I'm introduced to you!' She glared at Gidyon. 'You, apparently, are a cousin I've never seen or heard of in my life!'

It seemed to Gidyon that the tirade was going to continue long and loudly, but the old lady put both hands into a prayer position and touched her fingertips to her lips. It was a gentle motion and yet so sombre that it made Lauryn clamp her mouth shut with a snort of exasperation.

Gidyon cleared his throat awkwardly for the second time. He needed to say something but he was not sure what. Lauryn was still bristling with resentment, which he did not share, but it was clear some explanation was required. He ran his hand through his wet, untidy hair.

The old girl smiled. 'So like your father, my boy,' she whispered.

Like his father? Gidyon was baffled. He had liked the old woman straightaway but he was not at all sure about all this mystery.

'Um . . . I'm sorry, what should I call you?'

'Call me Sorrel. You may feel more comfortable using my name.' Her warm smile bathed him with security.

He pressed on. 'Sorrel. Something tells me I do know you but I honestly don't remember you. Perhaps you could explain all this.' He looked over at Lauryn. 'We . . . well, er . . . that is, I was told you were gravely ill and wanted to see me before you er . . . passed away. I don't know what to think now. I have no relatives and know of no cousin. I'm not sure why Master Galbryth brought us both here, or why you are welcoming us as though we should know each other . . .'

'I will explain everything. But first, please, you are both chilled and probably hungry after your long journeys. May I serve you the meal I have cooked for you?'

Gidyon regarded her properly. Silvery grey hair was neatly caught up behind her head. Her round, kindly face held nothing but warmth and reassurance, which her slightly rheumy brown eyes echoed. She looked a century in age to his young eyes but although she seemed a little frail she did not appear to be sick. What could he lose by accepting a hot meal after six days on dried meat and stale bread? She had said she would explain everything afterwards. He gave her a grin and stood up, offering to help.

Lauryn sagged on the other side of the table. She was hungry and she was tired and her anger was doing nothing except costing her more energy. The old woman obviously meant no harm; she was doing her utmost to be kind and Lauryn felt the least she could do was to accept her hospitality. Gidyon, she noticed, was one of those detestably nice boys typical of the Ferenyans. He seemed content to go along with this charade; though inwardly she acknowledged he was handling the situation with more dignity than she was. The Prioress would not be pleased with her behaviour. Now he was helping the old lady to serve dinner. He was handsome though, she would give him that. The Prioress would not like her thinking of handsome men either. She had plans for Lauryn to take her vows very soon and then she could trap her for good. She pushed away thoughts of the convent; the current situation was daunting enough.

The meal was delicious, like no other stew either child had tasted, and Gidyon made all the right noises to a beaming Sorrel, who took great pleasure in watching them enjoy her food. Even Lauryn had to admit it was a superb meal and the home-baked bread that accompanied it was unbelievably good. Hot fruit pie came out next, with lashings of rich farm cream.

The hungry children seemed unaware of Sorrel's penetrating gaze; she took in every detail as they ate.

Gidyon was his father all over again; he had inherited so many of Tor's physical traits. The girl, meanwhile, was full of repressed energy; so reminiscent of her mother. She did not yet show her mother's astonishing beauty, but she would. Beneath the extra flesh, Sorrel could see Alyssandra Qyn's exquisite features.

She opened a link and probed. The boy looked up from his pie. He smiled but looked puzzled, as though he had been disturbed. Ah, he is perceptive, she noted, even worlds away from Tallinor. That is promising. In Lauryn she met strength. The girl had shielded her mind without being aware she could. This augured well for the test to come. Sorrel dared not probe any further at this stage, lest she harm them. The pair had struck up a quiet conversation about their respective Orders so she chose that moment to clear the dishes and give them a few minutes to relax. It would be their last quiet time before what lay ahead.

She shook her head thoughtfully and Gidyon, ever sharp, noticed.

'Can I help, Sorrel?'

'No, my child. Stay by the fire and talk with Lauryn. I'll just clear the table and join you soon enough.'

Lauryn had already curled up by the fire and was soaking up its warmth like a cat. Gidyon sat down in the battered but comfortable chair opposite.

'What do you think?' he whispered, cocking his head towards Sorrel's disappearing back.

'Absolutely bonkers. What are we doing here? Who are you? Who in hell's flames is she?' Lauryn's tone was vicious.

He made a soft sound of admonishment at her curse. He was actually quite impressed with her ability to swear so confidently. It was enough to make old Abbot Muggerydge's toes curl up in his slippers.

'Well, yes, this is all very confusing, I'll admit, but she seems harmless and we're stuck here for the night, so let's just go along with it and we'll work out what to do in the morning.'

'How do you know she's not going to slip us a nice sleeping draught and bury us out on the moors?' Her eyes beneath all that plumpness were dazzling, he thought, as he openly laughed at her notion.

'Oh, it's lovely to hear laughter in this quiet old cottage,' said Sorrel, who had returned soundlessly to the fireside.

Gidyon pulled a face as though he'd been caught. Lauryn giggled in spite of her mood. She could not help but like him.

Sorrel made herself comfortable in the other chair and handed down a cushion for Lauryn. She cradled a mug of herb tea in her hands and considered the pair solemnly.

'I have a lot to explain to you both tonight. The story I'm going to tell you is long. I beg you to hear it all and not to interrupt me, for it is vital you hear it in its entirety and understand its import.' Sorrel's even tone expressed the gravity of her words. 'It is going to challenge you, and perhaps frighten you, but there is nothing to fear and I am here to protect you both.'

She paused dramatically, eyeing them both. Their eyes were wide with astonishment.

'Now hear me,' she began, as the flames danced and the rain drummed its rhythm on the small windows.

They said not a word until her tale was told.

When Sorrel finally stopped speaking, all that could be heard was the monotonous drip of water outside and the wind. It had stopped raining but neither Gidyon nor Lauryn had noticed when. Hours had passed and Gidyon no longer felt sleepy; he was more confused than ever but he was also excited. It all seemed far-fetched but the old woman certainly sounded convincing.

It was Lauryn who broke the silence. 'And you really expect us to believe that we are brother and sister? That we were born to enchanted parents who live in another world? And that you are some sort of sorceress who magicked us here?'

Lauryn was chilled to see the old girl nod. She hated her in that moment. She did not want to believe one word of this tall tale and yet it resonated too strongly with all her doubts and fears. Her alienation, her need for family, her desperation to know who she was and why she had been abandoned so young. The very mention of another world rang uncomfortably true in her mind; she refused to accept it but at the same time it felt like a relief. She was not strange; she really did not belong at Gyrton after all.

'Are you mad?' she asked Sorrel coldly.

'I wish I were, Lauryn, and then you could go back to your scriptorium, Gidyon could return to his precious Blues — which he will surely attain — and we could all get on peacefully with our lives. If I were mad I would not have to face the huge task ahead of us.'

'Us! You speak as though I have no choice.' Lauryn's voice was raised now.

'But you don't, my girl. Your father has called you home.'

'My father!' she spat, 'I have no father, old woman. If I did, he would be with me; he would not have given me up.'

Sorrel's calm enraged her more. 'He had no choice. We were all about to die at the hand of Goth if we did not get you to safety.'

Gidyon decided that if he did not intervene, Lauryn

might slap the old girl or run out screaming into the blackness of the night. She was trembling with a rage which threatened to boil over.

'Lauryn—'

'What?' she hurled back at him, daring him to try and placate her.

'I say we make Sorrel prove it,' he said quietly, not looking at the old woman but staring straight into the pretty eyes of the hard-breathing girl next to him. 'She needs to show us something which links us to this bizarre tale. I agree with you – it sounds ludicrous – but somehow I don't think Sorrel is mad and, to tell the truth, I've never felt like I belonged completely in the Order. I'm happy there but something inside me begs to hear her out; something inside me is tugging towards belief – as much as I fight it.'

He thought Lauryn might snap. She looked to Sorrel and back to Gidyon, her eyes blazing angrily.

'Are you hearing yourself? A few hours ago you were in a tavern flirting with some girl serving ale. Now you're prepared to what . . . ? Be transported through worlds? You're as mad as she is, Gidyon.'

She was getting sulky now. He preferred sulkiness to fury because it meant she was listening, however much she might hate what he was saying. He waited. Sorrel looked as though she had nodded off to sleep.

Lauryn finally looked at him. 'All right. She has to prove it.'

He smiled at her but she looked away again quickly.

'Sorrel . . . Lauryn has agreed. Prove to us that we are brother and sister. Show us something which links us back to your story of Torkyn and Alyssa.'

The old woman opened her eyes and regarded them both kindly. 'Gidyon, tell me what you brought with you on this journey, other than your clothes.'

It was such an odd question that he blinked a couple of times, as though trying to fathom it. Then he shrugged. 'Well . . . er, charcoal, a fresh tablet of rag paper . . . there's nothing else. I packed very light, Sorrel,' he said apologetically.

'Think harder. And whilst you do, perhaps I can ask you the same question, Lauryn.'

Lauryn sneered. 'I brought nothing but a fresh gown and a poetry book I have no intention of reading. You lose, Sorrel.'

Gidyon thought back as hard as he could. He pushed his hand through his dark hair and felt the bruise where he had banged his head on the bed looking for his paper . . . and then he remembered his stone.

'Well, I don't know if this counts, Sorrel, but I did bring along this,' he said, reaching into his pocket and retrieving the warm sphere. Its colours looked somehow brighter to him, almost as though they were moving inside.

'Oh!' Lauryn said and then wished she had not because both of them turned to look at her.

The old woman was smiling and nodding at her. 'And how about you, Lauryn?' she encouraged.

Against her better judgement, Lauryn reached into her pocket and pulled out her stone. It too was warm and the colours were brighter than they had ever been at the convent.

The two children stared at each other's palms. Gidyon could not believe what he was seeing. His stone was the only thing he had from his childhood; he could not remember a time he had been without it and, if he was forced to, he would have admitted that he had always considered it his talisman. His special possession; nothing else like it in the whole world. Except this girl had an identical one!

Lauryn was baffled too. 'I was told this stone was stitched into my clothes when I arrived at the boarding school.' She was careful not to mention which item of clothing. That should trick the old witch.

Sorrel smiled as she remembered. 'Yes, my girl, I stitched it into one of your mittens. You said that if you could hold it for the whole journey and keep it close, you might just be able to make it without crying all the way.'

Lauryn thought it unlikely she could hate the old woman any more than she did at that moment. It all came flooding back to her: standing on a frozen road, the wind biting through her cloak as she clung to her grandmother and begged her not to send her away. She had not remembered that scene in over a decade. She had shut it away so tightly, it had never been allowed to enter her consciousness. A few minutes ago she would have sworn blind she had never seen this woman before and yet here it was, roaring back in painful detail.

Gidyon was experiencing something similar. As Sorrel told Lauryn about her stone, he suddenly remembered the small child he used to play with. A little girl. A bright, cheeky, funny little girl who hugged him and told him she loved him every day. How could he have forgotten that? Why had he forgotten it? That had been his sister. He was there at the roadside when she was crying; they were all saying goodbye. He was leaving as well, to go to the monastery, but his coach was departing later. He could remember it now as though it was yesterday.

Gidyon felt suddenly choked. 'Lauryn . . . I . . . I do remember you.'

'No!' she cried. 'It's not possible. We are not brother and sister!'

'You are more than brother and sister; you were born just a minute or two apart,' said Sorrel seriously. Her face no longer held its genial smile. 'Your mother gave birth to Gidyon first. Torkyn Gynt, your father, held you, Gidyon, and he wept as he named you. And then you, Lauryn. You were so special to him. He said you were more beautiful than anything he had ever seen.'

Lauryn swallowed hard. No one had ever told her she was even vaguely pretty and now here was Sorrel telling her the father she had craved so long had considered her the most beautiful thing he had ever seen.

It was as though Sorrel could read her thoughts. 'You know, your mother is like a doll, a fragile, exquisitely beautiful porcelain doll, Lauryn, and when you were born you looked just like her.'

It was too much for Lauryn. She began to weep. Gidyon reached over, took her in his arms and hugged her tightly. He wept with her. She thought she could never feel this way again. She had family. Someone thought she was beautiful. Her own brother was holding her, comforting her.

Sorrel let them weep. It was an enormous shock for them. She felt grave fears for the pair and yet she knew they had what it would take to overcome the trials that lay ahead. She sensed their strength. Which was why she could tell them the rest when they turned their attention back to her, both looking at her from red-rimmed eyes.

'There is more,' she said and was relieved to see them nod, albeit reluctantly.

'Your father had no idea where I would take you on that wonderful yet terrifying day of your birth. He had to trust me. All he could give me as a token were the three Stones.'

Gidyon interrupted. 'You say there are three?'

Sorrel nodded. 'The third is safe, Gidyon. Fret not.'

Lauryn snuggled closer to her brother and asked Sorrel to continue.

'I believe your father imagined we would simply flee the region and get as far away from Chief Inquisitor Goth as possible. In escaping, we would not only save your lives but your mother's as well; even possibly his own.' She waited for the obvious question. It was Lauryn who asked it.

'And my mother agreed to this?'

'Your mother was bleeding to death. She would almost certainly have died before we could deliver you if we had not received help. We called upon the god of the forest, Darmud Coril, and he weaved a powerful enchantment to heal her. His spell put her into the deepest of sleeps and both of you arrived within minutes. Poor Alyssa, she never knew of your existence. Does not, I imagine, to this day.'

The children looked stunned but Sorrel misunderstood, believing them to be shocked by the fact that Alyssa did not know they lived.

'Our mother is alive?' whispered Gidyon.

'Why, yes. As is your father.'

'How do you know?' asked Lauryn.

'Your mother lives because Darmud Coril saved her life. I would have felt it if she were no longer alive. How do I know your father lives? Because of her,' she said and pointed towards the fireplace.

Gidyon and Lauryn swung around and were confronted by a floating, silvery-green apparition, who smiled sadly back at them. Sorrel hoped they would not be scared. Neither was. They stared in wonder.

'Her name is Yargo and she is a messenger from your father. She has taken a long time to find you. Already, Tallinese years have passed since he sent her.' Sorrel tried to explain further. 'Time passes strangely between our worlds. I hope I am right in calculating that for every year in Tallinor, almost two and a half moon cycles pass here. You children have been gone six Tallinese summers but you are already fifteen years old in this world. The Light knows what has been happening since Yargo left your father. Which is why we must hurry. He will already have set his plan in motion if he has asked for your return. He could be in trouble, or he could simply be waiting.'

There it was. She watched for their reaction.

'We're going there?' Gidyon asked, dreamily.

'We must,' Sorrel replied, trying not to hold her breath.

Lauryn spoke. 'Are we to be reunited with our parents?'

'That is the plan.'

'How did she find us?' Gidyon could not take his eyes from the floating Yargo.

'She listened for the Stones of Ordolt. They must have called to her. Let her speak now.'

Yargo's smile had not faltered. Now she drifted closer and was delighted to see the children did not pull away. Gidyon even reached out to touch her. She wished she could touch him. He was the very image of his handsome father. This was how Tor must have looked as a very young man.

'I have travelled far to find you. Your father had no clue where I was to search but the Custodian, Lys, has guided me. He was anxious that I should find you quickly. I am to tell you that he wishes you to return to Tallinor. We must travel together.'

'That's it?' Lauryn did not speak unkindly and she echoed Gidyon's thoughts.

Sorrel spoke, knowing Yargo would have no answer to this. 'She is only the messenger. If Torkyn Gynt has called you back, it means he needs you. Tallinor is in danger. Remember the Paladin I spoke of? Perhaps the Tenth has fallen. If so, time is short indeed.' She spoke carefully. 'I believe that you both sensed the fall of Figgis of the Rock Dwellers? You both suffered a fainting episode – you in the cloisters, Gidyon, and Lauryn while at work in the scriptorium. I gather you both collapsed about the same time, and for no good reason. I think it was the Heartwood reaching out to you, touching you with its plight.'

It sounded like gibberish to the children. So little was making sense.

'So how do we return to Tallinor?' Gidyon tried to make it sound a perfectly reasonable question.

'Yargo will take us,' Sorrel answered matter of factly. No further information was provided.

'What about the monastery? I have my Testings for the Blues. How long do you think this will take?' he asked.

Sorrel sighed. 'Gidyon, this is difficult for me to say and perhaps even harder for you to understand.' She paused. He did not so much as blink. 'The Blues are now the past. Everything until this moment is the past. Your destiny awaits you back in Tallinor . . . where you both belong.'

It was Lauryn who responded this time and again she controlled all emotion in her voice, speaking evenly and quietly. 'So we must forget about the lives we know . . . once again. Is that what you are saying?'

Sorrel nodded. 'I am. I am so sorry. Everything until here and now, this very second, has been crafted towards protecting your lives, which are so precious. Now we must face your destiny and bring you back safely to Tallinor.'

The children looked at one another and something passed between them, but Sorrel could not read it. She decided they could use a few moments to talk and excused herself to gather some items.

When she had departed the room, neither found they could break the silence. It was all too much to comprehend.

Yargo rescued them. 'Can I tell you about your father?'

They both looked at her with surprise. Her voice suddenly sounded less dreamy, more light-hearted; like the tinkling of glass strands in the wind.

'Please,' Gidyon said, relieved for someone to start some discussion.

And so she did. Whilst Sorrel pottered around in her small kitchen, humming quietly to herself, Yargo told them all she could of their father and it was not long before they had gathered he was the tallest, broadest, most handsome man who walked the Kingdom of Tallinor.

Lauryn could not help but laugh. 'You sound as though you're besotted by him, Yargo.'

'I am,' the messenger replied. 'I love him with all there is of me.' She realised she sounded sad again and immediately changed the subject. 'Did I tell you he keeps a pet bird?'

When they shook their heads, she laughed. 'Oh yes, a

magnificent peregrine falcon he calls Cloot. Cloot is magical too but I don't really understand how. All I know is that he is of the Paladin and is bonded to your father.'

Gidyon had been thinking whilst she spoke. 'Yargo, do you think it's critical that we return with you?'

She became serious again. 'I think, Gidyon, that your father loves you both so much that he would never ask you to return unless it was essential. He would never risk putting you in danger without dire need.'

Yargo fell silent as Sorrel tiptoed back into the room. The old woman regarded them both solemnly and waited.

Gidyon looked at Lauryn, then took her hand. He put it to his lips and kissed it. 'If Lauryn agrees, then we shall go.'

Lauryn felt afraid; she did not want the decision to rest with her. Gidyon's large blue eyes were holding her own. What was he telling her with them?

She pulled his hand to her lips and honoured him with the identical gesture. 'I'm not sure we have any choice. And I hate the scriptorium! I agree to go.'

Sorrel looked relieved. 'Thank you both.'

She was silent for a moment, then walked over to a trunk in the corner of the room. 'You will need to change your clothes. I've had these ready for years. Every six months, I re-do them to make them bigger. I'm sorry if they don't fit you well, but no one will notice, I promise.'

The children approached the trunk with trepidation and stared inside. Sorrel picked out a pair of dark brown breeches and a light-coloured shirt for Gidyon. She gave Lauryn a skirt with a draw waistband, which was handy considering Lauryn's girth. A loose blouse which tied at the neck completed her ensemble.

'What is the season, Yargo?' Sorrel asked.

'We shall enter in early spring,' the apparition confirmed.

'Then you'll need these,' Sorrel said, handing over a thick woollen jerkin for Gidyon and an equally warm shawl for his sister.

'I won't miss my itchy convent gown,' Lauryn remarked.

Gidyon thought it was wonderful to see her smile; she was certainly very lovely when she did. Sorrel took Lauryn to another room so both the women could change and Gidyon quickly climbed into his outfit. Not so bad, he thought; nothing felt too tight.

Yargo enjoyed watching him; he moved like his father. And his naked body was not unlike Tor's either. She smiled inwardly and wondered if the Custodian would scold over such indiscretion. When the women returned, both the children burst out laughing at each other. Even Sorrel shared a smile.

'Take nothing with you which relates to our world here. Check carefully.'

'What about our stones?' Gidyon asked.

'Oh yes, those must come with you, but nothing which belongs here.'

Lauryn took a deep breath; she wondered at the insanity of where she found herself and what she was about to do. She looked again at Gidyon for reassurance. Gidyon sensed her nervousness. He felt much the same.

'Are we all ready?' Yargo asked.

Her three travelling companions nodded and linked hands.

14

Orlac's Grace

Lys hated the Bleak; it was a place of nothingness between worlds. It was also her home.

The role of Custodian of the Portals had been passed down the women of Lys's line through the ages. Lys's own mother had been Custodian, as had her mother before her. Until Orlac's incarceration, however, the Custodian had not been required to live within the realms of the Bleak. The role had been more of a symbolic one: it was the Custodian's duty to guard the portals between the worlds, ensuring that nothing and no one could pass through without her permission. And no one did, for countless centuries.

But then Orlac had wreaked his vengeance on the Land. The Host had succeeded in Quelling the young god and imprisoning him within the Bleak. They had chosen the ten Paladin to hold him there, but when Darganoth consulted the Elders of the Host, it was suggested that the Custodian might also watch over both prisoner and the Paladin; she would be their sentinel.

The beautiful young Custodian had readily agreed,

understanding the plight of the Host and the need to find a solution. And when the notion of the Trinity had first been mooted as a potential method of dealing with Orlac, it was Lys who offered to enter the land which Orlac had devastated and set the complex plan in motion.

Lys's birthright to travel the portals was a great boon and helped enormously to minimise the inevitable damage that could be caused by tearing the fabric between worlds. Nevertheless, she was only permitted to physically enter and leave a world of men once. After that, she must rely on maintaining contact with that world through her spiritual presence. She had only the one chance to complete successfully the task the Host had entrusted to her.

Lys crossed the portals to Tallinor and remained there for almost a full year of moon cycles. She achieved all that the Host had asked of her but instead of returning triumphant she found that her heart was full of grief. No longer wishing to live in the beautiful world of the gods, she chose to make her home in the Bleak. Its atmosphere matched the depth of her despair at what she had been required to do.

And now she spent her time watching over Orlac, witnessing the brave Paladin falling one by one to his great strength. Only Themesius the Giant remained now, but instead of attacking the last Paladin, Orlac had withdrawn from the battle and was sitting quietly, apparently deep in thought. Lys did not understand why he had chosen to let the Giant rest at this crucial point.

Lys came out of her private thoughts and looked over towards the red mist which also inhabited the Bleak. Once a powerful god, the red mist was now all that was left of Dorgryl's physical form. The arrival of Dorgryl to her sorrowful plane of existence had not come as a surprise. Where else would the Host choose to banish a god who had plotted the downfall of his King, his own brother? The Bleak was the ideal prison for someone who thrived on the vitality of life and all the pleasures it had to offer. Yes, the only way to punish such a being was to remove everything he loved most: his looks, his indulgences, his freedom and especially his power.

It was fitting that Dorgryl would pay for his greed and arrogance for eternity in the Bleak. He had enjoyed greater privilege than most gods could ever want; more than most mortals could conceive of. And yet Dorgryl had wanted more. The younger of twin sons, he had craved the kingship which was his brother's birthright. He had plotted his twin's death and would have succeeded, if not for his own young wife's uncovering of his evil plan. Her loyalty to the King and Queen she loved had outweighed her love for her husband and so Dorgryl had been thwarted, tried and punished.

In her role as sentinel, Lys held herself removed from contact with the fallen god but now, against her better judgement, she felt the need to initiate conversation. She had noticed that Dorgryl had been taking an increasing interest in Orlac and that, combined with her curiosity about the young god's sudden inactivity, was over-whelming her better sense. Maybe Dorgryl would be able to explain Orlac's behaviour.

She came straight to the point. *Why do you think Orlac is so quiet?*

The elder god was more than happy to talk after centuries of solitude. The red mist shimmered. *Lys! Lovely to hear your voice.*

Dorgryl, I am not here for social conversation.

Oh come now, you beautiful creature. What else is there to do in this bleak place?

His play on words did not impress Lys. As for the compliments, Lys knew that beneath the smooth manner was the most cunning of minds, ever imagining ways that he might lull her into relaxing her reflexes or her own suspicions of him. There was no doubt in her mind: Dorgryl was up to something.

He had spent many silent centuries in the Bleak, talking to no one, not even himself. Now he seemed almost jolly, as though he had something exciting to look forward to. There was nothing in his pitiful existence to warrant such good humour. Which meant he knew something she did not, or at least he thought he did. She would have to maintain her guard; it was dangerous enough that she was conversing with him. Lys had promised herself she would never fall into the trap of treating Dorgryl with anything but extreme caution. Every word he spoke, every ingenious movement of his mind, was pre-empted. Dorgryl had almost toppled the King of the gods. He was never to be taken lightly.

Lys had often wished it was simpler to kill a god. It would have been a more straightforward way of dealing with Dorgryl and even with his nephew, Orlac, prince of gods. Instead, the King's brother and the King's son and heir were under her supervision. And as much as she despised the task, she intended that they always would be.

Like Nanak, Lys experienced moments of genuine sympathy for Orlac. Sometimes, like now, when he was quiet and his guard was down, she could touch his mind. Within it she discovered awesome sadness. This immensely beautiful god had been corrupted by grief. His ferocious anger and hatred for the Land he had grown up in stemmed from his discovery of who he really was. Heir to the throne of the Host, prince of gods, Orlac had been raised like a poor man's son, removed from his birthright. Lys understood his pain. He had been born to the highest level but was forced to grow up as a mortal. Worse, he had done nothing to deserve this fate. He had simply stumbled as an infant into the path of thieves.

Would there ever be a way to right the wrong? Would the worlds ever be returned to their true balance? What would happen should the Trinity's power be invoked?

Dorgryl interrupted her thoughts. *I am enjoying this . . . what shall I call it? Ah yes, this theatre which is unfolding before us. Orlac, the wronged god, fighting his way out of imprisonment. Your favourite of all mortals leaping off a ship during a mighty storm to possible death. That strange messenger drifting off secretly through a portal – I wonder where she is headed? And then there is the beautiful Alyssa; looks as though she's found herself a comfy spot as Queen. It is a most intriguing story, Lys, which is playing out in front of us. I wonder what will occur when all the parts collide? I feel titillated just thinking about it.* He chuckled.

Don't trouble yourself over it, Dorgryl, she answered coolly.

Oh but, Lys, what else do I have but this thoroughly enjoyable 'dramatic' to trouble myself over? It amuses me. But it doesn't amuse you, does it? I have to wonder why. What is the all-powerful Custodian afraid of?

Lys regretted ever starting the conversation but she needed an explanation for Orlac's inactivity. When the Ninth, Figgis the Rock Dweller, had finally succumbed, Dorgryl had howled with laughter. Themesius the Giant had bellowed his distress at losing his final companion; whilst Nanak the Keeper had slumped to the ground, unable to prevent the emotion of loss. Orlac, however, had shown no sign of triumph. He had simply sat down, rested his beautiful head on his knees, curled his perfectly muscled arms around his superb body and rocked himself in silence. He had uttered not a sound since the death of the rock-hearted Figgis. Orlac had quite simply stopped all activity; it baffled Lys.

She was forced to repeat her earlier question to Dorgryl; she needed to know if he could explain the younger god's silence.

Oh, well now, Lys, how am I supposed to know what a god is thinking, hmm? I may be one myself — a pitiful excuse for one in this place — but I can't conjure up a reason to satisfy your misunderstanding of our young friend's strange behaviour.

She believed him. How could he know?

Unless, of course, he continued, sounding a little sly now, *Orlac is simply being noble.*

Noble? What do you mean?

Well, when I was a fantastically handsome god and member of the royal family, there was a particular sport we engaged in. It was called Quyx.

I do know what Quyx is. I am a god myself, remember.

Dorgryl chuckled again. It jangled her nerves that he knew something she did not.

Ah yes, but we were royals, my dear, and we had a different set of rules.

He importantly shimmered deep red. She hated him but took a deep breath. *Oh?* she said, keeping her voice level. *Won't you enlighten me?*

He continued as though she had not spoken. *When the victor sensed he was about to deal the 'killing' blow, which would end the game, he would sit on the floor for a period and allow his opponent a time of rest. He gave quarter, you might say. This rest time was called Grace and it enabled the opponent to gather his dignity and prepare to 'die'. Quyx was just sparring sport, of course. This is different. This is a fight to the death.*

I see.

Dorgryl's tone was lofty as he concluded. *Though I'm not sure Orlac would understand such finesse, as he was barely more than a babe when removed from the Host.*

Oh, but I am sure, Lys replied, quietly excited. *All members of the Host have inherent knowledge of the ways of gods. You are right, Dorgryl. Thank you. I believe Orlac is falling back on instinct. He is giving Grace to Themesius.*

Glad I could be of service to you, Lys. Perhaps we could look at you returning a small favour—

Nothing is owed, Dorgryl, she replied harshly. *How long is the period of Grace likely to last?*

The god was sulky and refused to answer immediately. She waited. Finally he sighed. *I have no idea. Sunrise to sunset in Quyx – though how would we know in this forsaken place when a sun is lowering,* he snarled.

Lys snapped away quickly from his mind's touch and shielded herself. Dorgryl's mind was agile indeed; she must keep him away from the events taking place. He was correct, of course. Orlac was biding his time before he finished off Themesius, as he surely would. But his Grace bought them some more time. How long? If he abided by the sunrise to sunset rule, that could mean a full year cycle in Tallinese time. It would help, but they could not depend upon it.

She must speed Tor along. But first, she had to save him from drowning.

15

Adongo of the Moruks

The cold of the ocean angrily drank them up. Ryk clung
tightly to Tor's neck and Tor was aware of Locky holding
just as tightly to his arm and thrashing alongside him. Tor
had lost all sense of direction in the foaming, gulping frenzy.
The Colours felt hot and bright within; they urged him to
draw on them to lift himself out of the depths. But he was
confused. Which way was up? Worse, the face of Goth kept
swirling in front of him. He was swallowing salty water
now; and if he was, it meant Ryk and Locky were doing
the same. His only hope was that Goth was dying along
with them, somewhere in the ocean's cold depths.

Tor. It was the voice of a friend.

I must be sleeping if I can talk to you, Lys.

Not sleeping, drowning.

Maybe drowning would be a good thing.

*No, Tor. Use your power now and save yourselves . . . all of
you.*

For what, Lys? he said, sinking further.

There is no time for this, Tor. Call on the Colours.

Why? he demanded.

Your children have been found. They come to you. She closed the link and left him.

The mention of Gidyon and Lauryn snapped him back to his fragile life. He turned; could see Locky's eyes wide with panic, his mouth opening and closing as he used the last of his breath. Ryk must be dead, he thought, suddenly filled with despair. The boy was no longer gripping his neck as before. He summoned the Colours. In a moment they were breaking the water's surface; gasping great breaths, sucking life back into their chests and coughing out the salty death which had almost consumed them.

The Wasp was nowhere to be seen. Either they had been dragged far from it or it had sunk. The sea boiled around them but the Colours kept the trio safely cocooned.

Tor looked wildly around, still dragging in air and wondering if his chest might burst from the effort. He noticed some craggy rocks through the darkness. Land! They could probably reach it if he guided them closer. No time to think. He cast his mind towards the shore and willed them to safety.

He clambered wearily onto a ledge and dragged Locky with him. Ryk was slumped against his chest, unconscious. Looking around, Tor realised they must have reached an island for there was land stretching out beyond the ledge. Buoyed by this discovery, and the desire to see his children again, he pulled Locky to his feet and together, carrying Ryk between them, they limped towards the security of a sandbank. There they rolled onto the scraggy grass and sheltered in its natural dip. It offered some small but welcome protection from the howling wind.

It could still only be mid-morning yet the colour of the sky made it seem like evening. The storm would rage for a while yet, Tor could tell. He pushed the boys into the ditch and checked on Ryk; he was breathing, but raggedly.

Tor stood to get a better idea of the countryside around them. In the distance, he could just make out some kind of camp. He knew they could not make it there now. It would have to wait until his companions were stronger, and then perhaps they could approach the camp for help. Tor had to admit that he felt exhausted himself; it would do him good to rest awhile too.

He turned back towards the sea for one last look to where *The Wasp* had presumably sunk. Scanning the horizon, he noticed a small piece of wreckage in the angry sea, not far from the beach below. There was a dark figure clinging to it. Goth, curse him!

The so-called priest waved desperately. Tor could not hear what the man was calling out but guessed he would be begging for help. I will not save you, Goth, he thought. And I will not dirty my hands with your blood. The elements will take your life for me.

The piece of wood was swirling madly in the waves now. It was hard to fathom how Goth could hold on.

'Farewell, Goth,' Tor yelled.

The wind ripped his words away and threw them elsewhere. The man slumped and Tor watched the miniature raft being sucked hungrily back out to sea and then down the length of the beach. He watched until it was no more than a speck and he prayed that it might be the end of the man he hated most in this world.

With Goth in a watery grave, Alyssa would at last be free. With this hopeful thought, Tor slumped down beside his companions, exhausted.

*   *   *

He awoke with a start, not immediately aware that he had slept. He felt groggy and shook his head, as if to clear the mist from it. The storm had died around them, leaving just the angry wind and the rain, which had soaked them to their skins. When he tried to wipe the salt from his stinging eyes, he realised he was shackled.

His senses back on alert, Tor looked around. There were several other men chained up in the rain; they were swarthy and dark-eyed with angular faces and long limbs. He guessed they were of the nomadic people from the Exotic Isles, those Eryn had mentioned. They murmured amongst themselves in a language he did not understand. No one spoke to him, even when they realised he was conscious. Tor pulled himself to his knees and considered using his powers to free himself. Then he remembered Locky and Ryk. He should sit tight and wait to see if they were still close by.

He scanned the surroundings. From what he could tell, he seemed to be a long way from the sandbank where they had sought shelter the previous day. He had obviously been carried here and began to assume that he must have been drugged. It would explain his grogginess on waking; how else could they have moved him without him waking? He could remember nothing.

It was nearing dawn when someone finally came. The man kicked awake those few who were still sleeping and motioned for them all to stand. Tor did as he was told, having noticed the ugly whip curled menacingly in the man's hand. More men arrived. They looked like sailors. The fellow in charge addressed the prisoners in pidgin; Tor concentrated hard and managed to grasp at a few words. He need not have troubled himself. The man switched to Tallinese and introduced himself as Haryd, the first mate to Captain Blackhand.

'You, tall man, you took the wrong wave. You are now a slave and will act accordingly. Your name?'

There was no point in lying. 'Torkyn Gynt.'

'From?'

'Tal.'

The man laughed. 'We've never caught us an educated city man before. You will make me a big profit, Gynt. What are you doing here?'

'Surviving,' Tor answered and saw the whip twitch in Haryd's grip.

'No smart talk, Gynt. We punish slaves with fast mouths. You just answer my questions. I own you.'

Tor held his tongue.

'Which ship?' Haryd demanded.

'*The Wasp*. She sank in the storm.'

His captors looked shocked.

'You were on board?' Haryd said loudly, walking closer now.

'I and my two companions, yes.'

'What about Captain Blackhand?'

Tor was careful. 'Dead. Killed by his own hand.'

'You lie,' screamed the first mate. 'Blackhand, suicide? I don't think so.'

'I was there. It was not suicide; it was an accident.' Tor could almost taste the heavy silence around him now as all the men listened. Even the other slaves had stopped their shuffling. 'He was in the throes of his favourite sport of chopping off someone's hand, one of his crew. The storm was gathering and an unexpected wave buffeted the ship . . . it was the one that broke her, I think. He must have slipped because the axe ended up in his own chest. The last I saw of him, his guts were sprawled the full breadth of the sinking *Wasp*.'

Tor enjoyed the horrified look on his captors' faces as he crafted his tale.

Haryd managed to hold his nerves steady. 'What about the others?'

'All dead I would think,' Tor answered. 'Lightning struck the mast and set fire to the ship. It sank within minutes. I jumped with three others; two survived with me. I can vouch for no others.'

'What were you doing on *The Wasp*?'

'I had paid my passage to Cipres. May I ask where my two friends are?'

'One is dying, if not dead already; he happens to be a member of our crew. The older one is pretty enough that, in the absence of any whores, he will serve my men just fine.'

Tor felt his anger rise. 'I asked where they were. I am a physic, I can save the lad. As for Locklyn Gylbyt, it may interest you to learn that he is the brother-in-law of one Janus Quist, who I'm sure will be delighted to enter into discourse with you on how to treat his relatives.'

Tor should have seen it coming. He had not only spoken to the man in a contemptuous tone again but he had terrified him with the mention of Quist. Haryd's whip slashed across his torso and the pain of its bite into his wet flesh sent him back to the muddy ground. The lash came again, its sting flashing across his back now. The pain was immense.

He heard Haryd spit at him. 'You will never speak to me like that again, Gynt. From now on, if I address you,

you will reply with your eyes cast downwards. You are a slave. You have conjured a fine story to save your skin but it won't work, Gynt. You will be sold at Cipres in a few days, along with your arsesore companion. Now get up and heal the skinny lad because I need his services. And you are welcome to put a salve on the backside of your friend. I require him for sale, but I also need him healed and tight for my men for the next two nights at least.'

He saved some face with the last comment and the sailors laughed. Just as Tor was ready to wipe the smiles from their mouths, he heard a voice like velvet in his head. It reminded him of the day he had seen the girl, Marya, bridled and Merkhud had spoken into his mind for the first time.

Do not show yourself yet. It is not wise.

The Colours faded and Tor looked around him suspiciously.

Who speaks? he threw out.

I. Two men to your left.

Haryd was barking orders to his men and one of them hauled Tor to his feet. He took the chance to seek the owner of this smooth voice. A tall man was staring at him intently, the whites of his eyes glistening in his dark face in the dim light. He nodded slowly.

Who are you? Tor whispered as he was dragged away.

I am Adongo of the Moruks.

Tor was shocked. *Paladin?* He was pushed into a tent.

The Fifth. We shall speak later. The link snapped shut.

Ryk was sprawled on the ground in a corner of the tent, shivering with a high fever. Tor pushed away the revelation of Adongo, though his mind swam with its meaning. He asked that his shackles be removed.

'You do anything stupid, slave, and we'll slash the boy's throat,' growled one of his captors. He motioned for the other to free Tor. 'And I don't mean this one. I mean our whore,' he added and grinned nastily close to Tor's face.

It would be so easy, Tor thought to himself as he searched the shallow eyes. But killing was not his intent. He had always promised himself he would not use his powers to bring death . . . but that had become unavoidable recently. He could still see the blood pumping from the massive wound in Blackhand's chest. And it would be easy to kill this man too; to kill all of them. But Adongo had warned him not to show himself yet. He would wait and learn more from the Paladin.

'Thank you,' he replied, not feeling polite.

The boy was burning up. He would die before the day had reached full sunlight, Tor was sure of it.

'My bag. Do you remember there being a bag with me when you found me? A leather sack?'

The man looked at him dumbly. Tor tried again.

'It was strapped around me when I swam ashore. Dark brown. It must have been found with me.'

The man said nothing but a slight tilt of his chin sent the other fellow scurrying out. He returned not long afterwards with Tor's bag. Relief washed over him but he said nothing, just took the bag from the sailor. Tor did not need the satchel; he had just remembered it and wanted the security of knowing he had it safely back in his keep. He pretended to rummage through it. Perhaps there was something in there which could help. The contents were such an odd assortment.

He deliberately muttered aloud. 'No, not here as I thought. Has anything been taken from here?'

Both men shook their heads.

'Well, what I need is not here,' he lied. Adding an edge of frustration he said, 'Could I have some damp linens at least?'

The second sailor disappeared again. The other picked his nose, entirely uninterested.

Tor laid his hands on Ryk and summoned the Colours. He had to make it look as though he was testing the boy's temperature. It was easy to wield his power to force the fever down but he could sense much more damage; something more sinister. In his fear, Ryk had fled deep within himself. Just the shell remained; his terrified spirit was hidden away and slowly dying.

Tor thought quickly, recalling information he had read in Merkhud's books. Before he could act, he must get rid of these men.

He addressed them. 'The boy is dying of a disease I've encountered only twice before. It is especially nasty.'

Both men took a step back.

'I'm going to need some help,' Tor added, sounding matter of fact.

'Not from me you don't,' one said. The other shook his head.

'Well, he'll die then. Haryd said I must save him.'

'You said he's dying anyway,' grumbled the more senior sailor.

'Yes, that's true. But I can probably save him, though it will take several hours and some help.'

Neither man moved. He played his card.

'All right. Fetch me one of the slaves from outside. Not just any one. The tall one, two to the left of where I was chained. I need someone strong. He also looks dumb and won't ask too many questions.' Tor smiled as though sharing a private joke.

The sailors fell for it. The senior one even winked at him. 'Watch him, Bluth,' he said, leaving to find the slave.

Adongo of the Moruks was led into the tent looking surprised.

Tor sliced open a link. *Just play along*. It amazed him that they could understand one another when they spoke different languages. He wondered also why he was able to link with the Moruk when he was unable to do so with Saxon.

Happy to, Adongo's smooth, deep voice replied.

'I won't be removing his shackles,' the sailor said loudly, shoving Adongo towards Tor and Ryk.

'I understand. It won't be necessary anyway,' Tor said. 'However, if you value your life, I would recommend you don't tarry. If this boy so much as sneezes on you or even near you, you could suffer a similar fate.'

The man looked horrified.

'I am hardly likely to escape, but you can chain me to that tent pole if you want,' Tor said.

'How come you won't get sick then?'

'Because I have been exposed to this before and I did not become unwell. I must be safe from this disease. Many people are but we don't understand why. You may also be immune, but then again you may not be so fortunate. Take your chance, Beryd . . . is that your name?'

The senior man nodded. But he was persistent; he gestured towards the slave. Tor picked up on his thought and answered the question before it was asked. 'And I'm presuming that he just doesn't matter.'

Beryd grimaced. 'Yes, he does. He is leader of his tribe. He will fetch a good price at Cipres.'

Tor needed to get him out of the tent. 'Well, leave us both shackled and remain outside. I'll call you once the fever breaks. When that happens, we will all be safe,' he lied again. Beryd clearly needed pushing. 'Or you can take your chance. Victims eventually bleed to death from the nostrils, eyes, ears, cock, arse.'

The colour paled from Beryd's face and he yelled out an order to his mate. Tor and Adongo were quickly shackled to the post; Adongo remained manacled but Tor's hands were left free, although the chains on his legs were so short his captors knew he could not reach beyond the round tent.

'We'll be outside,' Beryd said, covering his mouth and nose.

Tor nodded and busied himself with showing Adongo how to press the damp linens to Ryk's body.

To their unbelievable good fortune, Ryk stirred at this moment and gave a half sneeze before sliding back into his feverish stupor.

Beryd and Bluth fled.

Thank you for coming, Tor said.

I'm not sure I had any choice.

No, I mean for re-emerging.

So do I, the man said evenly, *though I am not your bonded Paladin.*

I realise this. Do you know who is?

I'll know when I meet them, he said cryptically.

Has Lys given you a name?

Only that the person is young, Adongo said, avoiding the question.

Tor noticed the man's deliberate vagueness. He would not push it. They could discover more about each other later.

Do you know who I am? Tor asked, hating the pomposity of the question.

You are the One.

I prefer you did not think of me that way.

We all have our part to play. I am Paladin. You are He.

Tor sighed. It was useless arguing the point further. *Adongo, why did you warn me to hide my powers?*

The man grinned. *These sailing men are scared of enchantments. They kill anyone whom they suspect of aiming magic at them. My race call it 'fra-fra' — these men are scared of our beliefs, our culture, our magicks.*

And in Cipres?

I have never been there, Adongo said, looking at his chains.

Of course, I'm sorry. Where did they capture you?

Many leagues away. We are a nomadic people but the pirates know our traditional routes. They come with fire and arrows and slaughter our brangos, burn our tents. They killed my woman . . . my twin daughters. He smiled sadly at Tor. *But they cannot kill my memory of them.*

Tor had nothing to say which could offer any comfort. Adongo's dignity reminded him of Cloot. The chieftain noticed his companion's awkwardness.

You did not bring this grief upon me, and if it had not happened, I would not be able to fulfil my destiny as Paladin. I accept my lot.

You shouldn't have to. Tor's bright blue eyes blazed his anger. At that instant, he could have throttled Lys and her brutal manipulations.

The man shrugged. *Our life as Paladin is all about sacrifice. As I said, I don't believe I have a choice. Their deaths were swift. They felt nothing. Only I felt pain and I am grateful for that mercy. But let us not dwell on it. Please . . . the child,* he pointed to Ryk.

He is remote from us, Tor answered, embarrassed by his own relief at moving on from Adongo's suffering. *Ryk is in shock. I sense he's still with us but he will die if he does not return to his senses quickly. The fever I can stop but I have to find Ryk's spirit and bring him back to himself.*

The man nodded. *What can we do?*

It's dangerous. I don't even know if it's possible. I want us to link and then you must anchor me to that link inside you. I shall send myself into Ryk and see if I can find him.

Adongo's eyes widened with surprise. *It is not a reasonable plan.*

Tor grinned. Why did everyone always hate his plans? *It's the only one I've got.*

The swarthy man shook his head. *Too dangerous. I cannot.*

Are you frightened?

Not for me, he said abruptly. *For you. I am not permitted to allow such risk.*

Then I shall have to take the risk without you, Adongo. Pity, I could use your strength. This was unfair of Tor and he knew it but he had no choice. Ryk must live. *Just keep an eye on the guards for me then.*

Adongo stretched out his hand to hold Tor's arm. *Wait. I will help.*

The Moruk would never know how grateful Tor felt at that moment for he really had no idea of how to carry out this complex task. Wasting no time, he locked onto the link and cleared his mind.

The man twitched a grim smile. Tor looked at him questioningly.

This reminds me of when we did battle with Orlac, Adongo said, kneeling beside Ryk. *We would hold each other's minds as safely as we could, like this, and still our combined strength was not enough.*

It was a chilling statement.

Tor laid his hands on Ryk once again, summoned the Colours and felt himself disappear.

He found Ryk cringing. The boy screamed out when he felt someone so near. Adongo too heard the shriek and strengthened his hold on Tor via the link. He resisted the urge to peek towards the tent flap; he would hear the sailors before they entered.

Hush, Ryk, Tor soothed. *It is only I.*

The lad was confused and his terror stopped him being able to sort out his thoughts or even realise that Tor was there with him . . . inside.

You must follow me now, Ryk.

I'm frightened. He'll chop my hand off and feed me to the giant eels.

Ryk. Tor's voice was firm.

Yes?

It was only a whisper. He pushed on. *Captain Blackhand is dead. The Wasp is sunk. And you are lost. If you follow me now, I can take you back to where we need to be. Do you understand?*

The lengthy pause troubled Tor. He wondered how long Adongo could keep him safe like this.

Ryk, do you hear me?

He's dead? We're not drowned?

We're alive. In a spot of bother, but we can handle it. First, we need to be together . . . and awake. Will you follow me? I promise I will not allow anyone to harm you.

What about the bother?

So he was paying attention. Good lad. *I could use your help with it, to be honest.*

Ryk allowed Tor to take his hand and lead him back to consciousness. As Tor re-entered his own body, Adongo's eyes snapped open at the sound of the tent flap. Haryd came striding in, his henchmen following.

Adongo was still holding a damp linen and had the presence of mind to dutifully hold it out to Tor, who was breathing hard as he recollected himself.

Take it . . . Go through the motions, Adongo hissed across the link.

Tor sighed, stretched his back as though he had been on bended knees over the child for too long and casually looked up as Haryd arrived. He laid the towel on Ryk's forehead. He felt dizzy with the effort of appearing normal.

'Why do you need this slave?' Haryd barked.

Tor shot a look at Ryk and noticed his face was twitching and his eyes were fluttering behind their lids. The boy was back. He was asleep but safe and healing. Now, he must deal with the angry sailor. He stood with effort, careful to keep his eyes lowered as instructed and also mindful of showing Haryd that he was still chained.

Adongo remained still and silent on his knees.

'I have given the child a sleeping draught which will help lower his fever, sir. I believe, with some care, he will pull through for you.'

'So, we've learned some humility have we, mighty physic?'

'Yes, sir,' Tor mumbled, wanting to unleash the Colours which were still sparking inside him.

'But you didn't answer my question, slave.'

Tor had to think what it was. He needed rest.

Explain what I am doing here, Adongo hissed.

Tor grasped at various thoughts which drifted across his mind. 'Sir, I told your men that Ryk here is extremely ill with a disease which could be fatal to others. My apologies, I was wrong. He does, however, need to be kept moving constantly through this night or he will succumb. I am hoping that between the Moruk and myself we can keep him on his feet and not trouble your men . . . sir.' His eyes flicked to Haryd and back to the ground.

'I can't imagine why you'd care about my men's sleep, Gynt, but you are right about the fact that I don't care about you, this Moruk here, or this child. However, if he can be saved, he may turn out to be useful. So continue. Tomorrow we march.'

He turned to leave, his whip twitching. 'Oh, and Gynt – I won't be needing the whore tonight. I'm tired. He will be brought here for you to attend to.' Haryd smirked.

'Thank you, sir,' was all Tor could bring himself to say as they left.

He must have collapsed, for he felt himself being shaken. It was actually the noise of the chains clanking together which caught his attention, then everything else began to fall back into place and he found himself looking into the concerned face of Adongo.

What happened? he asked.

I know not. You are weakened by the boy's healing, I imagine.

Ryk. How is he? Tor held his own head as he moved into a sitting position, cautiously for fear of the dizziness.

See for yourself, Adongo suggested.

Tor looked over into the corner and saw Ryk curled up in a natural state of deep sleep.

He even spoke. Said to thank you for finding him, for bringing him back.

I'm surprised he could remember anything, Tor replied, closing his eyes again.

He may not recall any of it when he wakes truly. But he will be fine. There is no fever. His colour is normal. If he is permitted to sleep today he should be recovered in time for the march, Adongo confirmed.

Ah, the march. How long will it take?

I would guess three days.

Adongo, are you able to reach my sack?

The Moruk passed the bag to Tor, who still felt too queasy to move. He remembered seeing a small vial in it when he first looked at the contents on the day he left the Heartwood.

He opened his eyes to slits and searched for the small glass tube. His fingers found it; he desperately hoped it contained what he suspected it may. Pulling out the cork stopper he smelled the liquid and was instantly reminded of the dingy room at The Empty Goblet where he had once performed an amazing healing on a man who was now a falcon.

'Cloot,' he whispered sadly. 'Where are you?'

Tor sipped the clear liquid and the arraq slipped down his throat. Its effect was immediate; suddenly Tor felt as though he had slept for days. Strength returned to his body and his head cleared. He sipped again, remembering what Dr Freyberg had said about not taking too much at once. After a final slow sip, he returned the vial to the sack.

That is some potion, Adongo commented, amused and impressed.

A simply berry, tiny and rare, Tor said, recalling Freyberg's description. *They bloom only during Thaw and for a short season. The raw berries are poisonous – just a few drops of the juice can paralyse and a berry or two can kill – but if you boil them down to a syrup, you get this revitalising liquor. I am amazed that the same vial I was given many years ago, and had forgotten about, is now to be found in this sack.* Tor shook his head with wonder. *The Heartwood provides.*

He changed the subject. *Adongo, how is it we can use the link?* he said, standing and stretching, amazed at his own fresh vigour.

The Moruk considered this for a moment. *Though I was the Fifth to fall, I was the first to be recruited to the Paladin. I believe I opened the original mindlink between us when we were assembled. Perhaps this was a special quality given to me, which may be why I can link with you.*

Tor nodded. It seemed feasible. *One day we will return to the Heartwood and you will be able to talk with all of your Paladin companions. It is the most magical of places.*

Adongo's face lit up with a smile. *I shall look forward to returning there with you, Tor.*

They had no time to enjoy this thought. Footsteps warned them before the flap of the tent was ripped back. It was Beryd.

'Is it safe?' he barked.

'I think so,' Tor said, pretending not to be sure.

'The Moruk must be returned,' he said, striding in with two others. He addressed Adongo in the pidgin language Tor had heard earlier and the chieftain quietly stood for his chains to be removed from the central post.

Do not show them your powers, Adongo cautioned.

Why don't we just escape?

Lys told me it was important I get to Cipres with you. She cautioned that we must not draw undue attention to ourselves.

Yes, she always says that and so far I've never managed to obey that rule, Tor answered ruefully as Adongo was led off.

He heard Adongo laugh inside his head and it eased his troubled spirit.

Beryd was looking at him. 'What are you grinning about?'

'Just recalling freedom and the last brothel I visited,' Tor said, grabbing at the first excuse he could think of.

'Well, if whoring's on your mind, you'll be pleased with this visitor,' Beryd said, as Locky was shoved brutally into the tent. The boy landed on the floor and immediately pulled himself into a crouched position, manacles and chains clanking as he did so. 'Fix him up. Then you return outside.'

Tor nodded, eyes riveted on Locky, who refused to look at anyone.

'Make it quick. My men will be back in a few minutes,' the sailor ordered.

Locky was trembling. Tor could see livid bruises on his face.

'Talk to me, Locky . . . please.'

The lad looked up, eyes blazing with hatred. 'The first man who tried to touch me when I was seven, I killed. Now I'm going to kill Haryd.'

The venom in the statement was real. Tor believed every word. He reached once again for the arraq. There was nothing he could physically do to help, and he sensed that Locky would not permit anyone to help even if they could. He wanted to retain his anger. He could survive the hurt and humiliation if he kept his hatred strong.

'Sip this. Two sips only.'

'What is it?'

'A rejuvenating potion. We march tomorrow for three days. It will keep you strong.'

He thought the lad might refuse so was relieved when Locky held out his hand. He took the first sip and looked suspiciously at Tor.

'And another one,' Tor encouraged.

'Is Ryk all right?' Locky asked, taking a second invigorating drop into his mouth. 'Can I keep this?'

'No,' Tor admonished and was relieved to see Locky's mouth twitch with the rascal grin he remembered. 'Ryk's sleeping. He was knocked around a bit in the sea, but yes, he'll be fine. I just hope he'll be fit enough for tomorrow. How about you?'

The awkward moment had passed. Locky felt more at ease to talk now. He handed back the vial reluctantly.

'Light! That stuff's good. I feel as though I could march for a week.'

'I'm glad. We must stick close now.'

'Will they allow it?'

'Yes. I've told them who you are. Quist's name carries immense power. Even if they don't believe me, they won't risk it.'

'Janus will be merciless,' Locky said. 'But they're lucky they'll have to deal with only him and not my sister.'

'She will never know, Locky. Is there anything I can do for you?'

'Not unless you're prepared to get me drunk or give me the magic liquid again.'

Tor knew Locky would be all right. He was a tough lad and would take succour from his desire to avenge himself on these men. But now they must return to the other slaves.

As though their captor had read his thoughts, the tent flap was ripped back yet again. It was Haryd this time. 'On your feet.'

Locky stood, eyes defiant. Tor willed him to offer respect, even if it was pretence.

'Don't look at me like that for too long, boy, unless you want your back to be even more sore than your arse. I can have it arranged through the courtesy of my whip here.'

Locky looked down. He said nothing.

'Sir,' Tor said, hating the humility he had to show, 'your crew member Ryk will be fine by tomorrow. Could you allow him today to rest?'

'Only him. You two, back outside.'

Tor pushed the Colours back, promising himself that one day he would see Locky settle with this man. For now, he must listen to Adongo and prepare for Cipres.

16

Grievance

They had been marching for two days and most of a second night now, stopping only for a brief rest each evening. Their food ration was meagre but thankfully their captors left the prisoners much to themselves. They marched in a chain gang, supervised by men on horses and two wagons, one leading, the other bringing up the rear.

Tor did not mind the marching. It gave him time to himself. He kept open the mindlink with Adongo, though the chieftain spoke only when spoken to. He made no trivial conversation, which suited Tor. Locky was also silent, keeping his thoughts to himself, but he definitely looked brighter since the administering of the arraq and seemed glad to be on the move. None of the sailors had come near him since he had been given back to Tor. Nevertheless, Tor did not rate their chances against the famous wrath of Janus Quist, even with this new respect.

As for Ryk, it was as though nothing had happened. He had awoken the following morning with no memory of the events immediately preceding the moment they had leapt from the ship. The boy did not speak of

Blackhand's punishment; he recalled nothing but the boiling sea and attributed his good fortune in being alive to the man he now knew as Torkyn Gynt, not Physic Petersyn. Despite Haryd's orders, Ryk lavished attention on his saviour whenever the sailor's eyes were averted. He was now cooking for the men and Tor was grateful for the extra meat and bread the boy managed to smuggle to them with their gruel. Tor asked him to look after Adongo too. It puzzled Ryk but he did as asked. Anything for Torkyn Gynt.

It was cold, though not bitterly so. Winter was just about upon the Exotic Isles. There was much excitement amongst the slaves over the raft crossing to the mainland, which took an entire day. The initial buzz died down though as the hours of being chained standing upright on the small craft took their toll. By sunrise on the fourth day, the slaves were standing on the jetty of the Cipres docks, awaiting transport to the market.

Haryd was happy. Today was the main slaving day and he intended to make quick sales, purchase berths for himself and his companions on an outgoing ship and be away from Cipres by nightfall. He was not taking any chances on the story that Locklyn Gylbyt was Quist's brother-in-law.

Tor decided he must act soon to ensure Haryd did not escape his due. His powers must be revealed now, whether Adongo approved or not.

'Locky, would you know where to find Quist?' he whispered.

'I've never been here before but I have directions from Eryn to the inn he favours in Cipres. However, I imagine the chains and manacles may give me away.'

Tor grimaced at his friend's sarcasm. 'Trust me and pay attention.'

He watched Haryd, who was busy giving orders. Even though the man was far away, Tor's exceptional hearing picked up everything. The slaves were to be loaded onto carts and Haryd was currently negotiating with someone to provide them. Tor's main concern was that Haryd was occupied. His henchmen paid scant attention to the slaves who had been made to sit together in a tight pack.

It was now or never. Tor weaved his Colours and watched the iron of Locky's manacles melt away. Locky had not noticed; he too was engrossed in watching the haggling up front. So much for paying attention, Tor thought. He performed the same trick on the chains which held the lad's wrists. The boy was free. Now they had to move carefully.

'Locky,' he whispered again.

'Shhh,' the boy hissed back. 'I'm trying to hear what their plans are for us.'

Tor groaned. 'I can hear every word. Would you like me to tell you that we're to be loaded in carts shortly and taken to the western end of the main market? Would you also like me to mention that your arms and legs are no longer chained?'

Locky's head whipped down to look at his ankles and he pulled his hands in front of him. He was about to exclaim but Tor's voice stopped him. 'Not a word! Move slowly and use all your disappearing talents. Melt away and find me Janus Quist.'

Locky did not respond. His mouth was wide; his eyes too, with disbelief. Tor glanced towards Haryd and did not have to hear the conversation to know the men had struck a deal. The slaves would be loaded immediately.

'Go!' Tor said, softly yet urgently.

Locky's eyes turned to him now. 'Who are you?'

'Your friend. Now go.'

He watched with relief as the young man flexed his fingers and toes, preparing to creep away. The order to stand was given and the men began struggling with their chains to get to their feet.

'Good luck,' Tor whispered and grinned at Locky, who was already disappearing between the tall bodies of the slaves towards the back of their column.

Adongo, Locky is free. Tell your people to keep it quiet.

He saw the man nod. *I will pass the word.*

Tor was concerned that the other slaves might start to look around at Locky. He should not have worried. A hand reached for the empty chains on the ground. Its owner's lips parted into a grin and Tor watched him pass the chains carefully back down the line. Someone at the back would get rid of them.

'Good magic,' the man said, struggling to speak with the little Tallinese he knew. He was pleased when Tor nodded and grinned back.

Then they were herded forward and loaded onto two carts. Haryd had already turned his back on the prisoners. Probably heading for an alehouse, Tor thought. That suited him. Beryd, Bluth and the two other men who had been left behind to escort the prisoners to the market were not sharp; hopefully they would not even notice Locky's disappearance until they were actually there.

Tor's luck held. The carts rumbled away from the busy jetty and began to bump their way through the docklands. He could see the main city not far away. Beautiful buildings of pastel-coloured stone were enhanced by the watery sunlight which heralded the end of Deadleaf and the commencement of winter. Even the houses which crowded up the hillsides were picture-pretty with their pale colours. Standing alone on a huge outcrop of rock was the palace of Cipres. It was a breathtakingly elegant building with a row of tall, pale minarets, all of different soft colours. Their curved roofs were patterned with gold which caused them to glint constantly. It was an incredibly feminine-looking palace. And why not? It was home to a Queen.

The marketplace was located at a distance from the beautiful city and it was only a few minutes before they turned into the main arena on the western fringe. It was a lively, colourful place, thriving with people calling out their wares, their prices, their purchase desires. The carts rumbled on past into a secured area. Here the men were unloaded and told to sit in a group once again.

Tor wished Locky good speed and withdrew into himself to wait.

A few hours later, guards arrived, as did the Master of the Markets – a dumpy, overweight man known as 'Master Lard', a name which Tor considered most appropriate. Lard was not unkind though. He ordered the men's wrist manacles to be removed and a pot of salve was passed around to ease the inevitable sores which the leg irons had caused. He spoke the pidgin language so the nomads could understand.

'You have good fortune today. Each first day of the full moon, her majesty Queen Sylven visits the slave markets. It has been her tradition throughout her reign and she

will be here later today. Her presence brings luck to the
slaves. You will all find good homes today.'

Tor was surprised to see him smile kindly at the men.

The slaves murmured amongst themselves. Adongo
still kept his peace.

Master Lard continued. 'You are the first batch of slaves
into the compound; the rest will be arriving during the
morning. It will be far more crowded soon so make the
best of this space.' He chuckled but no one joined him.
'Each main slaving day – again, you men are fortunate in
your timing – we hold a Grievance Council. It gives slaves
the opportunity to air their complaints to our city fathers.
Cipres has a code of conduct for caring for our slaves,
which begins with the conditions of capture. The city
fathers will hear all reasonable complaints and make a
judgement, which will be final. I'm sorry, just being
captured is not enough to warrant a hearing.'

He giggled but his attempt at humour was met with
stony silence and he quickly hurried on. 'Ahem . . . so,
do we have any official grievances? Please raise your hands.'

Tor was unable to understand most of Lard's speech
but Adongo quickly summarised it for him. The chieftain raised his hand in the air and Tor followed suit.

'Ah, right. Well, you men come over here. The rest of
you, if you would please remove your garments. The
buyers need to see all of what they're purchasing. Ahem
. . . warts and all.'

He giggled again and turned to Tor and Adongo, who
were flanked by Bluth and Beryd. Tor could see Haryd
making his way towards them.

'And you are?' Master Lard asked in Adongo's own
language.

'I am Adongo of the Moruks.'

'What is your grievance?'

'My captor, Haryd, killed my wife and two children though I offered to surrender myself without a fight.'

'Oh dear,' Master Lard tsk-tsked to himself. 'Well, that is indeed a gripe we must hear out. Yes, you may present to the city fathers. Please return to your place, remove your clothes and I will call you in due course. Thank you.' He smiled anxiously as Adongo turned to rejoin the group.

'My name is Torkyn Gynt,' Tor said amiably, trying to put the nervous man at ease. 'I am a physic from the Royal Court of Tallinor,' he lied, 'and I had paid transport on *The Wasp*, which sank during the great storm off the Exotic Isles. In saving myself and two others, I was captured by Haryd despite the fact that I was a guest on board his captain's ship and had paid good coin for my passage.'

Lard frowned. This was a set of circumstances he had not come across before. 'I see. And you say *The Wasp* sank?'

'Yes, sir, to the best of my knowledge. The captain was already dead. All the crew, bar the one who survived with me, died in the storm.' Tor stared into the little man's face. 'He was the cook,' he lied. 'An amazing young lad who works magic with food.'

'Really?' exclaimed Lard, impressed. 'Well, I can't think of anyone more important to survive a sinking ship,' he said, rubbing his ample stomach. 'The palace is seeking a new cook. What did you say his name was?'

'Ryk. He is descended from the famous Savyls of Ildagarth. He even worked in The Tapestry kitchens there.'

'Good grief, man, are you serious? Even we have heard of the great Savyl chefs of Ildagarth.'

'I am serious, sir.'

'Well, where is this cook of such impeccable blood-line?'

'You must ask Haryd, sir,' Tor said politely and pointed manacled hands towards the furious sailor approaching.

'What happens here, Master Lard?' Haryd bellowed.

Lard wobbled with fright. 'Haryd, is it? Er, good. Um . . . this man here has brought grievance against you, as has Adongo of the Moruks. I deem both complaints be heard by the city fathers. You have no objection, I trust?'

'None,' growled Haryd, staring hard at Tor. The look was a threat.

One of Lard's staff whispered into his master's ear and Haryd took advantage of Lard's attention being momentarily diverted. 'Just remember the boys, Gynt,' he said nastily.

'Master Lard,' Tor said.

The fat little man turned his attention back to them. 'Er, yes?'

'Didn't you want to speak with Haryd about the young cook, Ryk Savyl?'

'Yes, indeed. Sailor Haryd, would you be kind enough to have the lad brought to the palace immediately. We wish to discuss something with him.'

Haryd glared but nodded and ordered his men to make the arrangement straightaway.

'Oh and Haryd . . . er, sir,' Tor said politely. 'I'm not sure which other boy you were talking about.'

Haryd sneered. 'Quist's make-believe stepson, of course. He'll be sold in two shakes of a duck's tail, Gynt.'

'Not sure he's available, sir.' It was Tor's turn to smirk. 'May I be excused to undress, Master Lard?'

'Indeed you may,' the Master of the Market said, waving

Tor away. 'I shall call your name shortly but there is a change to today's schedule and I must inform these men about it.'

Haryd strode along the rows of slaves, searching for Locky. His face was a picture of rage. 'Where is he, Gynt?' he howled.

Tor shrugged. All the other men kept their eyes downcast.

Haryd suddenly looked terrified. How could the lad have escaped? What if the story was true? He had already found out that Quist was in town, staying at his favourite haunt. Gynt looked confident. Perhaps there was some truth to the story. If so, he was in serious trouble. Thoughts of escape flashed across his mind; he could leave the slaves and the proceeds of his other precious cargo and preserve his life, for surely Quist would not spare it. Just as he was considering how he might quietly make his way out of the compound, trumpets sounded. He saw that extra guards had manned the gates and were standing to attention. No one would be allowed to enter or leave this area without official permission now. He was trapped. What was going on? Master Lard's quavery voice enlightened him as he made a new announcement.

'I have just been informed that Queen Sylven is making her visit to the slave market much earlier than planned this morning. Since the market does not officially open until midday, we have only you men to present to her. Security is high so please refrain from making any sudden moves or calling out. Such behaviour will not be tolerated near our Queen. You will all kneel and place your foreheads to the ground until further orders. The Queen's carriage approaches. We are doubly honoured today by her majesty's decision to hear grievances on behalf of the Council and make judgement. Now, please kneel and remain silent.'

The naked group of slaves did as instructed. Tor's pale body stood out sharply amongst the swarthy skins of the Moruks. They remained with their heads to the ground for some time, hearing voices and the sounds of footsteps passing by – guards, no doubt. When they were finally bid to kneel upright again, they were confronted by a glorious carriage adorned with jewels, its sides covered with artful veils. They could not see beyond the billowing layers, though they guessed Queen Sylven sat behind them.

In fact, the Queen was lying on a bed of plump cushions, sharing a private joke with one of her senior handmaidens about how well hung that particular man at the front of the group was. She put her finger to her mouth to hush the servant from laughing too loudly, though her own eyes were filled with mirth. Then her attention was caught by the white man. She could not see his face, which was hidden from her line of view, but his chest was broad and muscled. It was rare to see a white man for sale. She would enjoy seeing him stand up naked, but she kept that thought to herself.

At that moment there came the noise of angry voices from outside the compound. She could see guardsmen moving towards the scene and her own head of the guard followed after, ordering his men to close in around her majesty.

Her own man returned with information. 'It is the captain of *The Raven,* your majesty. He is a good man. Fearsome but honest. He says he has a serious grievance to present which involves these sailors who are selling their slaves today.'

'I see. What is your recommendation, Klug?'

'Your majesty, he has brought us many fine things, this captain. The quality of his goods is normally exceptional and, to my knowledge, his prices are always fair. He is held in high regard by the Caradoons and feared by other pirates and slavers.'

'Then we can assume his grievance is justified?'

'Yes, your majesty. I would suggest that Captain Quist would be unlikely to bring any small claim into your esteemed presence.'

'Allow him in. I shall hear his grievance.'

'Very good, your majesty,' Klug said and, with a movement of his hand, indicated that Quist, three of his men and Locky were to be permitted entry to the compound.

Haryd felt his stomach turn.

Tor was not allowed to look around but guessed from Haryd's face what had occurred. He had to struggle not to smile. The three strode into view. Locky winked at him and Tor clapped eyes once again on the memorable patched face of Janus Quist.

'Watch him!' Quist said to his men, before moving to pay his respects to the Queen. His three men closed menacingly around Haryd, who was now dearly wishing he had never laid a finger on Locky. He did not even like boys. He preferred his sex with women, hard and rough, but he had felt desperate that night and his men had urged him on. They had been stuck on the island for weeks without word from *The Wasp* and had taken no women slaves during this time. The chieftains were getting clever, sending out scouts and putting their women and children into hiding before raids. Only this chief had refused to send his family away. And he had paid the ultimate price for that arrogance. Pity. The woman had been young and beautiful, as were the two girls. They would have made his nights far more pleasurable than the abusive lad had done. What could he do to find his way out of this situation?

Haryd watched Quist come to a halt before the Queen's sparkling coach.

Lard made his announcement. 'Her majesty Queen Sylven will now hear grievance. Would Adongo of the Moruks, Torkyn Gynt of Tallinor and Haryd of *The Wasp* please step forward.'

Naked but unabashed, Adongo and Tor walked side by side to where Lard pointed.

Inside her cocoon of veils, Sylven's attention was riveted on the tall white man. What a glorious specimen he was. As one might imagine a god, she fancied. She sat up to see him better. Not only was he fantastically handsome but his body matched his face . . . and, oh my, such arrogance. He was staring straight at her. She was not used to such behaviour but she rather liked his forthrightness, the fact that he was not cringing like Haryd. She marvelled at the incredible blue of his eyes and wondered, briefly, how it would feel to have him make love to her.

She dismissed the thought. Old Lardy was speaking again and she must pay attention.

'We will hear from Adongo of the Moruks.'

The tall chieftain stepped forward. He began to speak and his voice was deep and measured. She noticed that he wasted no words, showed no unnecessary emotion and held himself regally. He spoke perfect Ciprean which took everyone by surprise. 'My wife and two daughters, one of them not yet nine summers, were murdered by this slave trader, Haryd, your majesty. They were not taken as prisoners but summarily executed for no reason other than the pirate did not like the way I looked at him.' Adongo paused. It was effective. 'He dragged them in front of all our people, your majesty, and stabbed each in the heart. He kept the child until last, forcing her to witness her mother and elder sister dying horribly before her. But she was brave, your majesty, and would have made a fine elder of our tribe one day. She made no sound and gave no satisfaction to her killers. She turned to me with the knife in her chest and her lifeblood gushing over her dead mother, and spoke her final words: "Father, I was born in blood from Mother and now I die with her blood mingling with my own. Avenge us." She died quietly, your majesty.'

There was silence as Adongo's listeners, awestruck by his composure and calm delivery, took a moment to realise he had stopped speaking. Looking directly at Haryd, the chieftain added, 'There was no reason for their execution, your highness.'

Lard nodded, shocked by the horrific tale. 'Queen Sylven will consider your grievance once she has heard all the complaints. I call Torkyn Gynt.'

The white man stepped forward, all of his lean, muscled body now on direct show to the Queen.

Sylven, disturbed by the chieftain's story, was surprised and relieved to hear amusement in this man's voice. 'To be honest, Master Lard, although I do have a grievance, I just thought it would be worth my last moments as a free man to be this close to such a beautiful woman.'

Poor Master Lard nearly fainted at the audacity of the

comment. He was surprised to hear a deep gurgle of laughter from behind the veils.

'And how do you know of my beauty, Torkyn Gynt, when the Queen of Cipres never goes unveiled in public?'

Despite the barrier between them, he was staring directly at her with those arrogant blue eyes. 'Your majesty, your taste alone gives away your beauty. Your palace is the most breathtaking building I have seen, and I have travelled far and wide. Your city — what I could see of it from the slave cart — is exquisite and I would give anything to roam its streets. No, my lady, my guess is that your beauty is not only unrivalled in this Land . . . but anywhere in our world.' She could see his eyes glinting with wicked wit.

Tor turned back to Lard. 'Should I outline my grievance now, Master Lard?'

Lard could only nod.

Tor proceeded to tell his story again. When he had finished he bowed to the veils.

Lard responded. 'Er . . . her majesty Queen Sylven will consider. Um . . . Captain Quist, please.'

Janus Quist stepped forward. 'Your majesty, I claim grievance against Haryd of *The Wasp*. My young brother-in-law here,' he said, tapping Locky on the shoulder, 'was working his way across to Cipres aboard *The Wasp* to be with me. When it sank, he escaped with Physic Gynt but, together with Gynt and another of the ship's crew, was captured by Haryd and his men. He was used forcefully as a whore by Haryd and his men and raped repeatedly on the night of his capture. If the physic had not stepped in, I believe he would no longer be alive.'

'Thank you, Captain. Queen Sylven will consider.'

They all waited in silence for her command.

Sylven felt confounded to begin with. It appeared that all of these stories intertwined and led back to Haryd, who was clearly an unscrupulous brute. She took the time to work out how she could unravel their stories and come to a conclusion which would ensure all felt fairly done by. Her eyes rested on Torkyn Gynt. There was something about him which fascinated her and it went beyond his disarmingly handsome appearance.

Sylven motioned to her maidservant that she would now pronounce her decisions. The word was given and Master Lard went through the protocol of informing the audience to pay attention. The Queen spoke.

'Captain Quist, I believe the grievance truly rests with your brother-in-law. You must concede to him the demand for settlement of the complaint against Haryd. Such behaviour is intolerable, particularly as the boy was not fair game for slavers and his captors would have known this.'

Quist nodded his agreement.

'Yet I feel that Adongo of the Moruks has a greater right to grievance than the boy and so I award to him the first chance to best Haryd. If Haryd survives, he must face the grievance of your brother-in-law. However, to compensate you for waiting your turn, I award all proceeds of the sale of the slaves in this group to you. Meanwhile, your brother-in-law is free.'

'And Torkyn Gynt, your majesty?' asked Lard.

'He is not a slave. He is free to leave Cipres immediately.'

She noted Tor's face twitch. Was it with pleasure? She could not tell but she intended to find out.

'Adongo of the Moruks,' the Queen called.

The chieftain stepped forward.

'I cannot free you. You are a slave, owned now by the captain, and only he can free you. But I can offer you the chance to avenge the death of your loved ones. Will you fight?'

'Yes, your majesty, I will fight.'

'Then let the contest take place now, before the midday trading.'

The audience was over, though the Queen would remain at the marketplace to ensure her decrees were met.

Tor, Quist, his men and Locky gathered in a huddle around Adongo, whilst Beryd and Bluth allied themselves with Haryd. They looked nervous. If he failed, they would face a similar fate.

Locky introduced the captain to his friend. 'Tor, this is Janus Quist.'

Quist clasped Tor's hand in the Tallinese manner. 'Locky has told me all about you and your connection with Eryn. She has asked me to help you find what you seek. I am at your service. What is it I can do for you?'

Tor looked at the man who had threatened Saxon's life and stolen Cloot. He was not a man to be trifled with. There was no point in hedging.

'Do you remember stealing a falcon from a Kloek outside a stracca den in Caradoon?'

Quist pulled his hand away as if he had been stung and stared at Tor. His eyes narrowed. 'And what is it to you if I do?'

'I have come a long way to get the bird back. You stole it from me. It did not belong to the Kloek.'

Surprise registered in Quist's face but just then the

Queen's head guardsman called the proceedings to order.

'There is no time for this now,' Quist said. 'We shall talk later.'

'I'll be waiting,' Tor replied gravely.

They turned back to Adongo. He had tied a colourful loincloth around his waist.

Quist spoke first in clipped Ciprean. 'What is your choice?'

'Of what?' Adongo said calmly.

'Weapon, man! Did you think you were going to fight with fiddlesticks?'

Tor tried. 'Adongo, you chose to fight Haryd. Do you know how to fight?'

'I am not a fighter, Tor. I am Paladin; a protector.'

Quist shook his head and walked away, muttering about riddles.

'Adongo, you must choose a weapon. This is a fight to the death.'

'No weapon is required,' Adongo said. The man was truly frustrating.

'How will you defend yourself?' Tor's voice betrayed his concern.

'In the Moruk way,' was Adongo's final comment on the subject.

'Haryd of *The Wasp* chooses the cutlass,' the guardsman announced. 'And Adongo of the Moruks chooses . . .'

He stopped as he realised the man standing in the centre of the compound held nothing in his hands.

'Adongo of the Moruks, you must choose a weapon.'

The chieftain stood silently, looking every bit as regal as a king. His eyes were closed and his long, lean arms hung loosely at his sides. He ignored everyone.

Tor spoke to him via the link. *Remember your destiny — the young one whom you must help.*

My bonded one is almost here, Tor. I sense it.

Then you must not risk death. He could hardly put it any plainer.

I will survive. But Haryd will not die at my hand. Nor will he die at yours.

It was a veiled message. Adongo's charcoal-coloured eyes were open now and fixed firmly on Tor. He was warning him not to interfere with his powers or by any other means.

Tor shook his head; he felt helpless. Haryd was brandishing two cutlasses. He was barefoot now, wearing only breeches, no shirt.

'Fight!' called the guardsman.

Haryd began to circle the Moruk, swinging the blades in a menacing rhythm. He looked comfortable with them. Adongo still did not move; once again the eyes were closed in the lean face.

'What is he doing?' Locky groaned.

'We have to trust him,' was all Tor could think of to say. But it was of no comfort even to him.

Haryd continued his circling, trying to guess what the Moruk might do. However, he was not a man of patience or foresight. True to his impulsive character, he made a run at his enemy, screaming his intent, both weapons lifted high above his head.

Just as the pirate was a moment from striking Adongo down, the chieftain leapt astonishingly high into the air and somersaulted backwards. As he did so, he kicked and one of the cutlasses went flying. His other foot connected with his rushing opponent. Haryd hit the ground hard, his chin taking the brunt of the impact.

It was a terrible landing and the audience groaned at the sound of bone breaking. Adongo was almost back in the same spot and, frustratingly for Haryd, standing still again, his eyes closed, arms loose at his sides. He was breathing evenly, as though smelling the fragrance of blossom on the air.

'I'm not sure I just saw that,' Locky exclaimed.

Quist stood with his mouth open in awe.

Is that the Moruk way, then? Tor said.

It is, came the measured reply.

Haryd was back on his feet. He rubbed at his swelling jaw; one arm hung broken and useless. He moved the remaining cutlass to his other hand with purpose, ignoring the pain. Murder was written on his face. He said something in pidgin. The other slaves watching looked horrified.

What did he say? Tor asked.

It is very bad to curse a Moruk's mother, Adongo replied calmly.

Haryd was rushing forward again. Everyone held their breath.

This time Adongo fell low to the ground and with a deft movement swept Haryd's feet from under him. As the sailor crashed again to the dust, the Moruk leapt onto him, smashing into the low part of his spine, then lightly jumped away.

Haryd screamed in agony. It was brutal punishment. Several of the Queen's ladies looked away. Even Locky wished Adongo would hurry up and deal the killing blow, even though he dearly wanted that pleasure for himself.

But Adongo waited.

Haryd's breathing was horribly ragged now. He pulled

himself painfully to his knees and stared at his opponent, who had struck his by now familiar pose, eyes closed, arms loose.

This infuriated the sailor who, with one final blood-curdling bellow, hurled his cutlass directly at his opponent, barely steps away. Despite the terrible pain he was in, Haryd's throw was accurate and frighteningly fast.

Adongo caught the cutlass by the blade, eyes still closed. The reflex action brought rapturous applause. Anyone who had not witnessed this would never believe the tale. Not a drop of blood had been spilled by either party, though one of them was near dead.

The Moruk opened his eyes, tossed the cutlass to one side and leapt again. This time Haryd screamed for his life. Adongo landed neatly on the man's chest, crushing his ribs with a cracking sound that echoed throughout the compound. One of the ladies fainted.

It was enough.

Adongo bowed low to where Queen Sylven sat impressed behind her veils and then bowed to his men before rejoining them to sit in the dust.

The guardsman listened to Haryd's chest.

'He lives,' was all he said.

Lard nodded and spoke. 'Her majesty calls upon Locklyn Gylbyt.'

Locky ran to the Queen's carriage and fell to his knees. 'Your majesty.'

'Well, Locklyn, it seems you will have your revenge on this man. I, for one, am glad for you. What is your choice of punishment?'

'Queen Sylven, I choose that he ride the Silver Maiden.'

She was surprised. 'But you will have to wait for that

to be arranged. Why not a swift death by your own hand now, child? He is almost finished.'

'Your majesty, I will wait. A swift death is not enough for his sort. He needs to know fear and I have heard of this local custom.'

'It is a terrible death. I am assured a man dies a thousand times just imagining it. Are you aware of the entire custom of Cipres – that the person choosing this method must first take his chances with the Maiden himself?'

'I am.'

'Then you are the bravest of men. And I have no choice but to pronounce that your wish be decreed. Haryd of *The Wasp* will ride the Silver Maiden.'

17

A Royal Jest

Quist sipped his ale and eyed Tor, who was laughing with Locky while they chose from an exotic and unfamiliar array of food. The Queen had generously ordered that all the former prisoners be taken to the inn and fed properly at the city's expense before being offered passage home. But Quist was not interested in food right now.

This stranger, Gynt, who had his wife's energetic support, did not fear him as other men did. But then, why should Gynt fear him if he was not a pirate himself? No, if he was honest, it was not Gynt who bothered him so much as Eryn's friendship with him. In his years with Eryn, this was the first time Quist had felt threatened by another man. Eryn was a gorgeous woman, but she was also a former whore and now a brothel madam. Men were her business, but none of them had generated jealousy in his heart.

And yet this one's relationship with her hurt. A friend; that meant so much more than paid lover. Her message through Locky had been precise: *Please help him find what he seeks to the best of your abilities, no matter the expense, no*

*matter how much time it takes. Please also give him your full
protection.*

That was some request. Actually, it was more of an
order. She had not left any room for translation; her
meaning was plain. If he did not do as she asked, it would
be considered an insult to her – and that would never do,
for Janus Quist worshipped the very ground Eryn Quist
trod upon. He found it hard to tell her this, but a laugh
at one of his jests or a simple affectionate gesture could
please him for weeks.

He remembered the incident Tor spoke of very well.
Quist's memory was sharp at the best of times but his
recollection of the Kloek was very clear. He had even liked
the man. He had taken the falcon knowing it would fetch
a rare price. And it had.

How was he going to explain to Gynt that it simply
would not be possible to retrieve this creature? The bird
was gone and the proceeds now adorned Eryn's elegant neck.

Quist was a forthright man, known for his honesty. He
would tell Gynt how it was. Perhaps he could purchase
a new falcon for the man. It would be expensive but Light,
for Eryn's happiness, he would hang any expense, especially as his recent voyage had been so profitable.

'So,' Tor said, finally coming to join Quist at the small
table. 'Let us speak plainly. You must recall the falcon.
He is magnificent, I am sure no one could forget him.'

'I recall him.'

'I suppose it is too much to hope for that you may still
have him?'

'Yes.'

'You do still have him?' Tor was surprised. Could he
be that fortunate?

'No, I mean, yes, it is too much to hope. I'm sorry, Gynt.'

'So you've sold him. Please, tell me everything.'

Quist saw pain cross the stranger's face. His quest was real all right.

'I will. But first tell me, why is this hawk so special?'

'He's a falcon, Quist. We have been together for many years now. He is very special and he was given into my care. I must not forsake him.'

'I see.' Quist did not see anything. 'Can we not purchase a new falcon for you? I realise it will not make up for the years you had with the other one, but birds are easily trained; this new one would become a companion of equal stature.'

'No, you don't understand, Janus. He is more than that. I can't explain it. Please, just tell me everything.'

Quist sighed. 'We brought him ashore at Cipres one moon or so after leaving Caradoon. To be honest, I thought he might die on the voyage.' He saw Tor wince. 'He was very silent for a bird of that size. To my knowledge, he ate nothing at sea, but I think he liked being out on deck.'

'He was tied, of course,' Tor said.

The captain nodded. He could tell from Tor's tone of voice this was not going to be an easy conversation. Just the mention of the bird not eating made him look angry.

'We came ashore and, because he is what we call a "perishable", he was sold within a day of our arrival.'

'And to whom was he sold?'

'Well, you see, Physic Gynt, that's just it. I don't know. The bird was sold at market. He fetched a right good price but I don't go taking the names and lodgings of my buyers.'

'You cannot tell me that a peregrine falcon like Cloot is sold every day at market to the ordinary passer-by.'

'No. The man, who paid good coin, was a master falconer for sure.'

'Well, where would someone like that take Cloot?'

Quist shrugged. He could have saved Gynt all of this trouble. He really had no idea where to start trying to track down a falcon.

'Would you remember this man?'

'No. I did not sell the bird; one of my men did.' Now Quist saw grief flit across the physic's features. He had promised Eryn he would help but he was failing badly. 'Now look, Gynt, it's true I have no idea where your bird is, but you're right, there are not that many falconers around.'

'Where is your man? Why can't we start with him?'

'Ah . . .' was all Quist could say. He tugged at his eye-patch and then scratched at his beard.

Tor groaned. 'Tell me the bad news, Quist.'

'He died. He got involved in a boisterous game of dice, was accused of cheating and was murdered.' He shrugged apologetically. 'Though Basyl was a pirate, he never cheated at dice. They killed a good man.'

Tor nodded, as though resolved to his hopeless situation. 'Then we no longer have a score to settle, Janus Quist. Thank you for trying to help.'

Quist was unsettled by this sudden end to their conversation. 'No, wait, Gynt. I must offer recompense. It is more than my life is worth.' He smiled, then added, 'Eryn', and shrugged again.

Tor put his right hand on Quist's right shoulder, a Caradoon gesture for sealing friendship. 'You are a good man and she cherishes you. No, you owe me no debt. If I ever need your help, Captain Quist, may I call upon it? It may be a long time coming, but it could also be tomorrow.'

Quist returned the gesture and they stood facing one another, arms crossed in front of them and resting on the other's shoulders. 'Count on me any time you are in need,' he said and meant it. 'Good luck in your search. Where will you start?'

Tor smiled wryly. 'At the palace. I have an appointment to meet a powerful Queen.'

Tor was deeply concerned about Cloot. He had tried opening a link several times but it led nowhere; it was not dissimilar to the sensation he had felt when trying to reach Alyssa all those years ago. Alyssa had been blocked first by Merkhud and later by the archalyt. Tor wondered what could be blocking the falcon's powers. Of course, there was one simple explanation. He could be dead.

Cloot dead? No, it was unthinkable. Tor could not entertain such a frightening turn of events.

At that moment he felt the cold slice of a link opening in his head. It did not have Cloot's memorable signature. He recognised the magic of Adongo before the man even spoke.

So troubled you look, Adongo said quietly from his corner.

Tor turned towards him. *You don't seem so jolly either.*

It is time for me to leave.

Yes, I thought it might be. I am pleased Queen Sylven pardoned you.

Adongo nodded. *It was appropriate.*

So where now? Tor asked.

I search. I must find the one to whom I am bonded.

Will we meet again?
I feel sure of it. In that place you called the Heartwood.
Until then. Stay safe.

Adongo effected a farewell gesture; Tor responded in kind across the inn. He felt suddenly very alone and wished the tall Moruk could remain with him. It occurred to him to say so but Adongo was already crossing towards the door. He had obviously said his goodbyes to his men. He carried nothing in his hands. His brightly coloured robe was just a simple sheet of woven fabric wrapped expertly around his body, yet he looked like a king nevertheless. And then Adongo of the Moruks, Fifth of the Paladin, was gone.

Tor wondered if he would actually lay eyes on Queen Sylven at this meeting which she had requested the day after his release. It suited him to be summoned. Questions asked of various courtiers had led him to understand that the Queen admired birds of prey and kept a large team of handlers on her staff to look after her aviaries both here and at her winter palace in rural Cipres. It was a start. If Cloot had fetched such a high price, it was more than reasonable to suppose that he had been purchased for one of the royal aviaries.

Tor was led into a cavernous hall with exquisitely carved stone walls. It was very cool, almost cold in fact, due to the wintry chill which was beginning to descend upon Cipres. From this room high in one of the towers of the palace, he could look out over the beautiful city. Surprising himself after years of enjoying a hermit's existence, Tor believed he could live here and be happy. If it were not for the terrifying notion of Orlac breaking free, or Goth possibly being alive and still a threat to Alyssa, he might have asked the Queen for permission to settle in Cipres.

He smiled to himself as he peered out across the city. He would have liked to show Alyssa this place.

Tor tried to imagine what she might be doing this very minute. He knew Queen Nyria would never allow any harm to come to her and hopefully she had been given lodgings at the palace in Tal. Plus she had Saxon and Sallementro to watch over her. He reassured himself she was safe. Perhaps she was building a new life now? She would push the memories of his grisly death deep inside and she would triumph over that grief; he was sure of it. One day some other man would be incredibly fortunate to call her his wife. Tor grimaced . . . but she was *his* wife. Nevertheless, as far as she believed, her husband was dead and she was free to marry another. Could she ever love someone as much as she had loved him? Tor knew he could not love another woman so deeply. Still, that had not stopped him making passionate love to Eryn, had it? He should not begrudge Alyssa new love if she was fortunate enough to find it.

A servant tapped him gently on the shoulder and disturbed the path of his thoughts. Tor was glad to leave them; they were becoming too painful. The Queen's lady-in-waiting was a beautiful creature, tiny and dark of skin with a light, soft voice and wide smile. Light! How could he resist these gorgeous women? His musings on Alyssa were pushed back into a safe spot in his mind as Hela bid him follow her.

Guards pulled their frightening weapons aside to allow Tor and Hela to pass. They walked through numerous decorative and sumptuous rooms before climbing a flight of stairs, which Tor assumed would lead them into another tower. Tor had not thought it possible for anything to be more captivating than what he had already seen until they entered another suite of rooms. All the grandeur of the rest of the palace was left behind; these rooms were magnificent in their simplicity of colour and style. In her private living quarters, the Queen of Cipres had chosen to surround herself with uncluttered space. The walls of the reception room were adorned by a few beautiful paintings and one superb tapestry. It seemed darker up here but cleverly placed torches lit the room and wider arched windows let in plenty of light. The furnishings, although beautiful and sophisticated, were also practical and — as far as Tor could tell — chosen for comfort. A small, painted porcelain stove had been lit against the chill in the air.

'If you would wait here, Physic Gynt,' Hela said, softly.

She walked barefoot out of the room. Tor took the opportunity to look around but almost immediately a pair of great arched doors were opened from the inside. No guards in this area, Tor noted, though it was heavily secured outside.

Hela pulled back a set of heavy drapes and smiled. 'Queen Sylven will take audience with you now, sir.' She bowed politely to him, allowed him to pass and then closed the drapes and doors behind her as she left the room.

'Approach, Physic. Let me see you,' came a familiar voice; one used to giving commands.

Tor walked towards the voice. He saw the outline of a tall carved chair behind a fine curtain. He dropped to his knees and waited, sensing a practised eye casting over him. He realised he had shielded himself. Curious. The precaution must be habitual now.

'You may stand.'

He obeyed.

'And you are a real physic?'

'Yes, your highness. From Tal.'

'Ah, yes. I have only this morning received some troubling news from your capital.'

'I have been away from the city for many years, your majesty. I am not familiar with any of its tidings.'

'I see. Then you will be saddened to hear of the death of Queen Nyria,' she said.

Tor momentarily lost his composure. He was rocked by the casually spoken news and his face betrayed his shock.

'This information is disturbing for you, Gynt, I can see.'

'Madam . . . I . . .' He ran his hand through his hair. 'Queen Nyria was a wonderful woman. Was it her heart?'

'The communiqué did not specify details. As far as I can gather, she was thrown from a horse and died soon afterwards. Did you know her personally?'

Tor chewed his lip. 'Yes, your highness. I was Royal Physic to the King and Queen.'

The sovereign paused. 'Then I am deeply sorry, Torkyn Gynt, that I delivered these tidings to you so harshly. You obviously worked closely with the royal couple?'

'Especially with Queen Nyria, your majesty. But she was a fragile woman and I should not be surprised to hear this news. The Kingdom has surely lost one of its greatest treasures.'

The curtains opened and a young woman stepped out.

She was adorned in a jewel-encrusted gown with slippers to match. Her looks were similar to Hela's and her olive skin gleamed. She smiled to show teeth which were perfectly white, perfectly straight. Her lips and cheeks were coloured with rouge. The woman stepped towards him and spoke.

'I am sorry for you, Torkyn Gynt.' She laid long, elegant fingers on his arm.

Still fazed by the news, Tor did not immediately react to his own senses which spoke urgently to him.

'Come, sit with me. I wish to speak with you about happier things.'

Tor allowed the Queen to lead him to a beautifully carved window seat. 'Please,' she said gently and motioned for him to sit.

He did so but something nagged insistently at his mind.

'What business do you have in Cipres, Physic Gynt?' she asked, joining him on the window seat.

'Well, I . . . er, that is, I am in search of something.'

The feeling grew stronger. He looked closely at the woman sitting next to him. Her breasts were full and shown off to their very best effect by her low-cut gown, which itself was dazzling with precious stones sewn into the heavy fabric. Her perfume was rich and heady.

Why did he feel something was not right?

He dropped his shield and 'listened' as he liked to consider it. Then all his thoughts fell into place. He almost laughed.

'Your majesty,' he said, standing.

'Yes?'

'Oh, not you, my lady,' he said to the woman sitting

next to him in all her finery. 'I mean to address the real Queen Sylven, behind those artful veils.'

He heard a burst of delighted laughter and a clap of hands. This time her majesty, Queen Sylven, stepped out. She was not a young woman but Tor imagined every woman in Cipres would pale in comparison with her. Her natural olive complexion gleamed its health. She wore no false colouring bar the kohl that outlined her feline, almost black eyes which disclosed her exotic heritage. She was tall, much taller than the impostor, and devoid of jewellery. Her gown of rich cream revealed the flawless, polished skin of her neck and the tops of her arms but the rest of her body was modestly covered. Tor could not see her slippers but wondered if they matched her gown. Her hair was neatly pulled back into a thick single plait and he could see that it was still naturally black. She was utterly radiant and her height and slimness reminded him of Queen Nyria.

'How did you know?'

Tor smiled. 'That was a fine trick, your majesty,' he said.

'That is one of my favourite jests. Tell me how you knew,' she replied and quietly dismissed the jewel-encrusted impostor Queen with a nod.

'Well, if your state rooms are anything to judge by, then understated sophistication is your trait, your high-ness,' he said. 'I walked through fabulous halls and reception rooms on the way here and yet it was only when Hela brought me into your chambers that I realised I was seeing the true taste of Queen Sylven.'

'Go on,' she said, intrigued and amused.

Tor continued. 'Elegant and clean. Modest yet quietly

proud. Strong and practical. Devastatingly beautiful, a beauty which time cannot affect.'

Tor watched her smile at the last.

'I wish we had met when I was your age, Torkyn Gynt. I think I would have fallen in love with your easy charm.'

It was rare for Queen Sylven to lay open her thoughts in such a way but she found the man in front of her disarming in all respects.

'Age means nothing, your majesty,' Tor said and meant it. 'Queen Nyria, who was almost old enough to be your mother, possessed similar style and poise. Like you, she was a Queen in every aspect of her character. I cannot imagine you ever need to search for male companionship.'

This amused Sylven. 'My brothel is brimming.'

Tor's eyes widened. 'So it is true?'

She gave him a puzzled look and he continued. 'I heard a rumour many years ago that you kept a brothel. Is there no King of Cipres, or any likelihood of one?'

'Even if there were, I am sure you Tallinese could never understand that the royal brothel would not be disbanded.' She loved the look of confusion which swept across his face.

Sylven took his arm and guided him to sit down once again. He noticed that her hand was soft and unwrinkled. It was impossible to age this woman. She was certainly years Alyssa's senior, yet younger than Nyria. That would have to put her somewhere beyond thirty summers but before forty.

'Allow me to enlighten you about Ciprean royal tradition, Tor. May I call you Tor?'

He nodded. 'Of course.'

'Cipres has never been ruled by a man. As a consequence of tradition and centuries-old magic, the crown is always handed down to a woman. The Queen chooses her mate and, through secret powers of her own, ensures that a daughter is born. The lover is no longer required. The Princess becomes Queen at her rightful time. The Queen of Cipres has absolute power over all her subjects and she is taught to be magnanimous towards them; she is their protector and will see no harm come to her people. There are no poor in Cipres.'

Tor agreed. 'I can guess that from the homes I saw just briefly.'

'There are always less fortunate people, for many reasons. But we care for those who fall into trouble or despair. We give all our people the chance to better themselves. No child goes hungry. No one goes without lodging. All our people are educated. Our farms thrive.'

'We could all learn from the way of Cipres, your majesty.'

She nodded, knowing he meant this compliment. 'And, in return, the people give their absolute loyalty to the Queen.'

'Is there a Princess, your majesty?'

'Indeed there is. Her name is Sarel. She is presently but twelve summers. Still a girl, but her father was carefully chosen and Sarel will be a great Queen one day. For now though, I expect her to enjoy being a child.' She sighed. 'I fear my mother and grandmother never quite grasped the importance of being allowed to play and enjoy as normal a childhood as can be permitted for a royal.'

'You have great insight, Queen Sylven. I am sure that ensuring freedom for Sarel now will reward you in later years.'

'I hope so. She will have a vast and powerful realm to rule. She must have no regrets about her role.'

Tor looked wistfully from the window where they sat. 'I was thinking as I looked out over the city, your majesty, how I could easily fall in love with Cipres and live here.'

She looked surprised. 'But Tor, we would welcome you here with open arms. Physics are always in high demand.'

He shook his head. 'But I cannot, Queen Sylven. I have tasks ahead of me which I do not relish but which must be done.'

'I see,' she said. 'Well, I hope you will tell me more. Come, let us stroll the gardens together, and then why not join me for dinner?'

'I would be honoured,' he replied.

Much later that evening, while sipping sweet wine and munching on exotic fruits, Tor wished he really could forget the past and make a new life here. Sitting out on one of the many fine balconies of the Ciprean palace, shielded from the cool breeze by the tall, sentry-like trees and warmed by many braziers, he felt relaxed for possibly the first time in years.

He and Queen Sylven had spent the entire afternoon together and thoroughly enjoyed one another's companionship. Sylven possessed a sharp intelligence which Tor would have found attractive in any man or woman, and her wit was deeply engaging. He was in no hurry for the evening to end.

The feeling appeared to be mutual as Sylven ordered another jug of wine to be brought out to them. Tor stretched languidly and once again felt an appreciative glance sweep over him.

'You never did tell me how you worked out my fine trick.'

Tor knew it was dangerous to tell anyone of his powers, but his instincts told him there was no threat here, only friendship.

He took the risk. 'I am sentient, your majesty.'

She was pouring him another goblet of the sweet wine but stopped. His comment had obviously taken her by surprise.

'You jest, of course?'

'No, Sylven. It's true that I did make some crucial observations,' he grinned at her open mouth, 'but, in all honesty, I relied on my ability to sniff out magic. Congratulations, it is a fine trick.'

He took his half-filled goblet from her long fingers.

'Prove it!' she demanded, her eyes glinting with high amusement.

'Tell me how and I shall do it.'

'All right.' She closed her eyes. 'What am I thinking?'

Tor cast. He caught the thought and laughed. 'I'm not going to repeat it out loud but I shall be delighted to do that to you.'

Sylven shrieked. She was deliciously excited now. 'That's just you teasing. You couldn't know what I was thinking, you wretch.'

Tor was enjoying himself. It had been a long time since he had used his power for fun. The last occasion was as a child, when he had done whatever he could to amuse Alyssa and hear that wonderful laugh of hers. When Sylven laughed it was not dissimilar to the undisguised mirth of the young Alyssa and he enjoyed the gentle reminder of the woman he adored but could not have.

'No,' the Queen said shaking her head, 'you will have to do something much more dramatic.'

Tor dragged his mind away from Alyssa and back to the present. While he was thinking, the jug Sylven had ordered arrived and was put down in front of them.

The Queen was quick to dismiss her servant. 'Thank you. We wish for privacy now.'

'Yes, your majesty,' the servant whispered and discreetly disappeared.

'We are alone, Tor, show off your magic!' she commanded.

He decided to perform a trick which had terrified Merkhud but which he knew would thrill Sylven. In the blink of an eye, Tor disappeared. The Queen screamed with delight.

'Shh!' Tor warned, reappearing immediately. 'You'll have them running from all corners. They'll chop my head off before I have time to explain.'

Sylven's perfectly manicured hands covered her mouth but her eyes betrayed her excitement, and her complete disbelief at what she had just witnessed. 'What else can you do?' she whispered.

Tor shook his head. 'I am not a performing animal, your majesty. I have sentient ability; that's it. I can . . .' he searched for the words, 'sense things.' He did not feel it appropriate to explain the full breadth of his powers. 'And you, your highness, how far do your powers extend?'

'Tor, if I could do what you just did, I would be the most powerful sovereign of all the lands in all the world. I still cannot believe you did that,' she said, shaking her head.

'Your majesty, may I request that this be kept private

between us? I am not in the habit of boasting about my power.'

She grinned. 'Only to sovereigns?'

'No,' Tor said, leaning across and taking her hand. 'Not to just any sovereign, only indescribably beautiful ones.'

'You will stay the night with me, Torkyn Gynt. I should like to see in which other ways you can use this mighty power.'

If it had not been for the cushioning barrier of trees, the Cipreans would have heard their Queen's and her guest's laughter almost as far away as the city's centre.

18

Kiss of the Silver Maiden

When Tor awoke between Sylven's silk sheets, the Queen's side of the bed was cool. She had obviously arisen some time ago. He blinked and rolled over to stare through the doors leading onto her private balcony. It was beautifully cool and silent out there. The sun was not yet high and the colours outside looked watery and dreamy. He had slept long and deeply; the sleep of total relaxation.

Tor recalled the pleasure of the previous night and how much they had enjoyed the erotic finale to a grand day in one another's company. Sylven looked nothing like Alyssa but all the same she reminded him so much of his wife. Her joy in life and infectious sense of humour had consumed him and his years of grief and loneliness had been released during a passionate exchange. Sylven enjoyed men and she was certainly not shy about showing him how to please her.

Tor must have drifted off briefly again because this time he opened his eyes to the sound of quiet voices on the balcony. It was Sylven talking with one of her maids. He wrapped a linen around himself and stepped through the doors. Neither of the women were embarrassed by his semi-nakedness; the maid even looked appraisingly at his body.

The Queen made a sound of disapproval. 'Tor, you'll catch your death out here. Hela, fetch a wrap, please.'

Hela departed and was back in a blink with a beautifully weaved cloth of the finest wool. It looked light in her hands but once Tor threw it around himself, he marvelled at the instant warmth.

Sylven grinned. 'Galinga goat. Very precious, very rare.'

Hela put a steaming mug of chicana in Tor's hand and he raised it to his lips. It tasted amazingly good.

'And very expensive, no doubt,' he said, bending to kiss Sylven's hair.

The Queen accepted his affection and proceeded to sign some paperwork. While she read, Tor quietly sat himself down to inhale the crisp morning air. It was perfumed by the exotic flowers from the palace gardens he had explored the previous day. He felt comfortable and serene. He sipped his chicana and turned to watch Sylven.

The Queen knew his eyes were on her but did not look up. 'I do not enjoy the formal part of running a Kingdom, you know. I love getting out and being with my people but I despise all these papers and signings and treaties and . . .'

Sylven stopped at Tor's chuckle. 'It's a lot of work,' she admonished, reaching for a sugar-encrusted pastry.

Tor helped himself to one of the delicacies as well. 'I realise this,' he said, taking a bite. 'I'm laughing because you sound exactly like King Lorys of Tallinor. Oh, this is good.' He took another huge chunk.

'Really?'

He struggled to get the words out of his pastry-filled mouth. 'Yes, absolutely delicious.'

She shook her head. 'No, I mean about King Lorys! Tell me about him. I hear he's handsome and – forgive how callous this sounds – but he must also be very eligible now.'

Tor nodded thoughtfully. 'Yes, I suppose he is. Lorys is a good-looking man. Perhaps not as tall as you, your majesty, but he carries his kingliness with great nobility. He possesses a sharp mind and great wit, loves to hunt and race, adores his people . . . and complains incessantly about paperwork.'

The Queen smiled. 'I know how he feels. And is he true, Tor?'

'True?'

'Faithful.'

'Your majesty, I cannot answer that,' Tor replied, remembering how Lorys had looked at Alyssa the first time he set eyes on her. It had been a look of raw desire. 'He is a man, after all.'

'Indeed,' she said cryptically. 'Do you think he will re-marry?'

Tor finished his pastry and licked the sugar flakes from his lips. 'Now that question is beyond me. He is young enough at fifty summers. Finding a woman who would match him as well as Nyria would be a difficult task though.'

'Why? Surely there must be plenty of nobles only too happy to marry off their youngest and prettiest to become Queen of Tallinor?'

'Light, yes! But knowing Lorys as I do, or did a few years ago, I think he would prefer an unknown. A girl who would hold some mystery for the other courtiers. You know, I think he'd sooner fall in love with a girl from one of his tiny villages than a worldly city sort. Lorys and Nyria, as I understand it, were childhood sweethearts,' Tor added wistfully, almost as though thinking aloud.

'Have you ever loved anyone like that, Tor? I mean, friends first, true lovers later?' Sylven suddenly asked.

He did not want to answer this question and yet Sylven's directness demanded reciprocal honesty from him. 'I have.'

'Ooh,' she said, grabbing another pastry, loving the intrigue.

'I still do,' he said very quietly.

'I heard that! You still do! Who is she?'

Sylven noticed Tor's discomfort. He was being very honest with her; she liked this in him. Tor had intrigued her from the first moment she saw him and his combination of sophistication and naivety, strength and gentleness, arrogance and humility fascinated her. One moment he was a small, lost boy and the other a brave man who appeared to carry a great weight on his shoulders. And now he was revealing a long-lost love! It fitted him perfectly: the man who loved the woman he could never have.

'Is she not yours, Tor?'

'She will always be mine,' he replied, sadly. 'We just can't be together.'

'Why?'

'Oh . . . circumstances.'

Sylven was not to be put off by his evasiveness. 'Where is she?'

'Tal.'

'But she's not from the city, I'm guessing?'

He snorted. 'No. Alyssa is from a little place called Mallee Marsh; a more simple and uneventful village you will not find, Sylven.'

'And I'm also guessing that she's pretty beyond words?'

He summoned the face he loved. 'Golden hair. Green-grey eyes. Honeyed skin. Petite, funny, intelligent; she's just . . . adorable.'

'Now I'm jealous,' Sylven pouted.

'Don't be.' Tor smiled. 'You remind me of her in a curious way.'

'Thank you. I do believe that's a fine compliment. Oh, you know what?' Sylven's eyes lit with a wicked idea. 'I've just had a brilliant thought. Lorys and Alyssa.'

She watched Tor pull a face as she finished her pastry. 'I don't think so,' he said firmly.

She dusted the sugar from her fingers. 'Why not? She is all the things you described the King of Tallinor would want. A girl with no past – well, a past that the courtiers have had no involvement with. She is Tallinese and from a village – she is poor, I take it?'

Tor nodded.

'She's adorable – you said it yourself – and you also described someone who is very easy on the eye and clever. I think they make a perfect match. King Lorys and Queen Alyssa.'

Sylven raised her cup in a mock toast.

'I can't drink to that, your majesty. Alyssa despises the King. She hates him more than a true enemy of the realm could. She would never marry the King of Tallinor.'

'Every girl dreams of being Queen, Tor.'

'Not this one.'

Sylven was thoroughly enjoying this conversation and how it was unsettling Tor.

'Why would she hate a King whom you yourself have just described as almost perfect? What could he possibly have done to make a village girl hate him so much?'

There was a long and uncomfortable pause. Sylven wondered if she had pushed too far.

'He took me away from her, your majesty,' Tor said finally, his face no longer showing any sign of amusement.

Before she could reply, the city's bells began to toll. They both put down their mugs and moved to the edge of the concealed balcony. Sylven was glad the bells had saved them from wherever their discussion was going and was relieved to see Tor had lost that defensive look.

'Those bells sound urgent,' he commented.

'They sound death,' she replied.

He looked at her, puzzled. The Queen moved nearer and he put his arm around her and pulled her close. She enjoyed the sensation. Usually she banished lovers from her harem within minutes of performing their duties. She could not bear them hanging around or, worse, falling in love with her. They were servants, that's all.

Torkyn Gynt was different.

She had desired him from the outset; now she was discovering that she wanted his affections, not just his urgent lovemaking. Sylven wanted more of this man; all of him!

'Your friend, Locky,' she said and Tor nodded. 'He has demanded that the sailor, Haryd, undergo the Kiss of the Silver Maiden.'

'Yes. I did not understand it at the time, but there was so much going on with Adongo and then all his people being released that I forgot to find out more.'

Oh dear, she thought. Then this will not be easy for you to hear.

'The bells are tolling the Day Wait.'

'I don't know this custom, Sylven – I don't know any Ciprean customs.'

The Queen guided him back from the balcony to their comfortable seats near the small braziers.

'Kissing the Silver Maiden is the worst punishment in Ciprean law. It is a horrible death if it occurs, but the Maiden is not choosy about her victims. She kills innocents as well.'

Tor shrugged. 'I'm making no sense of this.'

'The Silver Maiden alone chooses who she will kiss and who she will not. Her kiss, when she delivers it, slices her victim in two, from head to toe.'

Tor looked pleased. 'I can't think of anything more suitable for Haryd.'

'No, wait, Tor. He who calls for this punishment must first risk the Kiss of the Silver Maiden himself. If she spares him, he is deemed truly aggrieved and the person who caused him grievance must then face her wrath.'

Tor looked stunned and a little confused.

She hurried on. 'Yes, I know what your next question will be. Let me answer it now. The Maiden has a complex series of locks which open and close at random. They allow the blade to pass through or not. The choice is hers alone.'

Now he looked aghast. 'You mean it's all down to chance? Locky is playing dice with his life?'

'Yes, you could say that. Which *is* why the Silver Maiden is so rarely called upon for her affection. Most who are aggrieved go for the simple sword thrust or a

flogging, depending on their level of grievance. But if
you wish to call for the highest punishment in the Land
and the most terrifying for your victim, then there is a
price to pay.'

'But what are his chances?'

'Slim,' she replied. Honesty was best. 'We do not tamper
with the Maiden. She has her own Keeper and he is a Queen's
man. I trust him completely. The Maiden in her past two
outings has not executed anyone. That is four people she
has spared. She is hungry for a kill now, I imagine.'

'Your majesty, with the greatest of respect, you cannot
allow this. Locky is still a boy.'

'A boy making a man's decision, Tor. He insisted. I
cannot refuse him; his grievance must be honoured. This
is Ciprean law.'

Tor looked angry now. 'When does this barbaric event
take place?'

Sylven ignored his intended insult. 'In a few hours,
hence the bells. Lorke needed some time to set up the
Maiden in the city's amphitheatre. Her blade had to be
sharpened and the locks oiled—'

'I don't want to hear any more of this,' Tor said, beginning to pace. 'This is terrible. What will I tell Eryn?' he
muttered.

'Who is Eryn?'

'Locky's sister. I am supposed to look out for him.'

'Tor, this is Locky's decision. Not yours. Not his sister's.
Even Captain Quist is abiding by the law.'

'Yes, it's easy when it's not your own flesh and blood.
Quist is married to Eryn; he is Locky's brother-in-law,
though he acts like the father Locky never had. Eryn will
never forgive her husband. Never!'

'Tor, you are ranting. You will just have to hope that the Maiden is kind. There is nothing you can do.'

'I will not stand by and watch your Maiden split Locklyn Gylbyt in half.'

His veiled threat was not lost on the Queen. 'If you use your magic, Tor – and that's still a secret between us – I will have no choice but to declare it. We in Cipres are more understanding than your own kind, but we do not tolerate use of magic openly.'

'I must follow my heart, your majesty,' he said, standing to leave.

'And I must follow the laws of my realm.'

'Is there a law against magic?'

'It must only be wielded by the Queen for her daughter,' she said sharply.

'Then perhaps I might have to taste the Maiden's Kiss myself, your highness. And it will be at your command.' He bowed slowly. 'I should leave now.'

'Yes, I think you should,' she said sadly and watched him dress and leave her chambers in silence.

Sylven was not surprised when, a few minutes later, the other recently arrived stranger was brought in by Hela.

'Your highness.' The man bowed low.

Obviously used to being in royal company, Sylven thought. 'I was expecting you,' she said.

'You have welcomed me into your palace, your majesty. I feel it is important that I pass on to you my experience of Tallinese life, as you have asked.'

'Indeed,' she said in her dry way, which could mean anything.

The stranger was not deterred. 'Queen Sylven, I must warn you against this man.'

'You mean Gynt? Why? You said not only yesterday that I would find it interesting should I invite him to the palace.'

Goth gave a short nod, almost a bow, to her accuracy. 'This is true. When you told me of his presence at the slave markets, I could not believe it was the same man. Suffice to say, I consider him dangerous. Trouble follows him, your highness.'

As this rather detestable, arrogant man grovelled before her, Sylven wondered if he knew of Tor's powers. She considered it unlikely. No, there was something more than that here; jealousy, perhaps.

'You were both at the Tal palace together, I presume?'

'You are correct.' The man attempted a smile but it appeared on his face as a sneer.

'But he is charming; most diverting, in fact.' Sylven enjoyed seeing his face twitch at that comment, not that the wretched fellow seemed to have much control over his ever-moving features.

His black eyes hardened. 'I would advise you not to permit him in the palace again, your highness. I wish that you would allow me to deal with him for you, perhaps with a small number of your guard,' he said.

'Deal with him?'

'Remove him, your highness,' he clarified.

'From Cipres or from life?'

'Whatever your majesty desires, I would be very happy to carry it out. I owe you my life, Queen Sylven. It is a debt I could spend the rest of it repaying.'

He had been in the palace for only a few days, since

his rescue, and already she despised his obsequious manner. She did not trust him one bit, but her mother had taught her always to listen, no matter who was giving the information. All she knew of Goth was that he was the former Chief Inquisitor of Tallinor who had fled when the Inquisitors had been disbanded. He had feared for his life, apparently. He too had been on the ship, *The Wasp*, which was wrecked off one of the small islands, but had not realised that others had also survived. Goth had said he had spoken only to the captain and the ship's boy, Ryk, during the voyage.

He had been shocked to learn that Torkyn Gynt had also been aboard *The Wasp* and was now in Cipres. He seemed to know a great deal about Gynt, though Sylven could tell Goth did not like him. He tried to hide it behind his clever words but Sylven was a woman who read deeply into people's eyes. She had inherited her mother's clever intuition for people and she could tell Goth was a dangerous man. No, she decided, she could not trust him, for beneath the polite, sycophantic surface there boiled something cruel and unforgiving.

It was Goth who had suggested she invite Gynt to the palace, advising her that it might prove interesting. He had not counted on her spending the night with him, of course, but then neither had she. Disapproval was written all over his pock-marked face and Sylven presumed some of the maids' tongues had been wagging. How else could Goth know of Tor's stay? His opinion did not trouble her, however; she was more interested in the former Chief Inquisitor's relationship with her guest.

They had not had the opportunity yet to discuss at length his knowledge of Gynt, though she fully intended to exploit it now. Once again, she wondered if Goth knew of Tor's magic.

What was the relationship between the two men? Was it jealousy for the affections of a woman, she wondered? Perhaps Alyssa? Surely not. The pretty Alyssa and the impossibly handsome Gynt were a perfect match. Why would any girl who had enjoyed Tor as a lover consider Goth? No, it could not be that. Anyway, Goth gave the impression of being celibate, eunuch-like even. He had made no improper advances to her female staff – or male staff, for that matter – nor had he visited any brothels during his few days in Cipres. So sex clearly was not his bent and she dismissed the idea that he might be jealous of the love between Tor and Alyssa.

Goth was watching her carefully. His eye twitched incessantly and when he licked his lips once again she had to look away. She could not bear to have him near for long; she dismissed him. She was not ready to listen to his ideas. He was very disappointed but tried to hide it and left quickly.

Sylven knew the day was going to be a difficult one. It had already started badly. She was angry at Tor's disobedience and his veiled threat to flout her laws. On the other hand, she found herself attracted even more strongly to that arrogant side of him. He feared no one; not even her. Now here was a man she could love.

Love? She had never thought she would fall in love with any man. Oh, she had entertained such thoughts when she was young but she had been trained well. She was to be the powerful Queen of a powerful nation. No man would ever rule it. There would be no husband; she would never be allowed to fall in love. Her mother and her grandmother, whilst still alive, had gone to great pains to assemble the finest harem for their Princess so that she would have dozens and dozens of men at her beck and call. The harem was to be constantly 'refreshed' with new faces so the young Queen-to-be would be kept interested and not become too close to any individual.

It had worked. Sylven had taken so many lovers over the years that falling in love seemed out of the question. Now, at forty summers, she found it amusing that she might have discovered love . . . and with a Tallinese! Torkyn Gynt *was* irresistible. Charm, beautiful looks and physique aside, he was fascinating. He matched her own brilliant mind and she imagined that she could never tire of his intelligence. And his magic powers astounded her. She could spend a lifetime being intrigued by those alone.

Sylven shook her head clear of such thoughts. Torkyn Gynt had just walked out on her!

Tor was furious. How could this whole thing have got so out of hand? Locky could have called for any punishment, from flogging to beheading, but no, he had to choose the one method which risked his own life as well. Now his quest to find Cloot had been set back even further.

Foolish! Foolish! Tor ranted to himself as he stomped back across the city towards the inn Quist favoured. Suddenly Cipres didn't seem so gentle of colour and beautiful to behold; it looked bright and dangerous. The stand-off between Sylven and himself did not help his humour either. He strode into the inn and demanded to know whether Captain Quist was up.

'Up and gone,' one of the serving lads said.

Tor left. Where should he go next? He made for the

docks. A captain liked to be near his ship, he decided. His hunch was right: he found Quist and his men preparing *The Raven* for departure.

'Quist!'

The captain looked over the rail. He waved to Tor but his face was grim. Tor ran up the gangplank.

The captain met him. 'You've obviously heard then?'

'How could you let him do such a thing?' Tor spat.

Quist's own anger kindled quickly. 'Are you mad, Gynt? Do you think I would have agreed to this? He told me he had requested a public flogging and then starvation in the cage. I knew nothing of this Silver Maiden until this morning when I had to sign some paper or other. I refused of course but the officials could not care less. Apparently it was simply a formality; the boy's choice remains. I am helpless,' he snarled back.

Tor would not be put off. 'So you are leaving, running away?'

Quist's voice was icy. 'I am readying my ship, Gynt. We were departing tomorrow anyway. I have to get home to Eryn. I may be carrying a body in my hold back to her. Do you think I look forward to this?'

Tor could not help himself. His frustration at Sylven's casual attitude and placating words turned to anger which he now directed at Quist. 'I'm surprised you have the courage to face her after this.'

It was too much for the pirate; he turned and hurled a punch. Tor's reaction was faster and he threw up his shields. Quist watched in surprise as his fist slid away through the air, twisting his own body full circle with the force. But he did not stop to wonder; instead he charged forward, head aiming straight for Tor's belly. The blow was meant to wind and hurt but did nothing of the kind. Quist found himself running into a barrier as hard as stone and he dropped unconscious to the deck of his ship. As he lay there lifeless, Tor bent to check how badly hurt he was. It was not serious: the captain would soon come around. No doubt he would feel somewhat dazed and confused, but he would survive.

Fortunately for Tor, no one had seen this furious exchange, for Quist had sent his men off on errands just as Tor was making his way up the gangplank. But now the men arrived back from their various tasks and spotted their captain slumped on the deck.

'What happened?' one cried, hurrying forward.

'He collapsed,' Tor lied. 'Let's get him to his cabin. I'm a physic and can help.'

Quist was carried to his chambers and laid on his bunk. Tor reassured the men that he would call them as soon as he had performed a physical examination. One especially persistent fellow he sent off to find some fresh water. It bought him the precious time he needed.

The captain slowly began to come to. Tor administered some arraq from the satchel he now habitually carried with him.

Quist's eyes opened. 'My head hurts,' he groaned.

'Here, sip some more of this,' Tor said, offering the vial containing the rapidly dwindling liquid. Quist did as he was told and made the effort to sit up.

The sailor arrived back, breathing hard, with fresh water in a jug.

'Dismiss your man; we must talk,' Tor muttered under his breath.

'Lurg, I'm fine now. Finish off your duties.'

Lurg looked edgy. 'Are you sure, Captain? You look right pasty to me, sir.'

'I'll be fine. Just a headache. I felt dizzy and stumbled.'

'Righto, Captain, sir. Call me if you need anything,' Lurg said, before closing the door.

Quist fixed Tor with a baleful stare from his one good eye. 'Now what exactly happened up there?'

Tor sighed. 'I'm sentient, Quist. I used my magic on you.'

'Aren't you the lucky one?' Quist replied, rubbing at his temple. 'Actually I feel better. That stuff is good, physic.'

'So people tell me.' Tor grinned. 'I'm sorry for hurting you.'

Quist shrugged. 'I would have hurt you, otherwise. I've survived worse.'

'Are you bothered that I am sentient?'

'No, but it seems you are. I heard that Tallinor had abolished the Inquisitors. Yet you are obviously still nervous.'

'You never know how people may react. I don't broadcast it.'

'Neither will I,' Quist said. He pushed his feet over the edge of his bunk and groaned. 'I would like such skills myself,' he added. 'So, Gynt. Can we use this talent of yours to save Locky?'

'It's my intention but the Queen has forbidden it. She knows, you see.'

'Do you talk in your sleep then?' Quist began to laugh.

Tor felt himself go red. 'Does everyone know?'

'They're all quite proud of you. I certainly am. Never

did get the opportunity to sleep with a real Queen myself, though I have my princess waiting back home.'

'You really love her,' Tor said, inadvertently thinking out loud.

Quist looked at him in surprise. 'Yes, Gynt, I really do. Why do you find that difficult to understand?'

Tor shuffled, uncomfortable about the fact he had lain in Eryn's arms just days ago. 'I don't find it difficult. I am incredibly fond of Eryn and always felt she deserved the true love of one man. And now she has it. I'm happy for you both.'

Quist grunted. 'She won't love me too much if I return with her brother's corpse.'

'No. Well, you'll have to trust me, Quist. I promise you I will not allow a hair on Locky's head to be hurt.'

'You're all we have then, because the lad's under very tight supervision. I'm not even allowed to talk with him. Not that he cares. He is driven by revenge and is not old or wise enough to know there are different ways to get even.'

Tor nodded. 'I'm going to the city square now. It's time for me to meet this fair Maiden.'

'I'll be right behind you. Just a few more things to sort out here. We leave tomorrow morning. You're welcome to come back to Caradoon with us.'

'I'm grateful, but I still have to find my falcon.'

Tor headed back into the city centre towards the amphitheatre. He felt brighter. He knew his powers could easily overcome the Maiden's locks, no matter how complex they may be. But he was still wondering what to do next about Cloot. Without Sylven to open doors for him, he had a mighty task ahead in tracking down a bird which no longer communicated with him. The region was dotted with dozens and dozens of tiny islands and Cloot could be on any one of them.

Again Tor wondered about the silence. He felt sure that if Cloot had died, he would have sensed it. Instead, the link between them was blank. Could it be the archalyt again? It had been a thin green sliver of the magical stone which kept him separated from Alyssa initially, and then the physical distance between them had maintained that barrier. However, the archalyt had started to lose its potency the closer he got to her location and by the time he had arrived at the Academie, even Alyssa had been able to sense him casting to her, albeit very weakly.

Now that he knew what the archalyt felt like, he could overcome it with ease. But he had tried this with Cloot and he could sense no archalyt barrier at all, certainly not one he had encountered before. Nevertheless, Tor maintained a permanent open link to his falcon . . . just in case. Cloot might be trying desperately to reach him and if the link remained open, something may just get through.

He felt suddenly melancholy at the bleakness of his situation. Cloot was lost, Locky was facing death, Nyria was already dead, and he had just had an argument with Queen Sylven. Inevitably, his thoughts turned to his greatest loss of all: Alyssa. But Tor was determined not to sink into feeling sorry for himself; instead he worked at conjuring a positive mood.

He recalled that Lys had told him the children were on the way. So Yargo had found them. He felt a surge of hope just thinking about the children and as he walked along the pretty streets of Cipres, he began to daydream about his son and daughter. It was a luxury he had not once allowed himself since Sorrel had fled the Heartwood with her precious charges.

They must be about five summers by now, he decided, and tried to imagine how they might look. Gidyon had been dark at birth so perhaps he resembled Tor. Lauryn was likely fair like her mother, although she had been bald when born so it was anyone's guess really.

He realised that thinking about the tiny, bald baby girl must have caused him to smile, for a woman walking towards him smiled back. The thought of the children's arrival made him all the more determined. He had to hurry and find Cloot and then get back to Tallinor. He presumed Sorrel would bring the little ones to the Heartwood for safety. Damn Sylven and her aviaries and damn Locklyn Gylbyt and his wounded pride – he did not need any extra troubles to keep him from his quest.

Tor pulled up sharply as he came into sight of Cipres' main square. It was a mass of humanity and activity, but he only had eyes for the amphitheatre just beyond, where a huge contraption towered above all the people. The Maiden winked her welcome at him as a watery ray of winter sun broke through gathering clouds and glinted off the vicious blade.

'And to you, Maiden,' he said under his breath, looking at the machine with awe.

Tor climbed up into the beautifully carved stone tiered seating to watch the preparations. One man – he assumed he must be the Queen's man, Lorke – was giving directions to a dozen others. Tor softened down the noise of the city about him and cleared his head to listen.

'. . . just a boy. The Maiden is parched for blood. I don't want the boy's blood on her lips or my conscience,' Lorke griped to a soldier.

'It is the Queen's judgement,' the man hissed.

'Yes, and it's because of her I'll obey,' Lorke grumbled, banging a final wooden pin into place on the Maiden's framework.

'Are you set?'

'We will be before the Fourth bell.'

'The aggrieved and the prisoner will be brought in at the Sixth. Her Majesty will arrive at the Seventh—'

'I know, I know. I'm the one who has been doing this for the past two decades, you fool. And the first kiss will occur on the stroke of the Eighth – I am well aware of the proceedings.'

'Good. Then stop your moping and do your job. I must report back to the palace. By the way, if a tall stranger who goes by the name of Torkyn Gynt approaches, do not involve yourself in conversation. Queen's orders.'

So, Tor thought, Sylven was taking precautions. He could not blame her. He should not have been quite so fast to boast of his powers. Merkhud's voice came back to haunt him as he sat and watched the final preparation for the Maiden's Kiss. As far back as when Tor was fifteen summers, the old man had warned him never to show-case his talents, always to keep them secret. He could not help but smile wryly; it had taken him barely a day or more to break that promise. By the time he had reached Hatten he was using his power with abandon, first to punch a bully in the belly and then minutes later to assist poor Cloot who was nailed to a post by his ear. Merkhud's warning had fallen on deaf ears then and clearly still did,

Tor decided. Just a little playfulness from the Queen and he had demonstrated his magics like a sideshow practitioner.

Tor shook his head at himself and his poor judgement. He looked up to see that the amphitheatre was gradually filling. There had to be a hundred more people milling around now than there had been just a short time ago and they were being joined by hundreds more, streaming in from the main city square.

A small man seated nearby caught Tor's eye as he looked around. The dwarf grinned at him and his grizzled face looked as though it was lit by sunshine. What a difference a smile makes to this fellow, Tor thought.

'Have you ever been to one of these before?' the stranger asked.

Tor nodded. 'To an execution? Yes. But I have not seen the Maiden before today.'

'Ah,' his companion replied carefully. 'This place will be very crowded soon. It is not often the Cipreans have the opportunity to witness the Maiden's Kiss.'

'So I gather,' Tor said. 'Are you a local?'

'No. My people come from a place so far away that you will see only a few of us wandering these lands.'

'Who are your people?'

Before the little man could answer, Tor felt a jolt on his shoulder and, turning, saw he had been joined by Quist and some of his crew. Tor looked back at his neighbour but the little man had moved on a few rows. Tor shrugged his shoulders to indicate he was sorry that their conversation had been interrupted. The little man from a faraway land smiled radiantly again and returned the shrug, accepting the apology.

'So what now?' Quist asked, dragging Tor's attention back.

'We wait. I shall make my move when I see my chance.'

'What will you do?'

'Interfere,' Tor said and grinned mischievously.

At the Sixth bell, a cart rumbled into the amphitheatre carrying a wide-eyed but composed Locky and Haryd, who was slumped in the back. As Locky stepped down the audience applauded. Word of this brave young man had spread quickly through the city. Haryd was helped out of the cart by some guards. He was unsteady and could only walk doubled over. When they caught a glimpse of his face, they could see he looked confused. Remembering the terrible duel with Adongo, Tor wondered how Haryd could stand at all.

One of the officials read out the grievance and the Queen's ruling, then filled in the time before her arrival by outlining how Locklyn Gylbyt found himself to be there this afternoon. This was followed by a bloodcurdling description of how the Maiden administered her Kiss.

Tor noted that Haryd seemed entirely dazed by the proceedings. Locky, meanwhile, did not flinch during the gory explanation.

Quist was nervous. 'He can't die, Tor.' It was the first time since they had met that the captain had called him by his first name.

Tor looked at him. 'He won't die.'

The Seventh bell pealed and within moments Queen Sylven's glittering carriage, carried by eight burly men, came into view. A small unit of guards surrounded it. She was shrouded by her veils once again. Even though they could not see their Queen, the crowd went into rapturous cheers. It took several minutes for the noise to die down. More formalities took place, another parchment was read out and then Locklyn Gylbyt was led to meet the Silver Maiden.

Tor allowed his Colours to blaze within. Just then, the Queen's head guardsman stepped forward and called out a short statement. Heads turned and people suddenly began talking all at once, debating this unusual occurrence.

Tor could hardly believe it. The Queen had summoned him publicly.

He noticed for the first time that there were guards surrounding him, all dressed as civilians. A clever ploy by Sylven's men. He should have been paying more attention. The man in charge politely asked him to come before the Queen.

Tor had no idea what Sylven was doing. All in the audience were watching him.

'I can use my magics down there just as easily as up here,' he whispered to Quist.

Without another word, he stood and followed the guards down the tiers of seats into the centre of the auditorium, where he was then allowed to approach the Queen.

Tor wanted this over and done with. He would save Locky and then be on his way in search of Cloot.

He bowed. 'Your majesty,' he said, with nothing more in his voice than the respect she was owed.

There was no one within close earshot and Sylven spoke very softly; his acute hearing picked up her words with ease. 'Last night was lovely.'

He smiled, but no one else saw for his head was still bowed. So these theatrics were just an excuse to be close to him again.

'It was for me too,' he replied.

She continued, 'Which is why it makes it very hard for me to do this.'

Before Tor could react, his hands had been pulled behind him and tied. He felt something being pulled over his head. Instinctively, he let his Colours blaze and pushed out with them.

Nothing happened.

Tor was dumbfounded. He became very still. He could hear a voice – it seemed distant – telling the onlookers why he was being bound like this. He could not focus on the words. He pushed again. Once more nothing occurred.

For the first time in his life, Torkyn Gynt was severed from his powers. The Colours were blazing; he could feel them. The power was there to use but when he drew upon it, it was ineffectual.

He turned wildly towards the Queen but was forced to his knees by the guards. 'I'm so sorry, Tor,' was all she said.

Meanwhile, Locklyn Gylbyt was being strapped expertly into the Maiden's embrace.

'The blade will fall at least once in every ten drops,' Lorke announced. 'Our Maiden has not killed in four drops and she is eager to deliver her Kiss. Are you ready, Locklyn Gylbyt?'

To his credit, Locky did not so much as pause. 'I am ready to taste her lips, sir, and know her judgement upon me,' he called out loudly.

Everyone in the amphitheatre cheered their support for this brave fellow.

It was hideous. Tor was reminded all too keenly of a similar scene nearly five winters ago, when an innocent man had been strapped to a cross and his body stoned until it gave up the life within. Except on that occasion, the crowd wept. This gathering had a festive atmosphere which his execution scene had lacked.

He loosed the Colours once again but realised it was futile. He had been moved away from Sylven's carriage, so he could not even communicate with her. Lorke was doing one final check on his charge; no doubt praying to his gods that she would not show any affection for the boy in her grasp. He searched out Quist, whose face was a mask of anguish. It looked as though he was already convinced the boy would die horribly.

Tor began to probe around the magical 'crown' on his head. But it was too late. There was no more time to search for answers.

Women in the crowd screeched as Lorke pulled the heavy blade to the top of its axis and then let it go.

The blade hit the first series of locks, all of which opened immediately to allow it to pass through.

The Maiden was thirsty for blood. Locky was going to die.

The blade was moving quickly now; it was already onto the fifth of the ten locks. It opened. So did the sixth.

And then Tor felt it. Glorious, exquisitely sweet power washed over him. He looked around and realised that no one but he could sense it. It was strong and focused, felt otherworldly. It hit the blade as it met with the ninth lock and there the silver metal stopped, shuddering monstrously. Locky was trembling in time with it.

There was a moment of shocked silence and then the massive crowd erupted into delight. Hats were thrown in the air; babies were held aloft; women dabbed at their eyes and kissed their neighbours; men hollered their pleasure that the Maiden had spared the lad.

The magic was still all around him. It was beautiful. Tor could feel it but he could not respond to it or even touch it. It brought tears to his eyes that he could not reach out to this person and offer thanks. The Maiden had not spared Locky at all. A profound magic had interfered and Tor desperately wanted to learn whose.

He looked to Quist, whose sailors had enveloped him in a bear hug. Tor felt relief replace all his previous tension and he even laughed aloud as he scanned the crowd through watery eyes for the dwarf he had spoken with earlier.

The man put his hand to his head and then to his heart before bowing to Tor, who realised that the little figure was the wielder of the otherworldly magic. And then, curiously, the dwarf held up nine fingers. Tor was puzzled for a moment, then it dawned on him that he was looking at Figgis of the Rock Dwellers, Ninth of the Paladin.

Tor wept openly now; not just because Locky was saved but because the Paladin were almost fully reemerged and gathering bravely, for his sake and for the real battle ahead. He must never forget the true purpose of his life. The Paladin had not, and now eight of them had bravely shown themselves. Only Juno and the lion-hearted Themesius, who, for the time being, kept them all safe, were still to emerge.

No one took any notice of the weeping man in the

strange, studded leather crown; no one except Queen Sylven, who wiped tears from her own eyes behind the veils. She hated to see this man so weakened. Sylven had not touched the headband since it was first given to her by her grandmother more than two decades earlier. She had hardly understood its use and had not even thought on it again until the previous night, when Torkyn Gynt had displayed a power that shocked her speechless. It had reminded her of her grandmother's warning and when Tor defied her, she went scurrying for that enchanted headband.

Queen Sylven had never before shed a tear over a man. Torkyn Gynt was changing her life in more ways than she could ever have thought possible. She looked away from his kneeling figure and at the new prisoner, now strapped into the Maiden.

Locky staggered past the elated crowd to Quist, but Haryd was not so fortunate. This time the Maiden intended to drink fully of her prisoner's blood. The blade dropped so quickly there was hardly any time for the more squeamish members of the crowd to look away. It passed through all ten locks without resistance and Haryd just had time to shriek his despair as the Maiden bestowed her Kiss of Death. His scream was cut off as his body was split efficiently in half, gushing its contents into a dark red mass on the amphitheatre floor.

For the time being, the Maiden's thirst was quenched.

19

A Truce is Called

At the Queen's pleasure, Tor was given a few moments with Quist and Locky. There was only time for a brief farewell.

They hugged and Quist looked Tor hard in the eye, his way of conveying his thanks.

'Travel safely,' Tor said.

Locky, still in a state of high excitement and satisfaction, said, 'Come back to Caradoon soon.'

Quist nodded. He said no more but gave Tor the Tallinese salute of farewell. It was a respectful gesture for a Caradoon pirate who rarely acknowledged any laws of Tallinor.

Then the guards were pulling Tor towards the cart, which he had to share with what was left of Haryd, covered by an inadequate sack. The crowd had dispersed quickly and the Queen had long gone back to her palace. As the cart made a slow circuit to turn around, Tor noticed that Lorke and his team were dismantling the Maiden; her blade had already been cleaned and returned to its special box.

Tor spent the night in a dungeon. He was not treated

badly there but it was cold and damp. To his surprise, he was presented with an exceptionally fine meal during the evening. It was small and served on a humble clay plate, but beyond that had no resemblance whatsoever to regular prison food. A small mercy from the Queen, he decided. It was delicious.

Afterwards, he slept fitfully on his pallet. He dreamed of Orlac. Tor watched him rise from the floor where he had obviously been sitting, though he could not tell where the god was located. The vision was hazy but the surrounds appeared cavernous.

The god stretched and spoke. 'It is time,' he said.

Tor strained to hear more but his attention was pulled away by the feeling of another's presence. The sensation was cold, not friendly. He had the notion of a red mist and an icy wind enveloping him; it reminded him of when he was travelling back to the Heartwood after leaving Cloot's body. There was something trying to reach him. In his sleep he shrank back. The presence felt evil.

Tor. It was Lys.

What is that which pursues me?

He is of no concern. He will not come close to you again.

He?

Lys sighed. *His name is Dorgryl. He is just an observer, Tor. Give him no further thought.*

Are you in danger from him, Lys?

He heard her laugh gently. Tor did not think he had ever heard her laugh before.

Dorgryl is no threat to any of us, Tor.

I saw Orlac. He said it was time. What does this mean?

That Themesius must face his final battle.

I see. How long have we got?

Not long. Her evasiveness in the past had often fired his anger but not any more.

I must find Cloot.

Yes, he needs you, she said cryptically.

He knew not to ask her to elaborate. *The children?*

Are safe. They travel towards you. You must get back to the Heartwood quickly, Tor.

The vision melted, Lys disappeared from his consciousness and he woke grumpy and stiff, wondering what the day might bring. How would he escape confinement whilst his head was bound by something which overwhelmed his powers? He passed the following hours niggling away at the magical binding.

By the time the sun had risen, he had begun to understand its complexity. He wondered if, like the archalyt, he would be able to overcome it once it was removed because he had begun to unravel its secrets.

Finally some guards arrived and helped him to his feet.

'Take his shackles off but bind his hands. Queen's orders,' the main warder said.

The fellows who would be escorting him to his next stop nodded.

'Where now?' Tor asked.

'To the baths,' one replied curtly.

The Queen's maid, Hela, met them outside a pretty, stone structure. It had taken several minutes to reach the baths on foot and Tor realised he was now well away from the prison complex and deep into the main palace grounds.

'It's nice to see you again, Hela.'

'Likewise, Physic Gynt.' She smiled warmly at him. 'I can take him from here,' she said to the two men, who left without another word.

She led him inside the structure to a small pool carved into the stone. Steam billowed off the top of the faintly blue water and a delicate fragrance wafted towards them.

Hela saw him inhale it. 'Nettle, mint, lavender and citrus. They will refresh you,' she said and began to remove his clothes. When Tor was naked, she took off her own loose robe and stepped into the water with him. 'Her majesty wishes you bathed before she gives audience,' she explained.

Tor spent the next hour being washed with great care by the attentive Hela. He could not imagine anything more delightful than the treatment he was receiving at her hands. Finally, when his skin was warmed and supple, she dried him and laid him on a table, then massaged his body for another hour, applying sensual oils.

A final dip and cleanse before he was shaved, his hair groomed and he was dressed into clean garments. Hela did not speak a word during this time and Tor was happy to receive her ministrations in gratified silence. Hela tidied herself and then, with a smile which said droves, asked him to follow her.

After passing through various halls and passages, Tor recognised the route they were taking. Before long they were climbing the familiar tower to Queen Sylven's private chambers. He was shown inside and left. He knew she would be standing on the balcony.

Sylven turned around and looked at him, her eyes apologising before her voice did. 'Let me remove those bindings for you,' she said. She busied herself untying his hands. 'Can I count on you not to do anything untoward?'

'Such as?'

'Hurting me.'

He was genuinely grieved. 'Sylven, I made love to you the night before last. How could I hurt you?'

She dug her nails into her palms. It would not do to allow her eyes to mist up in front of him. If her grandmother were alive, she would flog Sylven for showing such weakness towards a man.

The thrill of his touch made her lightheaded as he gently reached around her waist.

'Turn around so I can untie the headband,' she said, terrified by her own feelings.

Tor did so obediently. He was still angry at what had happened but after the visit from Lys, the vision of Orlac, finding out about his children's arrival — what was happening now suddenly seemed so much less important. He knew he had to exploit every opportunity to find Cloot as quickly as possible and Sylven was the key. That he was fond of her was a bonus.

'You must be angry with me, Tor,' she said, slowly untying the bindings at his head.

'I am.'

'Will you forgive me?'

'Yes.'

'Then I am indebted to you.'

The band fell free and Tor was connected to himself again. He summoned the Colours and cast out freely. He never wanted to feel that dislocation again.

'May I?' he said, reaching out.

Sylven handed him the soft leather band which was encrusted with dull black studs.

'Sylven, what is this?'

She turned to where the table was laid with wine and cheeses, fruits and savouries. 'Sit with me, Tor. Eat,' she said.

Tor wanted information but remained patient and helped himself to a plate of the food. He even allowed her to pour him some excellent chilled wine.

'We have a new cook in our kitchens,' she said, relieved and very pleased to see him at her table again.

Tor grinned. 'And is his name Ryk?' he asked, as last night's exquisite food suddenly made sense.

'Yes!' she exclaimed. 'How could you know?'

'It is not magic, your majesty, relax. Ryk was on board *The Wasp* with me. I came to know him well and like him very much. He comes from a long line of famous chefs from Ildagarth and I mentioned this to Master Lard on the day we were taken to the slave market. I gathered from his reaction that a good cook would be warmly welcomed at the palace.'

'Indeed,' she said. 'I can't remember eating any better. Those pastries yesterday morning were his and he even visited last night to insist that he prepare an evening meal for you. He seems totally enchanted by you, Tor. I'm beginning to wonder if everyone is affected by your presence in the same way?'

'Are you, Sylven?' he said, taking a sip from his wine.

It was rare that Sylven could not hold someone's look; she was never one to back down. But she did so now, looking away almost shyly. She simply could not admit out loud how good it was to see him back here and smiling. She was already imagining the night's sport in the bedroom and how much fun it was going to be.

She changed the subject, hoping her cheeks were not flaring with colour. 'Tor, I want to apologise again about yesterday. I do mean it and it's important to me that you understand I say it from my heart. However, I think you will agree that my decision was the right one. The Silver Maiden honoured Locklyn's decision to call upon her; she spared his life and endorsed his grievance against Haryd, dealing with the sailor in her harshest manner.'

She looked at him steadily now. 'I think we can say the very best outcome was achieved.'

Tor was not about to tell her the Maiden had had nothing to do with it. The contraption was nothing more than a deadly game of chance, with the odds stacking up against each victim with each unsuccessful drop of her gleaming blade.

Instead he gave her peace. 'Yes, you were right, Sylven. There is no need to apologise, because you showed me there was never any need to employ any magical powers to save Locky's life. I hope the fact of my powers remains private between us.'

Relief flooded through her. She had not realised how very important his acceptance and agreement was to her. Perhaps there could be a future for them?

'I will never share this knowledge with anyone, Tor. Your secret is safe.'

He raised his glass. 'To friends and true loves,' he said, thinking of Alyssa.

The Queen of Cipres smiled sensually. 'To true love,' she said and drank.

'Tell me about this headpiece,' Tor said.

Sylven explained all she knew of it. Tor listened carefully. 'Do you know what the black stones are?'

'Ah, yes. My grandmother called it . . . er now, let me get this right . . .' She tapped her manicured nails on the table. 'Midnight archalyt – yes, that's it,' she said, pleased with herself for her exceptional memory.

Tor nodded and continued to eat, betraying nothing. So it *was* archalyt. That meant he could overcome it. He just had to learn more about it.

'And how did it come into your family?'

'Oh, Tor, I hardly paid attention in the first place. No one ever thought it would be used. You can see how new-looking it still is. It has never been used in my two decades as Queen and I never heard of it being used during my mother's reign either.'

Tor could tell Sylven had no interest in this conversation but it intrigued him. He would learn more of this midnight archalyt. But for now, he masked his fascination and allowed the discussion to move to more trivial matters until their meal was complete and the wine almost finished. The Queen ordered another flask to be brought.

Tor stretched. The next few moments would be tricky.

'Your majesty, I have been honoured by your hospitality and personal attentions. But I must now take my leave,' he said graciously.

'You're leaving?' She banged down her glass, more from surprise than anger.

'Yes, your highness,' he said gently. 'When I set off on my voyage from Caradoon I was on a mission. I am searching for something. I became embroiled in all sorts of distractions, including a memorable day and night with a beautiful woman.'

She dipped her eyes.

'But my task is still ahead, Queen Sylven, and I no longer have the luxury of time to spare.'

'Whatever do you search for, Torkyn Gynt?'

'A bird, your majesty.'

'A bird?' She wondered if she had heard correctly.

'A peregrine falcon. He was captured and taken from me by mistake, then brought here and sold, as I understand it. I am on a journey to find him.'

She looked at him as though she hardly understood a word he had said.

He played his card. 'Perhaps you could help me, Sylven?'

'I can help?'

'Yes. You keep aviaries of hunting birds, do you not? He is a magnificent falcon. Perhaps the royal keepers purchased him. It is a thought, anyway,' he said hopefully.

Hela arrived with the fresh flask of wine and it seemed to snap Sylven out of her dreamy state.

Her voice was commanding again and her attention sharp when she next spoke. 'You are asking me to help you find your falcon?'

'I am.'

'I suppose I could,' she said, accepting a glass of wine from him. 'My very best birds are sent to the winter palace at Neame, in the foothills.'

'Would you allow me to visit there, your majesty? Perhaps a note from you would gain me entry?'

'Oh, I can do better than that, Torkyn Gynt. I shall come with you. We normally close up the city palace for several weeks at this time of year anyway. I like to spend some time in the hills. We shall go together and if my aviaries have your falcon, we will find him and I shall return him to you.'

It was more than Tor could have hoped for, but he needed for her to move fast. He decided to press his advantage. 'This is kind of you, Sylven. I am more grateful than I can show.'

She cut across his words. 'I'll make you earn it all right,' she said, with that familiar wicked sparkle in her eye.

It made them both laugh, though Tor's humour was forced. Sylven could never understand how important this was to him. 'Speed is critical, your majesty. Cloot – that is my falcon's name – and I have been parted for too long. If he is not at Neame, then I will be forced to search far and wide throughout Cipres and its islands.'

'Then let us hope he is as magnificent as you say, Tor, because such a bird would not have slipped past my men's notice and he will be at Neame. We can leave today if you wish.'

Tor could hardly believe his luck. 'That would make me very happy.'

20

Goth Hatches a Plan

The palace was suddenly a hive of activity. Goth had to ask around to discover that the Queen and much of her household was relocating to her winter palace. His small chamber was quite some way from her majesty's tower which meant that he was last to hear the news. The distance was very annoying. He needed to be closer to her if he was to ingratiate himself and influence her decisions.

Being saved by the Cipreans had been a stroke of great fortune. He had definitely thought his time was up and that the boiling sea would swallow him that terrifying day. He had waved to someone on one of the beaches as he was swept along in the current. It had been too dark to see who it was but after arriving at the palace and hearing the story of the other survivors from *The Wasp*, Goth had realised he had been waving to his enemy, Torkyn Gynt.

Goth had first seen Gynt on the deck of *The Wasp*, when the pirate Blackhand was about to chop off the young boy's hand. He had spent the days since pondering how it could be that Gynt was alive when he himself had witnessed the man's death by stoning at the hands of the city of Tal's executioner.

He and hundreds of others had watched Gynt's head split open by the heavy stones. The wound had bled a torrent and the man had died on the cross while his lover, Alyssandra Qyn, was forced to look on. Goth recalled how he had wanted to touch Gynt's corpse, to be sure he was truly dead, and how Xantia had mocked him. How could anyone live through such an event? Xantia had gloated. It was surely impossible and yet there Gynt was, standing on the ship's deck that morning.

Goth began to believe that Gynt could not die. The man had suffered execution by stoning and a deadly storm, but apparently neither had been able to take his life. But then he smiled. As a child, the fire had tried to take his life and yet he had lived through it, and the storm had done its damnedest to claim him too and yet here he was, alive and well and a guest of Ciprean royalty. It seemed he and Gynt were survivors. And life was taking some strange turns for them both.

When Xantia had fled Caradoon, Goth was still disabled by the effects of stracca inhalation. One of the many spies Xantia paid throughout the upper region of Tallinor had sent a message that the King's Guard was heading further north than usual. It was unclear whether the Guard had been tipped off as to Goth and Xantia's whereabouts, but Xantia was not taking any chances. She was surprised they had managed to stay hidden amongst Caradoon's population for as many years as they had; she knew it would be only a matter of time before the search was widened to even the remotest nooks and crannies of the Kingdom.

Goth, weakened by the painful desire for more stracca and the urgent need for security, had begged Xantia whether they might stay together. But the sneer on Xantia's face had been answer enough. Goth knew he was no longer of any use to her; he wondered what use he may ever have been. His role as Chief Inquisitor had been dissolved and he had been marked for death; he no longer wielded any power. Xantia was a clever woman; she would have worked this out long before she helped him to escape, which meant she had another agenda, a better idea for his use. Not any more though, it appeared. Once she heard the Guards were coming, Xantia had warned him of their approach, told him she had arranged a berth for him on *The Wasp*, thrown a heavy purse at him and then simply disappeared.

Before he departed Caradoon, Goth had dragged himself to the apothecary. He knew he would not survive more than a day on the ship without something to counteract the effects of the stracca working itself out of his body. Armed with a supply of arraq, he had found his way onto the ship and then ordered that he be left totally alone. He knew the next few days would be filled with the greatest of pain whilst the stracca withdrew from his body. He had to pretend he was ill but the ruse had seemed to work. The stupid cabin boy had not cottoned on to his problem and the captain had hardly wanted a priest at his table.

Goth laughed his high-pitched giggle as he watched the activity taking place in the main courtyard below. If only he had known Gynt was on board *The Wasp*, he would have taken the opportunity to poison him. He could have disposed of the body by dropping it overboard; Gynt would have vanished without a trace.

Yesterday afternoon at the execution, he had been excited to see the Queen's guards escorting Gynt from the amphitheatre gallery to the Queen's box. He had believed the time had come once again for Gynt to die, but it was not so. It seemed that Sylven was interested only in humiliating him; she had tied some kind of leather band around the physic's head. It must have a special significance for the Cipreans; Goth resolved to ask around to discover more, if he could find time.

His mind slid readily back to the grisly scene which had been carried out in the amphitheatre's arena. He had thoroughly enjoyed watching Haryd meet his end, although he would have preferred the lad to die too, particularly as both Gynt and the crowd were on his side. A pity he had survived; a good bloodcurdling scream from a lad was always fun, but then again Haryd had issued something akin to a woman's scream, which had caused Goth a rush of excitement. He had watched in fascination as the blade fell through the locks as cleanly as if they did not exist and then split Haryd's body in two, cutting off his death shriek. Goth had never seen such a sight; he wished he could have got closer to view the man's innards spilling onto the dust. He had joined in the crowd's cheering and wished that they were celebrating the death of Torkyn Gynt.

Goth desperately hoped that the Queen of Cipres could be persuaded that his expertise as former Chief Inquisitor was useful. If he could win her support, he would enjoy the benefits of her influence and be able to indulge himself with the lifestyle he craved. Most importantly, a position at the royal court of Cipres would provide him with the means to create havoc in Tallinor and perhaps even the power to kill Torkyn Gynt, should he remain out of favour with her majesty.

Then, after ending Gynt's life, he would devise a plan to re-enter that of Alyssandra Qyn. It may take him years but he did not care; he would see her again and revel in that fear on her lovely face. Goth barely understood his fascination with the woman. She was such a delicate thing and yet she commanded his attention. Those large searching eyes and that fragile body. He hurt her all those years ago but he had not managed to break her. The time spent smoking the stracca had given him insight. He realised he had handled her wrongly. She was not the kind of woman to be seduced by power. She would never be ruled by anyone and certainly not by fear. Alyssa would rather die fighting than submit herself to him. The vision of her struggling against him inspired Goth and he fed off it during his dark days and nights in Caradoon. But now he concluded that Alyssa too must die and by his hand, for it was she who had sentenced him to death in Tal's Great Hall.

Goth remembered how he had tracked down Gynt and Alyssa to the centre of the Great Forest. He had arrived in time to see her newborn baby's corpse in its shallow grave. He had kicked at the leaves covering it and laughed at her grief. Was that the moment she had hated him most? Yes, he decided. Not even the rape could compare to a mother's wrath. He giggled again. He would relish the opportunity to end her sad and miserable life.

A familiar figure, tall and gracious, appeared in the courtyard and dragged Goth's mind away from his dark thoughts. He was shocked to see Gynt smiling and chatting with the Queen's servants, particularly the one Goth hated most, the wretched Hela. Surely Gynt had not been given his freedom? Yesterday's investigations had revealed that the physic was cooling his heels in her majesty's dungeons. What could have happened to make her change her mind?

He watched with loathing as Tor helped Queen Sylven into her carriage, kissing her hand before climbing onto a horse to ride alongside. The royal party comprised many carts and beasts, maids, supplies and even that stupid boy, Ryk, whom Goth remembered from the ship. What was *he* doing at the palace?

There were too many questions to which Goth didn't have answers. Why had Gynt been travelling to Cipres in the first place? He had to find out. He could not be left to stew like this. If his plans were to work, he had to be close to the Queen.

Goth put his fluid mind to work, running along a number of paths, rejecting some and turning back to others, testing each of them for potential. He needed to follow the royal party, but he could not risk being recognised by Gynt. And yet, if he was going to kill him, he had to get close enough to do it. How?

Goth watched the carriages move off. He was not worried that they were leaving without him; there would be supply carts still to follow the main party so he could travel with those. Right now his problem was the danger of being recognised.

'I need a disguise,' he muttered aloud. 'But what?' he asked the walls of his chamber.

He turned to watch the procession once more, his eyes following the last of the carriages out of the main courtyard. His attention was caught by a black veiled figure, holding her robes up slightly so she could move freely and quickly about the yard below.

And then it hit him.

Sylven insisted that she and her personal serving staff never ventured beyond the palace walls without a veil. In addition, her women always wore full black robes outside the royal chambers.

It could work.

21

A Meeting at Dawn

Goth knew he must choose with care so that the stolen robe fitted him sufficiently well that his presence would go unnoticed by the Queen, but even more so by that bitch chief maidservant of hers, Hela. He despised Hela because she was not intimidated by him; even worse was her insufferable arrogance born from her close friendship with Sylven. And Hela had sharp eyes. She would pick out an intruder in an instant, Goth mused as he sat in the courtyard, pretending to read.

In truth, he was busy watching the comings and goings of the palace staff as they prepared to leave for their winter retreat. He estimated that the last of the wagons would leave around this time tomorrow. It was now mid afternoon and he still had not seen an appropriate victim.

One of the Queen's courtiers suddenly appeared next to him. 'Good book?'

Goth stopped himself from jumping. He had been concentrating hard on a woman who had just stepped back into the palace. She was too tall . . . the robe would have dragged on the ground.

'Er, yes. Most absorbing,' he replied.

'I don't doubt this afternoon sun is cheerful on your back after the cold.'

The silver-haired man was obviously in no hurry, Goth thought sourly. He forced a polite smile. 'Yes, indeed. You are not joining her majesty at Neame then?'

'Not on this occasion,' the courtier said cheerfully. 'I sense this is one of those times when she prefers not to be disturbed by royal duties. I got the distinct impression she wishes to be alone.' He winked.

Goth wanted to wipe the conspiratorial smile off the old man's face. 'Hardly alone,' he replied. 'I see that man Gynt is constantly at her side these days.'

'Well, quite,' said the man, choosing not to expand any further. The wink had been innuendo enough. 'I actually thought you may be going along?'

'I wasn't asked.' Goth decided now was as good a time as any to cover his intended tracks. 'No, I think I shall remain happily at the palace, soak up this sun in her majesty's absence and spend the time learning more about Cipres.'

'Good, good,' said the older man, finally deciding to move on. 'I'll see you at dinner then.'

Unlikely, you old fool, thought Goth. 'That would be charming,' he replied.

As he watched the man walk away he noticed a woman bending down to pick up a basket of recently delivered fruit. It was a large basket but she hoisted it onto her shoulder and stood to her full height. Goth's breath caught. There! He watched her turn and carefully measured her height and width in his head and decided her robe would be ideal.

He pushed the book into his pocket and followed the woman. He caught up with her as she rounded a corner heading towards the palace's vast cooling rooms.

'Good day,' he said casually and fell in with her stride.

'Hello.' She nodded from beneath her veil.

'I wonder, may I steal one of those oranges? I am mighty thirsty.' He desperately wished for once that he was attractive enough to immediately win a woman's attention. People like Gynt and that former Prime, Kyt Cyrus, did not realise how valuable an asset their looks were. Or perhaps they just took it for granted. He felt his face twitch as she turned her dark eyes onto his. She said nothing.

'Apologies,' he offered, all politeness. He even effected a brief bow. 'I am Almyd Goth, an adviser to the Queen. I am new to Cipres and to the palace and I hardly know a soul.' He tried to smile, knowing it was likely to fail, as his burned, twisted skin tended to turn any attempt into a grimace. 'Actually, it's quite lonely,' he added, hoping a pathetic tone might win the sympathy he needed.

Did she smile? He could not tell, but something seemed to lighten in those smoky eyes which regarded him steadily.

Goth did his best to turn on the charm. 'That basket looks awfully heavy for a girl to carry. May I help?'

He was heartened by her soft chuckle. 'This is my daily job.'

'Well, I come from Tallinor and around our palace, we don't allow the women to carry such heavy loads.'

'Perhaps they are not as strong as Ciprean women?' She was teasing him but she put the load down onto the ground. 'Help yourself.'

Goth did not want an orange. He had disliked them ever since that episode in Ildagarth when, inexplicably, instead of killing Gynt he had murdered a child who had offered him an orange. Now, bending down to select one of the fruit, he recalled how the child's blood had mingled with the juice of the oranges on the ground.

The woman chose one and handed it to him with a smooth, olive-skinned hand. He took the orange and bowed his head in thanks, noting that her height did indeed match his. Her robe would be perfect.

Her deep, almost raspy voice responded quickly to his courtesy. 'I am Elma.'

'Thank you, Elma, for this,' he said, bouncing the fruit gently in his palm. 'Are you sure I cannot help?'

She laughed gently. 'I will manage.' She hoisted the basket back onto her shoulder. 'Perhaps I will see you again at the evening meal.'

Goth had not expected this. 'Perhaps you will,' he said, surprising himself at how flirtatious he sounded.

That evening, rather than taking a tray of food into his chamber, Goth deliberately went looking for Elma in the communal staff dining room. He picked at a plate of food and found an excuse to linger by talking to the boring courtier again, but all the while his sharp eyes swept across the hall. She was not to be seen.

Making his excuses he finally extricated himself from the tedious old man and asked a dozen different women if they knew where Elma was. Most did not know her. Those who did had not seen her. Frustrated, his anger rising, Goth decided to search the servants quarters. He would probably face someone's wrath for the trespass but he was beyond being polite. He had only hours now. He needed Elma's robe and was prepared to enter her quarters and steal it if necessary. However, he preferred not to take that risk. His first plan was neater, if a little bloody.

Striding from the hall he was annoyed to feel a tug on his shirt. He swung around to see a young woman.

'You are Almyd Goth?' she asked tentatively, obviously fascinated, or perhaps horrified, by his ugliness.

'What of it?' he replied impatiently.

She mustered a sweet smile from a plain face. 'I am Elma's friend. She asked me to tell you, if I met you, that she hoped the orange was sweet.'

'Where is she?' he asked, perhaps a little too urgently.

The girl stepped back. He had frightened her. 'She is not well, sir.'

'Ah.' He was too fierce, he decided. He must hold his temper. 'Well, I'm sorry to hear that. Please convey to her my regret that we could not break bread together this evening, and I hope she will be well in the morn.'

She nodded and smiled. 'I shall tell her. She will be pleased.' The girl made to leave.

Goth caught her arm; felt her recoil. Her politeness did not extend to enjoying the touch of this hideously maimed man. 'Sir?' The fright was back in her voice.

'I was just wondering . . . would you take something to Elma from me?' He added a plaintive note to his voice.

'Of course.' She held out her hand.

'I have to get it ready. Come with me . . . er, please.'

He was surprised that she followed, but she did so obediently, first into the gardens where he picked a rosebud of soft yellow and then into another room where he quickly scratched out a note. He handed it to her.

'Elma will be moved, sir, by your attentions.'

'Can she read?' he suddenly had the forethought to ask.

'No, sir. I can't either,' she replied politely.

Goth only just refrained from knocking her to the ground. All that effort wasted. But he held the anger in check and fixed another leer on his face, hoping it might pass for a smile. He ignored the way she shrank back.

'Well, could you perhaps give her a message to go with this rose?'

'I will do that,' she said.

'Thank you. Please tell Elma that I would be honoured if she would join me for a cup of sweet wine.'

Her eyes widened. She giggled and then stopped herself.

'Why do you laugh?' Goth asked.

'Elma always attracts the strange ones,' she said and then realised the insult.

Goth was careful not to show any had been taken. 'Well, I am lonely and Elma was kind to me this afternoon. I would like to say thank you properly and perhaps I will have a new friend at the palace,' he said to the younger woman, almost choking on the syrupy words.

She lapped them up, pleased for Elma, he presumed. 'When?'

'How about very early tomorrow? We can share a sunrise together.'

The girl looked doubtful. 'She may not wish to come alone at that hour, sir.'

Goth had not counted on this. He thought quickly, reassessing the plan. 'Then you shall come with her. We can all be friends and watch the sun come up over Cipres.'

He should have been a poet, he thought sourly.

'That would be fine,' she said. 'We shall see you at second toll.'

'Excellent,' Goth said. 'May I suggest the old well . . . the one on the eastern side of the palace?'

He had already checked that this would be an ideal area. The well was no longer used so was only lightly guarded during the day. At dawn, it was likely to be deserted.

'Come as invisibly as you can,' he suggested. 'Let us not be seen. This will be a secret rendezvous,' he added, theatrically.

She smiled again. 'We shall be veiled to go outside, sir. No one will know who we are.'

It was exactly what Goth wanted to hear. 'See you tomorrow,' he said and took his leave.

The two women arrived promptly, emerging from the eerie half-darkness of the pre-dawn hours. Arms linked, they walked carefully and quietly, giggling softly now and then – probably about him, he thought. He watched them approach. Killing both at the same time would be impossible.

He hid in a clump of small fruit trees, waiting for them to pass him. As they did, he took a deep breath then stepped out and smashed the blacksmith's tool he had brought with him into the back of the shorter woman's head. She dropped without a sound.

Elma swung around, her face filled with horror, but Goth gave her no time to cry out. He was on her in a flash, one hand clamped to her mouth and the other pushing her towards the well. He pressed her against the wall with the weight of his body and ripped off her veil, triumphant to have at last what he needed.

'If you scream, or make any sound, I shall kill you. Do you understand?'

She nodded dumbly from behind the hand pushed against her face. Goth removed a large kerchief from his pocket and tied it very firmly across her mouth. Elma made no sound as he did so. He was impressed by her composure. He finally turned her to face him and saw that Elma was more than just plain; she was downright ugly. No wonder, he thought absently, that her friend had laughed. Never mind, it was certainly not Elma's looks he cared about right now.

'I must ask you to undress.'

A query formed in her eyes.

'Quickly, please,' he added and was relieved to see her reach behind to unbutton her robe.

She stepped out of it, naked. Goth hardly gave her shapely body a second glance. 'Give it to me.'

Elma obeyed. He noticed goose bumps on the arm which obediently held out the robe and it occurred to him that the fresh morning air would be chill on bare skin. Oh well, he thought carelessly, you won't feel much shortly.

Goth took the robe and tossed it onto the ground, on top of the veil. He had his disguise. Now he must cover his tracks.

Without warning, he grabbed Elma, twisted her round and bent her over the well. He knew its stone wall would chafe badly against her bare flesh but it would not be for long. He grabbed her hair, neatly tied in a convenient ponytail, and wrapped it around his fingers to hold her in position whilst he removed the blade he had concealed.

Elma began to whimper. He felt nothing but contempt for her.

He put his mouth close to her ear and her whimpering lifted a notch. He must despatch her fast.

'I know I inferred I wouldn't kill you if you obeyed me, but I'm sorry, Elma, I'm the most wicked liar.'

And with that, Goth viciously pulled her head back by her hair and passed the blade swiftly and deeply across her throat.

Blood spewed from the wound. The force with which a body emptied itself of its vital fluid never failed to fascinate, or satisfy, him. He stood as far away as possible so none of the blood splashed on his clothes or boots and watched Elma's life cascade in a violent gush down the well shaft. Her corpse followed it within moments.

Goth wasted no time, moving swiftly to Elma's prone friend, who had come to and was also whimpering. Goth believed her skull was already crushed sufficiently to cause death but he liked to be thorough. He turned the woman over and stabbed her once, a powerful blow directly into her heart, which stopped its beat instantly. Her body joined her friend's at the bottom of the well. The smell of decaying flesh would bring the busybodies soon enough, but by then, Goth thought, he would be far away.

He picked up the robe and veil and disappeared into the smudgy light of early morning as the second bell tolled.

22

A Fateful Cup

Saxon arrived in Cipres two days after Goth left the capital on one of the supply carts. It had been an extraordinarily long and frustrating journey for the Kloek as he tried to trace the steps of Pirate Quist. At Herek's insistence, he had travelled to Caradoon with a small group of soldiers. The arrangement was not to Saxon's liking, but once Herek knew that Goth still lived, naturally the Prime wished to do everything he could to bring the former Chief Inquisitor to justice.

Saxon and the King's Guard had found the stracca den abandoned. Saxon had expected as much; these people would have heard of the military's approach – no matter how small the party – long before the soldiers had hit the villages which considered themselves neighbours of Caradoon.

When Saxon had finally rid himself of the company of soldiers, sending them on their way to take news back to Herek, he too had hit on the notion of asking for information at the brothel. Unlike Tor, however, Saxon had been shunned by its owner. He was not even granted an audience. The Caradoons were suspicious by nature and news of a Kloek asking questions of one of their own was bound to provoke jaws to clamp shut. Saxon felt helpless. It had been several weeks now since Cloot's capture; the first qualms of this being a desperately hopeless chase began to niggle.

His distress must have been written all over his face when his request for a brief meeting with the madam was turned down for the second time for a young and gregarious member of the establishment took pity on him.

'Why so sad, Kloek?' she said, a tray of glasses balanced expertly on her well-rounded hip.

Saxon looked at her. Pert and pretty, she was. He was exhausted and it had been such a long time since he had lain with a woman. It was tempting.

'Cat got your tongue, eh?' the girl said, putting the tray down. 'Nobody is allowed to look forlorn here, Kloek. Do you have a name? Mine is Celya.'

'Saxon,' he said, before draining his mug. 'Time to go.'

She nodded. 'I'm sorry that she won't see you, Saxon.'

'I don't understand why. I only want to ask about one of the captains who may pass through here.'

'Yes, I know. I gather no one has bothered to inform you though that the man you seek is Madame Eryna's husband.'

Saxon was surprised. 'I see. Then her reluctance makes sense,' he said, scratching at his beard and feeling as though he had been kicked in the guts.

'You could use a bath, a shave and a good night's rest; all of which is available upstairs.' She picked up the tray again. 'Forget Quist. He and his wife own this place. You'll get no information here. That last fellow, a few weeks back, he got the same answer.'

So, someone else was chasing the pirate. That figured, Saxon thought. 'Which fellow?'

'Petersyn or something. A beautiful man. Made all the girls' hearts race in here. Each of us hoped he would pass the night with us. Tall, dark and those blue eyes. Light! What I'd give to roll between the sheets entwined in those arms.' She grinned wickedly. 'He got no answers about Quist, but I'll tell you this, Saxon. He was on a ship bound for Cipres the next morning. I know because I was delivering something to the docks and saw him aboard *The Wasp*. Good night, Kloek.' She winked.

Saxon wanted to kiss her. In her own clever way she had told him where to head next. Cipres! Who was the man she spoke of, he wondered. It probably did not matter to his quest, though he smiled wistfully. Her description had sounded like Tor Gynt. If only.

Saxon had gone directly to the docks only to learn that it was highly unlikely any more ships would be making the crossing now until Newleaf. Stumped yet determined, he had visited the inn at the docks and asked as many captains as he could find the same question: 'How much to take me to Cipres?'

Each time he was met by laughter or derisive comments. The season was over. The men had finished their business for the year and the docks would become a ghostly place for the next few months.

Towards midnight, the innkeeper had suggested he try a wizened old sailor slumped over his ale in a smoky corner. 'That silly old bastard Fawks has lost all his money again at hari. Wagered everything. He may make one last voyage. He's got nothing more to lose except his life or his creaky old ship and neither of those are worth much these days. Give him a go.'

Saxon had approached Fawks, plied him with liquor stronger than ale and extracted a promise that they would sail the next afternoon, come what may. Saxon refused to pay a single duke until they were seabound and then he had promised just about everything in his purse. It was all he owned but it was worth it. He would die searching for Cloot if that's what it took. He could not live as a soldier any longer. That was not his life. He was Paladin. He had a destiny and finding Cloot was part of it.

They had departed the next afternoon on a vessel that even Saxon, with his positive outlook, found difficult to imagine would last longer than one day at sea. But lasted it had. The weather had been surprisingly generous to them and with a small crew, scant provisions and only just enough fresh water to last them the voyage, the rickety ship had safely dropped anchor at the Ciprean docks.

Saxon thanked the gods who looked after him and paid the grinning Fawks everything but a few coins which he held back for a single good meal and a bed for the night. He felt incredibly uplifted as he began wandering the docks, until he learned the news that *The Wasp* had sunk without trace on its last voyage. His hope of following the lead of the stranger, whom he had nicknamed Gynt even though Celya had called him Petersyn, was dashed. But gradually he rallied. So be it. He was not following the stranger. He was chasing Quist. And Quist was not the one lying at the bottom of the ocean feeding the fish.

He began to ask questions. People here were not so suspicious. Travellers from many Kingdoms passed through Cipres. Strangers were commonplace. Answers did not carry a price. His spirits revived on learning that Quist frequented a particular inn and he immediately made his way there, hardly noticing the beautiful city around him, so intent was he on this mission.

He paid for a tiny room overnight and enjoyed a decent meal. The girl who served him the meal knew Quist but said he had already left for the mainland. His spirits sank again. He had missed him. That was it. It was over.

'He never stays long, our Captain Quist. Sells his goods and leaves immediately,' she said, putting his cheese down. She left.

Sells his goods and leaves, Saxon repeated in his head. He did not need Quist any more. He had a score to settle with him, yes, but that could wait. If he had sold his goods, that meant Cloot might still be found in Cipres.

'Wait,' he called out to the girl. He flipped her his last coin. 'Where would someone sell a bird of prey here?'

'At the market,' she said, pocketing the coin in her apron. 'The market has everything, including slaves. Quist would have sold his wares there.'

This tidy piece of information and his subsequent snooping had led Saxon to the conclusion that a falcon as fine as Cloot would almost certainly have been purchased for the royal aviaries. Which was why he found himself standing in the main courtyard of Queen Sylven's palace, wanting to put his fist into the face of one of her lowliest staff members.

'I'm sorry, Master Fox, but the main aviaries are not located here. They are all at the winter palace in Neame.'

He had already said this once and Saxon was tiring of learning the same information and facing the same polite but meaningless smile.

Saxon battled to keep his voice calm. 'I realise this because you have already informed me of it. Tell me, are you hiring any staff at the moment?'

'No, Master Fox. The Queen is now residing at the winter palace in the foothills and we will be winding down the household here until Newleaf.' He smiled again.

Saxon's fist twitched. 'What about help for the winter palace? Could you use a strong pair of hands at Neame?'

'Ah, well now, you would have to speak with our staff organiser, Jayklon. Thank you for your enquiry, Master Fox. Now, if you wouldn't mind going around to the servants entrance – one of the guards will direct you – I have a busy morning ahead. Good day to you.'

Saxon snarled at the man's retreating back. He got his directions and made his way to the servants entrance, where a queue of people waited, all apparently seeking work at either of the palaces. It took most of the day to shuffle forward to the front of the queue and by the time Saxon's turn came around, any lightness of heart had dissipated and a black mood had descended on him. He decided to lie.

'Right now, Master Fox.' The tired interviewer rubbed at his eyes. 'And what are you offering us today?'

'I am from Tallinor.'

'Of little relevance, I'm afraid,' said the wobbling fellow, whose many chins suggested he was probably quite hungry by now for a large meal.

'From the palace at Tallinor,' Saxon continued.

'Oh? Well, good. This is promising. And what did you do at the palace of Tallinor?' Fat Belly enquired, still rubbing his eyes.

'I was the head handler of falcons.'

'My word. What brings you here?' He had the man's attention now.

'This and that. I had a falling out. Water under the bridge. Right now, I seek work in your Queen's aviaries. I don't expect to be a senior member. I'll muck out cages if required. An honest day's work is all I ask, Master Jayklon, and in return you can rely on me to take exceptional care of the birds. I prefer them to people actually. And I am very experienced.'

'I see,' said Jayklon, sitting up and scribbling furiously onto some parchment. 'Right, there's some staff leaving tomorrow for the winter palace. Present this to a fellow called Hume and he'll sort you out the other end. Hungry?'

Saxon nodded.

'Well, give this to the kitchens and they'll provide you with a meal for today.'

Jayklon handed him a pebble with a mark on it. Saxon looked at it in his palm, his face expressionless.

'It's a token, Master Fox. It authorises the kitchens to feed you as one of the palace staff. You will be paid two dukes a day and all meals and lodging provided. You leave tomorrow morning at first light. Thank you. Next.'

Tor had kept his peace throughout the journey. It would not do to rush Sylven. As they rounded the curve in the hills and set sight on the beautiful soft grey stone of the winter palace, however, he felt impatient. Somehow he knew Cloot would be here.

Sylven was saying something about the surrounding countryside but he paid no attention. He cast. There, it was happening again, just like it had with Alyssa. There was a slight give to the dense nothingness he usually encountered when attempting to reach Cloot. Yesterday when he had tried, the resistance had felt softer. Now, in Neame, literally at the doorstep of the aviaries, the resistance felt softer still.

'. . . don't you think?' Sylven said.

'Pardon me, your majesty?'

'You haven't paid attention to a word I've just said. I am not used to this, Tor.' But she was smiling. 'Thinking of your falcon, I suppose?'

'I am, yes,' he admitted.

'Won't you tell me why he is so important to you?'

'I'm not sure you could believe it, Queen Sylven.'

She shook her head and pulled her veil down over her face. 'I shall hear your story yet, Torkyn Gynt. But for now, welcome to my winter palace.' The carriages pulled to a stop. 'Ah, I do love it here,' she said, leaning from the window and breathing in the cool air.

'The fires are lit and Belsyn awaits, your majesty,' the faithful Hela said as she helped her Queen step out.

'Thank you, Hela. Isn't it good to be back?'

Waiting at the palace gate was a short, roundish man with a genial face. He was rubbing his hands in front of him. He bowed low and with genuine honour for the Queen. 'Welcome back, your majesty.'

'Belsyn,' Sylven said, waiting for him to stand upright again. 'It is so good to see you again.'

'Everything is ready for your majesty, just as you like it. And we welcome your special guest too.' He bowed to Tor who was standing behind her.

'Come, Tor,' Sylven said. 'Let me show you my favourite playground.'

Just then a squeal was heard and a girl came running towards Sylven. Laughing, the Queen clapped her hands and hugged the child.

She looked at Tor. 'My greatest love of all. This is Sarel.'

He bowed to the child who would become the next Queen of Cipres.

Tor showed extraordinary patience during the next couple of days, amusing the Queen and pretending to be thoroughly fascinated by all she showed him. If it were not for the powerful feeling that Cloot was at Neame, he might really have enjoyed himself. The palace was a simple but very pretty structure, with Sylven's signature gardens surrounding it. Nestled in a breathtakingly beautiful valley, it was protected on all sides from the worst of the winter elements. Even in his distraction, he knew he was in an idyllic place.

Several days had passed since their arrival and Tor was anxious to search for Cloot. This restless night, he found himself standing at the window of Sylven's bedchamber, staring into the darkness towards the hills. He glanced over at Sylven, who was sleeping peacefully after a night of indulgence. Ryk's incredible feast followed by several helpings of Tor's body had finally sated her. He smiled. If he could only allow himself to relax, life could be very peaceful and happy for him here with Sylven. He knew she was in love with him; it was clear from the way her eyes followed him all the time. Her passion was fuelled by a need to be loved by him in return, but Tor knew that could never be. As long as Alyssa was alive and he had breath in his body, his heart belonged to her. He could never stop loving her or wanting her. Sex was different. He loved to please women and take his pleasure in return, but it was not love. He had discovered true love on the day of the Floral Dance at Minstead Green and rediscovered it at his reunion with Alyssa in the archive library at Caremboche. He had been consumed by love in the Heartwood for nine glorious cycles of the moon. And just before his body died from the executioner's stones, he had seen love returned from that balcony where she stood. There could be no one else for either of them. He knew she would never love another.

Tor stared to the west where he imagined Cloot slept in the forest aviaries.

He would suggest a picnic. Sylven would like that and it could be combined with a trip into the forest. Perfect.

Not far away from the same window, Saxon sat munching on a hunk of bread and cold meat. He had arrived earlier that evening and would officially commence work in the aviaries tomorrow. He had not wasted any time, heading straightaway to find the man known as Hume. Saxon knew it would not take the keeper long to realise that he had none of his promised skills, but then he would not need very long to find Cloot. Free the falcon and escape – that was all he had in mind now.

He had strung Hume along, talking about things he remembered about the King's four hawks. Much the same thing as falcons. Lorys loved to hunt with hawks and Saxon had been out with him on occasion and spent time talking with the two handlers. He had absorbed enough information to muddle through this first encounter with the head of the aviary.

Saxon asked Hume if he could see the birds. The light

was very low, almost dark in fact, but even though he could not see clearly, Saxon did not think he would have missed the fine peregrine falcon if he had been there. Disappointment knifed through him.

'Are these all the birds?' he asked, as casually as his churning emotions would allow.

'No. Two of the best ones are still out at the moment. My men took them out this morning to put in some practice before the Queen hunts with them. They're both new birds so we thought we'd blood them a few extra times so they fly well for her majesty.'

Saxon felt weeks of disappointment and a great load of despair lift from his chest. New birds. He was sure Cloot was one of them.

'How have you found the new ones?' he asked.

'Ah well, they're both peregrines . . . temperamental. I suppose you'd know all about that.' He tapped his nose and Saxon nodded as though he understood the gesture.

'One's going to be fine. The other is a magnificent bird but he's odd. Very withdrawn. I think he just needs some settling, though he has been here long enough now. I keep him in a separate cage actually; he's quite aggressive towards the others. When left alone he just sits very still. One of the boys calls him "The Dead" because he makes no sound; doesn't even move unless he has to. Definitely a strange one, but flies like a bird of the gods. Faster, stronger and more beautiful in the air than any falcon we've ever had here, which is why I'll persevere with him.

'I have to keep him permanently in the hood. He's only quiet if it's on. We made the mistake the first few hours of leaving it off and he nearly killed himself flying against the cage, tearing at himself and the other birds in a frenzy to escape. We've got him under control now though. I think he's forgotten freedom. He's fallen into the routine here. Queen Sylven will adore him. He hunts with such ferocious intensity; she likes her birds to be a bit savage.'

'Really?' Saxon could not care less whether she did or did not but he had to sound interested in her majesty. In truth, all that mattered to him was Hume's description of the strange falcon. It was Cloot. He was sure of it.

Back at the castle, well after dinner, the young lad who was the Queen's chef had called to him. Ryk had obviously noticed Saxon lurking around the kitchens, hoping for some scraps from dinner. Always happy to feed someone, Ryk had not minded pulling together a meal of sorts.

The boy even had a way with bread and meat, Saxon thought, as he sat outside that night beneath a starry sky. Without realising it, his gaze followed the same direction as that of Torkyn Gynt, west towards where Cloot may be.

Goth had lain low since his arrival the previous day with the final carts of provisions and people who made up the winter palace staff. There were enough of them milling around that he could slip away unnoticed. If he stayed far enough away from the Queen and her immediate servants, no one would question him. He was a reasonably familiar face around the city palace by now anyway, though he intended to draw no undue attention to himself.

Goth found himself a tiny chamber within a seemingly unused wing of the Neame palace. He could hide out there and wait for the right opportunity to don Elma's black robe and veil. Right now, inside the palace surrounds, the Queen's women were unveiled. His plan depended on them leaving the palace walls, when they would wear their veils.

Patience is required, he thought, drumming his fingers on the sill of the window which overlooked a courtyard where provisions were being unloaded. He must not attract any attention to himself. It did not matter if he was seen by some of the palace staff, but he did not want the Queen to know of his presence. The fact that he had not been invited to Neame meant Sylven did not trust him.

Goth knew she did not like him, but he was used to such a response from women. She was, however, intelligent enough to appreciate the value of his counsel. Whether she would take much notice of it was still to be seen, but her interest in hearing information and, indeed, considering advice from someone who had been a senior member of the Tal court was heartening. Goth appreciated the quick mind of the Ciprean Queen; even at that very first meeting, when he had begged an audience after being rescued by her guards, he had seen immediately that she was no fool. Her frank appraisal of him had obviously resulted in a similar impression and she had permitted his continued presence at the palace, yet kept him very much at arm's length. No formal appointment had been discussed on the few occasions they had met, but he had been asked by the Queen for a first-hand account of Lorys and the former Queen Nyria. Goth had been surprised at a more recent meeting to hear Sylven ask about Alyssandra Qyn as well.

And now she had taken Torkyn Gynt into her bed. Her

interest in Gynt was salt in the wound of hate for the physic that festered inside Goth. But she would not enjoy Gynt's attentions for much longer. Goth pulled out of his pocket the tiny vial with its even tinier amount of the palest of pink arraq. This liquid would be the undoing of Torkyn Gynt, he mused.

He had bought the tiny vial from the apothecary in Caradoon, at the same time as he had stocked up on supplies of the liquid to get him through the voyage to Cipres.

The wrinkled, shrunken old man behind the dilapidated counter had sold Goth the necessary supply of clear arraq to dull the pain of the stracca withdrawal. Then he had smiled malevolently and pulled another vial from under the counter. This one was tiny and curved and its contents were a very pale pink.

The apothecary held it up to the light. 'Clear for health, pink for death,' he said and winked. 'Both come from the same berry but not many people know about the pink liquid.'

'Poison?'

'The nastiest and swiftest of all of them. Very painful but lightning fast.'

'I'll take it,' Goth said.

'Ah, but it will cost you plenty. A thousand dukes alone for this tiny amount.'

'I have plenty,' replied Goth, adding more money to the pile already on the counter.

'Be careful with it, sir. Just one drop will kill a person.'

Now it was time to test the old man's claim for the pink arraq. Just one drop and Gynt would be out of Goth's life for ever.

*   *   *

Tor was up hours before the Queen. He had been unable to sleep properly and had fallen into a fitful doze, waking every now and then, longing for dawn. Before it had even announced its arrival across the sky, he was dressed for the day. When finally Sylven began to turn and make waking noises, he bent and kissed her.

'Sylven, wake up.'

'Why? Come to bed and make love to me.' She spoke in a sleepy voice, hardly aware of what she said.

'Come on, Sylven, I have an idea for today. You'll enjoy it.'

Her eyes opened to slits. 'Are you dressed already?' She groaned.

'Want to hear my plan?' he said, brightly.

Sylven cleared her throat. It was obvious Tor was not returning to her bed this morning. 'Tell me,' she said and yawned politely.

'A picnic in the forest. Sarel will love it!'

'Sounds nice,' she mused, her head falling back onto the pillow. 'It's still dark outside.'

'Will you join me?'

She finally shook herself awake. 'I shall get Hela to organise everything.'

'No, I will. You take your time and get ready.'

He heard her groan again as he left.

Saxon and two other men were put to the task of cleaning out the cages. Hume had asked him to pitch in because the rest of his men had already been despatched this morning with most of the birds.

'I need everything spotless for her majesty. I've just heard she's coming into the forest today for a picnic and she'll almost certainly want to see her aviaries. Tomorrow she'll probably want to go hunting,' he said apologetically.

Saxon had not minded; he preferred a task which would not show his incompetence.

'Where's that difficult falcon you spoke of?' he asked, as though making conversation. 'Don't want my head bitten off whilst I clean the cages.'

'Oh, you won't have to worry, we always keep his hood on and he's silent then. He came in late last night and is out again; we'll show him off in flight this morning for the royal party.'

'I see.' Saxon felt the sharp pain of disappointment again.

Hume read it wrongly. 'Oh, you'll get your go with him. Think you can change him, eh? Help these men first and then I'll meet you at that northern copse at noon.'

'Right,' Saxon said, reassuring himself it was only a few hours to go.

He finished his work much earlier than Hume had anticipated but did not want to be around when the Queen's party came through, so he washed up and disappeared into the forest. He could kill an hour here before meeting at the rendezvous point. It was a good chance for some solitude and time to formulate some sort of plan for making his escape with Cloot.

Saxon chose a comfortable spot under cover of some bushes and sat down to munch on some cheese he had saved from his early breakfast. He slipped deep into thought, turning over ideas on how to get himself and Cloot out of Neame, back to Cipres and onto a ship. It was a tall order when he had no money and would soon be a fugitive on the run. Cloot could fly but he would be on foot and vulnerable. Perhaps he could steal a horse from Neame and gain some time?

Suddenly footsteps interrupted his thoughts. Coming into the clearing, his back to Saxon, was a man. It struck Saxon that the man was behaving furtively; he kept looking around, as if checking whether he was being followed. The Kloek could not see the stranger's face but he took in that the man was not especially tall though fairly broad across the shoulders. He had the vague notion, from the man's gait, the way he held his head, that this was someone familiar, but no name came to mind and the thought dispersed.

As he watched, the man pulled off his warm, long-sleeved jerkin. This was odd. It was cold in Neame. Saxon smiled at the curious behaviour and put down the apple he had been chewing. This would be interesting, he thought; there was something strange going on here. He could see the fellow was not young from his bared arms, although Saxon's experienced eye, honed over years in Cirq Zorros, told him those arms had once been well muscled. He sensed there was strength in that body still.

Saxon suddenly felt awkward sitting amongst the bushes watching this person engage in tasks which were obviously personal. He decided he should announce his presence and was considering what he might say so as not to startle the man completely, when the stranger pulled some black garments from the sack he had been carrying.

They looked like a robe and veil, Saxon thought with surprise. What could the man want with what was obviously women's attire?

Still with his back to Saxon, the man put on the long black robe over his own clothes and set the veil over his face. Saxon shifted for a better look and disturbed a small creature who broke cover. The noise made the stranger spin around. Saxon held his breath. It was too late to say anything now. He would have to remain hidden. All he could see were two small eyes staring through the slits in the veil. Saxon knew he was well covered yet those fierce eyes disconcerted him.

Then the stranger sat down in the clearing, obviously intending to remain there for some time. Saxon could not move without revealing his presence yet if he stayed under cover he would be late for his meeting with the other falconers. He did not care about Hume or the temper he was bound to get into if his new handler did not turn up, but he was desperate to learn whether Cloot was among the birds. But there was nothing to be done about his tardiness today. If he revealed himself now, it could have serious consequences. He had no idea who this fellow might be, but if he wielded any power at all with the Queen, Saxon would lose his best chance of tracking down Cloot.

Resigned to a lengthy wait, Saxon turned his attention to working out why the man was hiding in the clearing in the first place and in such strange garb. The man appeared to have disguised himself as one of the Queen's personal servants. What reason could he have to do so, unless he meant to cause harm?

Goth, oblivious of Saxon's presence, was turning over in his mind the frighteningly simple plan. Disguised as one of the Queen's serving women, he would join the picnic party later that morning. He pulled the tiny vial of arraq from his sack and held it up so the sunlight glinted through its palest of pink contents. Goth chuckled softly and slid the vial into a pocket in the robe.

Even Saxon's untrained eye recognised that the only thing likely to be contained in such a tiny glass vial was poison. So who was this fellow planning to kill? It had to be the Queen. There was no question of Saxon leaving his post now. He had to find out what the stranger intended and, if necessary, prevent him from achieving his evil aim. Just when Saxon thought he would have to let out the cough which had been tickling his throat for the past few minutes, the man stood, gathered up his sack and hid it behind a tree. Then he crept out of the copse and carefully picked his way back into the open, in the direction of the site where Saxon knew the Queen's picnic was to be held.

Saxon followed. It meant he would have to wait longer still for a glimpse of Cloot, but if he was able to foil this man's murderous intentions and save the Queen's life, she might listen to his request to reclaim the falcon.

He may yet be able to get away from here with Cloot and himself in one piece.

They were welcomed by the head of the aviary, Hume, who immediately launched into a lengthy apology for the absence of his new man. Tor paid no attention. He could see two men on the rise of a hill, with three birds. All were falcons; two of them of similar size, the third much bigger. It could be Cloot, but from this distance he could not tell.

He cast and felt something give in the usual blankness. His heart leapt . . . but his concentration was interrupted as Sylven and her man stepped up next to him and he had to give them his attention.

'Tor, this is Master Hume, head of our royal aviary. He has agreed to take us through the entire complex so you can search for your falcon. Right now, he wishes to give us a demonstration of his newest birds. He thinks I will enjoy them. Do you mind?'

'Not at all, your majesty,' Tor replied. 'Please – I would be fascinated to watch them myself.'

The keeper bowed again and signalled. They watched the first bird launched into the air. It flew beautifully and then, at a single command, it returned to the handler's thick glove.

Hume looked at his Queen. 'Your majesty, this next bird is the one I'm excited about. He is very special.'

Once again he gave the command. The handler pulled the hood off the bird's head and threw the falcon into the air. It lifted off with strength, its wings beating powerfully.

'Ah,' he heard the Queen say, 'this one is majestic.'

'I'm glad you like him, your highness,' Hume replied, bowing again.

The falcon dived and swooped elegantly.

Tor instantly recognised the familiar flight. It was Cloot.

Tears welled in his eyes as he cast to his friend. *Cloot, you old rogue. There you are at last.*

The falcon faltered in the air.

'Oh, what's happened there?' Sylven asked.

Hume cleared his throat with embarrassment. 'Ahem . . . he is a little feisty, your majesty. We are training him still.'

The link was strong now; the falcon was reciprocating the bond.

Cloot. Don't come back to the handler. Stay up there, Tor said.

Tor? came the deep and gentle voice, almost too frightened to ask.

Tor began to run towards Cloot. He could hear the Queen calling to him but he cared only for the falcon above.

'Cloot!' he screamed aloud now, so all could hear. 'Fly, you beautiful falcon. Fly away.'

The handlers were incensed by this stranger yelling at their bird. Hume caught up with him. 'Physic Gynt, sir. My falcon is nervous enough without you frightening it.'

'He's not nervous, fool – and he's not your falcon either. He's mine!' Tor snarled. He surprised himself with the visceral emotion in his voice.

'Tor?' It was Sylven. She looked alarmed. 'Are you not well?'

'Never been happier, Sylven,' he said, ignoring protocol. 'That's my falcon up there.' His grin was fierce.

The handlers called out as Cloot climbed even higher into the sky. 'He's not returning, Master Hume. He's not responding at all.'

'This is terrible. That bird cost us a fortune,' Hume said, glaring at Tor but unable to say too much; after all, the man was a guest of the Queen.

'You won't catch him now,' Tor said with glee. He snatched at the hood which dangled from the handler's hand. 'Is this what you use to keep him quiet?' he asked.

The man nodded dumbly. The hood was fashioned from leather and studded with the same midnight archalyt which had prevented Tor using his powers to save Locky from the Maiden's Kiss.

'Can I keep this?' he asked the Queen but was already pushing it into his pocket without waiting for her answer.

'Now, let me prove this is my falcon. You men – give your call, summon him.'

They tried again and again but Cloot continued to circle higher and higher above.

When they shook their heads in failure, Tor made his move. 'Watch this,' he said.

He reopened the link and felt it lock freely onto Cloot.

I've been shipwrecked, almost drowned, captured as a slave and now I'm having to play royal paramour . . . all to find you.

There was a long pause. Tor wondered if Cloot was changed in some way, if he had lost his ability to speak. But then he heard the voice again. *Well, don't you just have all the fun.*

Tor laughed, surprising his audience. As far as they could see, all he was doing was staring at the bird; he made no attempt to sign or call out to it.

Cloot, show them we belong to one another. I have to prove it. Fly to me now.

The voices around him intensified their enquiries but Tor turned and put his finger to his lips to hush them and they fell silent. Looking up, they watched the superb falcon turn on itself into what seemed an impossible stoop, then drop like a stone from the sky.

'It will never pull out of that,' one of the handlers said.

'He is the most amazing flyer I've encountered in my time,' Hume said, his voice filled with awe.

Cloot was racing towards them at a reckless speed.

'Step back, your majesty,' Tor warned. Everyone else followed his advice too.

In a matter of seconds, the falcon slowed from its breathtaking speed, turned its body and put its bright yellow claws out to land. Tor needed no protection as Cloot alighted on his outstretched arm; his prayers were answered. Cloot flapped his wings once and turned to stare at his handler. Tor burst into laughter once again at the accusation in those piercing yellow eyes.

Thanks for finally turning up, Cloot said, the familiar sarcasm thrilling Tor.

Tor kissed the side of the sharp beak; behind him he heard the others make noises of revulsion. *We shall never be apart again, old friend.*

Cloot grunted in his head. *Don't make wild promises, Torkyn Gynt.* He ruffled his feathers and stared balefully as the Queen approached.

I love you, Cloot, Tor said, then closed the link and smiled serenely at her majesty.

Sylven's hand was on her hip. 'Well, well, well. I suppose I have to give you this prized falcon then?'

'He is mine, your majesty, and you did promise.'

'Yes, I did, Tor. He is yours.'

'What about him?' he said, motioning towards Hume.

'He does as he's told,' she replied.

She dismissed the men, who left looking disgruntled. Hume looked murderous.

Tor surprised her by dropping to one knee, his head bowed. 'Thank you, Queen Sylven, for your generosity. You will never know how much Cloot means to me or how precious it is to have him back.'

There was such tenderness in his words, so much vulnerability, that she wanted to reach out and touch his thick dark hair. Here was the little boy in front of her now; a few moments ago he had been all swaggering arrogance, now he showed such humility. She loved these different aspects of him and she wanted to hug herself that she had this man with her in her bed. Yet, at the same time, she felt very alone. She sensed that the euphoria of having found her soulmate would be short-lived.

Instead of saying all that was running through her mind, she touched his shoulder. 'Come, Tor. Let us celebrate with that picnic you promised me.'

He looked up at her and her heart skipped a beat at the sight of those bright blue eyes; a colour she swore she had never seen on a person before and never would again. Torkyn Gynt was as beautiful as the gods they painted in the murals on the walls of her palaces. Yet he was real. Her very own god. She let him take her arm and lead her back towards their chosen picnic spot.

Cloot, we shall meet later. I have to spend some time with her majesty now. I shall speak with you tonight. Head for safety and freedom high in those trees for now.

Cloot took off towards the trees. There was much to say but it could wait just a little while longer. Tor was obviously in a prickly situation.

Sylven felt compelled to ask the question that was brewing in her mind. 'Does this mean you will leave me now?'

Tor was startled by the direct question; it stopped him in his tracks. He looked searchingly at her. 'I must.'

'You have your falcon again. Why can't we enjoy more time together?' The Queen hated to hear the plea in her voice.

'Because I have found what I came here for. And now I must return.'

'To her?' she snapped, despising the jealousy which grabbed at her throat. She was Queen; she could command him to stay. She could have him thrown back in chains and kept her prisoner if she so desired. What was wrong with her? She sounded like a child of twelve summers.

'Alyssa?' he asked and then shook his head. He spoke gently, 'No, Sylven, not to Alyssa. I am not permitted to be with her. You know this.'

He could scarcely believe it but the Queen was crying. Her party were waiting for them at the picnic spot but this needed delicate handling. He guided her behind a convenient tree and took her into his arms and hugged her. For all her poise and strength, all her power as the ruler of a mighty realm, she was weeping for the love of a man – the one thing she had assured him she did not need. She had a harem full of men, all awaiting her pleasure. She could use them as she wished and cast them aside, as he fully expected she did.

'Sylven, hush, please. This is not right. You know I must go. I have explained—'

'You have explained nothing!' she snarled at him, pulling herself roughly from his embrace. 'You talk about your destiny but it means nothing to me. I don't understand any of it because you have not told me anything. You walk into my life, bed me, take my heart and then you think you can just walk away.'

Tor looked at her with incomprehension. He repeated in his mind what she had just said and couldn't help but echo the words, 'Take my heart?'; he spoke softly but she heard. She pushed him and turned away, still weeping.

Tor's voice was almost a whisper. 'What can I tell you that will make it easier?'

'Why?'

'Why what, your majesty?'

'Why can you not love me? Be with me?' She was trembling with anger now.

Tor gave her the full respect she deserved, by speaking only the truth. 'Because I do not love you, Sylven. I love another. I cannot give my heart to any other woman as long as she is alive.'

'Then I shall have her killed,' the Queen said, petulance spilling into her passion for him.

'You will not win my love that way. You will never win it. Alyssa and I are destined for one another. I will never marry another woman. She will never marry another man or call him hers.'

When he needed to convince himself that his path would never cross hers again, he had tried to believe that Alyssa might build a new life without him. And yet now, with the thought of the children coming back and Cloot safe, he knew deep down that he wished she might never have another man in her life. Tor wanted her to suffer the pain he suffered every day in being apart from her. Because it was only through the pain that he could keep her love alive in his mind. And, in turn, her pain would keep him real, even though she thought him dead.

'Really?' the Queen said. 'She shall never take another? Perhaps you should read this, Tor.' She pulled out a parchment scroll from her deep pocket. 'I received it only this morning. It has come by way of the city palace with the carts which came in last night. It was written several weeks ago, I fear. The deed is done.'

She held it out to him, full of defiance. Was there also satisfaction in her expression?

He took the parchment. The situation felt suddenly dangerous and he wished he had just led her straight to the picnic and lied to her. Lied that he would stay, lied that he loved her and then he and Cloot could have escaped.

'Read it,' she commanded.

He did.

His royal highness King Lorys of Tallinor announces his marriage to Alyssandra Qyn of Mallee Marsh, to take place at the Royal Chapel of Tal in a private ceremony. The King hopes her royal highness the Queen of Cipres will join with the people of Tallinor in . . .

Tor could not read any further. The scroll was dated before the last moon. Alyssa was married to the man who had ordered his execution. She was Queen of Tallinor.

Tor felt as though he could no longer breathe. He crushed the parchment between his fingers and then he was on his knees, his emotions writhing agonisingly through his body. He began to moan.

It was a sound which tore at Sylven. Despite her anger and her terror of losing him, she kneeled beside him and held him as he whispered Alyssa's name repeatedly.

Cloot arrived overhead. The link broke open in Tor's head and he heard his Paladin. It was a voice of command now; no longer gentle. *Tor!*

She's gone, Cloot. Alyssa is gone, he moaned.

Gone? Dead, you mean?

She might as well be. She is married to the King.

There was silence for a moment and then Cloot was back in his head, strong and convincing. *Get up! Do you forget who you are? Do you forget you are the One? This very Land depends upon you; thousands of innocents don't yet know it but they depend on you for their lives. Stand up!*

Tor reluctantly pulled himself to his feet and took several deep breaths.

Sylven stood as well, still holding his arm, wishing she could take back all she had said and done. The pain on his face, in his trembling body, was too much for her to bear. She loved this man. He was the father of the child now growing inside her; a sister for Sarel, a second Princess for Cipres. Sylven wanted Tor as her Regent. What a dashing and brilliant royal couple they would make, if only he could be encouraged to forget this wench in Tallinor. She corrected herself – this Queen in Tallinor.

Sylven had taken the wrong approach and her anger had led her down a dangerous path. She must repair the damage now, bring him back to her side and gently show him that this Alyssandra Qyn was now in his past.

And Tor . . . Cloot said firmly.

Tor stood straighter. *Yes?*

Don't forget that Alyssa is still your wife. Nothing has changed that.

It was as though a shaft of sunlight had just broken through the overcast day and shone directly into his heart. Cloot was right. Alyssa was his wife and that still stood. *I won't forget it.*

Good, the bird said and flapped his wings. *Now take part in that picnic and go through the motions of the day. We must escape tonight. I sense our time is almost here. Be strong now.* Cloot flew off.

Tor turned to face Sylven. He could read a hundred apologies in her face but, before they could spill out, he put his hand to her mouth.

'No, wait! It is good that I am given this news. Thank you, Sylven. And now, I believe we have a picnic to enjoy.'

There he was, in control again, she thought. The man was an enigma. One minute on his knees in shock and then, as though some magical guardian had made him see reason, composed and strong again. Sylven shook her head. They would not speak further on this subject.

'My Queen?' Tor said and gallantly offered her his arm, gritting his teeth to stem the flood of emotion he was experiencing.

She linked her arm through his and together they strolled to where Hela and the rest of the servants had set up the glorious feast prepared by Ryk. Sarel was waiting to join them.

They refused tables and chairs, preferring to lounge on cushions and a rug. The Queen dismissed most of the staff, leaving just a handful.

Tor, feeling more in control now, pushed Alyssa to that safe place in his heart, as he had done these past years, to be retrieved at another time when he was strong enough to confront her. He had the Queen laughing and even blushing within minutes of taking their first goblet of fine, chilled Ciprean wine. It was a pleasant scene and Sylven could almost forget the ugliness which had taken place just moments ago.

Tor kept the conversation on safe ground. 'Why was your man Hume so grumpy when we arrived?'

The Queen wrapped a sliver of paper-thin meat around a fig and chewed. 'He was, wasn't he? Hardly the mood with which to greet one's Queen. He had hired a new man to start this morning and was cross that he had not turned up for the great "showing" of this priceless new falcon we had to give away to a foreigner.'

Tor lifted his glass and grinned. A woman, veiled like

her Queen and dressed in the full black of her retinue, came forward to top up his goblet. He thanked her and was momentarily arrested by her small, intense eyes, which were staring hard at him. They looked so menacing, he almost missed what the Queen was saying.

'. . . yes, well, you can't trust a Kloek, you know,' Sylven finished, also holding out her goblet to the servant.

Tor's attention was caught. 'A Kloek? Surely you don't get Kloeks this far north?'

The serving woman moved back to stand quietly at a polite distance from the sovereign and her guest.

Sylven sipped. 'Oh, we get all sorts passing through Cipres. But you're right, Kloeks are rare,' she agreed. 'Apparently he's a hunting bird specialist and most lately from Tallinor. He only arrived last night and was very keen to see this great falcon – which we now know is yours,' she said, pulling a face. 'So Hume was understandably angry that the man did not turn up at the showing this morning.'

'A Kloek with an interest in my falcon?'

'Well, I'm sure he didn't know it was yours, Tor. Do you know any Kloeks?'

Tor began to chew on a slice of delicious cold game pie. 'As a matter of fact I do. His name is Saxon Fox. You would fall instantly in love with him, your majesty. He is as tall as you, with wild golden hair and the face of a warrior. He is as broad as an ox with a heart as big. He was once a famous trapeze artist.'

Sylven made a sound of appreciation. 'Move over, Physic Gynt,' she said, her eyes dazzling him from behind the veil. They shared more laughter and Sylven began to relax. Perhaps she could win his love after all.

Behind his veil, Goth's face was a mask of hatred. He wished he could just pick up one of the sharp knives the stupid boy chef had sent along and plunge it straight into Gynt's chest.

He knew he had to calm himself. There he was; the enemy. Drinking and cackling with the Queen of Cipres and her acting like a bitch dog on heat. *Well, there will be no sport in the bedroom tonight, dear Queen,* Goth thought, and fingered the vial of poison deep in his pocket. *Your lover will be stone cold dead by then.*

His tiny, sharp eyes watched Gynt drink again and again from his goblet; he must choose exactly the right time to serve the poisoned wine. He needed both of them in a merry enough mood that the goblets could be passed almost unnoticed into their hands.

Slipping away from the other servants, Goth moved behind one of the carts which had carried all the provisions for today's decadence. He pulled a flask of a special sweet wine from the supplies. It was made only in this region, produced from a small grape which grew in tiny amounts each season. Exorbitantly expensive, it was considered by Cipreans to be the nectar of the gods. The Queen and her guest would not be able to resist it. He also pulled out two narrow goblets. These were exquisitely made from delicate glass, stamped with her majesty's personal crest. It was fitting that Gynt should die with his lips touching her crest as he sipped the poison.

Goth took the tiny curved vial from his pocket and broke the seal. He looked around furtively, but no one was watching . . . or so he thought.

*   *   *

Saxon was hidden behind a second cartload of provisions.

He blew out his cheeks. It was obvious the man was up to no good. He had to act. He could see the Queen and her guest reclining on some cushions not far away. They were laughing. The man looked familiar, but he had his back to Saxon and the Kloek's view was partially obscured by trees and the cart Goth was hiding behind. Saxon had heard of Queen Sylven's voracious appetite for men; he guessed this must be her current lover.

He watched as the impostor carefully placed the goblets of freshly poured wine onto a tray. Saxon moved closer. Now he could not see the guest at all, just the Queen. Goth tipped several drops of the poison into one of the glasses and Saxon made careful note of which one. He was preparing to rush the stranger in the veils to prevent him carrying out his evil task, but to his surprise the impostor moved back to the royal party, probably to ask the Queen's permission to serve this new wine. This was his chance. He ran towards the tray.

Goth hated leaving the poisoned goblet unattended, but there was a strict protocol for serving wine which he had watched over and again at the Ciprean palace. He must not endanger his plan with haste.

He motioned to the head maid that he wished to approach the Queen. She nodded.

Goth bent low to address Sylven and spoke in a disguised voice. 'Your majesty, I have some of your favourite Tolique to serve with the sweet course . . . if you please?'

'Yes, bring it . . . er . . . ?'

'Sacha,' Goth replied, unable to help looking towards Tor.

He realised Tor was watching him closely. Had he been recognised, Goth wondered? No, he decided, casting another furtive glance at Gynt. He cursed his foe silently before turning back to her majesty.

'Sacha, where is Elma, my usual bearer?'

'Your majesty, Elma has trained me to your precise needs. She is presently hunting down some special Mytal for you for tonight. She knows it is your favourite,' Goth said sweetly.

The Queen hardly paid any attention to Goth's explanation but Tor did.

'You know, there's something odd about that woman,' he said.

'I don't know her, she must be new,' Sylven said distractedly. She was plaiting Sarel's hair. 'My people are always training youngsters into specialist roles.'

'That one is hardly young, your majesty.'

'Hmm, true. But she seems to know everything that matters,' Sylven said, tying two plaits together.

'But who checks up on these people, Sylven?'

One of the plaits came undone, annoying the Queen, as did Tor's persistence. 'Oh, Tor, someone would have. Don't be so suspicious. What's wrong with her?'

'Her eyes – there's malice in them.'

'Rubbish!' Sylven dismissed the thought. 'Ah, here comes my Tolique. Now, Tor, prepare yourself for an extraordinary treat.'

Saxon had managed to switch the wine goblets, which meant the Queen was unlikely to die. But it still left the stranger at risk. He was about to throw himself into the peaceful scene and warn the two lovers of the danger, when a strong arm clamped around his chest and a large hand covered his mouth.

'You bastard!'

Saxon recognised the voice of one of the handlers from the royal aviaries.

'You're no falconer. I had my suspicions this morning and now here you are spying on our Queen!'

The man had a companion, who now came in front of Saxon and began to rough him up, punching him in the belly. As Saxon doubled over, winded from the punches, he caught a glimpse of the veiled servant handing the goblet containing the poison to the Queen.

No! That was wrong! Saxon had carefully switched the glasses. Why would the impostor have intended the poisoned goblet for the Queen's guest?

Saxon's panic lent him extra strength. With a mighty grunt he shook off both his captors and lurched out from the cover of the cart, yelling like a mad man. He watched in horror as the Queen, still smiling at her companion, clinked glasses and then took one long gulp.

It was only then his noise grabbed their attention and they turned towards him in confusion: the Queen, the impostor and . . . Suddenly Saxon felt as though his heart had stopped its beating. The man turning towards him was Torkyn Gynt. Hale, smiling brilliantly at some jest and bursting with life. Time seemed to stand still for Saxon as everything ordered about his world fell apart.

Then he heard himself screaming, 'Poison!' He saw Tor throw down his glass and turn to the Queen. No one paid any attention to the impostor servant, who crept stealthily from the scene and then began to run.

Tor kneeled alongside Sylven, calling to her, trying to

hold her attention. She was in agony, moaning and shrieking.

Sarel began to scream and suddenly people were running from all directions towards their Queen. Saxon arrived first.

Tor looked up, his brilliant blue eyes wild now. Saxon shook his head slowly. He was in shock; his mind in absolute turmoil. 'It can't be you.'

Sylven's body began to jerk and flail in its death throes. She screamed one last time before her eyes rolled back into her head and her lips turned purple. Tor ripped away the Queen's veils but it was too late. Sylven's body arched in one last horrific convulsion and a painful guttural groan came from her throat; her face flushed with the blood that was carrying death around her body. She bared her teeth through foaming spittle to form one final angry sound at the world and then she fell back, lifeless. The poison had done its work.

Tor also fell back, into Saxon's arms. He was breathing hard; he had tried to use his powers to save her but to no avail.

Hela kneeled beside him, almost rigid with shock beside him. She grabbed the child, Sarel, and held her close.

Tor shook his head. 'I . . . went inside. She was dead before I could do anything.'

Saxon held him firmly but could not believe it was Tor in his arms, warm and alive. The Torkyn Gynt he knew was dead, like the Queen now lying in front of them.

'I was too late, Saxon. Too late!'

The Queen's staff keened with despair, uselessly clutching at one another. It was impossible for them to believe that their Queen was dead.

Tor recovered first. 'Saxon, the servant – she's getting away!'

The Kloek was still in a state of shock and wonder. He had watched this man die by the executioner's stones. He had seen his body taken down from the cross and his broken face washed clear of the blood. The corpse had been wrapped in muslin and then Merkhud had driven away with it on an old cart to only he knew where. He was dead.

Torkyn Gynt's bright blue, very alive eyes communicated the need for urgency. Saxon pulled his scrambled thoughts together.

'That's no woman, Tor. Let's go – he'll head for the woods,' Saxon replied and then he was running; running alongside his old friend after the impostor who had tried to kill a man already dead, but instead had assassinated a sovereign.

23

A Desperate Escape

Goth's speed carried him into the cover of the forest before his pursuers had even begun to give chase. As he ran he went over events again and again in his mind. How could Sylven have got the poisoned goblet? He had been so careful to hand Gynt the doctored wine. It did not make sense.

He could hear yelling now behind him. He knew it would be Gynt but the idiot did not know to whom he gave chase. The robe was slowing him down and Goth realised he needed to dispense with it. He pulled it over his head and tossed it aside, instantly realising that he had forgotten to remove the arraq in its pocket.

He sneaked a look behind and felt his hatred instantly boil up. Pursuing him grimly was Gynt and his old sidekick, that once blinded but now all-seeing bastard Kloek. So that's what had happened! The Kloek must have swapped the goblets to protect Gynt. Yes . . . he understood now. His anger helped him to find new speed and he pulled away from the pair.

'Who is it?' Tor called breathlessly to Saxon, who was slightly behind.

It was Cloot who answered from up ahead. *It's Goth*.

Tor stopped in his tracks and Saxon caught up. 'What are you stopping for?'

'Cloot's just told me who we're chasing.'

Saxon looked immediately into the sky. Cloot had been found? He felt a fierce wave of joy pass through him. Tor and Cloot had been returned to him. The Paladin would not fail again; the Heartwood would prevail and the Trinity would be found.

'I've not seen the man's face,' Saxon said, returning to the conversation. 'Do we know him?'

'Goth,' Tor snarled and opened himself up to the Colours. This time he would kill him.

They picked up their pace again. In the distance, they saw the small figure halfway up a hill; Goth miraculously scaled its height with ease and speed. Tor remembered that night at Caremboche, when Goth had almost caught him and Alyssa; he recalled how fast the Inquisitor had run then, fuelled by his anger and his determination to stop their escape.

They had lost sight of him now. Breathing hard, they climbed higher and higher into the hills, with Cloot flying overhead and telling Tor which direction to take.

He's trapped! Cloot suddenly said.

Tor stopped; Saxon followed suit. *What do you mean?* Tor asked.

He's reached a waterfall. There's no way out for him, Tor. If he retraces his steps, he'll meet you. He heard the falcon chuckle. *He's all yours.*

Tor began to lope ahead again. 'Come on, Sax. We've got him trapped apparently.'

They climbed further; they could hear the rushing of water now as it hurtled over the edge of a precipice and crashed below. The air was damp with the mist from the waterfall.

Tor stepped through a narrow pass between two tall hills and came out on a high crag. There he finally recognised Goth; the man was standing at the edge, looking down.

'Goth!' he screamed, and the face he hated turned and sneered at him.

The former Chief Inquisitor certainly looked different; the once solid frame was slim now and gaunt. But he could not disguise his eyes and Tor was angry he had not made the connection when he first stared into those small, mean eyes at the picnic. He put it all quickly together in his mind as he watched the man's sneer overwhelmed by the prominent twitching of one side of his horribly scarred face.

The poison had been meant for him but it had mistakenly found Sylven. *Oh, Sylven, what have I done to you?* Tor's Colours burned inside, they wanted him to unleash them. But he had Goth cornered now. He could take his time.

Saxon rounded the crag and stopped, sucking in gulps of air. 'What are you going to do?' he asked, triumphant at finally having this man at their mercy.

Tor's own chest was heaving, more from hatred for Goth than exertion. 'I'm going to finish it here. He's killed enough people in his useless life.'

'Then do it, Tor. Finish it now.'

'He can't hurt us, Saxon. There is nothing he can do,' Tor said, walking forwards slowly. 'Do not fear him.'

Goth hurled a stream of abuse at him as he approached. Tor had to admire his courage.

'What are you waiting for?' Saxon called from the crag. He had no desire to look Goth in the eyes again. This was the man who had once taken his sight and beaten him savagely, leaving him for dead. He despised the man and could never forgive him for what he had done to Alyssa either. Saxon did not care if Goth suffered now – all he wanted was to see his life extinguished once and for all.

Goth fixed Tor with a look of scorn. He had never feared death. Now that it stared at him, he did not exactly welcome it but neither did he turn away, terrified. His clever mind wrapped itself around several options, none of them feasible. He was trapped. He could even see the falcon up there, circling, waiting for his death. He refused to give them the satisfaction of dancing around his corpse with glee. He could deny them that much at least.

Tor prepared to unleash the Colours and finally kill his enemy, but he faltered as a vision of Jhon Gynt suddenly entered his mind. He recalled how his father had abhorred all violence and had raised his son to show compassion to others.

'Killing is not my place,' Tor said, hesitantly.

'Then I'll do it,' Saxon said, pushing past him. 'And I'll enjoy it. I'll crush the last breath from him with my bare hands.'

Goth laughed and the girlish sound incensed Saxon. The man was remorseless. Even when facing obvious death, he did not plea for mercy. He simply laughed at them.

Then, to the disbelief of them both, Goth leaped off

the crag into the roaring torrent of water. 'Give my love to Alyssa!' he called and was gone. They could hear him howling, as if with joy, as he descended.

'No!' Tor yelled but it was too late; the man had disappeared from sight.

He and Saxon ran to the edge and looked over. It was high and Saxon felt momentarily dizzy. The height did not bother Tor. He stared intently at the churning waters below. How deep was it? Could Goth survive this? It was a mighty drop.

They watched and waited for any sign of his body to float up. Tor's keen eyes looked further down the rushing river, roving across the scenery below for any movement, any sign at all that Goth lived. There was nothing.

'What do you think?' Saxon asked, finally.

'I think I should not have hesitated,' Tor replied angrily, turning away.

'You think he could survive that? He's dead, Tor. By your hand or not, it no longer matters.'

Tor did not share Saxon's optimism. He cast to the falcon. *Cloot, can you fly over and see if there's any sign?*

The falcon silently obeyed.

'Goth seems to survive all adversity which comes his way,' Tor said to Saxon. 'I should have dealt with him the minute we arrived. He stood there and laughed at us and still I hesitated.'

It was true. Saxon could offer no consolation. Instead he spat on the ground in his unique Kloek way. 'I haven't formally welcomed you back from the dead yet, Tor.'

Tor felt awkward. 'It's . . . er . . . it's good to be back, Saxon.' He felt the familiar bearlike hug of the Kloek and returned the affection.

Cloot swooped down and landed on the crag. 'Hello, old friend,' Saxon said. 'I've travelled a long way to see you again.'

The falcon flew to sit on Saxon's shoulder, which brought the Kloek enormous satisfaction, whilst he gave Tor the bad news. *Nothing down the river that I can see. But there's pandemonium still at the picnic site, Tor. I think you should make plans to get away from here as quickly as possible. Accusations will soon begin to find their way to you.*

Tor nodded. 'How long has it been?' he said to Saxon.

'Since I left Tallinor, you mean? I set off the day after Queen Nyria died.' Then he looked mortified. 'Oh, Tor, I'm sorry. Had you heard this news?'

'And far worse,' Tor said, his face grim. 'Do you know about Alyssa?'

Saxon had never imagined he would ever have to consider Tor and Alyssa in the same sentence again. 'Know about her? Yes, she is safe; running her school at the palace and keeping up her duties to the sovereign, though I left her grieving for Nyria. Why? Is something wrong?'

Tor smiled ruefully. 'Well, she's certainly kept up her duty to the King in your absence.'

Saxon shook his head. 'What am I missing here, Tor? What's happened to Alyssa? And how could you know of it before I do?'

Tor sighed. 'Whilst you were travelling here, Alyssa became Queen of Tallinor. Sylven told me this morning after receiving formal notification between the realms.'

Saxon looked dumbstruck. It was obvious Alyssa's Paladin had not known of a relationship between Lorys and Alyssa, Tor decided.

The Kloek shook his head. 'There must be some

mistake. Alyssa and Lorys? No. She's been working with him, and the last time we spoke she mentioned that she had finally begun to look forward rather then dwelling on the past. Your death . . .' He cleared his throat, embarrassed. 'Your death was a terrible shock for all of us, Tor. Alyssa was lost for many years; she only began to come out of that grief and anger when Gyl came along.'

'Gyl?'

Saxon shook his head. 'So much to tell you. Gyl is an orphan whom the Queen took under her wing some years back. She put him in the care of Alyssa. It was as good for Alyssa as it was for the child – as you can imagine . . . since losing her own son,' he said, haltingly.

Tor said nothing; his face betrayed no emotion.

Saxon continued, keen to fill the awkward pause. 'Nyria asked her to form a school. Alyssa excelled with her teaching of the children and in her work for the Queen. And then, after a year or so, the King's private secretary died and Nyria thought it would be a good idea if she gave him Alyssa.' His last few words sounded ill chosen even to his ear.

'And she accepted?' Tor couldn't believe it.

'She fought it, Tor. Fought it hard. I have not been around the palace as much these last few years, but I know she was terribly unhappy about this new turn of events. She has done so well though. You would be proud of how she has really made something of her life at the palace. And everyone loves her.'

'Including Lorys, obviously,' Tor said with disgust.

'I know nothing of this. As I said, the last time we spoke was when I returned from Caradoon to tell her about Goth and how I had seen Cloot again. All she said was that she was trying hard to bury the hatred and move on. You were dead. It took so much of her energy to continue to hate Lorys. What was the point?'

'No point at all,' Tor agreed, standing. 'I just can't imagine how she made the leap from "I must try not to hate him" to "I want to marry you, Lorys."'

Tor walked back to the edge of the rock and looked again into the raging waters, ostensibly to see if Goth's body had surfaced, but in reality to turn away from the pain of his last sentence.

Saxon joined him. He put his arm on his friend's shoulder. 'Don't be too hard on her, Tor. You can't begin to imagine how much she suffered at your expense.'

It was true and Tor knew it.

'How long afterwards was it?' he heard Saxon ask.

He knew what Saxon meant but chose not to understand. 'What do you mean?'

'After the execution. How long was it before you returned?'

Tor felt again the full weight of despair and guilt he had suffered for so many years since that day he had reopened his eyes in the Heartwood.

'Almost immediately, Sax. Come, we must move fast – we must get back to the Heartwood. And I have a long story to tell you as we travel.'

24

A Disturbance in the Land

Alyssa thanked Tilly absentmindedly for the steaming cup of raspberry leaf tea. It was unlike her to be vague. Tilly took note that her mistress had barely touched her breakfast tray this morning and that the daily ritual of bathing and then brushing her hair for exactly one hundred strokes was not peppered with its usual lighthearted banter. And what was she doing up this early? Light! It meant they all had a long day ahead when the Queen rose at this hour.

It was true. Alyssa did feel distant this morning. It was not just that Lorys was away from her – on official business in Hatten – for the first time since declaring his love, or that life seemed suddenly incomplete without his blustering, irresistible company. No, it was not that at all. Today was definitely different, she mused, putting her cup down.

She had awoken with a start. Morning had barely announced itself and only a few bright slashes across the charcoal sky told her another late wintry day was emerging. Now, staring out of the window to the lush, heather-laden hills, she realised she was thinking of Tor. At one time he had been constantly in her thoughts; now she had to concentrate to put all the features of his face together accurately in her mind.

He had been so irritatingly handsome, had he not? She smiled. His dark, almost black hair, had been thick and straight and he had a habit of running his fingers through it when he was thinking. She recalled his strong jaw and the impossibly blue eyes in that lovely face, which had once made her heart pound simply by casting a glance her way. She never wanted to lose the memory of his face. And yet she had, to some degree. It had been four, no, five cycles since she had last seen it — smashed by the stones and gushing his precious blood. She had been forced to watch him die; had seen his chest heave in one last courageous effort to remain of this Land, and then he was gone. She would never forget his bloodied face.

His voice was gone for ever too, and that was almost the hardest part. She had loved his voice most of all; it was what she had fallen in love with first when he teased her as a young child across the link. A smile of regret played around her mouth and she inwardly chided herself for indulging thoughts of him.

Alyssa's life had been filled with misery and toil since early childhood. The only brightness in it was Tor. When she lost him the first time, she had found solace at the Academie in Caremboche. Alyssa denied that she had found complete peace there, because Tor had always been in her thoughts, but she had been able to escape through her work in the Academie archives and Saxon, Sorrel and even Xantia had provided companionship in those early years.

When Tor returned to her life it had been a gift from the gods, she was certain of it. And their short married life in the Heartwood had been blissful; truly the happiest period of her life. But it was so brief. Just long enough for her womb to quicken and her son to grow inside her; the same son who took his final breath so soon after his birth.

And then the misery and destruction began again. Goth came back to taunt her; followed by the crippling pain of witnessing Tor's execution and then the terrible loneliness of her life at the palace. If it had not been for the friendship of Saxon and Sallementro in those first two years, she was sure she would have ended her pathetic life.

But Tor was dead, long dead, and it did her no good to dwell on her first love. She was married to King Lorys now and Queen of Tallinor. She had a duty to Lorys and a future running this Kingdom alongside him, and, in truth, she had found love again. Alyssa would never have dreamed it possible, but she *did* love Lorys and he surely worshipped her. It had been a wonderful few months since they had finally been able to proclaim their love throughout the Kingdom and beyond. Alyssa considered Lorys as her salvation. She knew it was a strange notion after despising him for so long, but it truly was Lorys who had made her believe that her life was important to Tallinor and that there was a future for her here. She did not want anything to rupture this perfect life now that she had finally achieved it. She wanted to reign beside Lorys and be in his arms until their gods claimed them. It was true that she had known perfect love with Tor, and she would never try to compare her love for Lorys with that, yet in this marriage she knew complete peace for the first time in her life.

Tor was dead. Lorys was alive and loved her totally. She could not help returning that love and she told herself that she must learn to forgive the guilt she felt at odd times, like now, when Tor claimed her mind so powerfully and so unexpectedly.

It was only then she remembered what had awoken her with such a fright. The Land had spoken to her.

Alyssa pulled her rose-coloured silk wrap around herself more tightly and settled into an armchair to think. It was the sudden shift in the Land's power which had called her from her peaceful sleep. And that was why Tor had slipped into her mind. Clearly no one else had felt the shift or her young and excitable maid, Tilly, would have been near hysterical. No, Alyssa thought, this was connected with the Trinity somehow. The Writings of Nanak and the story of Orlac crept back into her thoughts. She had hoped she could put them aside when she started her new life with Lorys. How stupid of her! Orlac was coming back and this was a warning.

She felt suddenly cold and curled her fingers around the comforting warmth of her cup. She sipped the bittersweet tea but did not taste it; her mind was elsewhere. What could have caused the shift in the Land's balance, she wondered. Had the last of the Paladin fallen? Saxon was not here to ask. Her protector had been gone now for almost three moons.

Taking another sip of the cooling raspberry leaf brew, Alyssa accepted that the shift had to be connected with the gods. She put her cup down and touched her thumbs together to ward against bad luck, trying to dismiss the notion that the Tenth might have fallen. Surely she would have felt a tragedy as great as that deep in her soul?

Perhaps something had entered the Land and disrupted its balance? Surely not Orlac. Not yet! She stood and paced in an attempt to empty her head of the terrible vision of Orlac's escape, but still she spent another hour in distracted thought before finally forcing herself to dress. She did not feel any wiser for all the mind effort.

She chose a simple buttery yellow gown of fine wool, cinched modestly at the waist with her favourite chain belt. Although she preferred her hair plaited neatly, Alyssa did not want Tilly fussing around again, so she pulled her hair back with a clasp of polished antler. Her ablutions complete, she considered how to occupy herself at this early hour in a way that would stem any opportunity to think further about Torkyn Gynt, Orlac or anything connected with the Trinity.

She just wanted to be a happily married wife; a fitting Queen for her King. She did not want to think on the prophecy of Orlac's return. She took a deep breath and forced her mind to consider her options for the day.

She could tour the castle, possibly watch cook prepare the bread for the day, and then head up into the battlements to pass a few pleasantries with the guards. She knew this was where her popularity lay: the proletariat of Tallinor, particularly in and around Tal, was besotted with their Queen Alyssa.

Directly after their marriage, Lorys had made the wise decision to journey to the major towns once again, this time with Alyssa by his side. He knew it was the only way his subjects would accept a new Queen so soon after the death of their beloved Queen Nyria. It had worked. Alyssa's beauty and gentle, modest manner had captivated her subjects; she charmed everyone from the villagers to their children. And her obvious intelligence and wit made her equally at home amongst the aristocracy.

Alyssa fidgeted uncharacteristically, struggling to make a decision, when there was a soft knock at her door.

'Come,' she replied and moved to look out of the large window in response to the clattering of troops arriving in the main yard.

Her personal aide, Rolynd, made his apologies for disturbing her at this early hour. 'Your majesty, the troops have returned,' he said, bowing low.

'His highness?' asked Alyssa, her cheeks flushing as she whipped around from the window. She had missed Lorys dreadfully these two Eighthdays. No need for a stroll along the battlements on this chilly morning if he had returned. He would be her distraction. She could leave her crowded mind to itself and be entertained by his stories, his wonderful laugh and his limitless affection. His presence was all she needed to dispel this mood and increasing sense of anxiety.

'I'm sorry, your majesty, but apparently King Lorys will not be returning immediately. I am informed that he is paying a visit to Lord Tolly, who is gravely ill. The King's Guard has remained in Parkeston to escort his highness home afterwards . . .' The sentence trailed off as he saw the Queen's face display its disappointment.

'Thank you, Rolynd.' She turned away.

'Er . . . your majesty, the Under Prime wishes to speak with you. He is waiting in the vestibule.'

'Oh! Send him in immediately.' Alyssa brightened at the news that Gyl was back in residence. He too had been away far too long.

Rolynd bowed again and left, quietly closing the double doors into the Queen's suite.

Alyssa seated herself in her favourite chair over-looking the pretty walled garden which the King had commissioned for her and awaited the arrival of her other favourite man. She could hear his rhythmic foot-steps as he drew closer to her suite and she smiled, imagining the arrogant swagger and confident manner which caused most of the court's younger ladies to tremble with desire. Since his new appointment, Gyl seemed to have grown remarkably in stature, confidence and, above all, eligibility.

Alyssa had no intention of marrying Gyl off to any of these swooning ladies. She would know the right girl when she presented herself . . . and so would he. Gyl was a dreadful flirt and played with his admirers' emotions without hesitation. Alyssa gratefully noted, however, that he gave no special attention to any of them, which reassured her that he too was not considering early marriage. Light! The lad was just sixteen summers; he had a whole lifetime ahead to find the right woman to lose his heart to.

Alyssa conveniently pushed away the fact that she had fallen in love with Torkyn Gynt at the age of nine summers and was just fourteen summers when she threw him her posy at Minstead Green. If he had got around to asking for her hand that day, she would have said yes and happily married him by sunset. But that question was never asked. Merkhud had taken Tor's attention from her and then lured him to Tal, setting them all on a path to destruction.

Gyl was almost at her door. She could hear his voice now, joking with the guards Lorys insisted she maintain at the entrance to her chambers. Aside from the King, only Alyssa knew Gyl's true story. When Lorys had revealed his secret that he was the boy's father, Alyssa had immediately wanted Gyl to be told too, but she soon came to accept Lorys's conviction that they should keep it to themselves. At the time, there had been a great deal happening in Gyl's life and they had agreed it would be too much to tell him of his real background. But Alyssa knew they must not wait too long; keeping such knowledge from him could perhaps cause even more damage in the long run.

The doors opened and as Alyssa opened her arms to hug her son, all thoughts of the powerful disturbance which had woken her went out of her mind.

It was as Tor, Saxon and Cloot were journeying back towards Cipres that they sensed the shift in the Land's balance.

'Did you feel that?' Saxon said.

Tor's mind immediately fled to Orlac.

Cloot, has the Tenth fallen? Tor sounded alarmed; he was not ready for this news yet.

The calming voice of Cloot eased into his mind. *I don't believe so, Tor. It doesn't feel bad, just like some sort of disturbance, wouldn't you agree?*

He did agree, now that he dwelled on it. And then, as though sunlight had suddenly beamed through the cloudy skies, Tor's heart soared. He fell to his knees and opened his arms to the heavens. 'My children,' he said. 'They have returned to Tallinor.'

In the Heartwood, the trees, animals and its special magical creatures rejoiced.

'They are close,' Solyana said.

Arabella wept, overwhelmed by the knowledge that

the Land's most precious charges were returning to where
they truly belonged.

Sallementro, tuning his lute in his favourite stone hut in
the hills behind the Tal palace, felt the shift.

Adongo of the Moruks stopped in his tracks and closed
his eyes to listen to the Land.

Figgis the Rock Dweller, Ninth of the Paladin, on a
ship just docking at Caradoon, also felt the shift. He
resolved to travel south as fast as possible.

All knew the Trinity was gathering, finding its rightful
place, drawing its protectors back to their destiny.

Alyssa's true son, the one she quietly grieved for, felt the
wind knocked out of him as he rolled onto the ground in
Tallinor. Gidyon looked around in stunned disbelief and
took a few moments to steady himself and his breathing.
Sorrel had said they would arrive together but he had
known before opening his eyes that he was alone. So their
journey through the portals had not gone to plan.

He took another good look around. He was in a field,
which he shared with a few startled cows who moved away
briskly, disturbed by the sudden appearance of a stranger
in their midst.

He closed his eyes, shook his head and opened them
again. The cows were still ambling away. He was definitely no longer in Sorrel's cottage but sitting winded in
a field somewhere. All she had told them was true then.

Everything felt strange. It was not a bad feeling but
it was odd. His weak eyes were suddenly providing him
with perfect vision: he could see every detail of the lined
bark of that tree at the far edge of the field, further than

he would ever have thought possible. And the sounds of the birds chattering seemed somehow sharper. What was happening? And was this where Sorrel had spoken of bringing them?

Gidyon stood and took a deep, steadying breath. He had followed the shimmering green of Yargo as best he could, but though he remembered taking Lauryn's hand in the cottage, they had somehow become separated.

Where was she?

At that moment, a new sensation hit him. He felt cold slicing through his mind, like a blade. Then he heard her voice in his head. It was tentative. *Gidyon?*

He could not believe it. *Lauryn, is that you?*

Clever, eh? she said, more boldly now.

Very. How are you doing it?

Magic, she said and he enjoyed hearing her laugh. *We're empowered, like our parents – or were you not paying attention?*

This is all a little too much for me, he admitted.

She sighed. *I know. Are your sight and hearing different?*

Definitely; they're much sharper. I'm in a field somewhere. Where are you?

With Sorrel. She seems to think we're at a place called Harymon. And I'm told we're now going to make our way to another intriguing spot known as the Heartwood.

I see. Good idea. And what about me? He paused theatrically between each sentence for emphasis.

Lauryn had been determined not to like Gidyon but his gently ironic manner was charming. And knowing he was her brother, family . . . it was just too precious and she could not help but feel a strong bond of affection towards him already.

Well, this was all your idea, Gidyon, remember? Sorrel tells me that you must make your way to the Heartwood as well.

Has she offered any suggestion how? Do I leap on the back of one of these vaguely suspicious, but not so friendly, cows and ride there?

Lauryn enjoyed his jest. *Just get there somehow, as fast as you can. Wait . . .* He felt the link remain open but there was silence.

Lauryn?

I'm here. Listen, Gidyon, I'm to tell you this is serious. She wants you to be very careful. Stay away from anything which smells of trouble. Don't draw attention to yourself. She has sewn some money into your left pocket. It's not much; you may have to earn your way with odd jobs. But you have to hurry.

Ah. Well, do thank Sorrel for that superb help, he said, sarcastically. *Can she give me a landmark at least?*

There was a pause again and then Lauryn replied, *Head towards the city of Tal but get into the Great Forest as soon as you can. There's a village called Axon at the point of one of the forest's fingers apparently – I'm not sure exactly what she means by that. And you're going to love this. No laughing. A wolf, a donkey or a priestess will be waiting there for you. Trust them and follow.*

He did laugh. *You will visit again, won't you?* he said. *I just can't wait for the next instalment.*

You can do this too, you know, Lauryn replied.

How? he demanded.

Well, I just reached myself out towards wherever you might be.

Oh, totally simple then. Textbook magic.

I can't really explain it any better than that! Sorrel calls it the link and although she cannot link with us, we obviously can with each other. You must practise.

I will, as I earn my keep shovelling dung, tilling the soil and whatever else a person of my lowly status does in this place.

How do you know that?

What? How to till the soil?

No. I mean how do you know we are of lowly status?

Lauryn, perhaps you haven't noticed but she's dressed us as peasants, not courtiers or scholars.

Sorrel says you're right. And one more thing – apparently our memory of home will fade. She assures me it will help us to become more like the Tallinese.

I'll forget all I've learned for the Blues? Gidyon was horrified.

As I understand it, she replied and he felt the link close.

Gidyon put his hands on his hips and looked around him again. A donkey indeed! This was a dream, surely? He was going to wake up soon and laugh about this. He had ridden north to see a dying grandmother – now he was here. He *was* going to wake from this because he had something important to do back at that place he came from . . . but for the life of him he could not, just at present, bring to mind what that important task was.

He shook his head. No use lurking here, he decided and Lauryn had given him his instructions. He would be pleased to be with her again. She was his sister; what a lovely notion after years of it being just him. And he liked her. So, in order to reach Lauryn, this Heartwood place was where he had to go.

He made for the edge of the field and stepped over the low wall there, into a laneway. He had no idea which direction to head in. He dug into his pocket, breaking through Sorrel's stitches, and found a coin. On one side he noticed there was a dragon; on the other, what looked like a ghoul. He flipped the coin into the air and trapped it between his right palm and the back of his left hand.

'Right,' he said to the uninterested cows. 'Demons or dragons?'

When none of his new friends even turned to look at him, let alone answer, he chose dragons. Lifting his right hand, he saw that it was indeed a dragon.

'Then left it is,' he said brightly, not understanding one bit how he had reached such a conclusion. Gidyon began to whistle as he strolled down the lane towards his destiny.

Sorrel looked at the girl, her expression one of enquiry. Gidyon was meant to be with them. She felt very anxious that he had been separated. She had spent fifteen years in a different world waiting to bring her charges home and it had gone wrong already. If anything happened to him . . .

Lauryn, on the other hand, sounded jolly. 'He seems all right. He's on his way.'

Sorrel nodded. She must not give away that she was worried. 'Good. Then we must be on our way too. Help me with this bag, my girl. We have a long walk ahead of us.'

The similarity of this journey to the one she made with Alyssa so many years ago was not lost on Sorrel. And the likeness Alyssa's daughter shared with her mother was uncanny, despite all the spare flesh she carried on her frame. Lauryn would be as beautiful as her mother one day.

Lauryn slung the light cloth bag across her back and took the old girl's arm. She had not wanted to come – it had all seemed like a dark jest back in the cottage. But now that the magic had proved true and she was here, she felt excited.

She had parents here. Lauryn hardly understood any of what Sorrel had told her, but she was keen to suspend disbelief and even give up all of what had been her life before, if it meant she could meet her parents and belong. If this was her birthplace, then this was where she wanted to be. There was a lightness to her step that morning which she had never felt before.

'I have some money,' the old girl said. 'Not much, mind, but it will help us along. We can live frugally, though you may have to work.'

Lauryn nodded. Work? What could she do? Scribe, perhaps? She decided not to let it trouble her. There was more than enough strangeness in her life right now to bother about the least remarkable bits. She would let Sorrel make that decision.

'There should be an inn at the next village, if my memory serves me right or the thing has not burned down in the past few years.'

'And we'll stop there?'

'Just for tonight. We'll get ourselves together and set off properly tomorrow. I'm anxious about Gidyon. We should not have been separated like this,' Sorrel said, shaking her head, breaking her promise already.

'Well, there's nothing we can do, Sorrel. He had no idea where he was, so we just have to trust he will get to where you need him to be.'

'Practical, like your mother,' Sorrel replied.

'And will she be there . . . at this Heartwood you speak of?'

'My child, I honestly don't know. Your father has called us back; that is all I know for sure. I am answering his summoning.'

25

Duntaryn's Secret

Figgis admitted to himself that it was his own fault; he should have sensed the danger but he had been too enamoured by the feeling of freedom. It was grand to be back in Tallinor after so long, so many centuries of oppression, pain, frustration.

His normally lightning-fast reactions had failed him. So many thought Rock Dwellers were slow and witless; perhaps because of the gnarled, overhanging brow and the thick lips and wide mouth which were typical of his race. This assumption was entirely wrong, however. Rock Dwellers were slow at very little except running. They were not fleet of foot, although they possessed great stamina in their short legs, which could carry them over long distances and up an almost sheer rock face.

No, not slow of mind or reaction at all, but today the Ninth of the Paladin had simply been enjoying being Figgis again and, he realised with disgust, had let his guard down.

Until that moment his journey had been uneventful. He had travelled swiftly down through the north since arriving at Caradoon from Cipres, sleeping in the fields and eating whatever he could forage for. He did not feel the cold nor did he experience the hunger pangs of the ordinary man. He was a Rock Dweller and travelling rough was no hardship for his kind.

He had skirted all the townships and the villages through the Midlands but it was the sleepy and sparsely populated village of Duntaryn which proved his downfall. Deciding that he needed to pick up speed, he had chanced the quicker route through the main thoroughfare instead of following his instincts and the stream that meandered around the outskirts of the village.

He should have sensed trouble, should have seen it coming. It was enough that Duntaryn was a spooky place, its main street shrouded by dense hedgerow and overhanging trees. There was a strange atmosphere as he entered the village and he felt hidden eyes boring into him.

The sack had been thrown over his head expertly. If he was a normal-sized man, it would not have hindered his arms as it did, but being a Rock Dweller – or a dwarf, as they preferred to call his kind – he could do little more than struggle helplessly. Firm hands picked him up and a blow to the head stopped him struggling further. It brought thunderous pain and he had thought dimly how it was a fallacy that Rock Dwellers had skulls of stone. Figgis lost his bearings and his consciousness.

Now, conscious but with eyes deliberately closed, he reflected on how the disaster had occurred because he had been deep in thought. The meeting with Torkyn Gynt in Cipres had been unexpected. Figgis was glad to have helped with the young lad, Locklyn Gylbyt. That Maiden contraption was ludicrous. How could such a thing ever be considered a just resolution to a dispute? Oh, but being able to look into Gynt's eyes had given him strength just when he was beginning to feel the whole quest was pointless.

He was the One; the reason they had strived so long. And their pain and suffering had not been in vain. This man would save all worlds when he assembled the Trinity.

It did not matter to Figgis that Gynt may not have known that the small man he briefly spoke to in Cipres was the Ninth Paladin to die bravely on his behalf. All that mattered was that he had completed the first of his tasks and now he must find his charge quickly. The boy needed his help; Lys had said so in his dreams. She had urged him to stow away on the ship to Caradoon and get himself this far; she continued to push him. He was the boy's guardian. It was his most vital role of all as Paladin.

Suddenly cold water shocked his eyes open; someone had tipped a bucketful over his head, which still throbbed. He made himself lean up on his elbow to face the group of whispering men standing over him.

'A dwarf, all right.'

'Don't see his sort in these parts. I thought dwarves were fable.'

'He'll bring the crowds.'

Figgis looked at them unblinking. The smoke from their pipes in this confined space made him want to gag; so did his headache.

'Can you speak?' one said.

'Good day, you dung-breathed thugs,' Figgis replied in his own language, which he knew none here would understand. This group felt dangerous; he decided to play stupid until he had worked out what to do next.

The first speaker blew out smoke and grinned, revealing more gums than teeth. He was built like a stone shed. 'He speaks!'

A younger man said, 'Try him on Tallinese.'

The first man nodded. He addressed Figgis, enunciating his words with the greatest of care and pausing between each one. 'Do . . . you . . . understand . . . Tallinese?'

'Yes . . . I . . . do,' Figgis replied, though again in his own guttural language. Then he spoke a stream of what seemed nonsense. He kept it low, almost placatory, but he enjoyed using every insult known to his race. His long dead mother would be turning in her tomb if she could hear him speak such vulgarity, he thought.

The man sighed. 'It would have been good to hear him beg in Tallinese,' he said with some regret.

Beg? What was this about? He could see there were five of them now that his eyesight had adjusted, and he realised he was being held in a farm building of some kind, probably a barn. They had turned away from him and were murmuring amongst themselves. Figgis closed his eyes and feigned dizziness; maybe he could get them to believe he was sleeping, which would encourage them to speak louder. Gradually he allowed himself to slip over until he was prone on the ground again, his head on the offending sack.

'Leave him,' he heard the first speaker say. 'The main thing is that we have our sacrifices.'

The conversation continued quietly but Figgis's exceptionally sharp hearing picked up every mumbled word of it.

'How is the girl?' The same man, he seemed to be the leader.

'She's all right.' A new voice.

'I mean, does she suspect anything?'

'I can't tell. Ory may know more. He delivers to the family.'

'Ory . . .'

'Yes?' Footsteps, presumably Ory's.

'Does the girl know anything?'

Figgis heard scratching before Ory spoke. 'No . . . I don't believe so. I saw her yesterday. She seems her usual contrary self. She could guess, of course. She's no ordinary-looking person and this is no ordinary time of the year for these parts.'

The leader seemed to ignore what Ory had said. 'What about the parents?'

'They're not her parents, Scargyl.'

'It matters not to me. With the dwarf here, we have a perfect union. It's shaping up for the best ceremony we've had since I was a lad. I'm only just old enough to remember the Giant.'

'They say he took his time dying.' Figgis recognised the voice; the man who had told Scargyl to ask if he understood Tallinese.

'He did that, Truk. He gave us very good value that spring solstice. Tasted all right too.'

Scargyl, Truk, Ory. Two more to account for. Still, Figgis thought, their number was irrelevant compared with what he had just discovered. So he and some girl were destined to be the highlight in some grisly death ritual on the spring solstice. How many more days before the solstice eve? He thought hard with his blurry, aching head and settled upon the figure of two.

Two days to plan his escape or Orlac would triumph.

*   *   *

Gidyon had been walking for several days. He had taken Sorrel's advice and kept himself to himself. When entering a village, he would spend a few coins on bread and fruit. Fresh water seemed to follow him in the bright, fast-flowing stream he had kept to his left for all of his journey.

As a result of his meagre diet, his money was holding up. And, in an inspired move, he had managed so far to convince the people he ran into that he was mute. It was an old trick he recalled playing as a child, but he could not quite remember when and on whom. Each day his memory of his past dimmed further and with it his fear of it failing him.

Being mute meant that people invariably lumbered him with the label of being stupid as well. It suited his purposes though. He could point at what he wanted and hold out his money in his palm, so the person serving could select the right coin. Gidyon had no clear idea of the value of his money but he was beginning to get a grasp on it. He would have to drop the mute affectation shortly, however. Though his money was adequate for bread and fruit, he would need to earn some more if he was to find a bed to sleep in – a luxury he longed for after many nights spent in fields. He also needed to ask for directions to this Axon place. By listening to the chatter of people around him in each village, he had worked out that he was essentially on the right path, though it was probably time to swing more to the south.

He promised himself that at the next village he would have a voice and he would find himself an odd job for the day and a bed for the night. There were quite a number of people coming and going on this road and he caught bits of conversations about a festival being held at

Duntaryn in a few days. He reckoned this would be the next village he came to. A festival could be fun, he thought to himself.

Try though he might, Gidyon had not enjoyed any success in opening a link to Lauryn. It frustrated him that she called upon him with such ease and yet the magic evaded him. Through Lauryn, Sorrel told him to keep peace with himself, that it would happen in time.

They seemed to be travelling in a slightly more comfortable style than he was, staying at inns each evening. Lauryn sounded excited that they had spent one whole day picking the redberries and frostfruit of the region, from which the famous preserves favoured by royalty were made.

My fingers are purple, Gidyon. You should see them.

I hope to soon, Lauryn. It was lovely to hear the joy in her voice. She had seemed so sullen and argumentative when they had met.

Sorrel wants to know where you are now?

I've recently left Churley and am heading to another village which I believe is called Duntaryn. It should bring me further south, more in line with where I need to be, I gather.

There was a long pause. *Gidyon . . .* Lauryn sounded serious. *Sorrel says that Duntaryn is a strange place. When will you reach it?*

Tonight, I hope. Why?

Another pause. *She says to sleep in a field, well away from the village. If you can avoid it altogether, do so. If you can't, pass through quickly and don't linger.*

What's this all about? Again he had to wait whilst Lauryn related his question and then received a response.

Sorrel says — in her usual cryptic manner — that the spring solstice is not a clever time to be a stranger in Duntaryn. She refuses to give me more information but insists you don't try to find work there, or even stop there at all if you can help it. Just walk straight on to the next main village, which is Mexford, but try to make it to Fragglesham as soon as you can. There's a good inn there where you can stay. There will also be work there. Axon is just a full day's walk from Fragglesham. We're almost there, Gidyon, just stick to the plan.

All right. But I don't understand this fear of Duntaryn. I hear there's a festival on there.

Sorrel knows more than us. We should listen to her.

Yes, that's true. So, it's another cold night under the stars for me.

Sorry, Gidyon, but . . .

They both said it together: *It was your idea!* and they laughed.

I'll talk to you tomorrow then.

Sleep safely, Gid.

He felt quite lighthearted after their conversation. Even the notion of spending another night curled under a bush did not make him feel irritable, though it was a long, dusty walk and well and truly dusk before he reached the outskirts of Duntaryn.

Evening began to slide in around him and suddenly the wooded laneway felt slightly more dangerous. A wolf howled in the distance, which sent a shiver through him, and the shadows began to grow tall and ominous. By nightfall he was feeling edgy and very alone and desperately wished he had the power to open a link with Lauryn and hear her voice.

Just as he had convinced himself to walk through the

night and put this village well behind him, he saw a lantern swinging in the near distance.

Gidyon reacted instinctively. 'Hey!'

He could tell its carrier had turned by the way the lantern swung around.

'Who is out there?' It was a woman's voice. She sounded alarmed.

'A traveller. I'm sorry to frighten you.'

'I've got a stick!' she warned.

The wolf howled again.

'I won't harm you, miss. I'm weary, hungry. Actually, I just need somewhere warm to lie down. A barn, perhaps.'

'Let me see your face,' she said.

Gidyon approached, walking slowly, not wanting to scare her any further. He stopped a fair enough distance away that she would not feel threatened.

'Closer,' she said.

'I promise I mean no harm. Er . . . I can pay.'

'You have a kind voice, stranger. There is no malice in it. Yes, I trust you but I would like to see to whom I speak.'

Gidyon stepped forward a few more paces. He could only just see her outline. Her face was in shadow from the glare of the lantern.

'Ah,' she said. 'A face to match the kind voice.'

'Thank you. My name is Gidyon . . . Gidyon Gynt.'

'I am Yseul. I live at the cottage over yonder.' She pointed and he could make out the dark shape of a dwelling. Candlelight flickered very softly deep in the cottage.

'Is there a barn here, Yseul?'

'Yes. Right over there. You are welcome to share it

with the two pigs, the cow and the three goats.' She giggled. Now that he concentrated, he realised it was a young voice.

'Are you er . . . married to the farmer?'

'Farmer! The ox, you mean. No, I am not married to anyone, Master Gynt. No one owns me. But I have to work for the ox and his fat wife.' She suddenly stopped.

Gidyon was unsure of what to say next. He ran his fingers through his hair and was glad when she came to his rescue.

'My turn to say sorry. I did not mean to alarm you. They are not very pleasant people. Feel free to stay the night but don't get caught, or if you do, don't tell them I allowed you to sleep there.'

'What will happen?'

'They will flog me. He enjoys it. She enjoys watching but I've learned not to cry any more and give her the satisfaction. It happens often enough but I try not to give them an easy excuse. Follow me.'

Gidyon took a deep breath. He felt the slice of the link opening and responded. *Not now, Lauryn. Can we talk later?*

The link closed immediately; he felt bad, especially as they had agreed to talk the next day.

He followed Yseul and they tiptoed into the barn.

'You must leave early,' she cautioned. 'Don't stay around these parts. Duntaryn is not a good place for strangers at any time, but particularly now,' she added.

Gidyon still had not seen her face properly. She made to leave but he reached out and took her arm. 'Yseul, can I at least pay you something for your generosity?'

'No. But you can take me away with you.' It slipped out; she had not meant to say this.

'What . . . are you a prisoner?'

'Of sorts,' she said, sadly.

As the lantern swayed, its glow crossed her face. He had a fleeting glimpse of dark hair, olive skin, curiously light eyes.

'Thank you, Yseul,' he whispered.

She did not reply but he could hear a gruff man's voice bellowing her name into the darkness.

'I'm coming!' she called back.

Gidyon climbed the ladder to the top of the barn, dug himself into the sweet-smelling straw and lay down gratefully. He touched his stone, which was in an inside pocket close to his chest, and noticed it was hot again. He was too tired to think on what it might mean. If Gidyon had understood the significance of the Stones of Ordolt, he would have known it was warning him. Instead he fell asleep.

He woke very early after a long and deep sleep during which he had dreamed. A woman he never actually saw had spoken to him. She did not tell him her name but she urged him to wake and put this village behind him. She also told him that his protector was close. He did not understand any of it.

Gidyon sat up and smiled to himself. First Sorrel and then the girl, Yseul, had spooked him; now he was dreaming up other women frightening him off.

The sky was just lightening; he could see it would be a lovely, crisp day and after such a refreshing sleep he felt glad to be alive. All notion of danger had passed and his belly was rumbling. He promptly forgot about the dream. He had not eaten a hearty meal in days and if he was

going to walk for the next twelve hours or so, he needed
a breakfast. So what if everyone kept warning him about
Duntaryn? It was just a sleepy old village. He would get
some food into himself and then he would start his trek
south east to Axon.

He dusted off the straw from his clothes and then heard
someone enter the barn. He ducked down.

'Are you here?' she whispered. It was Yseul.

Gidyon's relief was huge. 'Yes,' he called back softly.

'You must leave. Quickly.'

Yseul climbed the ladder. She seemed terrified. Looking
at her now in the gentle morning light, he could see she
was roughly his own age. He had not seen it in that
moment of glimpsing her face last night, but she really
was an extraordinarily pretty girl.

'Yseul, what is all this about Duntaryn? Why are you
so scared?'

'No time to explain. I have brought you some food.'
She dug into her apron pocket and produced some warm
muffins and a pear. 'I'm sorry, it is all I could steal without
them knowing.'

'It is more than enough . . . after what you have already
done for me.' Gidyon stepped towards her but she backed
away.

'Master Gynt—'

'Gidyon,' he corrected gently.

Nervously, she looked back down into the barn and
whispered, 'Did you hear something?'

'I wasn't really listening. No, no, I don't think I did
hear anything.'

She nodded with relief. 'You know you offered to pay
last night . . .'

'Oh yes, of course.' Gidyon began to rummage in his pockets for the last of his coins.

'No, not money. I am wondering if you would repay one generosity with another?' she said, looking at him hard.

He noticed again how very light her eyes were. How strange, he thought, they were neither green nor blue. Grey would not be accurate either. They were almost sandy in colour.

He realised she was looking at him intently, waiting for his reply. 'Er . . . well, yes, I'll be happy to. How can I show my gratitude then?'

She smiled tentatively. 'I have a small brother. They beat him too. They are merciless towards him. Would you take him with you, wherever you go? I promise he will be no trouble.'

Gidyon had to run it through his mind again. What she had just said made no sense.

'You want me to take your brother away from you?'

'Yes, from this place. Take him anywhere. Keep him safe.'

'Yseul, won't you miss him?'

She smiled with great sadness and it hurt his heart to hear her next words. 'Where I'm going today, Gidyon, I shall miss no one.'

She turned to leave. 'He will be waiting for you in the trees behind the barn in a short while. Wait here a few moments and then leave by the back. Go as far away from this village as you can. Please keep my brother safe. His name is Gwerys.'

She paused, turned to look at him once more and then stepped up and kissed his cheek. 'Thank you for this.'

Yseul moved towards the ladder but Gidyon stopped her in one stride.

'Look, what is this all about? Do you have any idea how strange it sounds? All this secrecy, doom and gloom. What is going on in the village that scares you so much that you'd give a complete stranger the care of your brother?'

She searched his face. Gidyon thought for a moment she may cry but no tears appeared. She was a strong girl. He remembered the floggings she had spoken of.

Yseul took a deep breath. 'Each five cycles, the men of Duntaryn make a ritual sacrifice at the spring solstice. The custom is many centuries old; this part of the Kingdom is very superstitious.'

'Go on,' he encouraged.

'They believe that unless they give up lives to their stupid gods, their crops will perish. Well, that's how it originated. These days it's just an excuse to enjoy torturing some poor souls. It has no purpose; just killing.

'My great-grandmother, bless her soul, told me that once a new calf was slaughtered; but now they kill a child. And where they once used to drink the blood of a young female goat yet to be mated, well, they've somehow twisted that into being a virgin girl.'

She really did look as though she may cry now.

He felt the hairs stand up on the back of his neck. 'Yseul . . . are you telling me it's you they're going to sacrifice?'

She nodded and her eyes welled with tears but he saw her courage build as she fought them back. 'Yes . . . and some poor man, a dwarf, so I've overheard. He will represent the beast. In the old days it would have been an ox and they ate its flesh after roasting it. But they won't kill Gwerys!' Her light eyes burned with hatred. 'They can have me; my life is miserable enough that I will be grateful for its end. But not my brother. He is just five summers. He has a life yet to live if he can escape this place.'

'Now stop,' Gidyon said, not sure whether to comfort her or run. This was the most outlandish tale and yet Sorrel had tried to warn him; even the woman in the dream had spoken to him of the strangeness of this place. 'Why can't you escape with Gwerys?'

'They watch me all the time. I would get no further than the edge of the village before they caught me again. I tell you, I have not enjoyed my life. It can end for all I care. I care only for Gwerys and his safety. I am begging you to save him.' She did cry now; all her resolve fled.

'All right, get Gwerys. We leave now. All of us.'

Gidyon realised he sounded as though he knew what he was doing, but the truth was, he felt just as terrified as she did. It was too much to take in. Ritual killings, sacrifice, eating the flesh of a dwarf! What kind of world had Sorrel brought them to?

'We can't!' she whispered through her tears.

'We can!' he hissed. 'Where's Gwerys now?'

'In the cottage.'

'Dry your eyes. Go and fetch him on some excuse. Anything! I shall meet you where we arranged but I expect both of you. Trust me. I will not let anything happen to you or your brother. I shall get us away safely.'

He had even convinced himself. She nodded, believing his fervour.

'Now go, Yseul . . . and hurry.'

She left silently and Gidyon cautiously followed her

down a few moments later. He could see her stepping into the cottage. He shook his head. This could not be happening.

He let himself out of the barn and made his way across a small paddock towards a copse of trees. There was a tall oak; he hid behind it and waited.

His heart was racing; all thoughts of a big breakfast had disappeared. All he cared about now was Yseul and her brother and getting them all away from Duntaryn and its strange ways. He nearly let out a squeal when the link sliced open.

Lauryn! He leaped in before she could speak.

What's going on? she said. *I didn't want to disturb you again last night because you sounded like you wanted to be left alone.*

It was a tricky time when you dropped by. Listen, I'm in trouble.

Oh no, Gidyon, what's happening?

Make Sorrel tell me everything she knows of Duntaryn.

There was the expected pause. Then Lauryn's voice came back, a little shaky and confused now. *Are you captured, she says?*

No.

Then run. Sorrel says you are to get away from that village now and don't look back.

I can't, Lauryn. A friend, her name is Yseul, is in trouble and I have to help her.

A friend. You've only been there a night!

There's no time for this. Make her tell me.

He waited. Still no sign of Yseul and he began to feel afraid for her.

Gidyon.

Yes, he almost shouted down the link.

Sorrel says that on the eve of the spring solstice – that's tonight – the villagers make sacrifices. It's an ancient practice, which has been given up by all the townships and villages of the realm except Duntaryn, which holds close to the old ways. The folk are quite in-bred in this place, Sorrel says, and tend to not mix very much with the rest of Tallinor.

There was a pause and then she was back in his head. *The sacrifices were originally to the old gods but, to Sorrel's knowledge, the practice has become skewed and twisted down the ages. They no longer kill animals but people now. They believe that on the solstice eve all the spirits are loosed to roam.*

Pigs bollocks! he said and it made him feel better, momentarily.

Is the girl the virgin, Sorrel is asking.

Her name is Yseul, he said firmly. *Yes, she is. Her brother is the symbolic calf and they've got some dwarf who represents the ox.*

He waited while Lauryn repeated this to Sorrel, then she returned. *She says there is nothing you can do. You must leave.*

The hell I will. They're going to kill her. I've given her my word I will help her and her brother escape.

Lauryn began to berate him with Sorrel's warnings. He refused to pay attention. *Close the link, Lauryn. Leave me.*

I can't. What if something happens to you?

Leave my head free to think. Please, I beg you. Wait! I see her coming. Go now – we'll speak later. He was relieved when she closed the link without further argument.

Yseul arrived breathless, gripping the hand of a very small boy who was running alongside her. She forced a bright smile onto her face as she dropped to the ground beside her brother.

'Gwerys, this is the friend I told you of. His name is Gidyon.'

The child looked nothing like his sister, all fluffy-haired and freckled. But he had a sunny smile and his front teeth were just growing through. 'Hello, Gidyon,' he said.

Gidyon smiled back, though it was an effort. 'What happened?'

'I said there was a nest of new birds that I wanted to show Gwerys. The ox is too full from last night's liquor to realise the fledglings are yet to hatch in these parts. I hate him!'

'Me too, Yseul,' her brother said brightly. 'You told him a lie then?'

'Yes, Gwerys. We're running away from them.'

The boy spotted a beetle crawling over his boot and immediately lost interest in the discussion.

'What about the wife?'

'Oh, she's around but I just ran for my life. We must go. Please keep your promise, Gidyon, because if they catch us, they will torture him.'

'Let's go,' he said grimly, taking her hand. Gwerys allowed Gidyon to pick him up and together they began to run.

26

The Ritual

Figgis felt his body hit the dusty floor hard. He knew today was the day. Since his capture, they had beaten him every few hours. He had bruises on top of bruises and broken bones. He was a mess. Lys had deserted him. He would have the dishonour of failing the Paladin and crushing the Trinity. Not in all the time he had fought against Orlac had he felt this powerless.

Even his death in the battle against the god had won something – it had given the Trinity more time to prepare. And then he had been rewarded further with new life. Did Orlac realise that once he killed the Paladin, they were resurrected again? That they returned to whence they had first come – back to Tallinor, where it had all begun, to fight anew? How could Orlac know such things, trapped in the Bleak as he had been for centuries, constantly pitting his strength against the Paladin. But now Figgis may never get the satisfaction of seeing Orlac's face when he confronted the Paladin again for the final battle.

He coughed and blood splattered his already bloodied

clothing. He had only just learned why they beat him so often; he had heard Scargyl explaining to the younger men how the regular sessions tenderised the flesh. So . . . they intended to eat him. Well, Rock Dwellers did not make a good meal.

The joke would be on them, but he did not much feel like laughing now. The physical pain was intense but the agony of despair was far worse. Was this how it was to end then? Him a broken wreck, cooked by maniacal villagers who subscribed to some bizarre ritual?

No, he could not allow this to happen. He had to try something. Anything. But he had little to draw upon. Lys had told him that his magic would emerge as he needed it, but as yet he had felt nothing. He suspected that Torkyn Gynt had assumed it was he, Figgis the Ninth, who had wielded the power that day to save the life of Locklyn Gylbyt. But he had had no such enchanted powers at his disposal since re-emerging; he was merely the vessel through which a mightier power had been channelled. The Rock Dweller did not pretend to understand what had happened but he believed the magic had come from Lys, that she had used him as her conduit. The gods of the Host were not permitted to interfere in other worlds directly and he wondered whether Lys would suffer any retribution for her involvement that day. He also wondered if he would ever feel the surge of such magical power again.

He tried to concentrate with his blurry mind. He was Paladin. He was protector of the boy. That was his task: to bring this boy safely to the Heartwood. Lys, when she last entered his dream so many days ago, had told him that the child was close. With his hands and feet bound and his body incapable of movement, Figgis used his mind. He cast out strongly, fiercely calling on every ounce of strength which might still be in reserve in his broken body. He imagined a boy lost, frightened, confused, and he opened a link.

Gidyon was pushing them hard, running across open fields now. Thankfully, Yseul had her bearings and was directing them away from the village, heading south east, which was where Gidyon insisted they must go. Still their progress was slow and cumbersome.

Gidyon felt a link open fiercely in his mind. The effort to hold on to Gwerys, run fast and stay calm at the same time was too much. He screamed across it, *Not now Lauryn!*

There was a shocked silence but the link remained open. Then a man's voice, gentle but breathing hard, spoke. *This is not Lauryn.*

Gidyon stopped and fell over in the grass. He could hear Yseul asking if he was all right and Gwerys began to cry; he must have hurt himself in the fall.

Who is this who speaks? Gidyon whispered over the link.

He heard the heavy breathing again. Then a wave of coughing. The person sounded in pain when he spoke. *I am Figgis.*

Who are you? Gidyon felt chilled. Yseul was staring at him, confused, as she cradled Gwerys. He held his hand up to stop her speaking.

The Ninth, my child. I am your bonded Paladin, your protector.

Protector? Hadn't the woman in the dream used that term? She had said his protector was close.

You are here to help me?

Yes, Figgis said. *But I might need your help first.*

Yseul interrupted him. 'Gidyon,' she shrieked. 'What do you do? We are in danger out in the open like this.'

Figgis, please wait one moment.

Then he looked at Yseul. 'Forgive me, I tripped. Is Gwerys all right?'

She nodded.

He smiled at the boy in apology. 'Perhaps you should carry me, Gwerys,' and was glad the child appreciated the jest. 'Yseul, head for those trees over there. I shall come shortly.'

'Why not now?'

He struggled for an excuse. 'I have twisted my ankle. Please, just do as I say. Give me a moment and get yourselves out of danger.'

It worked. She picked up Gwerys and left him, running as best she could with the child in her arms.

Gidyon pretended to struggle to his feet and test the strength of his ankle. He felt fine. Only the shock of the man's voice in his head had sent him sprawling.

Are you there . . . Figgis?

Yes. Tied up, bleeding and going nowhere.

What?

Figgis coughed again. *Your name . . . Lys did not tell me.*

It's Gidyon. What do you mean, bleeding and tied up? Oh no, wait — tell me you're not a dwarf.

The man sounded defiantly proud all of a sudden. *I am of the Rock Dwellers. We are short of stature, big of heart.*

Oh no. No, this cannot be happening. You're the dwarf they're going to sacrifice.

How did you know? Figgis was caught off guard by Gidyon's knowledge.

Gidyon waved to Yseul and began to hobble slowly in her direction as he spoke. *It's a long story. But you could say I'm involved. Where do they hold you?*

In a barn, somewhere in Duntaryn. Where are you?

On the outskirts of the village.

Then keep going. Get away from this place, child. You are too important to risk.

I thought you were meant to take care of me.

I'm a little occupied, the man replied. *Forgive me.*

Right! Gidyon said, thinking fast and wondering how life had taken this strange path.

He called to Yseul. 'Stay here. I'll be back.'

'What?' she screamed. 'You can't leave us.'

'You'll be safe here. Just wait. I promise you I will return.'

'Where are you going?'

'Back.'

'To Duntaryn?' Her eyes were wide and terrified. He felt so sorry for her and wished he could hug her and make it all feel safe but Gwerys was standing between them, his own eyes accusing Gidyon.

Gidyon dropped to his haunches. 'Gwerys, I leave you in charge. You are the man here and must take care of your sister. She is upset so you must be the strong one, all right?'

The boy nodded solemnly.

'I am going back to Duntaryn to find someone. He will be hurt if I don't get to him first. Do you understand?'

He was speaking to Gwerys but his explanation was for Yseul's benefit. He just could not look at her grief-stricken face right now. He was scared enough.

'I shall look after her, Gidyon,' the child said.

'Good lad. I'll be back quickly.'

He chanced a glance at Yseul.

'The dwarf?' she asked.

He nodded. 'Don't move from this spot.'

And then he was running, retracing their steps and wishing desperately that he felt braver.

Figgis, he called. *Help me now. Keep the link open. Any guidance you can give will make a difference.*

Figgis saw the youngest one had been left to watch over him. That was fortunate. He asked the young man for a drink of water. Sullenly, the man obliged.

'I hurt all over,' Figgis said, hoping to start a conversation.

The youngster smirked. 'That's the point, dwarf. We have to keep you nice and tender for tonight.'

'What will they do to me?'

'I suppose it can't matter now to tell you,' the man said, enjoying the chance to frighten the victim more. He had not been allowed to administer any of the beating. It made him mad that they considered him too young to join in the violence, yet old enough to babysit the prisoner. At least talking about what was to come gave him some power over the dwarf.

'We're going to roast you,' he said, licking his lips for effect.

'I make tough eating,' Figgis replied.

'You won't be tough by the time we've finished with you, dwarf.'

'So is this practice peculiar to Duntaryn? I see I'm going to die anyway so it would be good to know why.'

'You are the beast,' was all the lad would say. He became more sullen.

Figgis did not want to be hurt any more. He had to stay calm and lucid for Gidyon's sake. He must not do anything to anger this lad watching over him. He tried a new approach: fuel the man's anticipation of what lay ahead.

'And the girl? I'll bet she's scared.'

The lad scowled. 'Yseul? She doesn't even know.' Then he smiled. Figgis saw the malevolence in it. 'I reckon by tonight she'll wish she had let me have her when I asked her last year. Then she wouldn't be a virgin. Saved by my prick.' He seemed to find this hugely comical and laughed happily to himself for a while.

Figgis played up to him. 'Well, lad, at least you've had women. You're a good-looking man; I'll wager you have no trouble with the ladies.'

The youngster turned to look at him. Good, he had his interest.

'You know, I'm so ugly – even for my own race – that no woman would look at me. Now you – you should not offer yourself to just anyone. You are a fine, strapping young man; be choosy,' he said, noticing the sudden swell of his captor's chest.

'That's right, dwarf. Fucking whore, she is,' he replied, not appreciating his own contradiction.

'So, what time does this all happen?' Figgis said casually. He had managed to push the pain aside; he was intent now on getting as much information out of this loose-mouthed youth as he could.

'Nightfall.'

'How many more beatings must I endure before then?'

'No more. You're done. You can stew in your own blood for a while, which should be running freely now within you. I just have to keep you alive long enough.'

Figgis felt his fury rise. Stay calm, he told himself. Think of Gidyon and stay calm. He reopened the link and heard, as well as felt, Gidyon's relief.

I thought you were dead.

Not quite, Figgis said softly. *Where are you?*

Drinking a quart of milk at the baker's. It's curdling in my stomach. Do you know any more?

Just a few more moments.

Hurry, Figgis. They don't trust me. They're beginning to stare.

I'll keep the link open.

Figgis coughed again to get his captor's attention. 'Do they perform it here . . . in this barn? Where are we anyway?' He held his breath.

'You are as thick as you look,' the man snarled. 'Do you really think Scargyl would perform the ritual in his own shedding?'

Scargyl! He ignored whatever the lad said next. *Gidyon! What news?*

Scargyl's barn . . . shed, whatever. Scargyl is one of the men who captured me. You're going to have to ask around.

Right.

The lad had stood. Figgis held his breath.

'I have to piss. Don't move or I'll make it worse on you.'

Figgis nodded and watched the young man open the timber door. Outside he could glimpse some of the village. *Gidyon . . . listen, I see hammers and anvils in this shed. I think Scargyl must be the smith. Go looking for the smithy. The*

*man watching me has stepped outside but the dolt has left the
door open. I see a butcher's shop, I think. Find the butcher and
look opposite — that's where they've got me.*

The man stepped back inside and closed the door. He
scowled. Figgis stayed quiet. The chat was clearly over.

Gidyon felt panicky. His thoughts were racing towards
Figgis but he could not get Yseul's face out of his mind.
Her expression, when he left, had accused him of betrayal.
But he had to do this and if she just listened to him and
sat tight, no one would find them.

He drained the milk from the mug and thanked the
woman, who eyed him balefully.

'Passing through Duntaryn are you, young sir? On your
way now?'

He mustered a smile. 'Yes, I have a delivery for Mallee
Marsh. Thirst got the better of me and someone back in
Churley asked me to give a message to someone here.'

'Oh? Is that right?' she said, uninterested. 'Better be
going now, sir. You don't want to be late into Mallee
Marsh. It's a full day, possibly more, from here.'

'Yes . . . um, excuse me, madam. Sorry to trouble you
but the person in Churley asked me to give a message to
a Master Scargyl. Would you know him?'

'He's the smith.' She looked suspicious now.

'Where is the blacksmith's place? I can probably call
in on my way out of the village.'

'It's in the other direction, sir. Perhaps I can give it to
Master Scargyl for you? Save you the trouble?'

'Oh well, that's kind but I was paid to deliver it to
him myself.'

She had returned to kneading the bread mix and

Gidyon hoped he would never feel the punch of those fists as she viciously dealt with the dough. She grimaced as she spoke. 'Follow the road back aways and go left at the crossroads. It's not far. Opposite Mekan, the butcher.'

'Thank you, madam, very much.'

He gave his best smile but she ignored it. Gidyon wasted no further time on her and departed, following her instructions. Sure enough he came to a crossroads, where he turned left.

For a village in the middle of the morning, the place seemed deserted. He continued walking and spotted the butcher's first. He stopped, looked across and saw the smith's a little further away. Tucked behind was a very small, old barn. Figgis had called it a shed. That was where he had to go.

Gidyon left the roadside and, with caution, made his way slowly around some tiny dilapidated outbuildings towards the barn. When he finally reached it, his hands were clammy with tension and he was sure anyone nearby could hear his heart thumping.

There was no sound from inside.

Looking around, he established there was only one door. No opportunity for a surprise entry then. He would just have to take his chances. Carefully checking that no one was watching him from the street, he tiptoed to the entrance, took a deep breath, firmly pulled open the door and stepped inside.

His eyes had to accustom themselves swiftly to the dimness inside the barn. Only a tiny window at the back afforded some muted light. He quickly took in the scene. A young man, older than him but not by much, leaped to his feet. On the floor lay another much older, shorter man, presumably Figgis.

'Figgis,' he said aloud. 'I'm Gidyon.'

'Hairy devils! Who are you?' asked the younger man.

'Oh sorry, I thought I just mentioned that. Gidyon Gynt. This is my friend and he's coming with me,' Gidyon said.

His sarcasm was lost on the sullen oaf, but Gidyon's victory was short-lived. He saw the oaf's eyes move from his face to behind him and turned swiftly to see three men approaching, all carrying weapons. One, probably Scargyl, was pounding a mean-looking hammer into his huge palm.

'Another stranger. Well, you'll do,' he said and they rushed Gidyon.

Groggy, he opened his eyes to the sound of soft weeping. He blinked and turned his head. To one side, he saw Figgis, curled up and prone on the ground. He turned the other way and his stomach twisted to see Yseul, her face beaten and bleeding. She was sitting up but was bound to a post. Nearby was Gwerys. He looked dead.

'Yseul!' Gidyon whispered.

She turned slowly. Her eyes were red.

'No more crying,' he said. 'Remember, you're the one who doesn't give them that satisfaction.'

'And you're the liar I trusted.'

That hurt.

'Is Gwerys all right?' he asked, not really wanting to hear the bad news.

'He sleeps.'

Relief swept through him.

'And Figgis?'

'They hung him up and beat him senseless. He is unconscious for all I know and care. Leave me alone, liar.'

'Yseul, you have to help me. Is it nightfall yet?'

'Twilight. Not long till we die, Gidyon.'

At least he had progressed to being called by his name again and not 'liar'. He would save them. He just had to think.

'Figgis!' he called. 'Figgis, wake up!'

No response.

'There is nothing to do but await our death, Gidyon. Be still.'

'That's it? That's your best effort?' he yelled at her. 'You're going to allow them to bleed you, kill your brother, roast Figgis and do who knows what to me?'

'Well, unless you have some magical powers that can get us out of here, Gidyon Gynt, I have no other choice but to wait.'

Her remark hit home.

Lauryn had said they possessed magical powers, hadn't she? How could he find them . . . tap into them? He had listened with awe to Sorrel's tales about his empowered father. Surely he had something of that in him?

He felt helpless. Without Figgis to press for more information, or Lauryn to speak to, he felt lost. Where was Lauryn? Why had she not linked with him? Damn his inability to open a link himself!

Yseul had looked away with disgust and was silent. They sat in the quiet for what felt like an eternity.

'Why you, Yseul?' he said eventually.

It was as if she had expected the question. 'My eyes,' she replied. 'I was picked out from a young age. I live a long way from here but Scargyl happened to pass through my village one day. He was a travelling smith then. Gwerys was still in a cradle. It was rare to see a child born with these strange, light eyes; it meant something to him. Back in the ancient times, when this village first began sacrificing people, the virgin they chose had very light, almost yellow eyes. It was prophetic for the thick-skulled Scargyl. He took me, just like that. One day I was living happily with my parents; the next I was a slave to the ox and his wife.'

'Why did he take Gwerys?'

'As a precaution. They needed the "calf", but I don't think that was the reason initially. Scargyl knew I loved my brother so, by keeping him, he was able to keep me prisoner in Duntaryn. I would never have left without Gwerys. Now it looks as though we can both leave this life together.'

'No, Yseul. It won't happen.'

'Stop it, Gidyon! You make my head hurt with your refusal to believe in the facts. In less than an hour, they will come and get us. We shall be dead within the following hour. Accept it and let me have my peace to say my prayers for my brother and myself. Just leave me alone.'

They came for them at nightfall, as promised. Tied as they were, struggling was useless, but still Gidyon fought as best he could. Gwerys woke and began crying immediately. Yseul refused to cry. In her silence she had found strength but there was little doubt her heart had already broken for her brother. She begged them to spare him. Her pleas fell on deaf ears. Figgis remained unconscious but the captors cared little for this fact.

As they were dragged outside into the dark, Gidyon saw a crowd of people had gathered. They were all draped in what looked like red sheets, with slits opened for the eyes. He could smell liquor and followed the scent to a pot simmering over a fire. The gathered were swaying and chanting words he did not understand. They were intoxicated.

He kicked the man pushing him. Strong hands propelled him forwards, almost into the fire. 'Do that again and I'll just open your throat here and now.' It was Scargyl, also clad in red.

Figgis, his arms and legs trussed with twine, was attached to a sturdy piece of timber lying on the ground. They left him there, cooling in the chill of the spring-time eve. His shivering brought him awake. He immediately opened the link.

I am sorry, my child. I have failed you. The link was weak.

Hush, Figgis. Save your strength for our escape.

It seemed a ludicrous thing to say but Figgis appeared to accept it.

Gidyon looked around wildly for any clues. They were in a wood, but standing in a large clearing. Small bonfires burned in a rough circle; probably to keep the wolves away, he figured. He could hear them howling in the distance. Gwerys began to scream as they tied him to a stone table. His would be the most ritualistic of the killings.

'Gwerys!' Gidyon shouted. The boy turned his head, terrified, towards him. 'It's just a game, Gwerys. Look at me – this is fun, isn't it? In a moment, it will all change and we get to tie the others up.'

The tiny boy's screams died away as this information

sank in. One of the men punched Gidyon in the stomach and he doubled up.

'Shut up, stranger.' It was the oaf from the barn. 'We want him scared.'

'I shall enjoy killing you,' Gidyon growled through the pain. He could not believe he had uttered those words. He had never killed anything in his life.

Yseul's voice could be heard above the chanting as she heaped curse after curse on the people around her. Her hair was matted and she looked demonic herself in her rage. Gidyon was glad her strength had surfaced. She would join him in the fight to survive, not accept death meekly.

The oaf slapped her hard. 'Wish you'd fucked me now, don't you, witch?'

Yseul stopped her tirade, turned her attention to the idiot in front of her and spat directly into his fleshy face. 'You'll wish you hadn't been born when he finishes with you,' she sneered at him.

'Who, him? The stranger?' the oaf said, wiping his face. 'Oh, I'm really scared.'

'You should be. He is the Gatherer of Souls.'

Those who heard this fell silent. Gidyon watched as the chanting stopped and a new murmuring began. It was hesitation, uncertainty. Yseul was preying on their superstitions. She was clever.

'Yes!' He took up the tale. 'I have come amongst you, hungry for new souls. What better time than the spring solstice, when Duntaryn does its worst? Are you ready to come with me?' He bared his teeth and looked at the oaf, who suddenly seemed a little less assured.

'Don't listen to them!' Scargyl's voice rang out. 'This is nonsense they speak. Proceed!' he commanded.

Gidyon watched, his moment of ferocity lost, as the log Figgis was attached to was placed on a specially constructed frame. He now hung horizontally, facing downwards towards the kindling to which they would soon touch a lighted taper.

Scargyl nodded. A roll of velvet was placed in his hands and the chant was taken up again, this time with real fervour.

Gidyon did not want to see what was contained in that bag. He held his breath as Scargyl unwound the silk which kept it tied, then unrolled the velvet to reveal an array of gleaming, vicious-looking implements, among them a shiny blade. Scargyl lifted it and held it aloft, then addressed Yseul.

'This is for you, my dear. It has been washed in purified water. You came to life pure and will go to your death pure and we shall drink your blood and be purified in turn.'

'Burn in hell, Scargyl!' she spat at him and then began her cursing again. She would not allow them to frighten her into submission. She would die fighting and cursing them.

Now Scargyl held up an even nastier implement, sharpened on both sides to a sinister point. He looked first at Yseul and then at the trembling Gwerys, who was silent now but for the odd whimper.

'And this is for you, child. We know you are pure. Your death will be swift, painless. It is the sacrifice we are required to make.'

Gwerys smiled nervously and looked over at Gidyon. 'Is it our turn yet?' He was trying to be brave.

Gidyon felt the world spinning. He had to do something.

Rage built inside him as he looked at Gwerys's trusting face. He could hear Yseul spewing her anger over the gathered and he admired her courage. Then he sensed a myriad of Colours rising up within him.

The link was open. Perhaps Figgis felt some of his rage, for he spoke to Gidyon. *Find your power now, boy. It is within you. Reach to it . . . for it reaches to you.*

Gidyon did not understand the dwarf's words. He thought he might faint as terror, tension and fury mingled into one. He saw the taper being lit; they would roast Figgis alive now. He saw the double-edged blade held over Gwerys's heart and saw the little boy still had his eyes firmly fixed on Gidyon, trusting him to save them. He turned and briefly glimpsed Yseul, her lips moving as she prayed for deliverance from this horror.

And then in a great gush the rainbow-hued rage spilled out of him. *Father!* he yelled and a monstrously powerful link opened to carry the word to its target.

27

Rage Unleashed

Tor and Saxon decided to press on through the night. Both knew they should be exhausted from their pace, yet they could not sleep. Cloot flew above, looking ahead. The moon was full and illuminated the road they marched along in silence.

Pain hit Tor so hard, he fell to his knees. The link hurt his mind and rainbow-coloured light blazed through him. *Father!* it screamed. And, through someone else's eyes he could see a terrifying scene: a child bound to an altar about to be slaughtered; a man tied to a roasting spit. That was no ordinary man.

'Figgis!' Tor yelled aloud into the moonlit night.

Saxon was already down at his side, confused by his friend's behaviour. Cloot swooped down in a rapid dive.

Across the link, Tor felt an enormous surge of power thundering from him, through him. He could not tell where it began and he ended, or where it was going.

And then it was gone. He was left prone on the floor, gasping as though taking his last breath of this life. His friends could only watch in complete bewilderment.

* * *

Scargyl raised the double-edged blade above his head and
joined in with the chanting of the village folk around
him; the sound built to a frenzy.

Those watching the stranger saw him suddenly arch his
back in some sort of silent agony; his mouth was wide open
and stretched back over his teeth but no sound came out.

Just a second or so later, as Scargyl prepared to plunge
the blade into the heart of the little boy, his robes exploded
into strange white flames. He was burning; screaming and
burning. Then everyone around him erupted into flames;
each red robe igniting the one next to it, passing on the
white flame with ease and speed. The clearing was filled
with screams.

Figgis felt like he was in a trance, but although he
could not see well, he could see enough to know what
was happening. *Finish it!* he commanded Gidyon.

And Gidyon did, unleashing the pure white power all
around, reserving the greatest bolt of it for the oaf, who
had so far escaped burning. He began to run but he could
not outrun the white flames which gave chase and licked
at his flying robes. His cries turned to a scream as he
burned, spreading the tongues of fire beyond the circle.

Now the trees surrounding the clearing began to burn.
The white flames, which were not repelled by cold or
wind or damp, spread with fury, moving through the
village of Duntaryn with such ferocity it was levelled.

The only people left alive that terrible night were
Gidyon, Yseul, Figgis and Gwerys. In a stupor, they
managed to untie one another. Gidyon picked up Figgis
tenderly and the dwarf touched his face.

It was necessary, child, he said, when he saw Gidyon was
trembling.

Weeping silently, Gidyon carried Figgis in his arms and, followed by Yseul who cradled Gwerys, the small group walked until they had left the burning village far behind.

Tor took deep, steadying breaths. He felt as though all the wind had been knocked out of him.

'What in the blazing Light was that all about?' Saxon asked, crouched next to him.

Are you all right? The falcon's concern was genuine.

I think so, Tor replied, cautiously. 'I witnessed the most terrible sight. I believe it was Gidyon,' he continued, with wonder in his voice. 'I heard him call me Father. He opened this powerful link and then it was as if our powers combined. Did . . . did you see it?'

Saxon shook his head. 'I saw nothing. One moment we were walking; the next you were on all fours and groaning as if the very breath was being sucked from you. Did Cloot see or feel anything?'

No, I didn't either, Cloot said. *I happened to glance down and saw you lying on the ground.*

Tor looked at Saxon and shook his head. 'No. Same as you. But what about that amazing white light?'

'Nothing but moonlight was falling on us, Tor. This was obviously a private experience.'

'Saxon!' Tor grabbed his friend's arm in sudden excitement. 'This whole journey I've been expecting to see my children as five or six year olds. The person who called to me, called me father – my son – he is a young man!'

'You're imagining it, Tor. All that sudden activity, the terror. What you saw – well, you still haven't explained it, but it obviously frightened you. The fear distorted things.'

'No, you don't understand.' Tor was back on his feet and pacing circles in the moonlight. 'It was a man's voice. My son is grown up.'

'Listen to yourself. How can that be? The baby . . . Wait a minute, what do you mean children? There is only your son, surely?'

Oh dear, Cloot said quietly.

Tor looked at Saxon. He suddenly felt guilty that he had not yet told the whole story.

'Let's take a break from our walk, Saxon. I have something to tell you.'

They sat at the roadside and shared some bread and cheese they carried. Neither was particularly hungry but the food gave them an excuse to busy their hands and mouths whilst Tor searched for the right words.

Cloot left to hunt, taking the precious spare time to feed on the small creatures which came out at night. He had not thought he would get a chance tonight and clicked his beak in delicious anticipation. He left Tor to the difficult tale.

Tor swallowed. There was no point in waiting any longer.

'Sax . . . you remember how when Gidyon was born, we were all weeping when the Heartwood's creatures were suddenly startled by a sound?'

'Yes. I remember I told you to wait. I went in search of Goth to head him away from Alyssa and yourself.'

Tor nodded. 'That's right. And whilst you were gone, I helped Sorrel to deliver a baby girl . . . a sister to Gidyon.'

Shock wrought its way across the Kloek's face. He spat out the bread he was chewing. 'And Alyssa doesn't know, does she?'

Tor shook his head sadly. He kept his eyes firmly on Saxon's.

'You bastard,' Saxon said. He stood. It was his turn to pace. 'You not only told her that the son who still breathes is dead, but she knows nothing of her daughter. You are a heartless man, Gynt.'

Tor allowed him to spend his anger. He had expected as much.

'Saxon, just be calm and listen. Please. Alyssa was dying at the time. The only way I could save my family was to support the lie. Sorrel disappeared with both children. She insisted that I should not tell Alyssa. It all made sense at the time — she promised me it was the only way to save the lives of the three people I suddenly loved more than anything.'

Saxon grunted. He was not convinced. 'And?'

'I went back . . . a day or so later. I could not live with myself: leaving Alyssa behind like that, half dead; letting my newborn children go off in the care of someone else.'

Tor could feel all the old distress and guilt rising in this throat. He took a breath.

'Anyway, I went back to the Heartwood. There was no sign of anyone. I don't just mean of Alyssa or the children, Sax, I mean of anyone having ever lived there. All trace of us had been wiped clean by the forest. Darmud Coril's influence, I suspect.

'Then I was captured. I was stunned to see Alyssa in Goth's hands. She didn't say a word to me from the moment she clapped eyes on me again. We travelled to Tal with a heavy silence between us, though in truth I was not allowed to even ride near her. In the city, as you know, I was thrown in a dungeon and she was cared for at the Queen's discretion. She was not permitted to visit. No words passed between us. No link. I was totally cut off from Alyssa. Even at the trial, all I could do was look at her. Then . . . well, you know the rest.

'Saxon . . . are you listening, man? Even if I had wanted to tell her, I have never had the chance. What do you think this is all about? I have called the children back to Tallinor. It is time they knew of their parents; met me, met their mother . . . They must play their role, if they have one to play.'

Tor held his head. The guilt was heavy in his heart.

Cloot arrived back and began to clean the gore from his beak.

It was Saxon who broke the difficult silence. 'Good feed, Cloot?'

Delicious! Cloot said and flapped his wings for Saxon's benefit.

Is all well? he asked Tor.

He knows the whole story now, Tor replied.

It is right that he does. He will help when the time comes, Cloot said matter of factly.

Saxon rounded on Tor. 'So where the hell have the children been all of this time? You can't expect me to believe you don't know?'

'That's the truth, Sax. Sorrel took them and she disappeared. I have never seen nor heard of them since that day of their birth in the Heartwood.'

Saxon continued to pace. 'And you thought they had stayed in the realm?'

Tor stood and dusted the breadcrumbs from his cloak. The food felt sour in his belly now. 'Initially I did. Later, as the years drew on, I figured Sorrel must have taken them from our Kingdom to another; which is obviously what she did do.'

'But then how do you explain your son being grown? A young man, you said.'

'I have absolutely no idea,' Tor replied, totally confused.

'Well, then it couldn't have been Gidyon, Tor,' Saxon said gently. 'Otherwise he would be around five or six summers; no more. Time does not pass differently in other Kingdoms.'

Of course, you are both assuming the children remained in this Land, Cloot said, eyeing Tor, no longer interested in his ablutions.

Tor looked at his falcon and Saxon noticed the sharp change in his body language.

'What did Cloot say?' he asked.

'He said we're just presuming that Sorrel kept them in this Land.'

Saxon snorted. 'And what's that supposed to mean?'

Tor looked again at the falcon. *What are you saying, Cloot?*

Just that there is every possibility she took them beyond our world, to another world, where time perhaps moves differently . . . It's just a notion.

Tor clapped his hands. 'Of course! Cloot is saying that Sorrel could have disappeared to another world altogether, where time maybe moves differently.'

Saxon shook his head. 'I think we're reaching here.'

'It makes all the sense in the world, Saxon. Open your mind! I left Sorrel with a dying woman, two newborn babies and the god of the forest. I have no idea of the extent of Darmud Coril's powers, but if he became involved, he could have sent them anywhere. It is plausible. Think about it.'

Saxon finally shrugged. 'Vaguely possible, I suppose.'

'Come on,' Tor said, a new vigour in his step. 'We must hurry now to the Heartwood; no time to waste.'

Once they had travelled a safe enough distance from the burning village and it was only a faint glow on the horizon, Gidyon made everyone rest. He held Figgis in his arms all night and listened to the dwarf's ragged breathing.

As the sun began to rise Figgis spoke to him. *Thank you,* he whispered.

It was frightening, Figgis. What have I done?

What you had to do. That village needed to be cleansed. You saved our lives.

I took dozens though.

All ready to meet their gods, I fear, Figgis reassured him. *It was an evil place, Gidyon. Please forgive yourself.*

I called to my father. I think I opened a link to him in my fear and my anger. I drew on his power, or something released mine . . . I'm not sure.

I met your father once.

You did?

Yes, not long ago. We were in a place called Cipres. You look so like him, you could pass for him.

Really? Gidyon felt uplifted to hear this.

We spoke only briefly. Two strangers, passing the time of day. I knew who he was but he did not know me.

I have so much to learn about.

That is why I am here. I shall teach you and I shall watch over you. You will never have to save me again.

So you are going to live? Gidyon said, relieved.

It takes more than a few broken bones to kill a Rock Dweller, my boy. Get me to the Heartwood and all shall be well.

He smiled a wonderful smile that made Gidyon feel safe and loved. He bent and kissed the little man on the forehead. *Thank you for being here for me.*

Always, Figgis said and drifted back into a painful doze.

Gidyon placed him tenderly on the soft grass where they had slept all night and covered him with his own jerkin. He hoped the rest would help to heal his friend. He would leave him quiet for a little longer.

Yseul was stirring. Gwerys still slept.

'Yseul,' Gidyon whispered, taking her hand and kissing it gently.

She opened her strange, sand-coloured eyes. 'We're safe, aren't we?'

He nodded gently. 'I promise.'

Yseul sat up and put her arms around him. 'Forgive me for all those terrible things I said to you. I owe you so much, Gidyon. I don't understand anything of what happened back there but—'

He hushed her words and stroked her hair. 'I always keep my promises,' he whispered.

She pulled back. 'Who are you?'

'The Gatherer of Souls, apparently.' He grinned.

'Don't mock, it was all I could think of. Oh, I was so frightened.'

'You were sensational. I drew courage from you, Yseul. You made me look weak by comparison.'

'Not in the end though,' she said, fixing him with her odd eyes.

He held her gaze. 'Would you believe me if I told you I hardly understand it either?'

She searched his face, as she had done once before in the barn. 'I do believe you. Strange events happen all the time. I trusted you the minute I saw you . . . I trust you now.'

'Thank you,' he said and meant it, because he really did not have an explanation which would stand much scrutiny.

She looked over at Figgis. 'What about him, your friend?'

'I shall carry him to where I am going. We will get help there.'

She nodded. 'Where *are* you going?'

'We're headed for a township called Flat Meadows and then on to Axon.'

'Oh, that's by the Great Forest. People are scared of the forest.'

'Scared?'

'Well, respectful is probably a better way to put it. It houses ancient mysteries. I believe what I can see with my own strange eyes.'

They both laughed when she deliberately made them go cross-eyed.

'And you, Yseul, where is home for you?'

'It's been so long, I'm not sure where to call home.'

He understood. 'Then come with me. If you have nowhere to call home, you might as well travel with friends.'

She considered it and then smiled sadly. 'It is very tempting,' she said, then she leaned towards Gidyon and kissed him very briefly, very gently. 'But this little boy here needs to know a real home. He needs a real mother and father who will love him. I think I must take him back to where he belongs.'

Again Gidyon understood, though he felt a flash of disappointment. 'Where is that?'

'Brittelbury. It is a week or more from here due east but we can journey slowly.'

Just then, as if by magic, they heard the sound of hooves. Several horses, obviously still spooked from the fire, had stuck together and were wandering in shock.

'Not on a horse it won't be,' Gidyon said, winking. 'Help me catch them.'

'Slowly,' she cautioned. 'They will be fearful.'

Somehow Gidyon sensed they would not be afraid of him. He did not know how he knew this, but he proved himself true when he gently called to them and was able to keep them calm and still whilst he approached. Of course he could not know that this way with animals was a talent inherited from his mother. A few minutes later, the horses were happily munching grass next to them.

'What about saddles?' Gidyon said.

'I used to ride bareback all the time as a child. I'm sure it will come back to me.'

He left her to squat down next to Figgis and ransack his pockets. He looked pleased when he returned. 'You have this,' he said, tipping a heavy pouch of coins into her hand.

Yseul peeped inside and then tipped a few out. 'No, Gidyon, this is a fortune to someone like me.'

'Trust me, he would want you to keep it and travel safely with your brother to your home. Is there enough for a saddle for each of you?'

'You don't know?' she asked incredulously. 'Gidyon, we could live more than well on this for several weeks. We could buy ten saddles and perhaps a few horses to go with them!'

'Then I am glad. You both deserve it.' He flipped a

single gold coin into the air. 'This will see us through. Promise me that you will stay at inns and be safe. Eat properly. Take the horses and sell them if you please when you get home. Just be careful.'

'I don't know what to say.'

'There is nothing more. I wish you would come with me, but I understand why you cannot.'

'I wish I could too,' she said.

He kissed her. It was the first time he had ever really kissed anyone properly. It was magnificent and he wanted it to go on and on.

'Are you sure we have to say goodbye?' he said when they reluctantly moved apart.

'You know the village where I live. Come and see me.'

He nodded. 'I will.'

She looked at him intently. 'No, you won't, Gidyon. There is no reason why you should. You are here for a greater purpose, I feel.'

Gidyon could not bear the thought that he may never see her again. 'Wait!' he said, this time digging into his shirt pocket. He found what he wanted and, for the second time, pulled her palm open and dropped something into it.

'What is this?' she said, glancing at the smooth, dull stone in her hand.

'This, believe it or not, is incredibly precious to me, Yseul. Promise me you will never lose it, never sell it, never give it away. It belongs to me but it will keep you safe until I come to collect it. There is my reason in your hand. One day, I shall come to claim what is mine,' he said.

She smiled. 'Then, as plain and curious as it is, I shall

consider it as precious as you do; as precious as your friendship is to me.'

It felt strange to be giving away his stone, his only tie to his past, but it seemed more important that Yseul should have something of him. Something that promised they would see each other again.

28

Lauryn's Journey

Everything seemed to be going smoothly. Lauryn was enjoying Sorrel's company, even though she was wary of the old girl; there was just something about her which suggested caution. Still, the daily conversation about herbs and plants fascinated her and even in this short time she had begun to recognise the flowers and grasses which Sorrel pointed out to her.

Sorrel was impressed with Lauryn's recall of which plant could help an ailment; there were even moments when she was stunned by the young woman's adeptness at suggesting her own combinations of herbs to achieve a different result. She would make a superb healer.

But mostly they talked about her mother. Lauryn never tired of hearing about Alyssa and was especially pleased when Sorrel commented on their strong likeness, especially as her mother was reportedly beautiful. She could hardly believe they did look alike; nevertheless, in the quiet of night she hugged herself when she thought about it. The tale she repeatedly forced Sorrel to tell was the reunion of her parents at Caremboche and their escape to the Heartwood.

'Where do you think this Goth is now?' Lauryn asked.

'Dead, I should hope,' Sorrel said with disgust.

'But you don't know that,' Lauryn suggested.

'No. The last I knew of him, he was hunting us all down in the Heartwood. Saxon, whom I've told you about, gave chase in order to lead the Chief Inquisitor away from where your mother was struggling to give birth to you, my child.'

Lauryn smiled, trying to build that picture in her mind.

'Saxon would have found a way to deal with him and, if not the Kloek, then your father. I'm sure of it,' the old woman added.

'Of course. I'm forgetting that you don't know anything that happened after this Darmud Coril you speak of sent you away with us. That's right, isn't it?'

'Yes.'

Lauryn considered this as they walked. 'So really, we have no idea what has happened to my parents since that moment. My mother could be dead,' she suddenly said.

'No, child. As I said once before, I would have known. We shared a great deal, your mother and I. And your father would not bring you back to a dead mother; I am sure of that too.'

'But how do we know they are even together? We don't know anything about their last fifteen years.'

Sorrel nodded. 'This is true but don't labour it, child. Time travels differently here than it does where we have come from. It has not been nearly as long as you think here in Tallinor. Let us try to think only good thoughts. This is hard enough without us anticipating the worst possible situation. Your father is alive. He has called you. One step at a time, eh?'

Lauryn could tell Sorrel was tired. It was only the middle of the morning and yet the old woman was struggling to speak and walk at the same time. Funny, she had seemed so much stronger and healthier in their own world. Here she seemed frail. Mind you, they had walked far; much further than Lauryn could ever recall walking before. In her old life — those little parts of it she could still remember — she knew she had been lazy, had embraced any excuse not to exert energy. Yet, in the past few days of solid walking, she had noticed her complexion was clearing, her clothes felt looser and even her humour was better. She needed no mirror to know these things.

It was a rare sensation, she realised as they walked the roads, to enjoy being Lauryn. It was a grand feeling and the only blot on her day was her brother's tone over the link.

Who was this girl he had to help, this Yseul? How could he have become so involved with someone, even as a friend, in such a short time? Lauryn grunted, but when Sorrel glanced at her, she ignored the look and kept walking. Gidyon had sounded anxious. Actually, that was what bothered her most of all. She was worried. Just when she had finally found someone to love and care about, he got himself in trouble and she was helplessly far away and unable to help. She wanted to open a link with Gidyon right this moment, but she dared not. He had made it very clear that he needed to be left alone to think.

The hedgerow was thickening and, as they approached a bend in the road, Sorrel stopped.

'Are you all right?' Lauryn asked, coming out of her thoughts.

'Someone approaches,' Sorrel said quietly. 'Lauryn, it

is important to say this now. Should anything happen to us—'

Lauryn cut across the old girl's words. 'What do you mean, happen?' She sounded alarmed.

'I mean, child, should we get separated, or if I am unable to travel with you for any reason, you must make your own way to the Heartwood. Do not wait for me. Do not even pause for me, no matter what might occur. Get yourself to Axon and into the Great Forest, to your father. Make haste.'

Lauryn could hear men's voices now and the sound of horses. They were moving slowly.

'Lauryn.' Sorrel insisted she listen. 'Do not tell anyone who you are or how you come to be here. Let them know nothing about your background. Lie if you must but get yourself to the Heartwood as fast as you can – alone!'

Lauryn could hardly miss the fear in Sorrel's voice but she had no time to ask more. Around the curve of the road appeared four horsemen. She and Sorrel moved to the grass verge, eyes averted, expecting them to pass.

'Who are they?' Lauryn whispered.

'King's men,' was all Sorrel had time to say.

The horses ambled to a halt. One of the men addressed them. 'Pardon me, ladies. Are you alone?'

'Obviously,' Lauryn answered, feeling nervous from Sorrel's caution. The old woman hissed at her.

The man got down from his horse and his men followed. He approached the two women and spoke. 'May I have your names, please?'

Sorrel curtsied. 'Forgive my granddaughter, sir. She is in poor humour today.' She glared at Lauryn to remain quiet. 'I am Sorrel, a herbwoman. This is Lauryn. We are travelling towards Axon.'

'I see,' he said. He looked at Lauryn. 'We are patrolling this area for a band of thieves. We lost sight of them last night.'

'Well, we haven't seen anything,' Lauryn said, hoping to bring the conversation to a close.

He ignored her tone and addressed Sorrel. 'Madam, may I suggest that you exercise caution in travelling alone with a young woman. These men have shown themselves to be ruthless. They already know they are dead thrice over for their deeds; they show no regard for anyone.'

'Are we in danger from them here?'

'Well, madam, the next village is not far. I would suggest you remain there today and perhaps join with a group who may be travelling to Tal or even Hatten. Safety in numbers. The road seems clear. We have made our presence felt so you should be safe.'

He smiled kindly. 'I am Captain Lyngos, by the way.'

'Thank you, sir,' Sorrel said, curtsying politely again.

Lauryn could not help herself. 'I would suggest travelling in a group would draw more attention to ourselves. At least with just the two of us, these men, should we encounter them, will quickly see we have nothing worth stealing.'

The captain turned back to her. 'Do you not?'

'No,' she replied, a little haughtily. 'My grandmother and I are on foot. We have one bag with a few items of no interest to anyone. We have so little money; it probably would not keep them in ale.'

'Young lady,' the captain said, eyeing her firmly, 'these men may take your grandmother's coin, but they may also decide to rob you of something more precious.'

It took Lauryn a moment to realise what he meant. He

was already on his horse and moving forwards when understanding hit and she felt herself blush with hot embarrassment.

'The Light guide you safely,' the captain said to Sorrel and they moved on.

When the guardsmen were out of earshot, Sorrel turned on her. 'You must learn to curb that quick tongue of yours. It will get you into trouble. You have no status here yet. That was a captain of the King's Guard and due your respect.'

Sorrel broke into a coughing fit which lasted some minutes. She could say no more.

By the time she was calm again, the incident was put aside. Lauryn was now worried for Sorrel, who was sitting on the ground from the effort of coughing.

'Are you sick, Sorrel? How can I help?'

'Not sick. Just old,' she said. 'It is almost my time.'

'Your time?'

'My work is almost done. I must see you safely into the care of your parents, then I can go to my rest.'

It all sounded too ominous for Lauryn. She changed the subject. 'Are you able to continue walking?'

'Help me up, child. We must be alert until the next village.'

Lauryn offered to carry her bag but Sorrel refused. Instead, Lauryn insisted she lighten the load and removed three apples to her own pockets and carried the small flask of fresh water. It made little difference, she was sure, but she felt better for doing something.

They covered the next mile or so wrapped in their own silent thoughts. Progress was slow but the weather was fine and it was a good road they walked. Lauryn began to relax. Sorrel was weak, there was no doubt about it, but she was a gritty old girl and made no further complaint. By mid afternoon, they sensed they were not far from the village of Hamptyn. Sorrel said they would have to stay overnight, even if they just begged the cover of a barn and a knuckle of bread from one of the farmers.

Just as she finished saying this, they rounded another bend in the road and were confronted by a small upturned cart. Lying at the side of the road was a seemingly lifeless man, his face covered in blood. By his side a lad knelt. He looked very distressed and, when he saw them, he jumped to his feet and started yelling. 'Help me, please! It's my da. He's dying.'

'Light!' Sorrel said. She did not heed her own warning and broke into a fast shuffle over to the boy. 'Quick, Lauryn,' she called over her shoulder.

Lauryn took in the scene. Sorrel had told her to be so careful and here she was rushing into a situation without care. Lauryn could see that something was not right here.

Sorrel dug a cloth out of her bag to clean up the man and see how bad his wounds were.

'Lauryn!' she yelled. 'I need some water.' Lauryn moved closer and handed Sorrel the flask. 'Use this. We can always get more.'

She looked at the boy. He immediately averted his eyes, though she knew he had been staring. There was not so much as a tear staining his face, for all his anxiety over his father. Something told her his antics were forced. He kept darting his attention behind her. No horse! That was it. That's what was wrong. Where was the horse which had been pulling this cart?

She swung around but it was too late. Three burly men were approaching behind her.

She screamed and the boy grabbed her. He was rangy but strong and his fingers dug cruelly into her arms. Sorrel began to scream as well as the wounded man sat up and grabbed her too, laughing.

'Let's see what's in this bag then, shall we, old lady? And if there's nothing worth taking, I'll help myself to something from her,' he said, licking his lips clear of the blood smeared all over them and eyeing Lauryn.

'No!' shrieked Lauryn, with clear understanding of his intentions.

One of the men dangled a rabbit in her face; its throat cut and still oozing the blood which had been smeared on the 'wounded' man's face. She tried to push it away but blood flecked her face in her effort. The men laughed.

'Take her into the woods,' the leader said, standing, one foot pinning Sorrel to the ground.

Sorrel found her voice. 'Run, Lauryn, run!'

The boy turned back and belted Sorrel so hard that the old lady fell backwards and lay deadly still.

Lauryn had been in shock to this point. But now she felt fury rising and, although two of the burly men had literally lifted her off her feet and were running her off the road into the copse of trees ahead, she began a titanic struggle. She screamed, kicked and bit whatever she could find. Fortunately, she found one man's ear and ripped the lobe clean off. He screamed and let go of her, but the other fellow still had a mighty grip. Her arm had gone numb from his hard hold on it. He slapped her.

'Get up, Belco!' he ordered. 'Help me get her away

from here. We can have some fun later and you can get your revenge. You had ugly ears anyway.'

Belco belted her too, for good measure. It felt to Lauryn as though he might break her arm by the cruel way he twisted it behind her back. Her head burned from the blow but she could still see the image in her mind of Sorrel lying on the grass, lifeless, and the first man rifling through her bag.

The leader arrived, the lad behind him. 'Where's my grandmother?' Lauryn screamed at them.

'Dead!' the leader said viciously. 'Which is what you'll be if you don't shut your mouth.'

Captain Lyngos and his men arrived at the rendezvous point. His chief, the Under Prime, was kneeling at a stream near where they had set up camp. Shirtless he stood up, flicking water from his hair and face, and used his old shirt to dry himself. The Under Prime was a good-looking man; he reminded Lyngos of Prime Cyrus from years ago. He possessed the same quick wit and intelligence, as well as the dashing bravado and arrogance which won the hearts of the ladies.

It had been hard to accept him as their chief at first. They could all remember him as the little boy who had been found chained to the palace railings. Now he was a man. Not exceptionally tall, but built strongly with a heart to match. He had earned their respect the hard way, beating all of them with sword, stick, fists if necessary. None of the men had made it easy but he had won through.

It was clear that the young man had not asked for this position. He was a favourite of the King and it had been dropped onto his broad shoulders with no choice but to accept. He had not pushed his role too hard; Gyl was intelligent enough to realise that he must take the business of leading men slowly. Trust had to be earned. With Prime Herek away, as his deputy he was in charge of the remaining company.

'Anything?' he said, striding towards them with his distinctive swagger.

'No, sir. All quiet. We have swept around from the back of Hamptyn and the only people we encountered were an old woman and her acid-tongued granddaughter.'

Gyl nodded. 'They're here, all right. But they're too clever for their own good.' He walked to his saddlebag and dug out a fresh shirt. 'All right, we break camp and set up a new rendezvous point and we'll go through this next ten miles with a fine comb.'

'Yes, sir.'

'Get your men fed and rested, Lyngos.'

The captain nodded and saluted, then turned to give orders.

'Oh, Lyngos, these people you met — was it wise to let them travel alone? How old was the girl?'

'I'd guess around sixteen summers, sir. Dressed plainly. They were on foot and insisted they had nothing worth taking.'

'Other than the obvious thing that fiends like these will not think twice about stealing,' Gyl said, shaking his head. 'Did you offer them an escort?'

'No, sir, I didn't. They were adamant that travelling alone suited them.'

Gyl believed the captain should have insisted, and Lyngos now realised he should have too. These men had killed many times and, having had the death sentence proclaimed on them over and again, had nothing more to lose. Rape was one of their favourite pastimes. An old girl and a young woman on foot would be easy pickings.

'Thank you, captain. Get some food into you.' Gyl dismissed the men and pulled on his shirt.

He knew the story of Alyssa's rape, which she had told him haltingly one rainy night a year or so ago. He could not recall why this tale had spilled out just then, but they had cried together over it and he had made her a promise then and there, that every woman in the Kingdom would be safe when he was Prime.

That comment from a young man had brought a smile to Alyssa's face. 'My brave Gyl. So you think you'll be Prime one day, do you?'

'I shall lead my men bravely and I shall die for my King if required,' he had said, leaping to his feet and grabbing the sword he was so proud of. 'And every woman will be able to travel the roads of Tallinor without fear!'

He remembered how his stepmother – the woman he now thought of as his true mother – had stood and hugged him hard. 'That is a fine promise.'

Gyl brought his thoughts back to the present and called for his horse.

'Carry on. I'll catch up with you,' he reassured the captain, who looked over at him enquiringly. 'I'll just see those women safely into Hamptyn.'

He hit the road at a steady canter.

Lauryn felt real fear now. 'What do you want from me?' she yelled at the leader.

'All it is that you have left to give us,' he said and laughed.

'Tie her to that tree for now, Belco. What happened to your ear, man?'

'She bit me,' Belco lamented, pushing Lauryn back against the tree trunk.

'Well then, you'll just have to bite her back later in a place she's never felt such pain before,' the man replied and grinned horribly at her.

Lauryn knew if she did not do something right now, it was over for her. These men would rape her, maybe torture her. Certainly they would not leave her alive. And Sorrel was dead! She could not dwell on that now, but Sorrel had forbidden her to linger, had urged her to flee at any sign of danger. And she would never see her Gidyon again, or meet her father, or be held in her mother's arms if she did not do something now!

With that rush of emotional thought, a new sensation flowed through her body. She felt it like a pulse and then she sensed the Colours; it was as though they were rushing through her. Suddenly she felt lightheaded and . . . powerful. Yes, that was it! She felt power. Not really understanding the sensation, or knowing what to do with it, she reacted instinctively when Belco bent her arm painfully back behind her for the second time that day.

Belco's body hit the tree opposite with great force and a sickening crunch. His body dropped to the ground, broken; his ear leaking a trickle of blood, which would stop shortly because his heart no longer pumped life.

The two other men had their backs turned, but the lad saw what happened and called out in shock. The men turned, their eyes flicking first to Lauryn, who was still untied, and then to Belco on the floor.

'Get her!' the leader cried and they rushed her.

Lauryn blinked, still struggling to understand how she had harmed Belco, and then she was running.

Sorrel's voice haunted her: 'Run, Lauryn, run!' and run she did, like a startled hare. She picked up her skirt and crashed through the copse of trees at a speed she never thought she possessed, but the men were in hot pursuit. She zigzagged, trying to throw them off, but knew she was making far too much noise, so she headed for open country, bursting out of the cover of trees and running across a field.

They spotted her, of course, and soon the lad was gaining on her. Lauryn stepped up her speed but the burning in her chest told her she could not keep this up; she might be able to outrun the two heavy men but not the lad, and he was all it would take to pin her down.

So she stopped and turned on him. Breathing heavily, she eyed him ferociously and it stopped him in his tracks. He approached cautiously.

'Don't take another step forward,' she said.

He lunged but found himself hurled high into the air; when he found land again it was with an assortment of broken limbs. He began to scream from the pain but Lauryn did not care. She turned on her heel and ran off through the field, with no idea of where she was headed, other than away from the scene of death behind her.

Gyl cantered around the curve of the road and scanned the scene. An overturned cart lay there, but had nothing in it, which was odd. Lyngos had made no mention of this either, but if the accident had just occurred, there would be lots of confusion, a terrified horse and its owner trying to calm it down. Gyl remained on his horse, cautious that this could be a trap.

Approaching slowly, he suddenly noticed a woman lying at the side of the road, her body roughly covered by a few branches. She was silvery-haired and clearly old. His heart sank. This was probably the old woman Lyngos had mentioned. With no sign of the granddaughter, Gyl could only imagine the worst. He punched his thigh, anger gripping him that this could have happened under his very nose.

He made a swift decision. If the old girl was dead, then there was nothing he could do for her. Right now, he might still be able to save her granddaughter.

With a kick of his stirrups and a cry of anger, he forced his horse up the small embankment and into the copse. He drew his sword and guided the horse carefully through the trees. It did not take Gyl long to find the smashed body of Belco. Once again he did not leave the safety of his high position. The man was dead, that was for sure, but he could not imagine what had happened here.

Witnesses had reported three men and a lad, so there were three outlaws still on the loose. He called out but received no response, so decided to head out of the copse and see what lay beyond. Emerging from the cover of trees, he looked ahead and saw two men running across the field. When he squinted he could see the golden hair of a woman bouncing wildly, running not that far in front of them.

Gyl spurred his horse into a gallop and gave mad chase. The men turned to see a King's man bearing down on them at speed and one peeled off immediately. Gyl pursued the other man, who was closing on his prey. The Under

Prime caught up with him quickly and slashed at the back of his legs, cutting through tendon and muscle and bringing the bandit to a screaming halt. It was not the leader.

Gyl did not even slow but pushed his horse faster, until he could reach down and grab the girl. She flailed in panic in his grasp. One moment Gyl had her cleanly up and onto the horse; the next, he found himself on the ground, which he had hit so hard he could see stars.

It took him what felt like a long time to roll himself onto his back, where he lay in pain, sucking in great gasps of air. Had the horse stumbled and thrown him? No! Gyl never lost his seat and certainly not from Bryx. He was the finest horseman in all of the company.

He lay there thinking unclear thoughts, wishing the pain would dissipate.

Where was Bryx? Where was the girl?

'Er . . . I found your horse,' a voice said.

Gyl opened his eyes to slits and turned his head painfully towards the sound. He saw a girl covered in mud. 'Are you all right?'

'In better shape than you, I believe,' she said, sheepishly. 'I fell into some sort of swamp. Can you move?'

'I'm not sure. Everything hurts. Did you see what happened?'

Lauryn lied. 'No. You must have fallen from the horse.'

Gyl pushed himself painfully to his elbows to regard her. 'The Under Prime does not fall from his horse,' he said, disgusted at himself.

'How do you feel?'

'Not good. May I ask for your help?'

Lauryn looked at the horse, unsure of what to do.

'The horse won't go anywhere. He comes at a command. His name is Bryx. And I am Gyl, Under Prime of Tallinor . . . I'd like to say at your service, madam, but it seems I am far from that.'

Lauryn smiled through the mud which she could feel covered all of her face and hair. The immense fear was falling away and the Colours were falling with it. She felt dreadful about what she had done to this man, who had obviously been giving chase to help her, but how could she have known that in those seconds of terror? Lauryn did not understand what she had struck out with, but it was effective; she knew that much!

'Where are they?' she said, letting go of the reins and approaching him.

'One's dead in the copse – I have no idea why or how. I felled another with my sword, but not mortally. The third ran in a different direction when he saw me. Light! If I had only kept my seat, I could have had them both under chain by now.' Gyl shook his head with disgust again. 'And apparently, there was a lad with them.'

Lauryn said nothing about the boy. 'Did you see an old woman at all?'

'Yes, I'm sorry. She is dead. They have much to answer for, these men.'

Lauryn bit back tears. She helped him to stand.

'Nothing broken, I don't think,' he said tentatively, leaning on her and gingerly testing his weight on his legs. 'Here, Bryx!'

He clicked his tongue at his horse, who obediently walked to his master. 'Let's get you back to Hamptyn and work out things from there,' Gyl said kindly.

'Oh no,' Lauryn said, pulling away. 'I'm not going back.'

'But what about your grandmother? Where are you going? You surely don't mean to go on alone?'

'My grandmother is dead. I am going to continue my journey to Axon and I definitely do mean to go alone,' she replied defiantly, remembering Sorrel's urgent warnings.

He looked at her. 'What is your name?'

'Lauryn.'

'And where do you come from, Lauryn?'

The question caught her by surprise. Sorrel had warned her not to say too much, so she blurted out the first place which came to her mind. 'Mallee Marsh.'

He seemed surprised. 'Really? That's where my mother comes from too. Why are you headed for Axon?'

'Why all these questions?'

'Lauryn, I am in charge of the security of the Kingdom. I have a right to know your business.'

'And do you think one young woman travelling alone could threaten the security of a Kingdom?'

This girl made him feel foolish. And she managed to achieve that whilst dripping mud from every inch of herself and staring at him from a mud-encrusted face.

'No, I don't.'

'Then thank you for your concern . . . Gyl, is it? I am grateful for your help but I wish to continue my journey.'

'I cannot permit you to continue alone.'

Lauryn felt exasperated by his stubbornness. And he was such a good-looking man. She did not wish to sit close to him on that horse of his, with her back against his chest; though then again . . .

She was completely confused by all these feelings and spoke sharply to cover it. 'Can you hold me against my wishes, sir? I have broken no law.'

Gyl knew he was clutching at straws. 'Axon is a-long walk from here, for a woman alone.'

'It would be no shorter if I was walking with ten others.'

Light! She infuriated him. 'Are you not scared of the outlaw who is still on the loose?'

Lauryn no longer felt frightened. If anything, she was more terrified by the powers which seemed to be at her command. She needed time to think on what had happened and how she had loosed such magic. Sorrel had insisted she go on alone should anything untoward happen. Well, it *had* happened and she would go on as instructed . . . if she could only escape this handsome man's interest in her. She was finding it hard to even look at him, with that shirt torn open and his broad chest revealed.

'No, I am not scared because I know you will track him down and keep me safe.'

Gyl smiled inwardly. How could she know him so well? A pity he could not see her face through the mud. He liked her strength.

'Do you know which way to head for Axon?'

'Perhaps you could show me,' she said. She wanted to wipe the mud from her hands on her skirt, but it may betray the nerves she felt at his keen interest.

Gyl knew he was not going to win this argument. He had a duty to his men and it was time he returned to them. He still had to pick up the felled man, sort out the body in the copse and start tracking the final villain in the pack. The Light only knew what had happened to the boy.

'The longer, easier route is back to the road and then head east.'

'There is another way, I'm guessing?' she said.

'Yes, over these hills. It's steep and very hard walking. But you will cut two days from your journey. Just head north east and you will see Axon nestling in a shallow dip next to one of the forest's fingers.'

'Then that is the way I shall head. It will also take me away from the outlaw, I believe. You will find him, won't you?'

'For you, Lauryn, I shall. Do you wish me to wait whilst you clean yourself up?' Gyl was beginning to think he would like to lay eyes on the girl behind this mask.

Lauryn was horrified. At least she had been able to hide her plump, plain looks behind the mud. And 'clean up' meant taking her clothes off. Certainly not!

'No, please. You have spent enough time with me. I am fine and thank you for the directions.'

'What about food? There are no farms or villages in that direction.'

Lauryn remembered the apples in her pocket. It was hardly a meal but they would suffice. She was anxious to be on her way. 'I'll survive,' she said and turned.

'If you ever get to Tal, ask for me,' he called after her.

She did not look back.

It had sounded like a good idea until she found herself on the moors. What would she not give for the strong back of Bryx and the broad chest of Gyl to lean against now? It was a comforting thought. She would hold that picture of the handsome Under Prime in her mind's eye. Lauryn was exhausted from climbing; she had not realised how much the day's terror had taken out of her. Alone, feeling lost and past being hungry, she wanted to cry, but she battled through it.

Finally, as dusk settled, she found a reasonably sheltered spot to rest, knowing the night's chill would descend
quickly. After gobbling down two of the apples, she pulled
her shawl tightly around herself and drifted into a deep
sleep.

In her fright and subsequent jumbled thoughts, she
had forgotten to link with Gidyon, but in this she was
fortunate. As Lauryn slept, Gidyon was unleashing an
awesome vengeance on the town of Duntaryn.

She woke uncomfortably just as dawn was breaking across
the moors. Bones aching from her cold, hard bed and
feeling nauseous from the lack of food, Lauryn cast.

Gidyon answered her immediately. *At last!*

She was grumpy enough without this sort of comment.
Really? Well, the last time I dropped by you asked me to leave.

She had not meant to react so viciously. In fact, Lauryn
would have given anything at that moment to feel his
long arms around her and hear his voice telling her that
everything was going to be all right.

*Good morning, Lauryn. I see you're in your usual charming
mood,* he replied, though not unkindly.

*If only you knew what's happened since we last spoke, you'd
be more gentle.*

That won his full attention. *What has happened? Are
you safe?*

It felt comforting to hear such fright in his voice. How
special it was to know someone cared.

Yes, I'm fine now. Sorrel isn't doing so well. She faltered,
fought back the tears again. *Oh, Gidyon . . . Sorrel's dead.*

She told him everything from the moment she and
Sorrel had encountered the overturned cart. He was silent

throughout. It was a shock for him to hear the terrible story.

What about you? What happened yesterday? she asked as an afterthought.

This was not the time to tell her, Gidyon decided. *Oh, it was all a misunderstanding. Everything is fine. Figgis and I are setting off now.*

Who is Figgis?

Long story, he replied. *How long do you think it will take you to get to Axon?*

That fellow Gyl said I'd be able to reduce the time by around a couple of days, so I'm guessing it must be roughly a two-day walk from here.

Keep the link open for me, Lauryn. Even if we're not speaking, at least we can both feel connected and together. Are you breakfasted and ready to leave?

Well, I have this lonely apple just dying to hit my belly.

She heard him chuckle. *You're doing better than us then! We have nothing. Start walking.*

It did feel so much better having him inside her head. After a long stretch, the final apple and a few sips of water which she found captured in the large leaves of a plant she remembered Sorrel saying made the best tonic for arthritis, Lauryn felt renewed. She pushed sad thoughts of Sorrel from her mind and resumed the hard trudge.

29

Back to the Heartwood

After a happy reunion with the Quist family, the three travellers spent barely a day in Caradoon. Tor was eager to begin their journey back to the Great Forest. There was no time to waste; he must find his children.

'And so again, goodbye, Tor,' Eryn said, squeezing his hand. 'Cloot is beautiful.' She smiled and whispered her next words. 'I envy his time with you.'

Tor looked to where Saxon and Quist were joking about the bump on the head which Saxon had sustained on their first meeting; the Kloek was pretending it still troubled him.

'Janus is mad for you, Eryn. He worships you.'

'I know. And I feel the same towards him . . . in my own strange way. I meant what I said at the wharf. Only Alyssa could satisfy you, Tor.'

Eryn instantly regretted her words, knowing he would punish them — as he did, taking great relish to embarrass her.

'Well now, that depends on what type of satisfaction you could be referring to.' He grinned.

'Hush! Do you forget my husband stands so close?' But

she was laughing at his teasing, loving that they could do this. 'Be careful with Locky this time, please.'

'I am sending him straight back, I promise.'

Eryn glanced towards where Locky stood, stroking the muzzle of his horse. He too was eager to be on the road with Tor and Saxon.

'He won't like it.'

'He's too young, Eryn. Still too eager to die bravely. He needs a few women in his life.' He kissed her hand. 'Then he will know that life is worth clinging to.'

The horses, which had been generously provided by Quist, made the travelling much quicker and it was only a day before they came to the southern-most point of Caradoon's reach.

It was a pleasurable ride, with Cloot flying ahead and Saxon, in fine form, regaling them with stories of Cirq Zorros and his life with the Shield.

The Heartwood calls, Tor, Cloot said gently, as they first glimpsed the finger of the Great Forest.

Tor could see that Locky did not want to leave. His request to stay with them was almost bursting from his lips. Tor jumped in before he could speak.

'Locky, you have been a great friend to us. Promise me you will take care of your sister. I don't doubt that next time we meet you will be a captain aboard your own pirate ship and every bit as good as Quist.'

Locky smiled sadly. 'Except it is not the sea that beckons, Tor. I wish to join the Shield.'

Tor nodded. 'So I hear. Give it another year, Locky, and perhaps Saxon here can speak for you. He drinks with the Prime.'

Locky's eyes shone. 'Is that right, Saxon? You really are close to Prime Herek?'

Saxon enjoyed the reflected glory. 'On my word. Beef up a bit, Locky, and keep up your study. I'll talk to Herek for you but not until you're fifteen summers, boy.'

'Deal!' Locky said and spat into his hand.

Saxon did the same and they shook on the promise.

Tor was relieved. He had no intention of dragging Locky into his world again if he could help it. He was safe with his sister, as far north as possible and away from Tal.

Saxon said the needful. 'Well, Locky. Let's see you on your horse now and headed home with the other two before we leave for the forest.'

Locky grinned and after giving the two men a brief hard hug, he waved to Cloot. It was a childish gesture and Tor was sad that Locky would never know that Cloot understood it very well and had even responded.

May the Light shine your path home safely, boy, Cloot called but only Tor heard.

They waved until Locky, leading the other two horses, had cantered around a bend in the road and they could no longer see him. Tor turned with Saxon towards the forest.

'Home, Sax,' he said, looking towards the sanctuary of the trees.

'It's good to be back,' the Kloek replied.

Shoulder to shoulder, the men walked towards the first line of trees, which whispered their welcome back to the Heartwood.

Standing on the fringe of the forest was Arabella. She wiped away tears of relief to see the two men she loved returning to her. The trio hugged before entering the darkness and serenity of the Great Forest.

The rest of Gidyon's journey to Axon was uneventful. He carried Figgis the whole way; something the little man found intolerable yet, at the same time, too wonderful for words. On the one hand, he felt humiliated at being so weak – it was painful to see a Paladin having to resort to being carried like a child! On the other hand, he just loved looking up into the face of the young man who not only had saved his life, but was now Figgis's reason for living. He was bonded to the boy and would protect him with his own life, until death released him.

Figgis had only spent a short while in Torkyn Gynt's presence but he was often astounded to see how clearly reflected the father was in the son. Gidyon was certainly his father again in looks, and even in the lilt of his voice and the way he carried himself. How they compared in personality was yet to be seen, though Figgis fancied the similarities would be strong. Gidyon had already shown the icy courage his father was famous for.

'Figgis, my friend, guess what?' Gidyon said chirpily.

'I hope you are going to tell me we are at Axon,' Figgis replied.

'We are. There's the signpost – one mile.'

Gidyon put his friend on the ground so Figgis could take a better look, then cast to Lauryn to let her know they had arrived. He felt pride at being able to do this; since the eruption of his power at Duntaryn, he had found it easy to open his own link to her.

The Rock Dweller looked at their surrounds for a

moment or two. Finally he decided. 'We must head straight into the forest from here.'

Gidyon shook his head. 'How do you know?'

'The Heartwood will help us. The whole forest will assist in guiding us to where I hope your father awaits. Let's go.'

Gidyon picked up his friend again and marched straight towards the trees in the distance. 'Won't be long now,' he thought aloud.

'Are you nervous, child?'

'No. Not nervous. Just full of anticipation. I've spent all my years wondering about who my parents might have been, why I was alone. This is the biggest thing to happen in my life.'

Figgis sighed inwardly, imagining what lay ahead. 'Oh, I think we might do better in time,' he said.

'Figgis, look!'

In front of them stood an enormous silver wolf. She waited patiently on the fringe of the forest, looking directly at them.

'I was told to expect a donkey, a priestess or a wolf . . . it's the wolf. It's beautiful,' he said in a reverential tone.

'That, my boy, is no ordinary wolf. Her name is Solyana.' Figgis's voice was thick with emotion. 'Please, Gidyon, get me to her.'

Gidyon almost ran to where the wolf stood serenely gazing at them.

Figgis threw his arms around the wolf's neck and Gidyon was shocked to see him weep into her thick fur. Solyana licked Figgis. It was a tender scene and he felt like an intruder. Suddenly he heard the wolf's gentle voice in his head. It was beautiful, like her.

Do not mind us, Gidyon. We have not seen each other in a long, long time. I am truly honoured to welcome you back to the Heartwood, child. This is your home always. The Heartwood will always protect and love you.

Gidyon was astonished. The wolf had spoken into his head with such ease and grace that he was without words. Instinctively he bowed low with respect for this magnificent beast. He assumed she must be Paladin too and had therefore also done her time of battle. He hoped he would live up to all of their expectations — whatever those expectations were.

Figgis was drying his eyes. The link was still open and Gidyon used it.

My . . . my father? he asked hesitantly of the wolf.

Awaits you, child. Come.

He was entranced by her. He picked up Figgis, buried his fingers into the thick, silver-tipped fur of his new friend and walked beside her into the Heartwood.

Lauryn had lost sense of time completely. Dizzy from lack of food, and exhausted beyond her own comprehension, she forced herself to put one foot in front of the other, covering ground slowly but steadily. The climbs had been the worst, but during them she had made Gidyon talk to her, sing to her, tell her funny stories — anything to keep her going. And for each climb she was rewarded with an easy run down the other side. She often fell, grazing her elbows and knees or stinging herself on thistles and nettles, but she stood up again with grim determination and continued. Each step brought her closer to the Heartwood; she would not give up now. Sorrel had died bringing her this far. She would make it.

Finally she glimpsed the sight Gyl had told her of: the natural dip of the land in which the village of Axon nestled. And, to the left, the Great Forest. She had not known she had anything left in her but she surprised herself by breaking into a trot. She did not fall down this time and she hit the flats at a hard run.

Gidyon had told her he and Figgis had arrived at Axon but after that, the link had disappeared. She did not worry; she was too close herself. She could smell the smoke of the village fires but she veered away from Axon and pushed herself harder towards the dark and mysterious trees.

Finally she stood on the forest's fringe. She was breathing very hard, pulling in deep drags of air. She bent and put her hands on her knees. Funny, they felt knobbly for the first time ever. She kept breathing. Steady it. Calm down. When she felt her breathing was easier, she stood up again . . . and saw it.

Munching nonchalantly on some grass and staring at her was a donkey. Sorrel had said to expect a priestess, a wolf or a donkey and she and Gidyon had laughed about it. Yet the old girl had spoken true. There was no mistaking it. A donkey was waiting for her.

Lauryn took a step forward and her legs felt like jelly. She dug deep. She kept her eyes — which were beginning to blur — firmly on the munching donkey and willed her legs to carry her to it. *Just get there,* she told herself with each painful step. *The donkey will help.*

She thought she might have reached out her hand to touch the animal but suddenly she felt hard ground come up and hit her. When Lauryn regained her senses, she realised she had fallen at the feet of the animal, which was now nudging her. She was so fatigued that she felt numb and the dizziness was ever present, yet the donkey insisted. Its velvety muzzle kept refocusing into her vision, imploring her with its persistent pushing. Using the animal for support, she dragged herself with an enormous effort to her feet and fell across its back, which felt warm and strong.

She thought she heard the trees whispering to her. It sounded in her blurring mind as though they told her to climb on the donkey. It sounded like a reasonable idea. With the aid of a tree trunk and some careful positioning by the creature, she miraculously hauled herself up onto its back and immediately fell forward, an arm either side of its neck and her head lolling against its mane.

Lauryn felt the beast turn gently and then pace slowly but surely into the deepening, safe green of the forest.

Amongst the tall trees of the Heartwood, Cloot found peace. The whispering of the leaves and swaying of the branches comforted him and he felt a sense of absolute security. He was home. Where he belonged. Where it was safe.

Below, Tor and Saxon spoke quietly. They had drunk from the fresh waters of the Heartwood's stream and eaten lavishly from the spread which the Heartwood had provided. They spoke of what lay ahead. As Tor raised the issue of how he might be allowed to speak with Alyssa again, he was interrupted by Solyana across the link.

Tor, she called gently. *I bring you Gidyon, your son.*

He swung around sharply. From the deep cover of trees and into the clearing padded the wolf, accompanied by two people. One was very tall and lean with dark hair, and Tor realised that he looked at a reflection of himself.

Both he and Saxon leapt to their feet. They had anticipated a lad but it was a young man who stood before
them, his hand resting on Solyana. She, rather comically,
was being ridden by a dwarf. But no one laughed.

It was Saxon who reacted first. 'Figgis!' he roared.

The noise shook father and son from their shocked
silence.

Tor took several tentative steps towards the child he
had held only briefly as a newborn. He looked into the
bluest of eyes, which regarded him intently, nervously.

'Gidyon?' he whispered.

The Heartwood became silent. All eyes watched the
son.

Throughout the long walk south to Axon, Gidyon had
tried to prepare himself for this event. Although he
thought he was ready to meet his father, he had been
wrong. Nothing could have prepared him for this spine-
tingling moment.

Solyana spoke gently to the man who had jumped up
at her voice. He looked stunned to see Gidyon. Gidyon
hoped his own face did not betray him, as he wondered
what the man had been expecting. He felt so nervous he
could feel his pulse pounding behind his ear.

There he was, the man he should now call father.

There was no mistaking that it was his father, of course.
Gidyon felt as if he was looking at himself in a decade's
time. Yargo had told Lauryn and himself that their father
was still a young and extraordinarily handsome man. She
was right: those intensely blue eyes pinned him to the
spot and refused him movement.

And then his father spoke his name. All his good intentions to remain composed fled at the sound of that voice

and he wept. The Heartwood watched its son crumple.

Tor reached his boy in three long strides and, without further hesitation, wrapped his arms around the child and shared his tears, lifting him so he could hug him close to his chest and tell him how much he loved him.

It was only when Tor and Gidyon finally let go of one another that they appreciated the silence which surrounded them; the respect which the Heartwood and its inhabitants had accorded them during this moment of reunion.

Tor's voice was choked with emotion. 'My son . . . we have much to talk about.'

Gidyon nodded, not trusting his voice. He looked over at Figgis and was surprised to see that his father's big, golden-haired companion was carrying the smaller man in his arms.

Tor cleared his throat. 'But first, there are introductions necessary. Gidyon, this is Saxon Fox. He is a Kloek and Sixth of the Paladin. He is bonded to your mother.'

Tor watched the boy's eyes spark at the mention of his mother before they darted to the Kloek, who strode over, still carrying the Rock Dweller.

Saxon bowed with a reverence Tor had not seen in the Kloek previously. 'Gidyon, I am honoured to meet you again.'

Gidyon felt lightheaded at the Kloek's graciousness. He responded in kind as best he could, and then hurried to make his own introductions.

'Er, Saxon . . . Father . . .' It felt both strange and lovely to address his father out loud. 'This is my Paladin. He is Figgis, the Rock Dweller and courageous Ninth.'

Figgis smiled at Gidyon's kind words through his pain.

He feared he would not be able to hang onto consciousness much longer but he knew he was safe in the Heartwood and in the arms of his old friend, Saxon.

'Saxon,' he said, struggling to speak, 'it is about time you took some of the weight off my feet.'

The jest, relating to their battle with Orlac, was not lost on Saxon and he enjoyed it loudly.

'Come, my friend, let us get you rested and well again.'

Cloot, overjoyed at being reunited with the Ninth, flew down to Tor's shoulder.

Tor took the opportunity to speak before the Heartwood reclaimed its precious charge back. 'Figgis, I am privileged to meet again with you. I owe you my deepest thanks for your help in Cipres.'

Figgis chuckled, despite the pain. 'It was clear you were otherwise engaged,' he said and liked it that Tor broke into a wide, bright smile.

'Indeed I was,' he said. 'Locklyn Gylbyt is safely returned to his family. We are in your debt.' He bowed then added, 'Before you enjoy the ministrations of the Heartwood, let me reunite you with another old friend.' Tor touched his falcon at his shoulder. 'This is Cloot of the Rork'yel. He is a shapechanger.'

'Cloot . . . ?' Figgis whispered with awe, then winced at a sharp wave of pain.

A chiming sound, which had been building during their conversation, now reached an insistent pitch.

'Come,' Saxon said, 'let us allow this miraculous place to work its magics.'

Saxon carried Figgis to where the Flames of the Firmament danced and weaved their shimmering, chiming colours. He placed the little man on the mossy ground beneath one of the huge oaks. Immediately vines appeared, tendrils snaking out from the undergrowth. Creaking with the effort, branches leaned down to cradle one of their own. To Gidyon's astonishment, he witnessed the trees of the Heartwood effortlessly lift Figgis into their tallest branches, to where they could no longer see him.

'Where has he gone?' he asked, shock plainly evident in his voice.

'To be healed,' Saxon said reverently.

Tor put his arm around his son's shoulder. 'The Heartwood protects its own. He is safe.'

Gidyon looked with wonder at his father and nodded. It was all too much to take in.

'Hungry?' Tor said, grinning.

'Ravenous,' Gidyon replied.

Well now, there's a chip off the old block, Cloot murmured to himself.

I heard that, bird, Tor answered and enjoyed hearing Cloot laugh again inside his head.

It was tricky for Gidyon to eat and converse at the same time but he managed to consume a vast amount of food whilst the words continued to tumble out. Tor and Saxon became silent as they listened with increasing dismay to Gidyon's tale of his journey since his arrival in Tallinor.

Tor stood and began to pace. When Gidyon had finished, his father continued pacing.

'All of them . . . dead?'

Gidyon nodded. 'I . . . I had no control. I didn't even know what I was doing. They were about to roast Figgis and murder Yseul. It just burst out of me.' He looked shattered as he admitted his handiwork.

Saxon grunted. 'We never used to visit Duntaryn when I was with the circus. It has always possessed a dark reputation. Good riddance to them.'

Tor grimaced. This was not the right message for Gidyon to hear.

'Killing is so final. It should never be the solution. Never!'

Gidyon threw up his hands. He had been feeling terrible about his deed for the past two days, and now he felt sick. He had barely had time to look at his father properly and already he had let him down. 'I didn't know I possessed the power to do this.' He ran his hand through his straight hair.

Tor felt dreadful for his son. He wanted to comfort him, tell him it was all right, but he could not find the right words. The boy had murdered a dozen or more people. His powers were obviously strong but he needed to learn to control them, rather than the other way around. He watched Gidyon run his hand through his hair again and recalled how Eryn had teased him about the same nervous habit.

Tor's voice softened. 'And this Yseul? What of her?'

Gidyon spoke shyly. 'She has gone back to her village. She will be safe now. I . . . I hope to see her again.'

Tor experienced a rush of emotion and affection such as he had never felt before. He did not want this precious child to leave the Heartwood ever again. This was a place of sanctuary; he was safe here. And his powers were dormant because there was no need to use them.

Outside the Heartwood's protection, Orlac loomed. They were still no closer to forming the Trinity and it frightened Tor that Lys said their time was running out.

Themesius would fall soon. Orlac would be free. Tor's private conversations with Cloot had revealed no further illumination. Between them, they had considered that the Trinity might be the three mysterious Stones of Ordolt. Or, as Cloot had suggested, it may well be the powerful combined presence of Father, Son and Daughter.

When Tor had mentioned this to Saxon, the Kloek had agreed but then had questioned Alyssa's role in the Trinity. Why would she have Paladin to protect her if she was not important? Tor was turning these thoughts over in his mind when Arabella called to them in alarm.

'Quick, Tor! Kythay approaches. He brings Lauryn. She is in trouble!'

Gidyon was first on his feet, but Tor held him back as the donkey plodded slowly into view. A young woman was sprawled heavily across its back, her head lolling against the creature's neck.

'Lauryn!' Gidyon yelled.

The three of them rushed towards Kythay, who stopped and allowed Tor to gently lift the girl into his arms. He was shocked to see there were flecks of blood on her stained clothes and she was covered with dried mud; he could not see her face beneath the crust of dirt and the lank hair which stuck to it.

He tried to pull the hair away from her face but it held. He looked around alarmed, not sure of what to do, only that she needed help.

Solyana commanded him: *Give her to the trees now.*

Tor laid the girl on the forest floor and the trees wasted no time in picking her up and then swooping her gently from branch to branch, tree to tree.

Tor soon guessed where they were taking her and began

to run, to follow them to the pool. Solyana overtook him and ran ahead; Gidyon kept pace with him whilst the others followed.

Cloot and Solyana were already at the pool when the others arrived, breathing hard.

Gidyon asked aloud what most were wondering. 'Is she dead?' His voice broke as he said it.

Tor watched the trees lowering his daughter into the water. The Flames of the Firmament burst into a blaze of chimes and Darmud Coril shimmered into view. Tor felt more confident now that the god was present.

It was Darmud Coril who answered Gidyon. 'No, son of the Heartwood, our daughter breathes still.'

Solyana spoke gently to Tor. *Leave her with us. The Heartwood's pool will rejuvenate her. Please, Tor, trust me.*

Tor nodded. 'Saxon, Gidyon . . . we must wait.'

Reluctantly, the three men returned to the clearing.

They sat close together and murmured anxiously about Lauryn's state. Saxon could see that both father and brother were distraught and so tried making conversation.

'Gidyon, it sounds as though you and Lauryn hardly know one another. Did you not grow up together?'

Gidyon considered the question and Saxon noted how like his father he was, to pause like that.

He answered the Kloek. 'Well, I suppose I must have known her all my life, but I can't really remember. It's so maddening. Sorrel told us that our memories of our former lives would begin to cloud; the truth is, mine has disappeared all together. Perhaps Lauryn may recall better than I. But I feel in my heart that we were not together until recently. How did you guess?'

Tor nodded. 'I was thinking the same, Gidyon. Perhaps

Sorrel deliberately kept you apart for safety. I have no idea myself, but I am sure she will tell us when she arrives.'

Gidyon looked at his father and Saxon, more worry spreading across his face. 'Of course . . . you, er . . . you don't know.'

'Don't know what?' Saxon asked.

Gidyon took a big breath. 'Part of the reason why Lauryn is in such a bad way is because she and Sorrel were set upon by thieves . . .'

This was not easy. He summarised Lauryn's story as best as he could.

'They saw an overturned cart in the road and a young lad beside a man who seemed to have been thrown from it and hurt badly. But when they tried to help, the man sat up and others from his gang cornered them. Sorrel screamed for Lauryn to try and escape. The last Lauryn saw of Sorrel was when one of the men punched her and she fell to the ground. Then the gang bundled Lauryn off into the woods. The leader joined them within a few minutes and when she asked after Sorrel, he said she was dead. Lauryn apparently flew into a rage and, when they tried to tie her to a tree, she loosed her powers at them.'

Tor held his head. 'Not more killing?'

Gidyon shrugged apologetically. 'I'm sorry, Father. She knows she threw one against a tree and he did look as if he might be dead. She managed to run and the others gave chase. The boy gained on her and she believes she just wounded him. She was upset when she told me all of this, of course. I think she was probably in shock. Like me, she had no idea she had such power within her.

'Her story goes that some King's man, an Under Prime or something . . .'

Tor looked at Saxon, who shrugged and said, 'Herek is Prime. I had no idea there was an Under Prime.'

'Go on,' Tor said to his son.

Gidyon shook his head. 'Well, whoever this man was, he was a soldier who introduced himself as the Under Prime. He happened along, gave chase to the men following her and got rid of them.'

'And?' Saxon prompted.

'Well, that's it. She went on towards Axon using the hills route, which is probably why she's half dead. She said that the Under Prime returned to his men, although he was unhappy about leaving her alone.'

'No, we mean, what of Sorrel?' Tor asked gently.

'Oh, I see,' Gidyon said. 'Well, this soldier told her that he saw Sorrel's body at the roadside and she was dead.'

Tor stood and began his pacing again. He was clearly upset.

'No, no. This is not right,' he said. 'This should not have happened. I had so much to ask her.'

'It is all I know,' Gidyon said, looking from his father to Saxon.

Cloot's arrival broke the tension. *Tor, meet your beautiful daughter,* he said across the link.

Saxon and Gidyon were surprised when Tor swung around. 'She comes,' he said.

At first Gidyon thought Tor meant Sorrel, but when he turned he found himself looking at a lovely young woman, who resembled Lauryn. This woman's hair was wet but neatly combed and the water clinging to it made it appear darker than it was. She looked gaunt; her arms were thin and her shoulders angular beneath the soft green shift she wore. Could this be the Lauryn he knew? Her

eyes were as he remembered them, he thought, digging
back into the blur. Then she broke into a smile; it was
tentative but there was no mistaking her now. That unfor-
gettable smile lit her pretty, now angular face into a rare
beauty. She looked gorgeous standing there.

'Lauryn!' he yelled for the second time that day and
left his father trailing as he ran towards her. He picked
her up and hugged her, twirling her around and thinking
how fragile she seemed.

She used the link. *I thought I had died and found Paradise
when I woke up to all those chiming flames. You could have
waited for me!*

Hush, we're together now, he said gently into her head.

He placed her back on the ground and she smoothed
down the simple garment which Arabella had given her.
She was ready to meet her father. She looked over at the
man who was standing very still, not far behind Gidyon.
He wore a look of shock; or was it anguish . . . or both?
He did not say anything; he simply stared.

There was no doubting he was Gidyon's father; they
were almost identical, though his features were more chis-
elled. Why had she expected someone much older? There
was not a grey hair on his full dark head. So tall, so strong,
so good-looking. Her heart flipped for a moment – yes,
Yargo was right: he was as beautiful as you would expect
a god to be. Was this truly her father?

The Heartwood was still.

Lauryn took a slow, silent breath. She must be brave.
'Greetings,' was all she trusted herself to say, however.

The man she knew was Torkyn Gynt stared back with
a wounded look in his eyes.

The golden-haired man standing behind her father

touched his arm and whispered something to him.

'This must come as a shock, Tor, I know. This is exactly how Alyssa looked when I first met her. Be brave, now. This girl needs your strength.'

Tor stared at the young woman in front of him; he knew she was not Alyssa – could not possibly be, of course – but his mind was playing tricks on him. She looked so much like Alyssa and he did not know whether to weep over her loss or at the gain of his daughter. He felt Saxon gently prodding him towards the girl.

Lauryn begged her legs to hold her steady as she let go of Gidyon's hand and stepped forward to meet her father. Now that they were this close, she noticed how impossibly blue his eyes were, even though they were filled with tears.

'I am Lauryn,' she said, struggling to keep her voice steady.

Tor's tears spilled over now and ran freely down his face. 'I named you, child, the moment your mother bravely birthed you, our most precious daughter.'

He reached out his arms and felt the Colours roar within as he pulled his beautiful child into his arms.

Orlac would never touch these children, was his last rational thought before he lost himself completely in the emotion of the reunion. He reached for Gidyon, who joined his sister and father. Solyana, Arabella, Saxon, Kythay and even Cloot melted away into the darkness of the trees, leaving the trio to embrace in their private sanctuary. Only Darmud Coril remained to watch over them.

The god sighed inwardly. *Almost there,* he whispered.

In the Bleak, Lys breathed out with relief. *Almost,* she echoed silently.

30

The Tenth Falls

Tor spent the next few weeks enjoying getting to know his children within the cocoon-like atmosphere of the Heartwood. The joy they brought was, at times, overwhelming. On several occasions Lauryn asked him why he was staring; and Gidyon noticed that his father often deliberately sat so near to him that their shoulders touched. He liked it but did not comment, for fear of chasing away his father's welcome attention.

For Tor, it was a remarkable time. Being able to see these glorious individuals every day made him want to burst into song. One day he did, to everyone's astonishment. He was happy; truly happy.

Lauryn was already in love with him. A daughter's love; so precious. He knew this by the way she seemed to delight in every moment of the day she shared with him and by the way she warmly accepted his affections. Tor sensed that this very beautiful daughter of his had felt her lack of parents keenly, and now that she had found it, she was terrified to let go of it. He would not allow her to lose it ever again.

Gidyon was different. He had arrived at the Heartwood as a 'complete' person; at ease with himself and his loneliness. Tor could see that he had a very good head on his shoulders. The boy was a leader, all right, and the power he commanded seemed to seep out of every pore. If Tor cast around Gidyon, without making actual contact, he could feel that power pulsating within the boy. But Gidyon was not aware of its magnitude. He was also unconscious of his classical good looks. His unassuming manner would stand him in good stead, Tor was sure of it.

The children enjoyed those carefree weeks hosted by the Heartwood, while Tor, Saxon and Cloot were reminded of those wonderful days with Alyssa after the escape from Caremboche. This time, however, they knew their days here were numbered, but for now it was a time of peace and of learning for the children.

Gidyon and Lauryn had much to catch up on about the story of their parents. Their memories of their childhood had gone now; even Lauryn's recall had dimmed to nothing of 'before Tallinor', as she described it. Neither seemed particularly troubled by this, though both suffered grief over Sorrel's death, especially Lauryn who had shared those first few days after their arrival with the old lady.

At Cloot's wise bidding, Tor began to inform the children in much greater detail about his past, their mother's past and what he knew of this strange journey he was destined to make. Saxon disappeared for a few days' foraging in the forest and Tor took advantage of this time to educate Gidyon and Lauryn.

This particular day, over a leisurely picnic, he picked up the threads of his story with the intention of finishing it. He spared them no detail and included all he could remember of his dreams about Orlac. If he thought the tale of Cloot's shapechanging had created intense curiosity, he was not at all ready for the barrage of enquiry which followed his telling of his more recent adventures. He brought them up to date, finishing with his journey back to the Heartwood, where he had come to await their own arrival.

Gidyon shook his head in disbelief. 'And our mother is now Queen of this realm?'

'As I am given to understand,' Tor replied.

Lauryn wasted no time in hitting to the heart of the matter. 'And how do you feel about that?'

Tor took a breath. He had promised them nothing but honesty at the outset. 'Devastation. Anger. Pain. Heartbreak.' He sighed. 'Perhaps understanding . . . I hope,' he added and smiled, a little embarrassed. That wound still felt very raw.

'There could be a mistake,' Gidyon offered hopefully.

Tor shook his head. 'No, son. I read the official notice; saw the royal seal which I know all too well. And your mother is disarmingly beautiful – like her daughter here.'

Lauryn wanted to pinch herself. She still could not believe anyone, even a biased parent, could say such a thing.

'Any King would fall in love with her,' Tor added very quietly.

Lauryn switched subjects quickly. 'What about Goth?' she demanded. 'What kind of threat is he to her, or to us?'

Tor took a sip of the sweet wine he held in a clay cup. 'Of this I am not sure. What I am sure of is that he will go to ground for a while. He will remerge to do more damage but I shall be looking for him this time. Your mother has been warned and is safe.'

'Father . . .' Gidyon said tentatively, 'in all this time, we have not yet talked about this Trinity you speak of and how Lauryn and I fit into the story.'

Tor nodded. 'You are right. I have not discussed it because I do not know what to tell you. I don't even know if you *do* fit into this terrible web being weaved about us; I am assuming you must.

'The Trinity eludes me, as it eluded Merkhud. But it is the only weapon with which we can fight Orlac and I have to keep searching for it – or all the suffering will have been worthless.'

'Could it be us?' Lauryn asked. The two men looked at her. 'I mean, the three of us, now that we are reunited?'

'Possibly,' Tor conceded. 'That was certainly my first notion. And yet I feel there would be a sign; an indication from the Heartwood, or even from Lys, to tell me that the Trinity is complete. But so far there has been nothing. It just doesn't feel right for it to be us.'

'What is your plan? Where will you continue looking?' said Gidyon.

'Well, first things first. I wanted you both to have this quiet time in the Heartwood. But soon we must move on to Tal. It is time we met with your mother.'

He looked unsure and Lauryn read his hesitation. 'How do you think she will receive this news?'

Tor grinned sadly. 'Your mother's wrath scares me more than Orlac's.'

The children smiled, but they knew there was probably some truth to their father's words, having got to know the feisty Alyssa through both Tor and Saxon's recollections.

He continued. 'I don't know, Lauryn. You must remember that your mother birthed you amidst great trauma and, above all, confusion. She had no idea that you had even been born. Worse still, she believes Gidyon to be dead; she saw what she was led to believe was his corpse. Can you imagine the pain of that?

'And now, seeing her dead son alive after all these years, then learning that she was tricked into believing only one child had been born, and discovering that I knew of you both and allowed you to be sent away . . . Just one of these lies would be enough to send any woman mad. We are about to hit her with all three.'

The children nodded.

'Finally, I am faced with confessing that I allowed her to watch me die. She loved me as deeply as I still love her and yet I permitted the trickery to take place. She witnessed the brutal execution of the one person she could love whilst she grieved for her dead son. How will she react to see me standing in front of her, when she realises I lied to her and betrayed her?'

Tor saw the dread and concern in their faces and tried to lighten the mood. 'I suggest we all wear armour!'

It won the smiles he wanted but he could see they were uncertain. 'Her anger will be directed at me, not you. She will be shocked to learn of your existence, but she will love you. I give you my word. You are her flesh.'

'We are your flesh too,' Lauryn cautioned. 'I will stand by you, Father.'

Tor felt a surge of love for this proud child. She would need that courage for what they still had to face. He wished that Lys would come to him. She had been absent for a long time now and he wondered at how much time they had left. He knew it would be short and he must use it wisely in training the children.

As Merkhud had taught him, so he would now teach them. Gidyon's power was vast but it was not under his control nor could he summon it easily. That must be righted. Lauryn, he sensed, would wield her power with subtlety but she must judge what to use and when.

He decided to spend another Eighthday in the Heartwood before beginning the journey to Tal. This would give him time to teach the children more about wielding the Power Arts. It would also give him time to gather the courage he knew he would need to face Alyssa once again.

While her children talked about her with their father, the Queen of Tallinor was tasting the custard which would grace that night's sweet course at the banquet which the King was throwing in her honour. It was her Name Day and when she had shyly admitted it several days previous, the King had insisted they put on a feast and a show for the city of Tal.

'Such extravagance, Lorys. Really, it is not necessary,' she had admonished, desperately wishing she had never confessed.

'Tush, my love. It is my pleasure to spoil you. I will hear no more against it and will leave it with your good self to plan with Cook. There must be plentiful food on stalls for all who care to come to the palace to pay their respects. And there will be wine and music and songsters. Sallementro can write a special song for you, Alyssa.'

'Another one?' she said, a groan evident behind her words.

'Any amount of them would not do you justice. I see the Maglieri Chorus is in Tal – a more beautiful group of voices I cannot imagine. They must sing for our people in a free concert.'

Lorys continued to outline his spontaneous plans but Alyssa had already stopped listening, knowing already that she would have to suffer another of the King's balcony scenes. She was only just recovering from the last one, on the day of their marriage, when it had seemed as though thousands of Tallinese had squashed into the main castle courtyard to celebrate their union. She had not enjoyed the experience.

Standing on that particular balcony had brought back the nightmare of Tor's execution all those years ago. It had shocked her that these memories could still affect her so profoundly and she had needed to steady herself on the King's arm whilst she pushed the rush of visions away.

That grisly scene aside, Lorys might enjoy the attentions of his genuinely adoring people but Alyssa still felt very awkward about being called Queen. She and Lorys had been married almost three moons now but she could not shake the notion that she was an impostor. Lorys simply laughed and kissed her to stop her talking when she broached the subject; but Nyria's perfume still permeated the chambers Alyssa had been given and that was how fresh the older woman's memory was in Alyssa's mind.

'Well, dab some of your own around,' Lorys had suggested. He was no help in this situation. He was so enamoured of his new wife that none of her gentle protestations had any effect whatsoever.

It made Alyssa nervous that the Tallinese had accepted her so readily after loving Nyria for so long. It was old Koryn, the King's manservant, who had commented quietly to her that the Tallinese memory was long.

'They have never forgotten that courageous young woman who proudly watched her lover die the worst of deaths. The people never held you to blame, my lady. They suffered with you at the thought of what that terrible Goth had visited on you and their hearts bled with you when Physic Gynt died.'

She had cried when he said this to her. 'Thank you, Koryn,' she had whispered, ever grateful for his wise and timely counsel.

'Let them love you, your highness. You are a wonderful partner for the King. They can see this. And you embrace all that is good about Tallinor: grace, elegance, a love of the village, a respect for its people, its creatures. You have opened five schools already, my lady. It won't stop there. The education of our young minds is the future, and yet you also hold close to the past with your knowledge of herblore and even your mark as one of the Academie. You are truly a fine ambassador for our Land,' Koryn had added.

The old servant had died only two days later and it was Alyssa who had grieved the hardest. His insightful words still echoed in her mind. She needed to trust his judgement – and her own ideas of how the new Queen of Tallinor should win the respect of her people.

She may dress in stunning robes, sleep between silk sheets and be bathed and groomed by a myriad of servants, but she was still, in her heart, Alyssandra Qyn of Mallee Marsh. Her closest staff begged her to be more lavish and to command them to do her bidding rather than politely request it, but such behaviour was not to Alyssa's liking.

Nyria had earned her respect over a lifetime and, although it might have sounded to others as though she commanded, that was just her aristocratic manner. And working so closely with Lorys as his assistant, Alyssa had learned that though he was King by right, he never behaved as though that right came to him unearned. Lorys believed that the sovereign must earn the respect of his people through action.

No, if Alyssa had to be Queen, then she would rule alongside her King in the only way she could. Her own way.

Which was why she was in the kitchens with Cook right now, her sleeves rolled up and her face gleaming from the efforts of crafting the perfect custard.

'How's this?' she asked, dipping a wooden spatula into the mixture and holding it out.

Cook loved Alyssa. They enjoyed a special relationship in which familiarity was important to both.

'Well, I can hardly tell my Queen I hate it, can I?'

'Speak plainly,' Alyssa said, grinning. 'I defy you to find fault.'

Cook tasted the fluffy yellow blob on offer. 'Well, well . . . it is delicious, your majesty.'

Alyssa clapped her hands. 'You mean it?'

'I do,' Cook replied, genuinely impressed. 'Now, turn it out into that fresh bowl – Jos will help you lift it – and let it cool for tonight. You learn fast, your highness.'

'I enjoyed doing this,' Alyssa said, wiping the back of her hand against her forehead.

Cook put her own spoon down firmly. 'I know. But you can't keep hiding down here. You belong upstairs.

And it's time you headed to your chambers and prepared for tonight. You have to look wonderful, not all red and sweaty. Come on — away with you, my pretty Queen, or I'll be in trouble with the King.'

Alyssa pulled a face. She wished she *could* hide down here in the kitchens. But Cook was right: she had to prepare herself for the evening's festivities. It was not that she was ungrateful for the people's attentions — she felt honoured and humbled by it all — but she also felt it was undeserved.

She wiped her hands clean and hurried back to her chambers, where she met Gyl coming the other way.

'Were you waiting for me?' she asked, surprised.

He bent to kiss her cheek. 'Mother, no one seemed to know where you might be. Is this normal for the Queen of Tallinor? Is it also usual for her to walk around the palace covered in . . . what is that? Flour?'

'Oh, stop fussing. Come back and share a cool ale with me.'

'Ale!' He burst out laughing.

She winked. 'Don't tell the King I've developed a passion for Tallinor's light ale. He's desperately trying to educate my palate with fine wines.'

'Our secret, I promise,' he said and followed her towards her suite of rooms.

Inside, she made him sit whilst she cleaned herself and ordered her favourite beverage. Gyl never failed to be surprised at her beauty when he studied her. Now, scrubbed and changed out of her working garments and into a soft shift, she looked like a young carefree girl. He knew Alyssa was still a relatively young woman at twenty-five summers; nevertheless, he also knew there were few women in the Kingdom, even those younger than her, who could hold a candle to her incredible looks.

He loved her very much and, although he would never forget the devotion of his beloved birth mother, Alyssa was now the woman he considered his mother. The first time he called her by that name, Alyssa had wept. It had just slipped out that first time but then it had stuck. He knew she loved to hear him call her mother and he cherished the fact that he could. Surprisingly, it had not been hard to think of her as his own parent.

Saxon understood and told Gyl to unburden himself of the guilt of loving another woman as a mother. The Kloek had assured him that the love between a mother and child was the purest of all loves and it mattered not whether they were of the same blood. That Alyssa accepted him as her son, and that he had not struggled to accept her as a mother, was proof enough that they had a special bond. What had helped most was Saxon's reassurance that his birth mother would feel free of her own burden of guilt for leaving him and could move forward in the spiritual planes and find peace.

'Anyway, who doesn't love Alyssa?' Saxon had laughed and slapped him on the back.

Gyl watched his mother now, curled up on her favourite sofa. That she was Queen seemed impossible to him at times, but the King was clearly lovestruck for his mother. They made a dashingly handsome pair and their laughter rang out often in the palace. They really were so happy and, after the grief following the previous Queen's death, it had been good for the people to lift their spirits at the sight of Alyssa's romance blossoming with the King.

'What time does it all begin tonight?' he asked, knowing the question would irritate her.

Alyssa pulled a face. 'At the seventh bell. You know, Gyl, it's going to take me years to get used to all this.'

'Nonsense, Mother. You are already most regal.' He bent to kiss the top of her head. 'You just don't know it.'

'Now you sound just like the King.'

She winced at the truth behind her words. Gyl was increasingly becoming more and more like his father and he would need to know about his background very soon. Their avoidance of the subject was asking for trouble, for the truth would surely come out eventually. Already some canny palace watchers had commented that the Under Prime was spending too much time in the company of his sovereign. *Not only does he walk and talk like him, but he even looks like him at times,* was one comment Alyssa had overheard. Such remarks bothered Alyssa; not because they were true but because Gyl did not know the truth. He deserved better.

There were undoubtedly petty jealousies around the palace with regard to Gyl's meteoric rise through the ranks to his position of Under Prime and the fact that such a young man was commanding so many older men. Thank the Light for Herek and his wisdom and guidance. The older soldier was solid and dependable but the best part was that Herek had agreed with the promotion. When she had questioned the Prime, he had surprised her with his candour that Gyl was the only man he would pick from the Legion right now to be groomed for the top job.

'He'll have to earn their respect the hard way, your majesty, but he's got what it takes,' he had told her. 'I believe he'll do the job well.'

'I hope so, Herek, for his sake.'

'Trust in him, my lady, as I trust your security to him as Queen's Champion. It is wise for Gyl to learn young. Should anything happen to me, then—'

Alyssa had refused to let him finish. She liked Herek very much. He was a plainly spoken man who wasted no words on obsequious flattery or superfluous conversation. He was intensely committed to his job and his brevity and seriousness was often misinterpreted. But she knew him to be the kindest of men and one who had cared for her during those early months after Tor's death. She also remembered how he had shown great compassion for Tor during his execution. Saxon held him in the highest regard too. She would not hear of Herek dying. Gyl would have years to grow into the top job.

The musicians, assembled under Sallementro's careful eye, played their hearts out for the King and Queen of Tallinor, who, much to all the guests' delight, generously led the boisterous dances. Sallementro slowed proceedings a little when he sang the special Name Day song he had written for her majesty; although it was a jolly tune with a rousing chorus which everyone quickly learned, Alyssa cried with pleasure at his beautiful lyrics. Now the music was gathering momentum again into a frantic Strip the Willow and the King and Queen had taken to the dance floor once more.

'Not around again,' Alyssa begged Lorys.

The King's laugh thundered around the Great Hall. 'You had better have bruises on those arms tonight, my beauty, or I shall order this all over again. You know the rules of Strip the Willow. No bruises means you've shirked your dance duties.'

'You are a brute, Lorys,' Alyssa called to her grinning husband as he mercilessly spun her around once more before letting her go to the next man in line. She made herself feel better by reminding herself that at least the balcony scene was done. The people of Tallinor had come, eaten, drunk, departed and were now making merry elsewhere. She had accepted their cheers and goodwill graciously.

Everyone was exhausted after the effort of Stripping the Willow so yet more mugs of ale and goblets of lightly chilled wine were brought out on huge trays for the royal guests. Gyl, whose men were peppered throughout the city to prevent the happy tavern festivities getting out of control, appeared in the Great Hall and walked over to his mother who was flopped in her chair.

'Don't you dare, Gyl,' she warned.

'The next dance is mine, your majesty. Surely you would not refuse your son, a simple soldier, in front of all these people?' he said and bowed low.

'I hate you both, you know that, don't you?' Alyssa said, murderously eyeing both Lorys and Gyl, co-conspirators; their smiles unmistakably born of the same blood.

'Last one, Alyssa, I promise,' Lorys whispered. 'Then I shall rescue you from this scene, take you upstairs and—'

'Come, Gyl.' Alyssa cut across Lorys, then whispered in his ear, 'I am not sure which is more exhausting, my lord, the dancing or thinking about what comes after.'

She stepped down from the dais, glaring at Sallementro who, clearly part of the conspiracy, had whipped up the music into another feisty village jig.

'Ah, the Dashing Demon. My favourite,' Gyl said, enjoying his mother's groan.

'I shall have Sallementro beheaded for this,' she replied, as her handsome son twirled her around in a series of nauseating spins. She had always considered this dance unfair on the women, who seemed to do all the spinning and none of the twirling.

At first Alyssa thought she had just spun once too many times, but the dizziness was quickly followed by crushing pain in her head. She must have stopped moving; she could not be sure. Had the music stopped too? Perhaps. Gyl was looking at her, concerned, offering a steadying arm. She could see his lips moving but no sound was reaching her. In fact, there was no sound at all, just a sinister drumming in her ears.

Alyssa, panic rising, searched for Lorys, who was already striding towards them, bewilderment on his face.

And then the drumming in her head stopped and she heard them: sounds which would live in her soul for the rest of her life. The heartwrenching shout of a man, followed by a horrible silence, and then a brief whispering between two men, but she could not make out any of the words. Then a terrible shrieking which tore at her mind; she had a vision of the Heartwood screaming. A far more intense pain hit her and she dropped unconscious into the arms of the King.

Pandemonium broke out in the Great Hall. All music and gaiety was abandoned as the Under Prime blasted orders to servants and pages to find Physic Kelvyn immediately. The King was stunned. He sat on the cool, stone floor of the Hall and shook his head with disbelief. She could not be dead, surely? He looked at Gyl, who shook his head briefly to show he did not know what had happened.

'Your highness, she breathes,' he reassured the King. 'Let us get her to her chambers.'

'You were both dancing and then she just stopped and went rigid,' the King whispered.

'I know. Come, sire, please,' Gyl urged, aware of all the courtiers, guests and gossip-mongers drinking in the scene. 'My lord . . .' He bent to release Alyssa from Lorys's grip. 'Allow me to pick up her majesty so you can escort her to her chambers.'

A shout from the back of the Great Hall broke the spell that seemed to have fallen upon the King. 'Yes . . . of course,' Lorys said and allowed the Under Prime to take the small, light body of his wife into his arms. 'Lead the way,' he said.

As they moved off, Lorys looked back to see where the shout had come from. He could just make out the twitching body of Sallementro lying on the ground, surrounded by horrified onlookers.

Gyl had seen the musician too; knew this man was almost as close to his mother as he himself was. He signalled to Caerys, the King's competent squire. 'Quickly, Caerys, find some helpers and follow us with Sallementro. They must have both taken some bad wine or something,' he offered hopefully.

Tor was showing Gidyon how to cast a glamour over himself. Lauryn was laughing. 'You're just blurring, Gid. Try harder,' she said.

'This *is* harder,' he complained.

'It's not really difficult once you know how,' his father encouraged. 'Just let go inside. Can you see the Colours?'

'Yes.'

'Let them swell. Allow them to consume you within but don't lose control.'

Gidyon was holding his breath in his effort to control the surge of power within.

'Relax into the power, Gidyon. You control it; not the other way around. Don't clench your teeth. Breathe.'

Gidyon let out all the air he was holding.

'Good,' his father said. 'Now, go through the steps I've taught you . . . take it slowly.'

He sensed Gidyon cast out superbly and, as he watched, his son changed into an old man. He heard Lauryn squeal with delight that her brother had finally mastered the complex spell and in the same instant felt a monstrous pain thump into his head. He was sitting cross-legged opposite his son; now he fell back, rigid, breathless from the pain.

Gidyon was writhing on the forest floor nearby. Lauryn had both hands to her head and was grimacing in silent agony, her eyes wide and begging her father to stop the pain.

Tor did not want to lose consciousness; he fought it, somehow opening a link to his falcon. *Cloot!* he screamed.

Themesius! was all he heard before Cloot fell off the branch where he had been perched and joined the other bodies on the soft turf.

Suddenly Tor felt the link slam shut and the most exquisite pain wrenched from his body, which lay contorted on the ground near his children. Now his spirit was soaring; freed from the agony of his body but bewildered — and afraid.

Cloot had called out Themesius's name. It could only mean that the giant had fallen. Orlac was finally free.

*   *   *

Saxon had felt the blast of pain and the shriek of a man in his head. Immediately he began to run back towards Figgis, now healed and whole again, who had decided to accompany him on this walk through the Heartwood. But Saxon only made a few steps before he collapsed. It was all he could do to drag in enough air to keep breathing. He lay on the ground, fighting the agony, begging for it to pass.

In another part of the Heartwood, Solyana and Arabella were also suffering.

Figgis was admiring an enormous oak, craning back his head to look to its very top, when the pain came. He fell backwards and lay there in an agony greater than that he had ever experienced during his battle with Orlac, but one which he recognised immediately. He wept as he imagined his great friend, Themesius, finally falling to the vengeful young god.

31

A Summoning

Tor was travelling again. He remembered this sensation from his escape from Caradoon, when he had been forced to leave Cloot's body and return to his own, but he was more frightened this time. He knew with certainty that he was travelling towards terror rather than away from it.

He stopped suddenly and found himself watching a magnificent, golden-haired stranger. Tor realised it must be Orlac, and the huge man nearby was Themesius the Giant. Strangely, Tor was privy to Orlac's words and thoughts, as though himself a part of the young god.

Orlac sensed that final hold over him give and he felt great sorrow for the giant who had been the Paladin's anchor over so many centuries. Orlac had overcome the members of the courageous group, one by one, with his mind's strength. But all the time this battle had raged across the enchanted link, somehow both he and Themesius had known it would come down to the two of them. And Themesius also had understood he would eventually be defeated.

In a way, there was a special bond between them. A

bond of hatred, no doubt, but a noble bond nonetheless and their respect for each other was deep. Which was why Orlac felt pity for his foe now: it took immense bravery to fight when you knew the battle was lost.

The pain became so intolerable for Themesius that he crouched to the floor and let go of Orlac's mind. The link was severed. The hold was gone. As the young god finally stepped free of the cursed ledge where he had been held through their magics for so many centuries, he considered how, in another situation, he and the giant could have been friends. Love and hate — there was such a fine line dividing the two emotions. In a different lifetime, in a different existence, perhaps all of them could have been something more than enemies.

He looked over at Nanak, the Keeper. 'Be gone, old man. You are done here.'

It was not said cruelly; he simply stated a fact. Nanak, his face a mask of despair, disintegrated to dust, which dispersed as the god walked through it to reach Themesius. He felt the need to say something to the giant; some last few words to respectfully herald his passing.

There was no longer any need for Orlac's mad giggle; it had been an affectation employed purely to annoy his captors and insinuate himself beneath the Paladin's guard. To laugh in your captor's face was to feel powerful. Orlac had learned this over the ages he had been imprisoned. He took no pleasure in seeing this strong man crumpled before him. In that moment, Orlac vowed to make Merkhud's man pay all the more for forcing him into this terrible humbling of those more worthy of his friendship than his spite. In the earlier days it had been easier to watch them fall. He recalled the beautiful one, the one known as Solyana, and how he had taken great delight in seeing her own failure reflected in her large, deep eyes. But now — the sight of Figgis's pain and especially that of Themesius made him feel the tragedy of the situation.

The giant was spent; Tor could see he was dying. Themesius rallied one last time to respond to his victor. 'It is not over, Orlac. This is the beginning of your end,' he croaked.

Tor expected Orlac to laugh, but when he spoke the god's voice was even and sober. There was no trace of arrogance.

'You have battled bravely, Themesius. I honour you and all the Paladin.'

'We will meet again,' the giant said. The last breath wheezed from his body and he winked out of the Bleak, his body disappearing from where it had crouched at the god's feet.

Tor heard Orlac sigh. It seemed genuinely laden with regret. He could still sense the god's thoughts, share in his memories.

Orlac was remembering the moment when his mortal father had died. The man had lived for centuries, a gift bestowed upon him by Orlac's true father, Darganoth, but when his final time had come, Orlac had sensed it. That Merkhud could escape his wrath had enraged him, the idea was unthinkable. But then, he had sensed a spirit within Merkhud that was not his father. That spirit had lifted itself from the body of his despised, cheating father and had gone . . . to where? To another host, no doubt, but Orlac did not know where or who. All he knew was that this person was now his enemy and would be the target of his revenge before razing Tallinor.

The moving of that spirit had created a powerful trace. He would always remember it. He had decided that it would serve the impostor well to see him as he stepped free, and so Orlac had summoned it, locking onto the unsuspecting spirit with ease and wrenching it free, dragging it without care to where he was. And he knew it was present now, could taste its trace.

Watch me now, impostor! he shouted.

Just as Themesius had vanished from the Bleak, so now did the Bleak itself as Orlac transported himself from where he had been incarcerated. Tor was carried along with him and saw that the god was now standing on a tall hill. The scenery looked familiar but there was no time to focus on anything other than the fact that Orlac had returned to the world he had been banished from centuries before.

Orlac's liberation was not Tor's worst surprise, however. The god spoke directly into his head.

I have brought you here to witness this, whoever you are. I know not your name, only that you are my mortal enemy and I will track you down. No power you possess can ever match mine. The hated Merkhud has escaped my wrath by dying, but you are his man and I shall make you suffer. You have become Merkhud in my eyes and you shall pay the price I demand.

Tor was frightened. His trust in the Trinity, his faith in Lys and even his courage seemed to seep away. Then he thought of Cloot, of all the brave Paladin, and how much they had suffered for his sake. From them he drew strength, found his courage again.

He stared at the god who, for Tallinor, was only legend and he understood why he had been chosen. Only his powers, combined with those of the Trinity — whatever it may be — could fight this strength.

He took stock of the god who stood before him and committed everything he could to his memory before he spoke in a measured tone.

As Themesius said, we shall meet again.

Orlac had sensed the remarkable change within the stranger. What power had allowed this man to find such valour at a time when he should rightly be cringing at the feet of a god? He could not imagine, but he was impressed. The man spoke like the Paladin, fearlessly. This would make their clash interesting. He acknowledged Tor's words with a nod, as two fencers might touch swords before a duel.

Now, go and hide. You may await my coming, he said.

Orlac felt the breeze blow around him now. He lifted his arms to embrace its reality and stamped his feet on the grass of the hillside where he now stood. He was back. Back in the Land he intended to destroy.

He flicked the spirit away and suddenly Tor was travelling again.

Tor had no idea where he was going, except that it was fast. When he finally lurched to a sickening stop, he heard Lys's voice.

Tor! How can you be here?

Tor's unexpected arrival in the Bleak distracted Lys's attention and Dorgryl took advantage of that split second of time. The mist of red whooshed past Tor's consciousness and was gone from the Bleak.

Lys—

But Tor did not get his words out.

No! Lys's scream was so loud that he cringed.

Tor instinctively turned away from her to follow her gaze. From the Bleak they were privy to all worlds and he shared Lys's horror as Orlac, still standing on the hillside in Cipres, was enveloped by a red mist. The god convulsed, then began to growl and thrash, his beautifully muscled body contorting into impossible positions. It was horrifying to witness.

Tell me it isn't so, Lys whispered, each word laced with terror.

I don't understand, Tor replied very softly.

Dorgryl has escaped. Orlac has broken free and Dorgryl has merged with him.

Tor turned his attention back to the shimmering, radiant presence in front of him. She was weeping.

This should not have happened. I have failed the Host, she cried.

It dawned on Tor that he was finally laying eyes on the Custodian, the Dreamspeaker who had manipulated all of their lives. She reminded him strongly of the only woman he had ever loved. That golden hair and that small, almost fragile-looking body. He was bewildered. *Lys, I see you.*

I know. You should not be here, Tor. How is it that you are here? Her words rushed out on top of one another.

Orlac. He took me from the Heartwood. We spoke briefly and then he pushed me away. I ended up here. What was that red mist? Was it the thing you told me would never concern me the last time I spoke with you?

Lys wept harder. Perhaps it was just the golden hair, or maybe the grey-green eyes he had glimpsed, or possibly the long fingers held in just such a manner that prompted him to say it. The words spilled out before he could pull them back.

Lys, are you related to Alyssa?

She lifted her head from her hands in a manner similar to how Alyssa had lifted her head as she stood on the balcony, forced to watch his execution. As Lys fixed his impossibly blue eyes with her own, Tor saw how familiar in shape they were.

I am her mother, she said firmly. The fear in her voice was gone; the Custodian was back in command of herself. *Come. This spiritual plane is dangerous for you and we have much to discuss.*

Tor re-entered his body and sat up with a jolt. His face filled with dread when he saw the bodies of his children and Cloot lying on the forest floor.

They all sleep a special healing sleep, Lys reassured him.

Tor looked over in surprise. She sat fully visible in the hollowed area of a tree.

How is it that I can see you even though I am not asleep?

She smiled sadly. *A special treat, shall we say. Do not ask me to move; I cannot. I am allowed to visit a world physically only once. I am only able to return if I keep contact with the trees: it is through the generosity of the Heartwood and the magic of its god, Darmud Coril, that I am permitted to be here in this way.*

Tor felt weak from the trauma he had just experienced but he wanted to be closer to her. He walked over to the tree and sat down opposite the shimmering Custodian.

She looked towards Lauryn. *Beautiful, like her mother.*

And her grandmother, he observed, gently.

She smiled.

Will you tell me the truth? he asked.

Predictably, she made him earn it. *What is it you wish to know?*

Alyssa – why did you abandon her?

I am not a mortal, Tor. I could not remain in Tallinor.

Then why did you come to Tallinor?

You will understand soon.

So Alyssa and I were meant to be together?

As designed by the gods themselves, she said, cryptically. *Be patient, Tor. All your questions will be answered.*

May I tell her?

That she has a mother who watches over her but never visits? A mother who is a god? Lys laughed. *I think you have enough on your plate with Alyssa, without complicating the issue further.*

Then will you tell her?

Yes.

When?

When the time is right for her to learn such news.

More secrets. Tor hated it. He sighed. He knew Lys would not change her mind for him, and she was right. Just thinking about how to approach Alyssa with the news that her son was alive and that she had a daughter she had never known about would be more than enough for him to cope with.

Tell me of Dorgryl, he said.

It was Lys's turn to sigh. *He tricked me. All these centuries he has fooled me with his petty conversations and moans about his existence, when in fact he was lulling me into believing he was helpless.* She spoke angrily.

Lys, you will have to explain from the beginning. I have none of the background; I don't know what you are talking about.

The Custodian took a deep breath. *Dorgryl is a former member of the Host. He was brother to King Darganoth and, like most younger brothers –* her tone was deliberate *– he coveted the crown.*

Tor nodded although her comment was lost on him. *Go on.*

He devised a cunning plan which would see the King dead and him crowned, but Evagora's announcement that she was with child threw those plans awry. Now Dorgryl had to rid himself of both King and heir.

Orlac? Tor asked.

As you know him, yes.

Dorgryl obviously failed then.

Only just, Tor. He came within moments of achieving his dark goal of slaying the King and the infant prince but, when the Queen announced she was with child, he hesitated. It was his arrogance which betrayed him: his own wife spilled the news to the King when she learned of her husband's treachery.

When he discovered his brother's betrayal, Darganoth refused to kill Dorgryl but there was no precedent to follow to punish him. Gods do not fight gods; they certainly do not kill one another, but Dorgryl was dangerous. Much too dangerous to be allowed to remain within the Host. And so Darganoth devised a plan to banish him to a place known as the Bleak; a place of nothingness. His spirit was banished from his own body and for centuries he existed only in the form of that red mist you saw.

She stopped to allow Tor time to consider what he had heard and hoped he would ask the right question next.

Tor's mind was racing. Every conversation with Lys felt like some sort of test. *You said 'infant prince'. So Orlac was no longer a babe in arms?*

Lys was pleased. She had taught him well.

You are perceptive, Tor. Dorgryl was banished a very short time before the child was stolen from Ordolt, The Glade.

Why did Dorgryl falter when he heard the Queen was with child?

Lys cheered inwardly.

You must understand, Tor, that births within the Host are often decades in the coming. Some couples live several lifetimes before they achieve a family; some never do so at all. For the royal couple to produce two heirs in such a short time was truly incredible, and Dorgryl hesitated. He did not know whether the child would be a son or daughter, of course, but his arrogance led him to believe that if he destroyed the entire royal family he would come out of it as the newly crowned King. In re-planning, he lost momentum and his secret was exposed by his wife, Yargo.

Tor was shocked at the mention of Yargo's part in this but he sensed time was too short to follow tangents. He must focus his attention on finding out more about Orlac.

And how do you fit into this, Lys?

She was impressed by Tor's strength of purpose. *Once Orlac had been Quelled, the Host needed one of their own to watch over him. Orlac is a god, but he is also a prince and, as such, he deserved respect and care. He was also dangerous and, because he was living as a mortal, his emotions and therefore his powers were out of control. The Quelling and then the enchantments by the Paladin were all we had to keep him safe from himself and the Land safe from his powers. At that time, we had no answers for a long-term solution.*

Then the Elders of the Host devised the Trinity. It was an audacious plan which is now coming to fruition, where you find yourself now. We always knew the Paladin could only hold Orlac for a short time. That we have survived so many centuries is testimony to the Paladins' immense courage and strength.

My role was to watch over all that occurred between the Paladin and Orlac, and to watch over you. As Custodian of the Portals, I have access to all worlds. When Dorgryl was thrown into the Bleak, I also became responsible for guarding him, although we did not really believe he was still a threat. How wrong we were.

Tor hurried her story forward. He was gradually adding new pieces to the jigsaw of his own life. *So what is Dorgryl's intention, do you think? What does he gain from merging with Orlac?*

A body to begin with. Dorgryl was alive only in spirit; his own body was permitted to wither as part of his punishment. He was forced to live only in his mind; the ultimate humiliation for a god. He showed not the slightest interest in his nephew's fate, until the moment Figgis fell. But then he began to comment on the progress of the battle. I should have suspected something then, but I just did not pick up on the signs. He is cunning, Tor. And he is far more dangerous than Orlac, because he is driven by pure evil.

At this Tor's head snapped up. He looked bewildered.

Lys shook her head in disgust. *I was stupid. I was the arrogant one. Centuries of imprisonment and I just assumed we had Dorgryl completely at our mercy; that he would never again be a threat, just a nuisance in my existence. Now, Tor, we face even greater jeopardy.*

Tor wrapped his long arms around his knees. *How bad is it?* he asked, not really wanting the answer.

How bad? She barked an angry laugh. *Dorgryl has possessed Orlac. Orlac is driven by a need for revenge and is single-minded about this; nothing will get in his way. At least we know his intentions. But with the addition of Dorgryl, with his agile and sinister mind, who knows what he might achieve in Orlac's body. With such power at his disposal, I am terrified for Tallinor and its world. I am terrified for all of us.*

You mean if he totally overwhelms Orlac?

She nodded, staring at the ground.

What does Dorgryl want? Tor said, frustrated now.

She looked at him with disbelief. How could anyone not know what the mad god wanted? *Power! He craves power. He lusts to rule. And if he cannot rule the Host, he will rule weak mortals instead. He will keep Orlac quiet by helping him to achieve his aims, but all the while he will be using Orlac to achieve his own agenda. What that is, I can only guess. His initial triumph is that he is free from the Bleak, as his nephew is free from his enchanted prison.*

Tor rubbed his eyes. This was too much to take in all at once. *So what do we do now, Lys?* he asked tiredly, desperately hoping she had an answer.

I must think on it. I will also consult the Host. For now, you must continue with your plan. Orlac knows of you but not who you are. He will need to spend time tracking you down. But Dorgryl knows more about you. He will lead Orlac to you and your family. We shall have to move much faster than we had originally intended, Tor.

They will not harm my children, Lys. I will die fighting them.

She mustered a sad smile. *Perhaps you might. I am sorry I have let you down, Torkyn Gynt.*

He reached out and touched her shimmering hand. *It was not your fault. You did not expect Orlac to summon me as he did. Could he do this again?*

You must shield at all times now. Remember his trace and keep all senses casting for it all the time. Even I am unsure of his powers now. Combined with Dorgryl . . . She shook her head in defeat.

I remember his trace perfectly. It felt familiar.

She did not answer this. Instead she pulled the branches

of the tree around herself. *I must leave you now, Tor. We may not meet like this again.*

He stood and bowed to her. *I am honoured to have met you in person, Lys.*

She smiled her radiant smile. *Be brave, Tor. We will triumph.*

Keep your promise to me. Speak with Alyssa.

She nodded once and then shimmered out of his world.

32

Possession

Orlac sensed rather than saw the red mist but, before he could react, it enveloped and entered him. The pain was immense. What was it?

He began to fight the invader. Growling and thrashing, he used everything he had within him to force the strange thing out. He must have wrestled with it for hours . . . he could not tell. When he lay on the hilltop, all his energy sapped, it spoke to him.

I am Dorgryl, it said, the voice deep and cultured.

Orlac spoke breathlessly. *What are you?*

I am a former member of the Host of the Gods. I am presently a guest of its son and heir. In between, I was nothing but anger.

Who are you? Orlac asked, stupefied by this intruder.

I am your uncle, it said, smoothly.

Orlac felt a familiar panic grip him. He recalled this sense of despair from the day he was Quelled by the Host. Were they here to destroy him already? Was this the messenger of death?

Get out! Orlac screamed.

The voice was amused. *I have no body of my own. Yours suits me. We are family, after all.*

Orlac tried to calm himself. He remembered how Merkhud's man had pushed away the fear to find control and he steadied himself, wondering how much the invader could share of his thoughts. He took some moments to consider. His guest remained silent. Orlac knew instinctively that he must not show his fear. He must play along, learn as much as he could.

What do you want, Dorgryl?

That's better, nephew, the thing said firmly. *I want to be your partner in destroying Tallinor. That is what you want, is it not?*

How do you know what I want? Orlac snapped.

I know because I have watched you for centuries fighting to get it. As each of those stupid Paladin died, I cheered. I only wished you could have heard me out there in the Bleak, with that wretched Lys watching over my every movement. But I was more artful than she could ever have imagined. I pretended not to notice anything about you, yet I fed off your triumphs, urged you on, yearned for your victory, boy. I knew you would do it. Knew you would win our freedom.

I won my freedom, Dorgryl, not yours.

Call me uncle, child. Your father and I are brothers.

Then why are you not counsel to his majesty . . . uncle? The last word was said as though tasting a poison.

An indiscretion. Darganoth felt he needed to punish me, make an example of me, Dorgryl sneered. *Darganoth felt threatened by me when we were children. We are twins, you know. It was a tragedy that the weaker child was born first. If I had been King of the Host, life would be very different for all of us.*

Orlac had recouped his energy. *You cannot stay in here*

with me. He began to struggle again, yelling for the creature inside to leave. He loosed his magics but still the horrible thing clung tightly within him. The pain of his own power loosed against him prevented Orlac attacking Dorgryl any further. He lay on the ground once more, panting. He had been possessed and now he was doomed.

Dorgryl waited. This was a shock for the youngster, who had not aged a day since he was Quelled. He must pick the right moment. He stayed still and silent, waiting for the young god to calm down again. When Orlac's breathing subsided to a more normal level, he made his move.

I can help, you know.

How? Orlac said sullenly.

I know the person whom you seek.

You know nothing! Orlac countered, angrily. At that moment he felt he could throw himself off the hilltop in despair. The fight over the centuries had been for nothing. This thing now held him in its power; he was trapped again.

I know plenty. I know the name of the person you summoned to witness your final blow to Themesius. I know what he looks like. I know the people he loves and who love him.

This won Orlac's attention. *How?*

He felt the thing inside him shift, as if to make itself more comfortable, as if it relished the chance to tell its tale.

I have not only been watching your progress but that of one Torkyn Gynt as well. It is true my first few centuries in the Bleak were spent in complete desolation. I was bitter and uninterested in everything. Dorgryl laughed harshly. *There was nothing to be interested in, except my own downfall. Lys told me a little about you but I cared nothing for your struggle. I could see you were there for eternity. And then you started to win and those stupid Paladin began to fall. I had to admire your single-minded commitment.*

When I learned your full story, I became intrigued. Perhaps you would topple your captors. I started to follow Merkhud; watched his interminable search although I had no idea what it was he looked for. Lys would tell me nothing.

And then one day I noticed that he had taken an apprentice: a young village scribe called Torkyn Gynt. It became clear that Gynt possessed rare magics; I presumed it to be the wild magic. He is powerful, though of course no mortal power can match that of a god. However, the Host believe he will save Tallinor from your wrath. All your enemies are relying on him. I shall help you find him and I shall help you to destroy him. Nothing would give me greater pleasure.

Orlac said nothing for a few moments. He carefully considered all that he had just learned from Dorgryl. *And you?* he said finally. *What do you get out of this?*

Fun! . . . And the chance to strike back at Darganoth. With your powers and my cunning, we can wreak havoc on Tallinor. It will be everything he fears. We will make all of its people suffer and you will enjoy your sweet revenge.

Dorgryl laughed. The sound had an edge of madness.

That's how I must have sounded, Orlac thought to himself. *But I was never mad. Dorgryl surely is.* He decided to push his point. *And afterwards, Dorgryl? After we have razed Tallinor, destroyed the Land, dealt with Gynt and all he loves — what happens then? What will you ask of me next?*

It was Dorgryl's hesitation, just for a moment, which confirmed for Orlac that he must never trust him.

You will help me. Together we will kill your father for the wrongs he has done you . . . and me.

How? It is my understanding that a god cannot be killed.

It is my intention to use his body as I use yours now. When you have helped me to achieve his possession, we will both be free of one another to do as we please.

Orlac considered again. He must tread carefully now. He was trapped. It was clear that Dorgryl had no intention of leaving his body for the time being, and he could not dislodge him. Perhaps there might come a time when his uncle was not so watchful and he could be rid of him. But for now he was stuck with his voice inside his head and his spirit travelling within him.

He decided he must be seen to be going along with the plan. He even grudgingly acknowledged that Dorgryl would be a boon in finding his enemy. Now that he was back in the Land, he must travel and live as a mortal. He had many leagues to cover and many fruitless years could be spent searching. With his uncle's knowledge, tracking down his target would be easier. He would make his own plans, though. He knew that he would have to destroy Dorgryl somehow, for he sensed the god would never leave him. The notion of possessing Darganoth's body was nothing more than a ruse. For now, though, he must be seen to be playing along with Dorgryl.

All right. But you will leave my body once we reenter our world. Orlac knew only too well that it was a hollow pact he was making.

Agreed. Dorgryl laughed maniacally again in Orlac's head. Orlac began walking down the hillside. *So, what first?*

Dorgryl was in his element now; plotting was his favourite pastime. *You must not rush into anything. You have warned Gynt of your coming. Let him stew on it for a while. Allow the anxiety to build within him.*

You misjudge him. He is not scared of me.

This is possible, Dorgryl replied evenly. *His life is not his own, it is true. It is committed to the moment when you and he will do battle — and you will. But he has friends whom he loves, nephew. Even better, he has a family he cherishes. His children and he have been reunited in the Heartwood. They represent his greatest joy but also his worst fears.*

Orlac, felt confused by the web of thoughts Dorgryl was weaving in his mind.

The senior god continued. *Do not go after Gynt immediately; go after the ones he loves first. He will be so busy trying to protect them that he will lose the offensive. Nothing will prepare him for the devastation of losing loved ones. He will be in no position to attack and will go entirely on the defence, which will give you the opportunity to destroy him.*

Orlac was impressed. Dorgryl's mind was indeed dark and clever. *Where do we begin?* he said.

Time is on our side, boy. First we find ourselves some fine surrounds to live within. I have been too long in the Bleak; I want some luxury again. We should take the chance to enjoy life before the killing begins. And I think I know just the place. Dorgryl was enjoying himself immensely.

Where?

A place called Cipres; we are not far from it. The country is in chaos because their Queen has been newly murdered. The place is ripe for the taking and its palace and riches will suit us perfectly. It will be an ideal location from which to plan.

To Cipres then, Orlac said.

His uncle chuckled, delighted with his day's work. He settled back comfortably into the body of the god he intended to destroy.

33

Unexpected Visitors

Alyssa sat in her favourite armchair and ignored the food laid out in front of her. Even the waft of Cook's special chicken broth could not entice her. Hunger was not her companion this evening. Her mind was preoccupied with the startling event which had occurred just over an Eighthday ago. She traced it over and over in her thoughts. She had been dancing and jesting with Gyl. True, she had been fatigued from the day's activities followed by the dancing, but not so exhausted that she should collapse so dramatically.

Physic Kelvyn had insisted on rest for several days. He had given her a vile-tasting tonic in which she recognised all the herbs of an infusion which would help her rest. She hated to take any stupefacient but with Lorys and Gyl grimly standing by, she had obliged.

Perhaps it *had* helped; her body did feel rested for the two days' forced confinement to her bed, although she hated the fussing. Lorys had left his own chambers to move into hers and she loved the way he held her close each evening and gave the order not to be disturbed.

Alyssa knew she had terrified him by passing out like that. She guessed it brought back horrible memories of Nyria dying in his arms.

She was not dying. But she knew it was not exhaustion either, nor could it be passed off as the result of a bad batch of quail eggs. It was a convenient excuse but highly unlikely, as no one but she and Sallementro had been affected. It was curious that Sallementro had shown the same reaction. Something had happened in the Heartwood; she was sure of it. It was the only connection between them. The only possible explanation. Which was why she had banished everyone from her chambers this evening, claiming a headache. She hated to lie but Lorys, much against his will, had travelled west on Crown business and now that the main fusspot had departed, she needed the rest of the attention to stop. She needed peace to think.

What could have happened to cause such a massive disturbance to the Heartwood that the shock should reach out this far to affect her and her Paladin? She wondered about Saxon, wherever he might be right now; perhaps he too had collapsed? And Cloot. Had Saxon found the falcon? Had the falcon felt the shift?

As she expected – and this time she did not fight it – her thoughts turned to Tor. She missed that lovely voice in her head. She would welcome his companionship right now; she felt very scared. She had avoided it for as long as she could, but as she sat there, the broth cooling at her side, she finally allowed the dread thought to surface.

The last of the Paladin had fallen. Orlac was free.

Was this truly the case? Surely nothing else would cause the Heartwood to scream and all those connected with it to feel its pain. And the voices in her head — had she heard Orlac delivering his killing blow?

Alyssa shivered. There was no other explanation.

She heard a soft knock at the door and her new, rather nervous maid tiptoed into the room and asked if she wished to see Sallementro at this late hour.

'Yes. Bring him in. I'll be right out. Dismiss everyone for the night, Tanya. I shall be needing nothing further, thank you.'

The maid bobbed a curtsy and disappeared. Alyssa took a few minutes to tidy herself, then stepped into her salon, where the musician stood at the window. He turned and smiled although his expression was sad. 'Are you well, your majesty? It is so good to see you.' He bent low and kissed her hand.

She did not let go of it. 'I feel fine, Sal. And you?'

They spoke as friends now.

'It wasn't quail eggs, Alyssa.'

'I know,' she replied softly.

'I don't understand it properly; I never really have. But I sense it was connected with the fact that I am Paladin and bonded to you.'

Alyssa stepped up and put her arms around him. 'I believe,' she said haltingly, 'that Orlac is free.'

She felt his body tense.

'Then you are in danger, my lady. I must protect you as I promised Saxon,' he said, not feeling especially brave.

'I don't really understand it either, Sal. I think that all of us involved in this strange quest are in danger now: Saxon, Cloot, you, me . . . all of those who may still be alive in the Heartwood.'

'What should we do?'

She sighed and let her arms drop away, then stared out of the window with him.

'Without Torkyn Gynt, I am lost, Sallementro. He was the One. He was the only weapon we had against this foe. I don't know who we turn to or even who we can tell. I would like to tell the King but I just can't see Lorys believing such a tale. Can you?'

The musician turned and put his arms on her shoulders. 'An Eighthday ago we were given a sign. I think we must wait for the next one.'

Alyssa grimaced. 'But who has the power to stop a rampaging god?' She felt a flutter of panic.

Sallementro surprised himself at his conviction. 'None of us. Which is why we wait, your majesty. Other forces are at play here. We cannot control them. They seem to control us. I am hopeful that Lys will visit soon and tell me what I should do next.'

'At least you have Lys.'

He ignored her bitter comment. 'Saxon would have felt it too. Wherever he is, I think we can count on his fast return to you. Let us wait for that.'

'And then what, Sal? The three of us fight a god . . . with what? My powers are stymied for ever.' She pointed to the green disc on her forehead.

'I sincerely believe we will be given a sign; we will be shown our next step.'

There was another soft knock at the door. Alyssa swung around.

'No one leaves me alone any more. Everyone thinks I'm about to die on them.'

She marched towards the door. 'Another Queen of Tallinor gone!' she said, hating the nastiness in her voice which was born of the fear she was suddenly feeling.

She pulled the door open and Tanya bobbed a terrified curtsy.

'Well?' the Queen said.

'Your highness, forgive my disturbance. This has arrived for you. The bearer said it was urgent and for your eyes only.'

Alyssa looked at the scruffy note in her hands. 'Who brought this?'

'Um . . . an old man, your majesty. He . . . er . . . he said I was to tell you that Rufus Akre's teeth finally fell out.' The maid shrugged. It was a stupid message but she had been directed to deliver it.

Alyssa was shocked. She covered her surprise with a nervous laugh. She had not heard that name in years. Rufus Akre, the lad with gravestones for teeth, who had so desperately wanted to catch her posy during the Floral Dance at Minstead Green. It was the day she expected Tor to ask for her hand. She shook her head with no understanding. Only she and Tor knew of Rufus Akre and his intentions.

Tanya held out the note. 'Um . . . the Under Prime spoke with the old man and said it would be all right for me to deliver this, your majesty. He says the old fellow is probably just batty and harmless. Gyl . . . er, that is, the Under Prime, your majesty, says he believes it could be a note from your father.'

Alyssa took the note, still shaking her head at the old memories which the name of Rufus Akre dredged up. She thanked Tanya and closed the door whilst the maid was still trying to effect another nervous curtsy.

'Not bad news, I hope?' Sallementro enquired.

Alyssa walked to her desk. 'No. But very strange,' she said, frowning and reaching for her blade to break open the sealing wax.

She read it, her eyes widening. 'Sal . . . it's from Saxon.'

'What news?' said the musician, hugely relieved.

'It's so odd,' she said, looking up. 'He wants me to meet him in the small wood just to the west of the palace.'

'Why?'

'Well, that's just it. He doesn't really say. There's someone he needs me to meet but he cannot bring this person to the palace.'

'You mean he's here . . . now? Waiting for you?'

'He must be.' She showed him the note.

Sallementro read it quickly. 'He's quite firm that you're not to bring anyone but me with you.'

'Now, isn't that bizarre?' Alyssa exclaimed. 'Why the secrecy? And why the odd reference to Rufus Akre? He doesn't know Rufus Akre any more than you do.'

'Who is Rufus Akre?'

'Precisely my point!' she said impatiently. 'Only Tor would dream up that sort of password to get my attention. And he's dead.'

The musician bit his lip in thought. 'Perhaps he mentioned him to Saxon at some stage and Saxon realised you would consider the name a safe code, one you could trust. He must have good reason to use it, Alyssa. I would trust my life to Saxon.'

She looked at him. 'I do trust him with my life. We'd better go.'

'How do we get out without being noticed?'

She thought swiftly. 'I know a way out.'

Sallementro hesitated. 'You don't think this is a trap? I mean, should we perhaps tell Gyl?'

She shrugged. 'It is Saxon's writing. He would sooner die than lead me into a trap, even if someone was holding a knife to his throat. No, I believe it is genuine, but I am certainly intrigued by the covertness. And, to be frank, Gyl is the last person to bring in on this. He's worried about me already; this would send him frantic. He would immediately order the Shield to search the woods. Gyl would not be able to tolerate such a shrouded message.'

'And the King?' he asked, reminding her of her status.

'The King is not here, Sallementro. I am the only sovereign in this palace right now and I shall do exactly as I please.' She grinned. 'I'll get my cloak.'

They listened at the door and could hear nothing. The palace was always quiet when Lorys was away. Alyssa was sure he single-handedly created all the noise and bustle of the royal household. She lifted the latch and opened the door slowly. Two guards sprang to attention outside, giving both her and Sallementro a fright. She had not expected to be supervised quite so closely.

'Your highness,' one said and nodded.

Alyssa composed herself. 'Who ordered this guard at my door?'

'Under Prime Gyl, your highness.'

'And you are?'

'Eamon of the Shield, your majesty.' He bowed stiffly again.

'Well, Eamon of the Shield. I am not a child, I am not sick and I will not be supervised like this. I simply fainted, for Light's sake! Now, I wish to take a night stroll with

Sallementro and I do not wish to be followed. Is that clear?'

'Yes, your majesty. I will inform only the Under Prime.'

She swung around. 'You will do no such thing. In fact, Eamon of the Shield, I shall go directly to him and tell him myself. Perhaps you forget that he is my son; he, like you, will do as the Queen commands.'

The guard was mortified. He nodded. 'As you wish, your majesty.'

'I wish,' she said and marched away.

Sallementro scuttled after her. 'So, you can be tough when you want to,' he whispered, impressed.

'Oh, you don't know the half of it, Sal,' she replied, stifling a laugh as they escaped the watchful eye of the Shield.

She led Sallementro towards the kitchens. Those people still up and around the palace were surprised to see her walking the corridors and especially at such a late hour. Alyssa adopted a haughty air and even gave a couple of pages some errands.

She is magnificent, Sallementro thought, seeing her through new eyes as the distinguished sovereign she had quietly become. She was not a girl any more; she was not even just a beautiful woman any more, or aide to the King. She is our Queen, he suddenly articulated in his head. She is truly aristocratic.

'Someone is going to tell Gyl. Too many people have seen us,' he warned.

'Let them,' she said over her shoulder. 'I am not scared of Gyl. And we will be long gone before he catches up with us.'

*   *   *

It was a boring evening. He did not feel tired enough to sleep but he was certainly tired of patrolling the grounds and battlements. His captains were already well in control of tonight's watch and Gyl felt decidedly redundant. He wished he had accompanied the King when given the opportunity, but he could tell that Prime Herek preferred him to remain behind to keep the command strong. He did his duty but he felt restless. And the Light strike him if his mind did not keep flicking back to that young woman heading off into the hills on her own towards Axon. He wondered what had become of her. Had she perished?

Lauryn – a pretty name. He wondered if the face matched. He shook his head clear of such thoughts and decided he would visit his mother. The episode on her NameDay feast was still bothering him. The Queen was in excellent health and this strange incident yielded no explanation around which he could comfortably wrap his mind. He had allowed Physic Kelvyn to pass it off as a mild poisoning from a batch of quail eggs gone bad, but he knew his mother hated eggs. She never ate them unless they were disguised in cakes or pastries.

And he had seen it in her eyes that she tolerated the explanation for his and the King's sake but inwardly dismissed it. And what about Sallementro? He had reacted at almost the same instant in an identical manner. Why was no one asking questions of this? When he tried to question the King, Lorys had not permitted any further discussion. Gyl realised Lorys could not tolerate any suggestion that anything might be wrong. Well, Alyssa was strong enough now. He would go up to her rooms to share some supper with her. Perhaps she might shed some light on the incident in private.

When Gyl arrived at the Queen's chambers, both of the guards he had personally posted were not there. He stopped a passing page and asked him to immediately fetch Eamon of the Shield. In the meantime, he knocked softly on the door. There was no response. He listened at the door. Silence. Gyl tried knocking again, wondering why no maid answered. Perhaps the Queen had gone to her bed early and dismissed her staff? It was plausible but did not explain the absence of the guards.

He knew the chambers would be unlocked. No one was allowed past the main guard at the bottom of this tower so the area was secure. He tried the latch and it gave. Stepping inside, he noticed only two candles burning; the rest of the salon was in darkness. He had just decided to peep into the bedroom, in case his mother was sleeping, when a man cleared his throat at the doorway. Turning he saw the guard.

'Ah, Eamon. Is it my imagination or did I not give orders for you and one other to keep watch here?'

Eamon was standing to attention. 'No, sir, it is not your imagination.'

'Then why, may I enquire, have you left your post?' He kept his voice even but inside Gyl was seething.

'Sir, Queen Alyssa dismissed us when she left her chambers earlier.'

'She dismissed you and you didn't think it appropriate to inform me?'

'Sir, the Queen forbade me to inform you. She made it very clear to us that she was going directly to speak with you, sir.'

Gyl felt unnerved by his mother's behaviour. Why would she undermine him like this? 'Well, she did not come directly to me. I have not seen the Queen this evening.'

Eamon's eyes flicked nervously from the Under Prime to the flagstones. 'Sir, she did say she was taking a night stroll.'

Light! This was getting worse by the moment. 'Was anyone with her?' Gyl asked, amazed that she would head out into total darkness.

'Yes, sir. Sallementro the musician was accompanying her.'

Gyl considered this. His mother never took night strolls, though he was glad to hear Sallementro was with her.

'Tell me, Eamon, did her maid deliver a note here earlier this evening?'

'Yes, sir. And the Queen left almost directly after.'

Gyl sighed. 'I see. Did she say where she was going for her stroll?'

'No, sir, she didn't. She dismissed her staff and us. She was quite angry, sir, that we were here on guard.'

'Yes, I imagine she was,' Gyl said, thinking aloud. He wished he could somehow get a peep at the note.

'You may go, Eamon. In future, soldier, your duty is to the Shield first and foremost. No orders are to override those of your senior officer. Is that clear?'

'Yes, sir, but the Queen was quite wrathful, sir.'

Gyl wanted to laugh. His mother wrathful? Ridiculous. 'Dismissed,' he said wearily. The soldier gave the Shield salute and disappeared quickly.

Gyl thought about the sequence of events involving the note. The old man who had delivered it had seemed rather pathetic. He had not begged an audience; had simply asked that someone might be kind enough to pass the note to the Queen. He said he came from the same district as she had and knew her father. He simply wanted to pass on some news. He had reassured Gyl there was no bad news contained in it; just a note from a father to his daughter. It had seemed harmless and it was only a note, after all. But where could she have gone? What was in that note?

Gyl knew that Alyssa would have to sneak out of the palace; she would be well aware that he would not approve of her leaving its safety in the dead of night. How would she do it? He thought on it a few moments and decided on the kitchens — it was an area of the palace she knew intimately and it had many exits.

He took the flight of stairs three at a time, startling the guards at the bottom of the tower. He simply could not have his mother, the Queen when all is said and done, in any situation which was not secure. It was his responsibility, as Queen's champion, to see to her absolute safety.

Cook stoked the smouldering fire for the last time that night. From now on one of the scullery maids or one of those rascal boys would be in charge of keeping the flames alive until dawn. She was exhausted. The King was due back in the palace tomorrow and she was planning one of her special welcome home meals, but the preparations were taking their toll so soon after the NameDay feast which had gone so horribly wrong.

Cook shook her head as she poked the flames into life. The suggestion that her quail eggs were bad was so preposterous she refused to give it legitimacy by even responding to such a claim. She blew on the new flames angrily. The eggs had been fresh that morning. There was more to her Queen's collapse than people were letting on. Still, it was none of her business.

She had heard that Alyssa, and indeed that musician of hers, were both well now and that was all that mattered. She straightened with a groan, trying to stretch her back. As she did, she heard footsteps approaching and whispering. Turning, she was surprised to see the Queen, dressed for outdoors, together with the same musician who had just been in her thoughts.

She smiled. 'Well now, my Queen. What brings you down here so late of an evening?'

Alyssa put her finger to her lips and spoke very softly. 'Hush, Cook. I'm trying to steal an hour for a walk. That wretched physic has me cooped up in my chambers and I am well sick of it all. I am in excellent health and I just want some fresh air. Will you help me?'

'Help you, your majesty? How?'

Alyssa took Cook's arm and, with that subtle move, brought her friend into the deception. 'Sallementro will keep me company.'

The musician pulled a face of resignation, as though he had no choice in the matter.

Alyssa continued. 'We shall sneak out through the cool room. If anyone asks you if you've seen me, please, please, I beg you, tell them you have not sighted me.'

'Why, my child?'

'Because I am tired of being fussed over and treated as an invalid. I simply fainted, Cook. I did not even eat an egg. The Under Prime has me under guard now, so I am making a stand and refusing to be subjected to this humiliation. I am Queen. I will walk in the night's fresh air if that pleases me.'

Her large, grey-green eyes regarded Cook. Who could resist them? It was heartening to see the Queen so high-spirited again, and what mettle. Well, they all knew she had it; she just had not shown it for some time.

'Of course, my dear. I saw nothing. I've been stirring up my flames and preparing to leave my kitchen for the night. If you came past, I did not see you.'

Alyssa kissed her friend on her fat cheek. 'Thank you, Cook. This means so much to me.'

'Well, disappear then, you two, before you get caught.'

Cook turned her back on them and gave one last poke at the now merrily burning fire which would keep a huge pot of her vegetable broth simmering through the night. She had no idea through which door the Queen and Sallementro departed but she assumed it must have been that in the cool room, as Alyssa had mentioned.

Once she had noted the arrival of the scullery staff and given directions for the few hours until dawn, she struggled out of her apron, hung it on the same hook where she had hung it for the last forty summers and stretched.

When she finally came out of a huge yawn, she noticed the Under Prime standing in the main doorway.

'Light strike me, sir! You startled me,' she said, hand to her heart.

'Apologies, Cook. You looked like you needed that yawn. I didn't want to interrupt it.' He winked, walked over to her and gave her a big squeeze.

She had a terribly soft spot for young Gyl; always had since that freezing morning when they discovered him tied to the palace gates.

'What's on?'

'Vegetable broth as usual, Gyl. Have a bowl.'

'I will later. It smells as delicious as always.' He dipped a wooden spoon into the pot and took a taste. 'Mmmm . . . the best.' Then he added, very casually, 'Cook, you haven't seen my mother tonight . . . recently, have you?'

Cook did not even hesitate. She was terribly fond of the son but his mother was her favourite. 'The Queen? No. I was just heading off to bed now, Gyl.'

'Oh, well, don't let me keep you. It's just that I need to speak to her rather urgently and I can't find her anywhere in the palace.'

'Don't you fret. Your mother always was one who needed quiet time. She'll be somewhere private, reading or writing.'

'Hmmm.' He eyed her. 'Probably. You head off.'

Cook threw a final glance towards the maid, glad that Nelly had not been around when the Queen had come in. The maid was the worst tittle-tattle in the palace and, like most of the younger women on the staff, was hopelessly besotted with the dashing Under Prime. She would sell her soul for a kiss from him.

'Keep those flames alive, Nelly, or I'll skin you in the morning.'

'Yes, Cook,' Nelly said, bobbing a curtsy.

As Cook departed she saw Nelly smile, not so shyly, at the soldier. With her back to them both, almost hobbling with fatigue, she blew out her cheeks with relief. That had been close!

Two figures made their way stealthily across one of the many courtyards of the Tal palace. Alyssa knew the routine of the guards well. She had spent many nights chatting to the soldiers in her determination to get to know those who served the King. She had quickly learned their names, their habits and absorbed their regular watch changes, even the route they took on their patrols. Her knowledge enabled her now to plot the precise moment of her and Sallementro's charge towards the tiny iron gate which would lead them out of the palace grounds. Once through they both leaned back on the stone wall outside, breathing deeply.

Alyssa began to laugh. 'Sallementro, this is fun.'

He could not help but smile at her delight. 'I am sure you won't think so when the King suggests my head be removed from my shoulders for permitting such folly.'

'Nonsense!' she said and slapped him with a backhand to his chest. 'You forget who you are with, musician! Come on.'

Holding hands, they crept up the small mound behind the castle, where she and Saxon often liked to sit and talk privately. Ahead they could make out the dark shape of the clump of trees.

'Can you see anything?' Sallementro whispered.

'No,' she said, dropping the hood of her cloak. 'Let's get closer.'

As she spoke, a tiny light suddenly glowed into life and was immediately extinguished. Someone not paying sufficient attention would never have noticed it. It reminded her of one of the Flames of the Firmament from the Heartwood.

'There!' she said, letting go of Sallementro's hand. She picked up her cloak and began to run towards where she had seen the brief glow.

Sallementro chased after her, suddenly feeling that

perhaps this was not such a good idea. He kept hearing Alyssa's words 'we are all doomed' echoing in his head and he felt unnerved. What would he do if this was a trap and someone tried to harm her?

His anxieties were washed away by a flood of relief when a familiar shape emerged from behind one of the trees. There was no doubting that it was the Kloek.

'Saxon!' Alyssa called, trying to keep her voice low but betraying her excitement at having him home. She threw herself towards him.

The Kloek had not realised how much he had missed his beautiful Alyssa. He could never think of her as anything but the fragile, almost childlike girl he had taken such delight in lifting from the crowd on that fateful night at Fragglesham. And now here he was, lifting her again with similar delight and enjoying hearing her squeal. The thrill, he knew, would be short-lived but he held that lovely moment while he could.

'My Queen. Congratulations on your marriage,' he said with respect, but hugged her hard as one does a loved friend. 'I am sorry to have left you for so long.'

He felt he ought to bow but she was clinging happily to his neck and he did not want to spoil it.

'You are fortunate. I shall not have you chopped into pieces, Kloek, because I am hopelessly in love with you, but you shall never desert me like that again,' she said, hugging him almost as hard in return.

Sallementro arrived. 'Sax!'

Saxon put Alyssa down gently and bear-hugged the musician.

Sallementro groaned. 'Mind my fingers, Saxon. I have to play tomorrow.'

The Kloek beamed and inhaled the night air. 'It is good to be home,' he said, putting his huge arms around both of them. 'Come with me,' he added and pulled them further into the stand of trees.

Alyssa gladly fell in step with him. She felt truly safe now. 'Saxon, what is all this mystery about? Sallementro almost didn't let me come to you because he was nervous it was a trap,' she admonished.

'He was right to be cautious, your majesty,' Saxon admitted.

'Alyssa, when we're alone like this, if you don't mind,' she corrected. 'So, cough it up. What is this terrible secret that you cannot reveal on palace grounds? You said something about a visitor?'

Saxon became suddenly serious. They were in full cover of the trees now and he felt his stomach flip inside. This was it, the defining moment. How would she react? Was she strong enough to cope with the truth? A dozen other nerve-racking thoughts crossed his troubled mind in the space of those few moments whilst his two friends stared at him. He hesitated a fraction too long and Alyssa's expression clouded. He saw concern flit across her gorgeous face in the moonlight which filtered through the branches overhead.

'What is it, Saxon?' Her smile had faded. She sensed trouble.

Cloot flew in silently and landed on the Kloek's shoulder. Saxon knew the bird came to offer support. He appreciated it and touched the falcon with thanks. He saw Alyssa's eyes light with joy again.

'Cloot! You rescued him?'

Saxon nodded. Words failed him but he knew he would

have to find them quickly. He reached up so the falcon could hop onto his arm, which he then held out to the Queen. She kissed Cloot, affection flowing effortlessly from her to Tor's falcon. 'Oh, Cloot. You're safe; you're alive,' she wept. 'Having you here somehow makes me feel like Tor is still with us.'

Saxon felt the hairs on his arms lift at those innocent yet chilling words. He looked over at Sallementro and shook his head sadly at the musician's questioning expression. Sallementro guessed bad news was coming. He took a deep breath, wondering what Saxon had brought home with him this cool night.

Cloot felt more nervous for Tor, who was hidden in the trees, watching the scene unfold.

Tor spoke to the bird. *I can't do this to her,* he said, his voice trembling.

You know that you must. Be brave now, Tor. Alyssa has more spine than you give her credit for. Risk her hate. You have no choice in this matter. Orlac is free — never forget this.

Cloot's mention of Orlac gave Tor the courage he needed. He recalled how the god had threatened to track down those he loved. Alyssa was one of the main targets. He must reveal himself in order to protect her. He must allow her to hate him to save her. He felt sick.

Lauryn and Gidyon flanked him and he felt their love washing over him across the link.

Don't be frightened, Lauryn reassured. *A woman can never hate someone she truly loves.*

Gidyon echoed her sentiments. *She will forgive you, Father.* Alyssa stepped away from Saxon and looked him in the face. He suddenly seemed very distant. She tried to read his expression: he was nervous. Cloot flapped away and Saxon cleared his throat, but it was Alyssa who spoke for him.

'Whatever it is, Saxon, the problem will not go away by remaining silent.'

He nodded.

'Is my father dead?'

'No, Alyssa. I have not met with your father. That was a ruse.'

She tried to make it easy for him; could see he was genuinely struggling. Sallementro stepped up behind and took her arm but she gently shook herself free. 'Then is it Goth? Are you afraid to tell me news about him?'

'I have news on Goth but that is not why I called you out at the dead of night. It was true when I said I have brought someone to see you.'

And then he shocked her by kneeling. He took her hand and kissed it. 'Forgive me, my Queen, for what I bring back to your life tonight.'

It was a fanciful thing for Saxon to say and a thousand warnings klaxoned in her head. Alarm raced through every part of her. Saxon was afraid. Why? He had brought someone with him but he was so terrified he could not bring himself to say the name.

Go now, Tor, Cloot whispered into his friend's mind. *Our hearts and love walk with you.*

Tor told the children to remain hidden until he called them, then he stepped out from behind the tree trunk. A twig snapped underfoot and he watched as the Queen of Tallinor swung around towards the sound.

Alyssa's mind was racing with possibilities of who the mysterious visitor could be when she heard movement behind her and spun to see who was approaching. She saw the figure of a man who must have been concealed behind the trees. She felt Saxon stand up behind her, felt his arms reach for her, but she stepped forward to avoid them. The shape in the shadows was tall. His silhouette was achingly familiar. She was holding her breath and she wondered why the others were not deafened by the sound of her heart beating. It sounded to her as though its thunderous hammering could reach back to the palace and wake all within.

The man took two steps forward. It was impossible, but he reminded her of someone it just could not be. When he spoke, it confirmed that her mind was playing terrible games with her. Surely she was dreaming? She was in the midst of a horrific nightmare. Why was Saxon feeding it? And why was that man in the shadows talking with Torkyn Gynt's voice and standing in Torkyn Gynt's distinctive way?

'Alyssa . . . it's me. It's Tor,' the man said.

Tor. She said his name silently in her head.

'But . . . but Tor is dead.' Her breath was suddenly ragged. 'Saxon, what is this trick you play on me?' she demanded, her voice quivering.

Saxon was at her side in one stride. 'It is true, Alyssa. He lives.'

Sallementro had to steady himself by holding onto a tree. He could not believe what he was seeing or hearing.

Tor took another tentative step forward. A couple more and he would be able to reach out and touch her. She was heartbreakingly beautiful, even in the dimmest of the silvery moon's light. And then he remembered whom he approached. She may be a little wild-eyed and breathing a little too shallowly, her chest moving like a startled sparrow, but she was the Queen of Tallinor. He was compelled to kneel and bow his head. 'Your majesty.'

His formality snapped her from her state of terror but Alyssa continued to stare in deepest shock at the man she had always loved. She could no longer feel her own body; it was numb. It was truly him: beautiful Torkyn Gynt, the father of her dead son. The man who had torn her apart with love and then died courageously to save her. She had watched those stones break his head open. She had witnessed his blood gush forth and his life spill out with it. She had spent years in despair trying to come to terms with his loss.

And then, out of nowhere, she recalled Merkhud and his strange behaviour on the day of the execution. Those bright grey eyes of his had stared at her for too long, as though wanting to say something important, and yet when he had spoken, all he said was that she should consider Sallementro a friend. And then he had blown her a kiss. Alyssa had thought his behaviour very strange and she remembered how Herek, who had been one of the guards, had commented on the old man's odd action.

Then an impossible notion hit her; it felt as though a hundred punches had landed in her belly at once. Had the old man won again? Had that conniving old goat somehow stolen Tor from the brink of death?

She turned to look at Saxon, but his head was lowered and he would not meet her eyes. Sallementro, who was clearly not in on this wicked trickery, also stared at the ground.

Alyssa turned back to Tor. He remained kneeling and it seemed he too found the grass more interesting than her.

Grief roared up and threatened to choke the last breath out of her. Pain, anguish, anger – her three old companions – returned with glee.

She found her voice. 'Stand up!' she commanded. 'Stand up and look at me, you betrayer!'

No one moved initially; her order had taken everyone by surprise. Then Tor stood.

'Look into my eyes,' she said.

Tor lifted his head. A cluster of tiny flames lit his face; they were never far from his call these days.

So it *had* been one of the Heartwood flames that she had seen earlier. Alyssa was trembling but she balled her hands into fists to steady herself. Once his face was illuminated by the flames, there was no mistaking who stood before her. Those impossibly blue eyes could belong to no one else but Torkyn Gynt. She could even make out the livid scar which ran across his head, a legacy of the execution stones.

The shock boiled over. Alyssa took one step forward and swung. No one expected it, not even Tor. How she was able to reach so high was anyone's guess but she hit his jaw so hard that he toppled backwards. And then the Queen began to weep; years of sorrow were loosed in a torrent.

Tor! Someone comes, Cloot called urgently.

Gyl had searched the palace and its grounds with no luck and was now understandably anxious. The Queen was definitely no longer within the palace walls and the castle gates were closed. None of the guards had seen her or Sallementro pass through any of the courtyards. So where was she? He found himself back near the kitchens but outside this time. He felt sure that if she was to steal away, she would use this area to leave from. But why did she need to sneak off at all?

Then he heard a muffled yell coming from the small stand of trees beyond the mount, as the small hill was known. He did not wait for back-up but ran as hard as he could towards the sound. He was the Queen's champion. If anyone had so much as touched a hair on his mother's head, the perpetrator would pay on the spot with his life.

Gyl was fast. He pulled his sword, crashed into the small clearing of the trees and was totally arrested by what he found. A tall, dark-haired man was climbing to his feet; he appeared to have been knocked to the ground. Sallementro was standing by him and there was Saxon — damn him all to hell, where had he suddenly arrived from? The Kloek was holding the Queen, who was crying.

'What in the Light happens here?' he demanded, his sword immediately at the throat of the dark stranger.

Saxon quickly spoke for all of them. Gyl looked wild enough to kill. 'Gyl, the Queen is fine. She has received some shocking news and is upset. We need to get her back to the palace.'

Gyl looked from Saxon to Sallementro. There was furtiveness here but he could not see their faces clearly enough to read them properly. He trusted Saxon with his own life and knew his mother did with hers. There was no reason in the world not to trust him now.

'You!' he said, pressing his blade against the stranger's throat. 'Who are you?'

Tor opened his mouth to speak but it was Alyssa who answered for him. She sounded regal and back in control.

'Gyl, he is a friend. He brings me news of the past. I expect you to treat him as you would any honoured guest.'

Gyl hesitated a moment but pulled his sword back and sheathed it. He walked over to Alyssa. 'Are you all right, mother?'

She mustered a smile but her eyes were still watery. 'I am sorry I hoodwinked you, son.' She touched his cheek. 'I just felt you were being overly protective. I am well. Will you escort us back, please?'

She turned back to Tor; her bright tone rang false. 'Come, old friend, we have things to discuss.'

'Er, your majesty,' he responded.

All eyes turned to him.

'I . . . I have travelling companions. May I bring them with me?'

Saxon closed his eyes with despair. If they thought that Alyssa meeting Tor again was hard, what was coming next was sure to break her.

'As you wish. All are welcome,' she said, a little too lightly, but her voice was steady and she kept her head high. She linked her arm through Gyl's and moved forward with Sallementro not far behind.

Pull your hoods up, Tor warned his children and they obeyed. They tiptoed from where they were concealed and walked alongside their father and Saxon, following the diminutive figure of their mother, the Queen of Tallinor.

Cloot remained in the copse. He did not envy them all what was yet to come.

34

A Time for Truth

The group arrived at the Queen's chambers in an awkward silence and filed in. Alyssa paid no attention to the two hooded figures who followed Tor. She was barely hanging onto her own composure as it was and did not care about the strangers who accompanied him.

'Gyl, thank you,' she said and kissed him. 'I am sorry for the trouble I have caused you. Can I press upon you once more, to muster up one of the maids? I am sure we could all use some refreshment.'

The Under Prime was so confused by his mother's odd behaviour and her strange visitors that he complied without argument.

Saxon followed him out of the Queen's rooms and called to him.

The soldier turned on him. 'You owe me an explanation, Sax. What the hell is this all about?' he asked in a grim whisper.

Saxon could tell Gyl was about as angry as someone could be yet he managed to control the emotion. The boy had grown up. He faced a man now and one who was due the respect his status demanded.

'I do owe you an explanation.' He shook his head. 'It's very complicated, Gyl, but trust your mother. This all harks back to her former life, before she was even living in Tal. I promise you, she is in no danger from these people. They bring news she will want to hear. Allow them some privacy. Sallementro and I will keep guard outside until you return.'

Gyl nodded, none the wiser for listening to his friend. 'No one goes in or out without my permission, Sax. Do we understand one another?'

'Very clearly, sir,' Saxon said and noted that Gyl looked suddenly abashed at the respect his former mentor was paying him.

'I'll be back soon,' the Under Prime said, in a less commanding manner and glared at Sallementro who had just come out of the Queen's rooms.

The musician sighed. The only comfort he could offer was that he was as confused as Gyl was. The musician closed the door softly behind him and hoped the King would return soon and, with him, sanity.

Inside the Queen's chambers the four stood in uncomfortable silence.

Alyssa waited for the door to close. Then, before Tor could say anything, she spoke, determined to wrest back control of herself and the situation. 'Will you introduce me to your friends, Tor?' Her voice was like icy shards dropping on him.

Tor thought of Orlac's warning on the hilltop and the

reality of his vengeance. They were still no closer to the Trinity. The Colours blazed inside him as he felt anger at all the pain and grief his life seemed to bring to others. Then he pushed aside his despair. Whatever else happened tonight, Alyssa would be given the gift of her children. He could do this for her. He ran his fingers through his hair, knowing there was absolutely no turning back now. But there was no easy way to say it; no gentle means of breaking such news to someone who had already survived one shock that night. He must tell the truth in all its stark simplicity.

'Alyssa.' He saw her stiffen at him saying her name but he pressed on. 'This is Gidyon and Lauryn . . . they are my children.'

The Queen's spirit died a thousand deaths. Children. So he had married and been given the gift of children, one which she had not been blessed with. So be it. She dug her nails into her palms and delved deep inside herself to find new strength. She was not going to cry at his news. She forced herself to turn towards the two people who stood silently near the window.

They pulled back their hoods and bowed. Together they said, 'Your majesty.'

The candle glow was low in her rooms, as she preferred at night, but there was absolutely no mistaking the son of Torkyn Gynt, who straightened now and stood before her. She drank in his appearance and fought back the recognition that this was how Tor had looked that day when he caught her posy of flowers. Fresh-faced and brilliantly handsome, the boy Gidyon even possessed identical, disarmingly blue eyes. She wanted to hate him and hate the mother who had borne him in love for his father, but she could not.

Gidyon stepped forward. He was in totally unknown territory now. He had no idea what his father expected, or when the truth would be revealed, but he could not allow his beautiful, tragic mother to stand before him and not touch her. He took her small, elegant hand, bent low and kissed it.

The Queen battled with her emotions. He was every bit as beautiful as his father. She could not look at Tor at this moment. Instead, she took a long, silent, steadying breath and pulled back her hand. She felt the kiss still lingering on it.

Now she turned her attention to the girl. This was a shock. Honey-golden hair gleamed against the perfectly oval face which sat above a petite frame. The Light strike her! Was she imagining it?

Before the girl could make a move or show her respect, Tor moved forwards to stand alongside the Queen. Alyssa could not bear for him to be this close. The conflict between loving him still and hating him passionately for his betrayal was raging inside her, but she was coping with rather too much just now to deal with it. Her eyes were riveted on his gorgeous daughter, Lauryn, whose own grey-green eyes regarded her nervously.

Tor touched her arm. It was an intimate gesture and she felt as though that part of her arm sizzled from the contact. His voice was soft now. 'Alyssa, does Lauryn remind you of anyone?'

The words caught in her throat but she forced them out with an effort. 'Dare I say that . . . Lauryn reminds me of . . . of me?' she said, finally looking into those blue eyes.

And now the unthinkable. He reached his arms around

her and brought her close against his chest. How could she allow this? How could she permit this man whom she wanted to despise to touch her with such familiarity? Tor kissed the top of her soft, golden-haired head. She felt weak at his touch . . . but welcomed it.

'She should remind you of yourself, my love. She is your daughter . . . our daughter. And Gidyon is our son.'

There. It was said.

Frozen silence reigned for what felt like eternity as the Queen's mouth opened and shut again and her sad eyes darted from son to daughter and back. The children did not know what to do so they remained quiet; it was best to take their lead from their father right now.

A soft knock was heard at the door. It brought Alyssa out of her trance-like shock. One hand went to her hip; the other covered her mouth to stifle any sound. Tor saw her gulp. She closed her eyes and composed herself. He had watched her do something very similar on the day of his execution. He knew she would survive this. She was brave and strong.

The Queen looked at no one. In silence she went to the door, opened it and allowed her maid to enter with a tray.

'Hurry, Nelly,' she said. 'Over on that table is fine. I'll take care of it.'

The girl quickly placed the tray where she was told and scurried out of the door, forgetting to curtsy. The Queen did not notice. She turned back into the room, lacing her fingers together as if by doing so she could force all nervous movement to stop.

'How can this be, Tor?' she said, surprisingly evenly. 'If these were the children I bore in the Heartwood, they would barely be out of infancy.'

'May we sit, your majesty?' he asked. 'We have travelled a long way today.'

'Please,' she offered. 'My apologies. Lauryn, perhaps you might pour everyone some wine.'

Lauryn was relieved to have something to do. She felt as if she was about to explode and if it were not for Gidyon in her head, calming her down, making her show patience, she was sure she would let everything spill out. She nodded, smiled a little nervously and walked to the table, past the Queen, who stiffly sat on the window bench.

'Now tell me,' she said, looking hard at Tor.

While Lauryn passed around goblets of wine, Tor began to relate the story of the children's birth. Alyssa felt as if her heart was breaking and the grief she had stored inside for so long flooded her body. As Tor's soft voice told her of what had happened after the birthing, she began to cry.

Gidyon could no longer bear it. He dared to move and sit alongside the Queen, taking his mother into his arms and holding her close as she wept for the son she thought was dead and the daughter she had never known about.

Tor's voice broke too. Slowly, he told his terrible tale, about the ordeal of trying to find her again, only to discover she had been captured by Goth. When he spoke of the execution, he faltered and it was Lauryn who comforted him and encouraged him to finish.

Finally Tor explained Merkhud's Spiriting.

'I guessed only tonight that it was you in Merkhud's body, wasn't it?' Alyssa said, her eyes sore and red from her tears. Her nose was running too; she must look a fright, she thought.

'I . . . I just didn't know what to say to you. There were so many people around us.'

She nodded, resigned to her life of ongoing sorrow. 'Go on.'

He told her everything. How he had been brought back to life; how he had flown within Cloot to track down Goth; Cloot's capture; the voyage to Cipres; how he had finally found Cloot and then, on returning to the Heartwood, had finally been reunited with his children.

Alyssa sat cradled in her silent son's arms; when the words came out she could not believe how calm she sounded. 'Where have you both been all this time?'

Lauryn realised the question was being addressed to her. She shrugged. 'Sorrel took us to another world, a place where time passes differently. Neither of us can remember, I'm sorry. Sorrel said we would forget . . . and we have.'

Alyssa shook her head sadly. 'Sorrel,' she said. 'So she took you both away?'

'With the help of the Heartwood,' Tor said quickly. 'To safety. Alyssa, can you recall what a terrifying time that was for all of us?'

'I can't. I don't remember anything from that time really, except being happy with you in the Heartwood and then the reality of your execution. In between is just a blur.' She turned to look at Gidyon. 'I saw your tiny dead body.'

Tor spoke gently. 'You saw a glamour, Alyssa. It was meant to make you believe your baby was dead . . . for your own protection, Lys said.'

'I hate Lys,' she replied and it was clear she meant it.

Tor wondered if Alyssa would say that if she knew who Lys was to her. He ground his teeth with anger at how Lys played with their lives.

'Where is Sorrel now?' Alyssa suddenly said.

The three travellers looked to each other awkwardly. Tor spoke. 'We believe she is dead. Like Merkhud, her time was up, I think.'

A new wave of sadness swept through Alyssa. Another death. Another loved one gone.

'How much more of this is there, Tor?'

'There is more but it can wait. You now know what I came here to tell you and I should leave.'

She was startled. Leave?

'No,' she said, 'I will not permit it. You will all stay here and we shall talk some more.'

The Queen shook her head again with disbelief as she regarded the two children, now on their feet. 'I am so glad you ca—' She could not finish. She began to sob.

Tor, Lauryn and Gidyon put their arms around her and shared her sorrow for all that they had lost as a family.

After seeing to his mother's wishes, Gyl did a quick round of the Guard. He was too fired up to return to the Queen's chambers just yet. He trusted Saxon and Sallementro; knew they would not allow any harm to come to her.

He turned to his paperwork and began to sort out some of the messages from the surrounding districts. He was pleased to read that the King was making his way back to Tal and should arrive the following day. Just as he was giving orders for a party of the Shield to greet the King a day's ride from the city and escort him back, he heard a disturbance.

'See to that, Brash, would you,' he said.

The man left the guardhouse and returned a few moments later. 'It's an old woman, sir.'

'Well, give her some soup, man, and get someone to show her the outhouse where she can rest up.'

'Sir, she demands entry to see the Queen.'

Gyl swung around. 'The Queen?'

'Yes, sir.'

'Do you know what the time is? Send the old twit on her way. She can make her request through the normal procedures in the morning. Don't bother me with this.'

'Sir, she looks half dead. I don't think she can walk another step. She . . . er . . . she says, sir, that she is Queen Alyssa's former guardian.'

'Pigs bollocks! Someone will suffer for this,' Gyl said, his night's frustration spilling over. 'Where is she?'

'At the main gate, sir.'

'Right,' he said. He strode off, muttering. 'If you want something done properly, do it yourself.'

At the main gate, he found a small, very frail-looking old woman. She seemed vaguely familiar but he dismissed the thought in his anger.

'Now, look, madam. It is past the thirteen bells. Her majesty sleeps,' he lied. 'And we have no intention of waking up the Queen to speak with you. Do you understand?'

The old crone pointed a long, bony finger through the iron grille and croaked at him. 'You are the one who does not understand, young man. Tell the Queen it is Sorrel. She will permit my entry at any time of the day or night.'

'I will not do any such thing,' Gyl said, furious with the night's proceedings and people who seemed to think they could usurp his authority and do precisely what they wanted with palace security. 'Go away and return tomorrow.'

She ignored him. 'Is Saxon Fox here?'

'Sax?' That surprised him. 'Look, who are you?' he asked, realising too late she had already told him. He glanced around at the men, who looked everywhere but at their leader.

The old woman was gracious enough to say nothing more. Gyl considered his position; he felt he was handling this badly. In fact, he had handled the whole of the night badly.

'Fetch the Kloek,' he said to one of the men, wearily. 'He is outside the Queen's chambers.' He turned back to the old woman. 'If he vouches for you, you may enter.'

The children munched on the cheeses, nuts and fruit which were on the tray and talked quietly at one end of Alyssa's long salon. They were both relieved that the dreaded meeting was behind them.

Lauryn was taken aback at how very young and beautiful her mother still was. Why she had imagined someone much older, she could not think. Her mother had not touched her yet, but Lauryn instinctively sensed she was frightened. Frightened of all the pent-up emotions. She needed to be seen as one who was in control. She was Queen of this realm, after all. And they had plenty of time to get to know one another. Lauryn was looking forward to it. For now, she was just pleased to see her parents talking to one another.

Tor and Alyssa sat in the window seat, the drapes drawn so they could speak in private.

Tor deliberately kept his hands wrapped around his goblet. He dared not put it down for fear that his empty hands would try to find hers. That was too dangerous.

There was a painful barrier between them. It was called Lorys.

'I feel I ought to congratulate you, Lyssa . . . on . . . on your brilliant marriage.' Then he felt stupid for saying it.

Alyssa was aching inside at being so close to him yet unable to so much as touch him. When he called her Lyssa she had to bite the inside of her cheek to stop herself from crying all over again.

'Don't, Tor. I can't begin to explain—'

'Please . . . you don't have to. Truly. You saw me die. I cannot imagine how you coped alone for as long as you did. Losing a child, losing me, losing all of us from the Heartwood . . . I hope he makes you happy,' he said, trying to mean it as he looked directly at her, which was hard enough in itself.

'Yes,' was all she trusted herself to say, although she allowed herself the luxury of staring into those eyes she had loved for so long.

He broke the difficult moment; moved from what stood in the way of him holding her close again. 'The children are magnificent, Lyssa. They are strong and brave. Both possess great powers – Gidyon especially. We have created two very special people, even if . . .' He could not finish.

Alyssa rescued him; tried to sound bright. 'They are wonderful. I feel badly that they have seen me in such a state. I hope I can get to know them more fully. I hope you will stay a while?'

'They should stay, but I do not believe the King will welcome me with open arms.'

They let that subject rest. Alyssa had not even thought so far ahead as to consider how the King might react to all of this. She was finding it hard to come to terms with it herself. It felt so unreal.

'Tell me about Gyl,' Tor said.

'I adopted him several years ago now. He was found outside the palace one morning, chained to the gates . . . a forlorn little thing, he was. Nyria took pity on him immediately.' She saw him smile as he remembered how Nyria had always taken pity on all children. 'She gave him to me to care for. He was young enough to still need a mother, and I was still hurting from my loss and needed rescuing. He was my saviour. He and Saxon, Sallementro, Nyria . . . and later, Lorys.'

'He loves you very much.'

'The King loves me deeply, Tor.'

'No, I mean Gyl.'

'Oh.' She felt embarrassed. 'Er . . . yes. Gyl and I are very close. He is distressed about me because I collapsed last week. I felt this strange shift in the Land's force—'

Tor did take her hand now; he could no longer bear not to touch her. 'I did too. All of us did: the children, Saxon, all those in the Heartwood.'

'It is Orlac, isn't it? He has broken free?'

'Yes. He summoned me.'

She gripped his hand hard. 'You have seen him?' She was alarmed.

'We spoke. He intends to kill us all.'

'Sweet mercy,' she whispered. 'What about the Trinity?'

'I called the children back to Tallinor because I hoped they may shed some light on the dark secret. But I am no closer to knowing, Alyssa. I am afraid for them . . . and for you.'

'What are you going to do?'

'This first,' he said, reaching to touch her forehead.

She made a surprised sound as the gem fell away into his hand and she felt connected to her powers again for the first time in many years. He sliced open a link in her mind. It felt wonderful to have Tor back in her head again.

And this second, he said, putting his lips to hers. When she did not pull away he kissed her gently.

I needed to do that, to tell you that I have never stopped loving you. And, because I love you so much, I release you from all duty to me. You are in the most difficult of situations and I did not come here to complicate matters any more than I have to. I needed to warn you so that you might be protected whilst I decide on my next move.

She was about to reply when there was a knock. Saxon announced himself and said he had a surprise for them.

'Not another one,' Alyssa muttered, emerging from behind the drapes. 'I am not sure my heart can take it. Come!'

The door was opened by Sallementro. Saxon's arms were full with what looked like a huge bundle of rags.

The bundle moved and everyone stood in surprise.

'Sorrel!' Lauryn squealed.

Pandemonium broke out in the room.

35

Revelation

Saxon laid the old woman on one of the huge sofas. Her
eyes were closed and her breathing came in difficult rasps.

Tor could see Sorrel was dying in front of them; each
breath drained her life. Nevertheless, he asked the others,
who had crowded around her, to give him some room.
Saxon and Sallementro, feeling helpless, returned to their
positions outside the door.

Tor laid his hands on her. He felt the Colours sparkle
within and learned very quickly that she was not long for
this Land. He looked at Alyssa and shook his head sadly.
As he made to stand, the old woman gripped his hand.
When he looked at her, it seemed that the beautiful smile
which suddenly spread across her wizened face was just
for him. She whispered something so low that only his
superior hearing could decipher it.

'The Trinity eludes you?'

He nodded.

'It is close, child. Look to the forest. The Heartwood
protects its own.'

Her eyes closed; it seemed she had passed on to her

gods. Lauryn, despite her best efforts, began to cry and Gidyon offered her the comfort of his big arms once again. He shared her sorrow.

'She still lives,' Tor said, softly.

Sorrel confirmed this by opening her eyes once again. 'Where is Alyssa?'

'Here, Sorrel. I am right here,' the Queen said, bending down beside Tor and taking the old woman's other hand. That she had any tears left tonight seemed impossible and yet they flowed for this woman whom she loved.

'Ah, my girl. So beautiful. Look at you,' Sorrel said and even managed a dry chuckle. 'Queen of Tallinor . . . who would have thought?'

Alyssa whispered to the old girl, 'Sorrel, don't tire yourself now. May I get the physic for you?'

'No, child. The best physic Tallinor ever had has already seen that my life comes to its close now. I needed to see you one more time. I have returned to you what is yours, Alyssa. These children were stolen from you only for your safety and theirs. I hated leaving you, my girl, but I had to protect you and their precious, precious lives. Will you forgive me?'

Alyssa could not reply. Tor pulled her close and gave her the strength she needed to nod through her tears.

'Don't speak, Sorrel. Save yourself,' she begged.

Sorrel coughed raggedly and then drew another rasping breath. Lauryn looked away. She could not bear the old woman's suffering; felt guilt settling on her shoulders for leaving her for dead.

The old girl steadied herself and answered Alyssa. 'But I must speak, my Queen. Time is short. I have struggled to get here because I have one more thing to do before my spirit goes. It is the most important of all my tasks.'

Sorrel closed her eyes to gather the very last of her strength. When she opened them, they were glassy, as though she was already moving on and away from them.

'Tell us, Sorrel,' Tor encouraged.

He motioned to Gidyon to move Lauryn away; he could see she was deeply upset by this scene.

Gidyon helped Lauryn outside of the chambers. They both needed some air and relief from the tension in the room. 'Are we allowed outside?' he asked the two men who waited there.

'We shall come with you,' Saxon replied, glad to have something practical to do.

Sallementro agreed heartily and the four of them made their way to another part of the tower where they could talk quietly on one of the balconies.

Back in the Queen's chambers, Sorrel gripped Tor and Alyssa's hands with newfound strength and pulled them towards her.

'Hear me well,' she croaked. 'There is a third child. A son. Born after I sent you away, Tor. He was weak, almost dead. Darmud Coril granted me the boon I begged of him. He took the child; promised to keep him.'

She wheezed again, her strength waning. Her listeners were too stunned to speak; too numb to notice that her grip was loosening.

It was Tor who recovered first. 'Where is he, Sorrel? Where is our son?'

She spoke in the barest of whispers now. 'I know not. Look to the Heartwood. His name is Rubyn.'

She sighed out her last breath, dying with a soft smile on her face.

'Sorrel!' Alyssa shrieked at the dead woman. 'My son
. . . my son.'

She felt the Green closing around her, welcoming her
to its haven, pulling her into its depths where she could
be safe. Where she could escape from all this heartache
and grief.

And then Tor was with her, inside her head. He spoke
softly, knowing he must gather her back gently. *Don't go,
Alyssa. Do not run from this, I beg you.*

*Our child, Tor. Abandoned. Left to die in the forest. That
was his body I saw!*

She sank deeper into the Green.

*Not dead. Alive. Cared for by the Heartwood. Kept safe by
the god of the forests. Rubyn lives and we have to find him; we
must find him. Oh, don't you see, Alyssa, my love? Rubyn
completes it.*

She wanted to push him back, to stop him talking to
her. Stop him trying to make her fight. She had taken
too much battering and this was the final blow. The Green
beckoned. She would flee to its peace.

*The Trinity, Alyssa. Think! It is our children . . . three of
them. They are the Trinity! Rubyn completes it. Not me, not
you — them! We have to find him now, before it is too late.*

Trinity . . . ? she faltered; she could feel herself being
pulled away from the Green.

Yes. Gidyon, Lauryn, Rubyn. He waited. Then he added,
Your children need you, Alyssa.

She hesitated.

I need you, Alyssa, he added.

And somehow that was what she needed to hear. She
turned from the Green and followed his trace; came back
to where they sat in her room, holding hands with a dead

woman. Except that Sorrel was no longer a woman. She was dust.

Tor looked at Alyssa, elation sparkling in his bright blue eyes. *The Trinity is found*.

She smiled back at him. *We are found*, she whispered, terrified of the import of her own words.

Outside, high in the trees, a falcon called triumphantly into the night.

Far away, the Heartwood heard its own and rejoiced.

The story concludes in
Destiny: Trinity Book Three

By
Fiona McIntosh